# NEVER TO RETURN

## A Wild Fens Murder Mystery

### JACK CARTWRIGHT

# ALSO BY JACK CARTWRIGHT

**The DCI Cook Murder Mysteries**

A Winter of Blood

A Secret to Die For

**The Wild Fens Murder Mysteries**

Secrets In Blood

One For Sorrow

In Cold Blood

Suffer In Silence

Dying To Tell

Never To Return

Lie Beside Me

Dance With Death

In Dead Water

One Deadly Night

Her Dying Mind

Into Death's Arms

No More Blood

# NEVER TO RETURN

# JACK CARTWRIGHT

# PROLOGUE

"It's freezing," Simon gasped, as one of his new trainers sank into the mud at the shallow edge of the River Witham. His mum was going to go bananas. He would be grounded for sure, and for a week at least. However, if he voiced that thought, Gavin would hear it, and then Simon's life wouldn't be worth living. Plus, Julie Lansbury was watching, so he couldn't back down now.

"Come on, Simple Simon, you big girl. I thought you said you'd done this before?" Gavin called out from the safety of the bank.

Simon stared up at Gavin, the largest of the three boys, who flicked a lock of blonde hair from his brow and took a pull on the joint he had rolled. He stared back at Simon, defying him to argue, daring him to voice his complaint. Because he knew Simon wouldn't. He never fought back. Until now, that is. Now he'd show them.

"I have done it before," Simon protested with one foot resting on the paddle board and the other sinking deeper and deeper into the stinky, brown mud. If it wasn't for the paddle, which he had jammed into the river bed, he would have toppled over, much to their delight. "I did it when we were in Saint Lucia last year. But the water was clear and warm, and I had sand between my toes. Not freezing cold filth and this muck all over me."

"Just get on with it," Gavin said, taking another pull, and Julie smiled. "You told us you can do it. So, show us."

"I can prove it. I've got photos. My mum took loads."

"Is your mum in them?" Dave asked, sitting up from where he lay on the bank, his hair being tended by Tess Mitchell, the quieter of the two girls, but just as pretty as Julie Lansbury.

"Some of them, I suppose."

"Is she wearing a bikini?" Dave asked, braving a playful slap from Tess.

"Oh, leave off, Dave," Simon mumbled.

"Your mum's well fit," Dave continued. "I have absolutely no idea how a woman of her pedigree could conceive an imbecile like you. I bet she wears a thong, with her tight bum all hanging out as well."

"Dave, stop it," Tess said, and she shoved him away, much to the delight of Gavin, who picked up where Dave left off.

"I've seen her topless," Gavin said.

"You what?" Dave said.

"You have not," Simon argued.

"I have. She sunbathes topless in your garden. I saw her last summer, lying on the lawn behind that old greenhouse in your garden."

Simon wanted to argue. He wanted to contest it, but he knew the only time his mum ever sunbathed in that particular spot was when she wanted to get rid of her tan lines.

"There. See?" Gavin said, lying back on the grassy bank beside Julie. "He hasn't got anything to say. I can picture her now–"

"I'll tell them," Simon said, hearing the venom in his voice and regretting the threat before he'd even finished speaking the words.

"What did you say?" Gavin said, sitting up and shoving Julie out of his way. He climbed to his feet and strode towards Simon with purpose, his eyes narrowed and dark. He stepped into the water, then lowered his voice to a pre-pubescent growl that only the two of them could hear. "You won't tell anybody anything, paddle boy."

Gavin Forbes was a lunatic. His whole family was. He wouldn't think twice about getting wet or muddy, and he certainly wouldn't think twice about hitting Simon, especially if Julie was watching. Then again, maybe if Gavin punched him, it would work in his favour. But the idea of being hit was not a pleasant one.

"I might," Simon said, and he took another step back into the water, nudging the paddle board out with him. But the river deepened and he lost his balance, letting go of the paddle, the only thing that was keeping him upright. The water splashed as Gavin surged through the shallow water behind him, leaving Simon with only one escape route; the paddle board.

He clambered on and lay as a surfer might, paddling with his hands to get away. He was freezing. The winter had been hard, and everyone was talking about the joys of spring. But the bloody water was still cold enough that his body began to shiver.

"What did he say, Gav?" Dave called.

"He said something about my mum," Gavin lied, glaring at Simon, daring him to contest it. "Why don't you come here and say it again?"

But Simon was already too far from the bank for Gavin to reach him. The current caught the tail end of the board and began to turn him, pulling him further out into the middle of the river.

As if in victory, Gavin raised the paddle Simon had dropped into the air. "Oy, Simple. You forgot your paddle, you loser."

Then he tossed the paddle away into the long reeds.

For a fleeting moment, Simon saw them all stand. They were laughing. He turned to see where the river was taking him with the sudden dread that follows a very bad idea. And by the time he looked back, they were running along the riverbank. He'd gladly suffer a beating from Gavin if they could help him get to land. He peered into the murky water, wondering if he should jump in, but cowered at the thought.

That was when he realised, he'd made a terrible mistake.

The river dragged him further away, so fast they couldn't keep up.

"Help me," he called out. "Call someone."

But they didn't shout back. To his utter dismay, they all came to a stop, breathless, some of them doubled over to catch their breath.

And then they slipped from view. He passed beneath Five Mile Bridge, spying a man walking across. No, he wasn't walking. He was running. He stopped to peer down at Simon and stared in dismay.

For a brief moment, Simon was worried the man might recognise him, and try to help. But he didn't. He just ran off towards the little car park, rendering Simon completely alone.

The riverbanks bore tall reeds, impenetrable. He was moving now. Really moving. He clung to the board, searching ahead for one of the little boats that often cruised the waters. But it was late. It would be dark soon, and anyone who had been out on the river would have returned by now.

He brought himself up onto one knee, adopting the stance a surfer might just before they'd stand and carve the waves. He shook with fear at the task ahead, and the cold, and hot tears streamed down his face.

He saw nobody. No movement at all. Ahead, the river turned towards Bardney. Everything was exactly how he'd planned it.

But he didn't make it to Bardney. The weight of the board and his body combined, along with the momentum he had built up, took him out of the current and into the swirling waters on the inside of the bend. He managed to grab onto some reeds, and the board turned and came to a stop. If he let go, the river would take Simon around the bend and into the faster water.

*Here*, he thought. *This is where it happens.*

He peered up over the tips of the reeds, gauging the distance to the bank. Twenty feet at least. It was the perfect spot for what he needed to do. The weeds would tangle around his feet, and he knew the water was deep enough. He would drown and they would never find him. He pictured the board floating on without him. All the way past Bardney and on to Boston. It must be fifty miles. Fifty miles of meandering river for the police to search. They would never find him in time.

It was perfect.

Tying a few reeds into a knot, Simon managed to create a loop to slip his hand through. He lay with one arm outstretched and the current tugging at the board. It was all he could do to hold on and keep his balance, finding that if he lay flat on his front with his arm in the reeds in the water, he could get comfortable while he contemplated his final moments.

But the water was cold and dark, and the thought of slipping into it terrified him into submission. He could do nothing. It was the final hurdle, and he hadn't the courage to do it.

As the huge sky above him paled, then darkened, and the birds that had soared above returned to their nests, sleep took him. It came in fitful bursts. Sometimes he woke in a panic and called out. Other times, he would come around knowing exactly where he was, how helpless his situation and how much of a failure he was.

Twice, he woke and nearly lost his balance, but the fatigue that had been brought on by fear and tension soon took him again. He shivered and shook with the cold, and his arm was numb, though he dared not let go.

"This is it. There's no turning back now," he said aloud, but to himself. He sobbed, stared up at the sky, and shouted in anger, "Why me?"

"Simon?" somebody whispered in the darkness.

"Hello?" he called out weakly. "Is somebody there?"

With no nearby towns to pollute the sky, the night was as dark as he had ever seen it. Darker, he thought. The darkest night. There was no moon, or if there was, it was elsewhere. He would have given anything to see the moon. To have some light, albeit weak.

A shape appeared, or so he thought anyway. He blinked into the gloom in the direction of the gentle lapping he could hear. "Is anybody there?"

A bright torch light flicked on and swept across the water, blinding him so that he had to raise his free hand to shield his eyes.

"Help me," he called out, resigning to being rescued. "I'm over here."

"Simon?" a voice said. The hand that grabbed his arm felt familiar. Bewildered by the ordeal and the thought of being saved, he couldn't even speak. He was safe.

But then the hand tightened on his arm and forced him off the board.

"Help," he said, as his face plunged into the water. He pushed up for a gasp of air. "Help me, please."

But the hand found the back of his neck, and the next words Simon Bird uttered were lost to the freezing cold water of the River Witham. He screamed and thrashed for all he was worth, fighting the urge to breathe, holding on for just a moment longer. *There must be a mistake.* He reached up to pull the hand from his neck, but it was strong. Stronger than he was.

And then it came. This was it. This was how it was meant to be. His miserable life was over. He wouldn't have to endure his mother's bitter tongue any longer, or his father's pitiful cries. He wouldn't have to put up with the random beatings from Gavin, or the vindictive sneers and laughs from the girls.

This was it.

He fought it, but that was just instinct. That was his body in its fight for survival. His mind fought a different battle. His mind had come to terms with its fate. Where his body saw death, his mind saw escape. An end.

Peace.

# CHAPTER ONE

DETECTIVE SERGEANT BEN SAVAGE WAS FROM FARMING STOCK. Generations of Savages before him had all worked what the Romans had called the golden soil. Lincolnshire soil. His father's farm spread as far as the eye could see, and although it had been producing crops for the Savage family for nearly two hundred years, the heritage didn't stop there. The Romans had worked that same soil, and the Iron Age folk before them. Farming families, strong and resilient.

Though, as far as Ben was aware, he was the first of the Savages at least to break the mould. He was the first to reject his expected vocation, and had ventured into the police force, driven, but with trepidation.

His house formed the southern arm of a U-shape and had been given to him by his father on his twenty-first birthday. His father occupied the central house while his two brothers, who had carried on the tradition of Savage farmers, lived in the third arm.

Such was the brutality of Ben's work schedule, and the often uncompromising effort required of the three Savage farmers, that their paths seldom crossed.

Today, though, was different. A rare lull in investigations had allowed Ben the time to drop in to see his father, and what he saw had alarmed him. For a man in his seventies, his father, Joshua Benjamin Savage, was as sprightly as any forty or fifty-year-old man. A life in the fields had kept his body fit and able, and his hands just as Ben remembered from his childhood seemed as large and strong as shovels. But it was during his previous visit that Ben had, for the first time, seen a decline. Nothing major, but evident. A slight tremble in his father's hand. A groan as he sat down.

He was getting old. Damn, he was already old. Most men stopped working at sixty-five, yet here was his own father still grafting as hard as any of the hired hands. And although he had always seemed it to Ben, he wasn't a machine.

That was why Ben's visit today was different. It wasn't a quick drop by to borrow something, as it often was. It was a visit to make sure his old man was still up for the job.

He knocked three times with the old, brass knocker. He could have just walked in. After all, he did grow up in the house. But there was a respect of privacy the three households shared. It was six-thirty a.m. and his father would have been up for a good two hours already. Breakfast would have been dealt with and cleaned up. The dogs would have been fed. And his father would be in his office, checking off the tasks for the day, readying himself to distribute the day's work to Ben's brothers and the farmhands.

The front door swung open, and his father was already walking back to his office by the time Ben stepped inside. There was no greeting, as was often the case. He didn't mean anything by it. It wasn't rude or impolite. It was just his father's way. He didn't waste words.

"Taters going in, Dad?" Ben asked, as he entered his father's office.

Although Ben hadn't followed in his family's large footsteps, he had worked on the farm right up until he joined the force and still helped out on occasion. He knew the timetable. He knew what had to happen, rain or shine, and he knew all too well the consequences of not meeting the schedule his father had crafted in the half-century he had run the farm. It was springtime, and the potatoes had to be planted.

"I've got Johnny Grouch coming to take care of it," his father said, referring to a local farmhand who was trusted by many of the local farmers, and had been working on the Savage farm since before Ben was alive. "Checking up on me, are you?"

"I don't think you need any checking up on, Dad. Do you?"

"Twice in one week. Something's wrong," his father said, without looking up from where he was pencilling comments into his diary and adding notes to the notebook he carried with him.

"I just came to say hello. I don't see you much," Ben replied. "Are the sheep being moved?"

"All under control. They're going over to Bozeman. Jeff is going to fertilize the fields."

Bozeman was the name of the field he used to hold stock on a temporary basis. The grazing fields would need fertilizing if they were to produce hay and silage later in the year. Each of the fields had names. Bozeman was part of a small farm his father had bought nearly ten years ago. Every field had been named after a town in Montana, USA, due to some link with the previous farmer. There was Billings and Helena, both of which were ideal for grazing, and Livingston, which was given over to rape. And then there was Bozeman, a small field in low-lying land that was as picture-perfect as any postcard Ben had seen. But, from a farming perspective, it wasn't really suitable for much more than holding stock on the occasions it wasn't flooded.

"What about James?" Ben asked, referring to his other brother.

"Spraying the cereals. He'll be out for a few days."

"And you?" Ben asked, getting to the real reason he was there.

His father laid his pencil down and sat back in his chair to stare up at Ben, narrowing his eyes.

"What about me?"

"Are you getting out there this year? I imagine there's plenty to do in here."

"I'll be out there," his father said. "I've a team drilling the rape. I want to make sure it stays on track. Weather's closing in."

"They know what they're doing though, Dad. You don't have to be out there—"

"While there's life in these old bones, Benjamin, I'll be out there. Is that why you're here?"

"No," Ben lied. "Like I said, I just thought I'd say hello. Can I help at all?"

Snapping his diary shut, Ben's father pushed his chair back and stood, using the desk for support. It was these little things that Ben was noticing more and more. And it wasn't like his father was a small, frail, old man. He was still taller than Ben's six-foot-something, and even broader.

*He'll fall one day*, Ben thought. *And when he does, it'll be like an old oak crashing through the forest.*

The Savage farm was one of the largest in the region of North Kesteven. As a result, the assets alone would be enough for the next four or five generations to live comfortably. Despite the wealth, his father's house still bore the same wallpaper, the same floors, and the same facilities as it had when Ben was a child. Only his father's office had changed. It hadn't been updated as such. Rather, it had regressed. There were oak panels on the walls, laden with tall bookshelves filled with leather-backed books. The desk was an antique, and the furniture wouldn't have looked out of place in a nineteenth-century gentleman's club. It was only when his father was halfway out of the room that Ben drew his attention to the desk.

"Dad?"

He stopped and turned in the doorway. It was as if he resented Ben being there suggesting he was too old to carry on. He was defiant.

"You forgot your notebook," Ben said, holding the older man's gaze.

He never went into the fields without his notebook. With more than a thousand acres of fields to his name, each one a critical part of the farm's ecosystem, the notebook was vital. No man, not even a younger man like Ben or one of his brothers, could remember everything that had to be done in every field on every day.

The old man grumbled and sauntered back into the office, snatching up his notebook.

"See yourself out," he said. "There's work to be done."

# CHAPTER TWO

Hugo Bird was as far from being entrepreneurial as a man could be, in the eyes of his family at least. In fact, it was safe to say that if ever his mother, god rest her soul, or even his wife, who was still very much alive and kicking, was asked to summarise Hugo in a single word, he was sure that word would have been *lazy*.

Although now that he came to think about it, he was sure that neither of them, even his mother when she had been alive, could manage a single-word sentence. It was rare that his wife Sally could ever tell him about her day, or ask their son how his day had been, without venturing into such a monologue that saliva built up in the corners of her mouth. His mother had been the same, he mused, as he looked down at his little boat, moored up in Lincoln's Brayford Pool. Rarely had she been able to have a quick chat with anybody, despite always telling Hugo's dad that she was just popping into the garden to have a quick chat with Iris, their neighbour.

"A quick chat?" his dad used to say to himself with a chuckle that wobbled his belly. He would shake his head at the very idea of a quick chat, tut, then mutter, "Dear oh dear," and return to his spot in the newspaper, or more accurately, *The Racing Post.*

These days, his father would have been called a Refuse Attendant, or something along those lines. A bin man, that's what he had called himself. Proudly too. And he had every right to be proud. Despite several short spells in Her Majesty's Prison Lincoln, and a slightly longer career in Pentonville, his father had managed to find work that paid the bills, just about, and afforded him the freedom to indulge in the gee-gees. That was, after his nap of course.

Glancing up at the hustle and bustle of the ancient city of Lincoln, Hugo considered the professionals walking with purpose on their way to their jobs, their careers. Some of them probably had families to support. They might even earn enough to save for holidays, something Hugo's father had never been able to do. Any extra cash was always lost on a horse, and on those rare occasions he had managed to get lucky and win something, the money was spent celebrating the win, rendering the whole exercise pointless.

A young couple walked across the little dock towards him, the man helping his partner onto the jetty, and Hugo wondered if they were his clients.

Sally had baulked at the idea of him referring to his customers as clients. He remembered her scowl the first time he had used the word.

"Clients?" she had said, scoffing. "You run a bloody tourist boat up and down the river. You're not representing them in court."

For a little while after, he had been disheartened by her cold words and sharp tongue. But the more he had thought about it, the more he wanted to use the word clients. That had been a few years before. When he was just starting out. When he would spend his weekends fixing up the boat, helped on the odd occasion by his son. Those were the days when Hugo would announce his plans and his visions for the finest tour boat in Lincoln, and tell Sally how one day he would take them all on a holiday. Mostly because he had never been abroad himself, but also out of pride.

He would be the first in his family to take his family away. He would be the first in his family to have his own business. People would bid him good morning. They might look at him with respect.

Sally had rolled up when he told her. "You'll end up a bin man, just like your dad," she had said. "There's nothing wrong with that. But a man like you, well... You need to know your limits."

Cold words again. Always the cold thumb pressing down on his forehead. Quashing his dreams. But she hadn't complained when he had presented her with the flight tickets, had she? No. She hadn't complained when he had left the travel agents with a brochure for a four-star hotel. Four stars. Not three. It wasn't like the place they had stayed in Skegness that time. It was a proper hotel. He could have gone to five stars, but he had wanted to keep some money to get them both something. A keepsake. A memory. Something they could remember with fondness, and something he could look at with honour.

"Mr Bird?" the young man said as the couple approached.

He was an Asian man wearing expensive but loose clothing. The type Hugo imagined wouldn't look out of place on a tourist in Milan or Naples. A crisp shirt, clean, beige pants, and leather loafers.

"That's me," he replied, and with a dramatic wave of his arm, and his most charming smile, he presented his vessel. "Call me Hugo," he said, as he climbed on board behind them. "I'll be your captain and guide today. Sit, please. Make yourselves comfortable."

They took their places on the scatter cushions Hugo had bought at a charity shop to decorate the floorspace with. He had considered buying proper seats, but they were expensive, and besides, they limited the number of passengers he could take. It was, after all, only a fifteen-footer. The scatter cushions were less formal anyway. His clients could sprawl out in between the sights. Or enjoy a picnic lunch together. Hugo would stand at the helm, looking on with swollen pride.

The young girl turned her nose up at the choice of seating, but after some gentle encouragement and enthusiasm from her partner, she settled into a corner, making a show of adjusting her skirt as if Hugo might steal a glimpse at what he shouldn't.

As if he would do that. *Spoiled little cow*, he thought to himself.

He cast his roving eye along the length of her bare legs as she slipped off her shoes and flexed her toes. The sight was tantalising for a man like Hugo. She was a delight to take in, visually, at least, and as she rested her head back, closing her eyes against the springtime sun, Hugo imagined her. He would have bet that beneath that little, flowery dress, she was just like Sally had been back in the day. Toned, supple, and fiercely sexual.

*And a complete bitch*, he thought, smiling inwardly at the young man who now tended her toes with a light massage. *Just like Sally*.

It was at that moment he decided he would make it his goal to turn her opinion of his boat around. He wouldn't be dissuaded by a little princess. By the end of the tour, she would be eating out of his hand. He knew how to charm the girls. He hadn't lost all his youth. Not yet. She would then go on to sing his praises to all her friends. That was how it worked.

He would be remembered as the best tour boat guide in Lincoln. Maybe Sally would hear it being said one day. When it was too late.

The fact was, and it was something Hugo often considered, that he might have been able to buy a larger, more glamourous boat. He might have even been able to have a helper. Someone to drive while he gave his historic tour pointing out the sights. There was so much he could have done, if he hadn't spent most of his money on a holiday in an effort to prove to his moaning wife that he could make a success of his little venture. That, and paying for all the extra tuition his son needed. If only Hugo hadn't passed his father's genes onto his son. If only he hadn't met Sally in the first place. He could have been a millionaire by now.

He'd show them, though. His journey would be longer, and fraught with financial challenges. But he would get there. And then they would see.

"I'm Harry," the young man said. "And this is Debbie."

"Debbie Harry?" Hugo repeated, smiling at them. But they obviously didn't get the joke.

"No, I'm Debbie. Debbie Glover. This is Harry," the girl repeated, her tone indignant.

"Right. Gotcha," Hugo mumbled, as he turned the key in the ignition and prayed the old diesel engine would fire up first time.

It did, although not without a great plume of smoke clouding the sky.

"She's just warming up. I'll give her a minute or so and we'll be on our way."

"Is it just us?" Harry asked, clearly the more pleasant of the pair.

"Yep. Season's only just started. Come summertime, I'll be fully booked, so you're lucky."

"Lucky?" Debbie said to herself, but loud enough for Hugo to hear.

Cold words. Hugo could deal with cold words. He was a master at dealing with them. He might not have a degree, and he might not be a millionaire yet, but when it came to insults and put-downs, he was Teflon. Nothing stuck.

"Don't you worry, little miss," he said, as he eased the choke back and steered the boat he'd named *Sally* from its dock for the last time. "You're on the finest tour boat in Lincoln. Sit back and enjoy the ride."

# CHAPTER THREE

The sky was a bright blue, unmarred by clouds, when Detective Inspector Freya Bloom peered through her window that morning. An eighties playlist was playing on her phone and she was putting the finishing touches to her makeup when her phone vibrated once. A message flashed up. It was Ben telling her he would be ready in a few minutes. She glanced through the window again, peering out across the fields to where Ben's house stood beside that of his father's and his brothers'.

Still fairly new to Lincolnshire, the small farmworkers cottage she rented from Ben's father was in dire need of redecorating and some modernisation, and she had intended on getting it done. If anything, it would be her way of saying thank you to Ben's father, who had agreed to a much lower rent than the market rate. But the winter had been cruel, and the investigations she had dealt with had been crueller still, leaving her very little time to take on the project.

In the six months or so since she had been in Lincolnshire, leaving behind a cheating husband and his adorable son, Freya had dealt with five murder investigations. That didn't seem a lot compared to her previous position in South London, but when she factored in the associated paperwork and the less-murderous investigations, she had been busy. She had made her mark on the county, and in return, it had made its mark on her.

'Be there in two,' she replied, before applying what she considered to be enough perfume to turn heads.

She stood and checked her reflection in the full-length mirror, one of the few installations she had made in the cottage. It had been her original ambition to bring a little class and culture to Lincolnshire. To show the locals that one could stay warm and dry and still look great. However, after six months and a brutal winter, that theory was close to being quashed. She slipped on her new Barbour jacket, pulling an accompanying scarf about her neck, tying it to reveal enough of her neckline to draw Ben's gaze, yet still keep her warm. A little chill on her chest was worth it to catch his wandering eye.

With just two fields between them, she often shared a ride with Ben. It was a good time to discuss an investigation, and being Lincolnshire born and bred, Ben usually drove. However, today would be different. Today, Freya was driving. Having left London in the family motorhome and setting up a rudimentary home on a nearby beach, Freya had been forced to rent a car. Somehow she had endured the winter having only once planted the little Toyota into a twelve-foot-deep roadside dyke.

But now she had her own wheels. Her independence swelled as she climbed into her new Range Rover and felt the comforting rumble of the engine through the leather seats.

A few minutes later, she pulled up outside Ben's house, sounded the horn, and then checked her reflection in the rear-view mirror. But Ben's front door wasn't open, and she was about to give him another blast of the horn when she saw him wandering across from his dad's house, his expression sombre and thoughtful.

"Well?" she said, when he had opened the door and climbed

inside, and not even mentioned the seat she had preheated for him.

"Oh, sorry. Morning," he mumbled.

"Wow. Somebody looks like they need a coffee. Rough night, was it?"

"Eh?" he said, and stared across at her for the first time, and in response, she waved her hand across the plush, tan leather dashboard, presenting her latest.

"What do you think?" she asked.

"Oh, the car. Yeah, it's nice."

"Nice?" she said. "Nice is a word you use to describe a sandwich or a salad. Nice is a word you use to describe somebody who is polite but lacks personality. This is a Range Rover."

"I can see that. It's very nice. You'll be very happy in it," he replied. "As long as you don't have to drive it off-road."

"It's an off-roader."

"It's an off-roader if I was driving it," Ben replied. "But you? I'd stick to tarmac. Or bumpy tracks at a push."

"Are you saying I can't drive?"

"I'm saying you put a little Toyota in a twelve-foot dyke a few months ago. A car that weighed less than DS Gillespie's lunchbox. This is two tonnes of super-charged V8. Stay on the roads."

"You really are a grouch this morning. Is there something you want to tell me?"

"Only that coffee sounds like a good idea," Ben replied. "Sorry, it's just been a weird couple of days. How was your weekend?"

"I'd like to tell you it was enlightening, fantastic, and more. However, I feel that my enthusiasm will be crushed. So I'll keep it to myself, for now."

He didn't rise to her comment. Instead, he huffed, leaned forward to turn off his heated seat, and then gazed out of the window. It was enough of a hint for Freya to just drive, so that's what she did. Had Ben's mood been a little more like himself, upbeat and responsive, she might have put her foot down on the long farm track up to the main road. But he had already made a comment on her driving, and something about this complete shift in his demeanour told her he had something on his mind.

"DC Gold is off this week," she said, deeming the conversation neither personal nor intrusive.

"Yeah, she texted me," he said. "Something about a course DCI Granger has lined up for her."

"It's a Family Liaison course. Doesn't bode well for us."

This caught his attention. He turned from the window and stared at her quizzically.

"Why doesn't it? She's just bettering herself. There's always some kind of course to go on."

"It's a sure sign she's thinking about altering her career. It's a different pathway to DS. If she had any inclination to make DS, she'd be sitting the Sergeant exams."

His expression was hard to gauge.

"She's soft, Ben," Freya told him, only too aware that he and Jackie Gold had been friends since childhood. "Maybe becoming a Family Liaison Officer would be a good move for her. She has all the skills. She might even go far with it–"

"She's always wanted to be a detective. She's talked about being in major crimes for as long as I can remember."

"Are you sure she wasn't just following you, Ben?" Freya said, then winced, realising he wasn't in the mood to be pushed.

"What's that supposed to mean? I've told you before, there's nothing between us–"

"Only because you don't want it to happen. I wonder if she would say the same thing."

"She's a friend, Freya–"

"When did she join the force?"

"A little while after me, I think."

"Right," Freya said. "I think she's grown bored of waiting for you. I think she's looking to move into something a little more suitable for her circumstances."

"Her circumstances?" Ben said. "What are you talking about?"

"She's a single mother. If it wasn't for her mother helping her out, picking Charlie up from school, from football, or piano, or whatever it is he does, then she would have had to do it. There's no way she would have been assigned to a major crimes team. She did it to be closer to you, Ben. That's all I'm saying."

"That's utter rubbish," Ben said. "She's her own woman. She does what's right for her. She's not the type of woman that will throw away everything she's worked for at the drop of a hat. She's not the type to make life-changing choices to be close to someone, especially not me. If she is looking to move towards becoming an FLO, then she'll have her reasons."

"Yep," Freya said. "I couldn't agree more."

"Good," Ben replied, although his expression suggested he was dubious of her agreement.

Freya indicated, then pulled into the station car park, making use of the rear cameras to reverse into her spot, something her little rented Toyota had never allowed her to do. It was when she had applied the parking brake that Ben spoke again, clearly unsatisfied with her answer.

"Go on then," he said.

"Go on then, what?" she asked, knowing full well that the more agitated he became, the more he would enter into a conversation. Even his sharp, snappy tone was better than the brooding silence he had been in.

Ben sighed impatiently. "What're Jackie's reasons?"

"Me," she said. "If, as you say, Jackie wants to alter her pathway, then I would suggest that I've had some part to play in her decision."

"How the bloody hell have you managed to turn this around to be about you?"

"Do you take dinner around to her house to discuss investigations?"

"Eh?" he said, clearly not following. "No, of course not–"

"Did you spend Christmas with her? Curled up in front of your fireplace, just enjoying each other's company?"

"No, you know I didn't. I spent it with you," he said. "Oh... I see where you're going with this."

With one hand on the door handle ready to climb out, Freya leaned closer to him, and lowered her voice, "Have you seen each other naked?"

She climbed out. Usually, they finished their heated debates over the roof of Ben's Ford or Freya's Toyota. But the Range Rover was too tall for Freya to do that. Ben, being six-foot-some-thing, was perfectly fine to peer over the roof. But Freya, in all her five-foot-eight inches with heeled boots, struggled. So, she met him across the bonnet of the car, and smiled.

"That was an accident, and you know it," he said. "I didn't know you were looking up my towel."

"I wasn't looking up your towel, Ben. But it was pretty hard to miss."

There it was. The first semblance of a smile he had shown since she had picked him up.

"It wasn't a compliment," she added. "What about the time you crept into my house and spied on me?"

"I did not creep into your house and spy on you. I let myself in and made some coffee. How the bloody hell was I to know you'd be walking around stark bloody naked? And why do you always have to bring that up? I'd almost forgotten about the incident until then."

She smiled at the memory. At the time, the incident had been somewhat embarrassing, yet equally as thrilling.

"What I'm trying to say is, you don't do that stuff with Jackie. She's grown bored. She's moving on. It's not something we need to concern ourselves with just yet. But it's good to have that kind of thing on our radars."

"She's not going anywhere. You're reading too much into it."

"Want a bet?" Freya said, and couldn't restrain the laugh that slipped from her mouth.

"A bet?" he cried, shoving himself off the car and making his way toward the building. "The last time I lost a bet with you, I ended up wearing nothing but a bloody pinny in front of half the station, a nutjob pathologist, and a bloody crime scene investigator."

"It wasn't half the station," Freya added, meeting him at the front of her car to walk beside him. "It was just the girls. But that's a good point."

"What's a good point?" Ben asked, holding the door for her. Even in the midst of a heated debate, Ben never forgot his manners.

"Jackie *has* seen you naked," Freya said, stopping in the doorway to smile up at him.

"As have half of Lincolnshire, no thanks to you."

"Maybe that's the reason she's moving on," Freya replied. She smiled then sauntered past him and up the stairs. "Maybe she's disappointed?"

# CHAPTER FOUR

THEY HAD ONLY JUST PASSED BENEATH WIGFORD WAY, THE exit from Brayford Pool, and Hugo was about to deliver the first part of his tour, when Debbie moaned for the first time.

"Why did we come this early? Nothing's even open yet."

"What do you mean nothing's open?" Harry replied, in a calming tone that Hugo knew to be tried and tested.

In many ways, Hugo thought, the couple were very much like Hugo and Sally had been. They were in a new town, and Harry wanted to see the sights, learn the history, and see Lincoln from a new perspective. And all Debbie wanted to do was check out the local Primark, which would, no doubt, be very much like all the other Primarks.

"There's no-one about. It's only seven o'clock."

"We haven't come to see the people, Debbie," Harry explained. "We've come to learn about Lincoln. There's tons of history. Did you know, the cathedral was the tallest building in the world at one point?"

"The tallest building in the world? That's only because it's on a hill. It's not that big."

Hugo smiled to himself, and thought it best to move on to the next little snippet of information. At least he knew Harry would be interested.

"This bridge we're approaching," he began, "is the oldest bridge in the UK with houses still on it. It's called High Bridge, and it was built in the twelfth century."

"The twelfth century, you say?" Harry said, trying to enthuse Debbie, but with little effect.

"It's amazing, isn't it?" Hugo continued. "That's been there for nearly a thousand years. It always makes me wonder, if walls could talk."

"It's not really a thousand years, is it?" Debbie argued.

"It's pretty close," Hugo said.

"No. If it was a thousand years then that would mean it was made in..." She squinted, clearly doing the maths in her head. "One thousand and twenty-two. The tenth century. You said it was built in the twelfth century, so that's only eight hundred years."

"The twelfth century was pretty much a thousand years ago," Hugo explained.

"It wasn't," she said. "Harry, tell him. You're good at all this stuff. If it was the twelfth century, it would have been built in twelve-something-or-other."

"No, babes," he began, using that same tone as before. "Twelfth century means it was built in eleven-something. It's the twelfth century. The thirteenth century began with twelve-something."

"No," she argued. "Now you're just trying to make me look stupid."

"Babes, come on," he said. "Don't be like that."

But she was stubborn, just like Sally. She folded her arms and ventured into what Hugo assumed was the first stage of sulking. He'd have his work cut out if he was going to bring her around.

"It's not that well explained," Hugo told her. "I always get them mixed up too. There's some refreshments in the cool box, if you fancy a drink."

She said nothing. She didn't even look his way.

"And some wine," he added.

That got her attention.

"Wine?"

"Yeah," he said.

"Is that allowed?"

"My boat, my rules," he lied, knowing the council would revoke his licence if they caught him. But the chances of them doing so were slim. "Let's just get out of the city, and I'll open a bottle for you. Nothing like cruising the Witham with a glass of vino as the sun rises."

"Now we're talking," she said, and she sat up to look ahead. "How long—"

"Until we get out of the city?" he finished for her. "A few minutes."

She was no longer sulking and Harry was helping by massaging her feet. Hugo gave him a sly yet knowing wink when the younger man looked his way.

"Where does the tour take us?" Harry asked, when they were passing beneath the last of the bridges and an open landscape greeted them. "We're being collected at Tattershall."

"Well, usually I spend a bit more time in the city. But, you know? The tour is flexible."

"Thanks," Harry said.

Hugo nodded at the cool box he had stowed behind the helm. "Help yourself. You'll find some plastic cups in there too."

Dropping Debbie's feet onto the scatter cushions, Harry crawled toward the back, where Hugo was. He found the bottle of wine, unscrewed the lid, and pulled out the little stack of cups.

"I keep it just in case somebody is celebrating or something," Hugo explained. "It's always a nice touch. Unexpected too, for the most part."

"Good job you did," Harry said under his breath, with a slightly reproachful glance over his shoulder. But Debbie wasn't listening. She was lying with her head against the side, eyes closed, and her arms trailing close to the water.

"There are some wonderful ruins along the valley, if you get the chance," Hugo explained.

"Ruins?" Harry repeated, as he offered a third cup to Hugo.

Hugo waved his hand dismissively. He daren't drink and drive. Not with clients on board. "Yeah. Abbeys. There were nine of them along the valley, before the reformation, that is."

"Reformation?" Debbie said, opening her eyes and accepting the cup from Hugo.

"You know? When Henry the Eighth led Britain away from Catholicism. It was back in the sixteenth century."

"Did he?" she asked. "So that's fifteen hundred and something?"

"That's right," Hugo said, sensing he had her on the hook. All he had to do now she had her wine was reel her in slowly, but delicately. "He wanted to divorce his wife, but Catholicism wouldn't allow it. So he created his own religion. I mean, there's more to it than that, but that's the crux of it. If it weren't for him, we'd all be Catholics."

"So why the ruins then?" she asked, and it was Harry who answered.

"He destroyed all the Catholic abbeys and churches. Entire monasteries were abandoned. It was huge."

"He's right," Hugo said. "We'll see some ruins in a minute. Ah, it's wonderful out here. To think, humans have been on these waters for more than two thousand years."

"No," Debbie said.

"They have. The river was different back then. It's been shaped. The coast was a lot closer too, but we've always been out here. It's the fresh water, you see. Humans need fresh water. We're just coming up to Washingborough. See that bridge? That's

Five Mile Bridge, that is. The remains of human settlements have been found on the banks here all the way back to the Iron Age."

"What century was that?" she asked.

"The Iron Age? Well, that began around 1200 BC."

"Ah, so that's the thirteenth century then?" she said proudly.

"No, sweetie. 1200 BC was about three thousand years ago."

"Three thousand years?" she said, her face twisting into utter confusion, as if at the very concept that there was even life before the year zero. Clearly she had no idea of what BC and AD meant, and a tour of Lincoln with a plastic cup of wine in her hand was probably not the best place for a lesson in the measurement of human existence. "But we're in 2022, right?"

Hugo gave her a wink. "All you need to know, Debbie, is that we've been on these waters for thousands of years. It's a wonderful thing."

They passed some distant ruins, and Hugo nodded at them silently to Harry, who glanced up at them appreciatively. Debbie was halfway through her second cup of wine when she suddenly sat up, as if something had just dawned on her.

"Where is it we're going?" she asked.

"We'll go down to Tattershall Bridge. About a mile from here. We'll just round this bend, and I'll open her up a bit. There's a lovely little place we can park up and you can get some breakfast before you go."

"Ooh, breakfast sounds lovely," Debbie said, and Hugo smiled inwardly.

He had turned her around, and as long as he didn't mess it up on the last leg of the tour, she would be singing his praises to all her friends. She might even post about Hugo and his little boat on Facebook. That would be a turnout. It was just like he had heard once on one of those entrepreneurial podcasts. Sometimes, the people who moan the loudest can become your biggest fans. If she posted something on Facebook, Sally was bound to see it.

Then she'd regret losing him.

Debbie leaned on the prow of the boat, something Hugo didn't really like, as it obstructed his view. But he let it slide, this time. It was as she was holding out her cup for Harry to top it up for the third time that she cried out.

"What's that?"

There was a panic in her voice. Her pitch rose by an octave, or perhaps two, and she grabbed onto Harry before Hugo could see what she had been pointing at.

"Stop the boat," Harry said, turning Debbie's head away. He stared back at Hugo, his face a picture of horror. "Turn around. There's something in the water. A body."

# CHAPTER FIVE

THE INCIDENT ROOM WAS ON THE FIRST FLOOR. THE MAIN stairs and the crummy lift were on the far side of the building, so most of the Major Investigations Team used the fire escape stairwell, as it brought them out closer to the incident room. They passed Detective Superintendent Harper's office, although neither of them had seen him for months now. DCI Granger had told Freya that he was sick, but to keep it under wraps. And although a few of the team had made suggestions on where he might be, or what was wrong with him, she had kept her word and revealed nothing. His office was on the right, followed by DCI Granger's office, the little kitchen, and then the washrooms. Halfway down the left-hand side was the incident room, a huge room that had once held two teams, but since Freya had joined, and her incumbent, DI Standing, had transferred to Lincoln HQ, the decision was made to operate only one team. The result was that Freya had inherited a few more direct reports, and she was slowly shaping the team into a talented unit of individuals.

The incident room door, however, still needed work. She had noticed it the very first time Harper had led her through it all those months ago. The hinges squealed like an injured animal, then slammed closed like a shotgun firing. That nobody had fixed it didn't surprise Freya. It was one of those things that irritated her then she forgot about until the next time somebody opened it.

The door squealed open, and Ben stood to one side to let her in first, ever the gentleman.

The hum of activity fell to a lull, and the ball of paper that was already in mid-flight when Freya entered was the only thing that moved.

It hit DC Cruz, the youngest of the team, square in the face, and DS Gillespie, a brash, rough and ready Glaswegian, did little to hide his smirk.

"Alright, boss?" he asked, then nodded to Ben. "Nice morning for it, eh?"

"Nice morning for what, Gillespie?" Freya said. "For chucking paper balls at Cruz? Or for going to get the coffee?"

"Eh?"

"I'm buying," she said. "I don't want that crap from the kitchen. I want proper coffee."

"You mean the wee coffee shop up the road?"

"I do. I'll have a flat white. Get everyone's order, will you?"

"Aye, boss," he said. He was so very overqualified for fetching coffee. In fact, by rights, it should have been Cruz who was sent on the minor errand. But Gillespie liked the girl behind the counter, and if Freya was right about Ben's mood, Gillespie leaving for fifteen minutes or so could only be a good thing.

Gillespie began taking the orders, turning a mundane task into an event, much to Freya's annoyance. But it was Monday morning. She didn't want to bring the mood down. Ben would do that on his own the moment somebody asked him a question.

"Who's having what, then? Eh?" Gillespie called, using his standard-issue notebook to take the order.

"Latte, please," Chapman said.

She was a sweet girl. Older than her years. She wore a knitted cardigan, thick-rimmed glasses, and was as plain as plain could be. But in Freya's mind, she was one of the best researchers she'd ever worked with. She'd take plain if it came in the form of a Chapman.

"Black coffee," Nillson said, retying her ponytail.

Nillson was fit and strong, and more masculine than Cruz in many ways. There had been a few times when she had demonstrated her ability to hold her own with suspects, and was a force to be reckoned with. "No sugar this time, Jim."

"Aye, gotcha," Gillespie said, making a note in his pad.

"I'll have one of those vanilla lattes," Cruz said, leaning back on his chair like a schoolboy. "Get them to sprinkle some chocolate powder on the top as well. Oh, and two sugars."

"Jesus, Cruz," Nillson said, disgusted at his choice. "You'll have a bloody heart attack."

"I'm a growing lad," he joked.

"You wait until you hit puberty, son," Gillespie said, writing the order down. "Then you'll be on the flat whites. That's right, eh, boss?"

He turned to look at Freya, clearly recognising that he hadn't really said what he had meant to say, and in fact had insinuated something entirely different.

"What are you saying, Gillespie?" she said.

"Aye, well... Nothing really. Just, erm, a flat white is a good choice, that's all. You know? Not as sweet as what he ordered."

"You might want to stop talking, Jim," Nillson said.

"Aye. Well, how about you, Benny boy, eh?" Gillespie said, turning the attention to somebody else. "Latte, is it? A wee sprinkle of the old chocolate powder, maybe?"

"Just a latte, Jim, please," Ben mumbled.

"Right, then. I'll be off, shall I?" Gillespie said, heading for the door.

Freya reached into her bag, collected a crisp twenty-pound note from her purse, and held it up. The door squealed open, slammed shut, and then less than ten seconds later, it squealed open and slammed shut again.

"Need this?" Freya said.

"Aye, boss," he said, and made his way across the office to her desk without once meeting her stare. She gripped the note as he took it, forcing him to look at her.

"Flat white," she said. "And stick a sugar in it."

"Aye," he croaked, his voice failing him. He was nearly as large as Ben, and, to most, would have been a formidable man to encounter. But Freya had seen men like him before. He was great to have on the team, but a short leash was required.

He slipped from the room again and the door crashed closed behind him.

"Right then, maybe we can get on with some work now he's gone," Freya said, hoping to raise a smile from the rest of her team. She opened her laptop and was rummaging through her bag for her phone when the door squealed open again. "For god's sake, Gillespie."

But it wasn't Gillespie. It was DCI Granger, and his face said everything she needed to know.

# CHAPTER SIX

"WE DON'T HAVE A NAME YET," GRANGER SAID, TOSSING A BLUE file onto her desk. Freya knew what the file meant. By the time the investigation was over, reports, photos, statements, and god knows what else would spill from the file. It would be her case bible. But for now, it was empty.

The rest of the team all stopped what they were doing and watched. They knew what it meant.

"All we know is that it's a young boy. Thirteen to fourteen years old. Found floating face-down in the river up near Tattershall. CSI are on their way, as is the medical examiner. I suggest you take your team and get over there before the circus begins."

"Who found him?" Ben asked, and despite the grim nature of the conversation, Freya was pleased to see him come out of whatever darkness he had been in.

"Tour boat. One of his passengers saw something. Freaked out. They've all given their statements to uniform on the scene."

"Anybody touch the body?"

"No. They saw him and called it in."

Granger was one of those men with oversized features. His hands were like shovels, and his ears seemed to have outgrown his head, reminding Freya of Roald Dahl's BFG, a thought she kept to herself. But it was his ears that caught her attention. They seemed to move as he spoke, as if he was grinding his jaw. And now that she thought of it, he was. His eyes shone, though he outwardly showed no emotion.

"We'll get down there, guv," she said, flipping open the file and finding just a single sheet of paper with the investigation metadata. The job number, details of the Senior Investigating Officer, and a large space where she would be required to fill in the blanks. "Chapman, can you man the phones?"

Chapman nodded. With her knitted cardigan and calm expression, Freya imagined she would have a bag of boiled sweets in her bag to keep her company, and perhaps a crossword or a puzzle book.

"Until we know the death is suspicious, we'll keep a low profile. We don't want to step on anybody's shoes, do we?"

"Divers will bring him out at Tattershall," Granger advised. "There's a little dock beside the bridge. And as for the cause of death, nothing's confirmed yet. But if you want my money, the bruises on the lad's neck didn't get there by accident."

Freya digested the information, wondering why he waited until now to divulge it.

"Thanks, guv. I'll give you an update as soon as I hear anything."

"Will Gold be joining us anytime soon, guv?" Ben asked.

He stared at Ben quizzically, as if he was reading further into the question.

"I thought I explained to DI Bloom," he replied. "She's away on a course this week. You'll have to make do without her."

Ben nodded, clearly hoping Granger could offer a little more insight into how the course came about. The news had clearly rattled him. He and Gold were good friends. Freya was well aware of how close they had once been, before she had arrived on the scene at least. Either that or whatever news had upset him at his father's house that morning had left him sensitive, which was totally out of character.

"Right, let's go," she said. "Nillson, can you take Cruz? We'll follow up. We may need to split up, so two cars is probably for the best."

Granger nodded his thanks and slipped from the room, as much as anybody could actually slip from the room with that bloody door.

"Shall we wait for Jim?" Cruz asked, clearly more interested in getting his hands on that coffee than actually waiting for Gillespie himself.

"He can follow us up," Freya said, and that twisted part of her savoured watching the disappointment spread over his face. "Unless, of course, you're more interested in your coffee than you are in progressing your career, DC Cruz?"

"Fine," he said with a schoolboy huff.

Nillson was already up and pulling on her jacket, which was the classic denim variety that did little in the way of adding any femininity. She tossed her keys in the air and caught them in a display of energy, the way Freya's ex-husband used to do when he was rallying the family to leave.

"Ben, you're with me. That okay?"

"Eh?" he said. "Oh, yeah. Sure. I'll just be a moment."

He left the room, letting the door swing closed with a bang.

"He's quiet," Nillson said to nobody in particular.

"Personal stuff," Freya said with a wink.

"Oh, the change, you mean?" offered Chapman.

Freya enjoyed having Chapman, Nillson, and Gold on her team. Her London teams had been predominantly male, and any females were usually working their way through the ranks but not yet close enough for Freya to lean on. She'd always had to adopt the leadership role. She did here too. Leadership was everything in a small team. But, somehow, in this team, the opportunities to get to know them as individuals were far greater.

Freya laughed at the comment. Perhaps Ben was going through a change. A mid-life crisis, albeit somewhat early.

"He'll be out buying a sports car next. A little, red convertible," Chapman added.

"Change?" said Cruz. "What change?"

Cruz was the very definition of naivety. Somehow, common sense seemed to pass him by. He had been so sheltered by his mother, with whom he still lived, and so too from life, and all the frivolities of youth. It had become a running joke that after at least two known incidents, Cruz had very little control over his bladder, especially when he was nervous or scared. But he took the jibes in his stride with a strength only gleaned from perpetual insults and banter. He'd be strong one day, and a good detective too, maybe. He had a thirst for knowledge and spent his spare time studying and watching crime documentaries, giving him an uncanny ability to call out little-known facts as if they were common knowledge and everybody should know them.

"Have you ever heard of the male menopause?" Nillson asked him, to Freya's delight. She loved to start a thread and let the team's banter take over, which was usually fed and driven by Cruz's lack of common sense.

"The what?" he said.

"The male menopause. The change. Mood swings and irritability."

He shook his head, pulling a bemused expression. "I haven't got a bloody clue what you're talking about, Anna."

"You will one day," she advised him. "When you look at little, red convertibles and women two decades younger than you, then you'll remember this conversation."

He looked at them all individually.

"Is this what you lot talk about?" he said. "You're mental."

"Why don't you ask your girlfriend? What's her name again?" Nillson said.

"Larson?" Cruz said. "Why would she know about the male menopause?"

"What's her actual name? Her first name?"

Cruz lingered on the question, clearly debating whether or not to go into details about his girlfriend.

"I just call her Larson," he explained. "Especially now she's been moved into CID. She wants to keep a good impression. You know? She doesn't want our relationship to get in the way, or for us to get complacent at work."

The three women all gazed at each other, then back at him.

"You call her Larson? Even when you're out with her? In public, I mean?"

"Yeah," he said with a casual shrug.

"And she calls you what?" Chapman asked.

"Cruz, of course," he said, as if it was obvious.

"All the time?" Freya said, feeling the need to join in.

"Well, yeah."

"What about when you're with friends?"

"Larson," he said.

It was on the tips of all their tongues, but someone had to say it, and Chapman phrased it as delicately as she possibly dare.

"What about when...you know?" she said.

But Cruz just shook his head.

"You know?" Nillson said, venturing further. "When you and her are getting it on."

"Getting it on?"

"Oh, for god's sake, Cruz," Freya said, just as the door squealed open. "What do you call her when you're giving her one?"

Ben stood in the doorway, eyebrows raised. He glanced up the corridor to make sure nobody had heard. The corridor must have been empty, as Ben turned back to face them all, then settled on Cruz, expectantly.

"Well?" he said. "I presume we're talking about Hermione here?"

"Her what?" Nillson said, and then stared even harder at Cruz, who shuffled his feet. "Hermione? Is that her name? Hermione Larson?"

"Yeah," Cruz mumbled.

"It's a beautiful name," Nillson said. "Why do you call her Larson?"

"You think so?" he said, enthused. "I like it too. But she doesn't want us to get too familiar at work. She thinks it might hurt her career if she slips up and calls me Gabby. So we just call each other by our surnames. I mean, when you think about it, it makes sense."

"Yeah, until you get married," Chapman said. "Then you'll both be Cruz. That'll get boring."

"Hold on, hold on," Freya said. "You still haven't answered our question."

"What question?" he said, and his face reddened.

"Come on," said Freya. "Give us all the details. What do you call her in bed?"

"And more to the point," Nillson added, "what does she call you?"

"Ah, come on, guys—"

"If you tell us, I'll let you stay until Gillespie gets back," Freya said, and his eyes flashed at the thought of that sweet coffee he had ordered.

"I call her my little witch," he said shyly. "You know. Like in the Harry Potter films. Hermione. She's a witch—"

"Yeah, yeah, we get it," Nillson said, unable to hide her delight. "And what does she call you?"

"Oh, come on—"

"How bad do you want that coffee, Cruz?"

"Ah, for god's sake," he said, looking to Ben for support, but finding him staring into space. Cruz pocketed his hands, searching for something to fiddle with, something Freya had seen a hundred suspects do moments before they were about to confess. "She calls me her little wizard."

Silence, at least three seconds' worth, during which Freya imagined all kinds of scenarios she would never forget.

"She...what?" Nillson spurted. "Her little wizard?"

"Don't laugh–"

"I'm not laughing, Gabby. I'm bloody mortified. All this time, you two have been casting spells on each other, and we've been sitting here with Harry bleeding Potter."

But Nillson wasn't finished. If Freya had been asked, she would have bet Anna Nillson had grown up with older brothers. At least two, but more like three or four. She had been the only girl. She wasn't afraid of getting stuck into the banter.

"Hold on," she said, grabbing hold of her denim collars and straightening them, ready to leave. "You don't dress up, do you? You know? Like Harry, and, erm..."

She was fighting the urge to laugh so hard that Nillson couldn't even finish the sentence.

"Hermione," Cruz said, as if there was nothing to laugh about. "And we've spoken about it."

They expected him to deny it. They expected him to blush and tell them all where to go. But he didn't. And the more time that passed with him failing to deny it, the more they believed he was telling the truth.

"I can't believe it," Nillson said.

"I'm staggered," Chapman added.

"What?" Cruz said. "It's just a bit of fun. It's not like we can actually do magic, is it?"

"No, Cruz," Freya said. "No, you can't."

"You can't tell Gillespie. Please. Promise. All of you. You can't tell him. If he finds out, he'll tell the entire station."

"Tell me, what?" a voice said from the corridor. And from

behind Ben, the big, lumbering form of Gillespie stepped into view. "Eh? I heard something about magic."

Everyone seemed to look to Freya, as if rank suddenly played a part in whether or not to divulge the information to Gillespie, and therefore, the rest of the station. But the risk of Larson hearing about it was too great.

"Nothing," Freya said. "It's just that Cruz had another of his minor accidents. Didn't you, Cruz?"

He stared between them, then down at himself, and he shrugged.

"I couldn't help it," he said. "It just happened."

# CHAPTER SEVEN

The journey was silent, and this time Freya didn't even bother trying to make small talk. Ben offered a few grunts here and there, telling her when to turn and how far out they were. They were a mile away, by his reckoning, when he spoke for the first time, and Freya understood.

"Sorry, Freya," was all he said to begin with.

"No need to apologise to me, Ben."

"I do. I haven't been the best company. I'm not quite with it."

"Anything I can help with?" she asked, as she felt how tense her body had been as her muscles relaxed. "Just say the word."

"There's nothing. But thanks."

"You know where I am," she said, trying not to push for answers, when all she wanted was to reach across to him and hug the big, daft brute.

He seemed to take a moment to collate his thoughts, or to work out what he wanted to say, or how to say it.

"I think my dad is losing it," he said, which was far from what Freya expected him to say.

"Losing it? In what way?"

"His marbles. You know?" he said, tapping his head. "His dad had it, too."

"Dementia?"

"Something like that," Ben said. "Never thought it would happen to my dad. Never really gave it much thought."

"What makes you think it?"

"Just the way he was this morning, and at the weekend. And now I come to think of it, he's been like it for months. Irritable. Forgetful. I think he knows it too. His hands were trembling. Like he was scared of something. I've never seen him scared. He always..."

He stopped, unable to say the words.

"He's always been your hero?" Freya offered, and he nodded. "He's your father. Of course he's your hero."

"You don't get it. You've only met him a few times. He's bloody strong. Not just physically. But mentally. He's solid. He can't lose it. I can't see it happen to him."

Ben pointed to a side road and she slowed. Freya checked her mirror to find Nillson's car, with Gillespie in the passenger seat and Cruz sitting in the middle of the rear seat.

"Look. So what? You've seen a few little signs. Even if it is something like dementia, and I'm not saying it is, it can take years to progress. Just keep an eye on him. That's what you do. You're his son. You have to look out for him. Yes, he might be the toughest old man I've ever met, but he is getting on. Most men his age have retired by now. In fact, it's not uncommon for men's health to deteriorate once they have retired."

"I think that's why he's pushed it so far," Ben said. "You know? Why he's worked so long. He knows it's coming."

"Has he ever spoken about it?"

"Of course not," Ben said with a laugh, as Freya brought the Range Rover up beside the little, white CSI van and came to a stop. "He barely says anything other than giving out orders and asking questions about the farm. But I think it's real, Freya. I've got this feeling. Have you ever had that? When something's wrong? You know it. You bloody well know it's wrong."

"All the time," Freya said. "Usually when I'm listening to Gillespie telling me about his weekend."

Ben laughed a little. That was as much as Freya could have hoped for.

"Keep an eye on him, Ben. That's all you can do."

"I know. But..."

"But what?" Freya asked, trying to read his expression. "You're worried that if he has it, then you might do too? One day?"

"I don't want to end up like that. And I don't want my dad to end up like it."

"What are you saying?"

He was quiet for a moment, then shook his head. "Nothing. I don't know. Forget it. Anyway, that's why I've been quiet. I've just been wondering what if this and what if that?"

"The farm?" Freya said. "You're wondering if you'll need to drop everything to keep the family going?"

"Something like that. My head's going bananas."

"I know what you need," she said, removing the cup of coffee from one of the two cup holders and taking a sip.

"What?" he asked. "A drink?"

"No. No, something far more cognitive than a drink."

"I'm all ears, Freya. Believe me."

"What you need is a good murder investigation to take your mind off things," she said, and pushed open the door to climb out. "Come on. You can lead this one."

# CHAPTER EIGHT

"What do we have, Doctor?" Ben asked the medical examiner, as he walked away from the grim sight of the body bag lying on the dockside.

"Well, if you want confirmation of death, you've got it," the man said. Doctor Saint was in his late fifties, early sixties. He snapped off his disposable gloves with what Ben could only describe as distaste. "But if you want a time of death, or cause of death, I'm afraid you'll have to see wait for the pathologist to open him up."

"But if you had to make a guess?" Freya asked.

"I don't guess, DI Bloom. But he has some severe bruising on his neck and on his arm, probably from fighting back. Given how and where he was found, he may have been held under the water until he was drowned."

"Wouldn't he have sunk below the surface?" Ben asked. "With the water in his lungs?"

"Eventually, yes. The body takes a while to expel all the air, and besides, the divers told me he was in amongst some long reeds which may have held him up. If I was pressed, I'd say he was killed between nine and twelve hours ago."

"I think it's safe to say he didn't drown accidentally," Freya said. "Given the bruising."

"Agreed," Saint concurred.

The dockside was just thirty feet away. Two white-suited crime scene investigators were crouched beside the body bag, and from where Ben was standing, the pale, white face of the young lad could be seen protruding from the open bag. He turned to find Gillespie, Nillson, and Cruz waiting for instructions. Cruz clutched his coffee while Nillson took in the scene. Gillespie, meanwhile, was watching Ben and Freya interact with the medical examiner. He was as experienced as Ben, but had the misfortune of reporting to DI Standing before he was transferred to Lincoln HQ, and as a result, Gillespie hadn't yet had the opportunity to demonstrate his competence, with Standing's famous narcissistic tendencies claiming any glory worthy of being added to his profile.

"You want us to get uniform to lock the place down, Ben?" Gillespie called out.

"Please, Jim," Ben replied. "Give me five minutes and we'll have a plan."

"A plan in five minutes?" Freya said under her breath, as Saint made his way towards his car, leaving the two of them alone. "You must have cracked it already."

"I haven't cracked it, as such, Freya. But I can see a few challenges we'll face," Ben replied, then waved over one of the diving crew.

The man finished the conversation he was having with another of his crew and strode over to Ben. His wetsuit still hung around his waist, and his t-shirt bore the branding of the Lincolnshire Police Underwater Search Team on the breast.

Ben showed him his warrant card. "DS Savage, this is DI Bloom. Were you on the boat?"

"Sergeant Cole," the man said, offering his hand for Ben to

shake, and then Freya. "I pulled him out. No sign of life. He was face-down in the water."

Cole was a tall man who, at first glance at least, seemed to exude confidence, and bore an almost superhero, V-shaped torso.

"Can you show me where, exactly?" Ben asked, retrieving his phone from his pocket and opening the map app. He zoomed in on their current location and followed the instructions given by Cole to trace the river back to where it turned north, less than a mile away.

"I've got a team searching the riverbed one hundred yards up and down from the spot, but if you ask me, he was swimming further up the river and the current took him."

"What makes you so sure?" Freya asked.

Cole stared at her, his face grim. "It's a natural spot for the current to take him as it neared the bend. Any further out and he would have been swept around the bend, and who knows? He might have been in the North Sea by now."

Ben nodded, more for lack of anything to add, as they all pictured the scene and imagined what the lad had been through.

"Photos?" Ben asked.

"I'll have them sent over to you," Cole replied, and Ben handed him a card with his contact details on it. "And I'll call you if we find anything. You can drive up there and look. I'd offer you a ride on the RIB, but I've got divers in the water. Maybe when they're done?"

Ben glanced across at the RIB, a small inflatable boat with a rigid hull and an outboard motor.

"I've got no interest in getting on a boat. But thanks," he replied. "I'm more interested in seeing where he got into the water."

"Well, you've got about eight miles of riverbank to choose from," Cole said.

"Eight miles?" Freya repeated. "Why so specific?"

"The city is eight miles away," Ben said. "There's a chance he could have fallen into Brayford Pool, and if he did, we'd have him on camera. It's more likely he entered the water somewhere between here and the city. The question is where and when, and who he was with?"

"Did you find any ID on him?" Freya asked.

"We haven't touched him," Cole said, holding his hands up in defence. He nodded back to the CSI team. "The last thing I want is her shouting at me for contaminating her crime scene."

"Her?" Ben asked, his eyes wandering to the pair of investigators, both of whom were hooded and masked. But one of them stood, pulled back her hood, and moved her goggles to reveal long, blonde hair and big, beautiful eyes. She removed her mask, while fumbling with her mobile phone, and paced up and down the dockside, savouring the fresh air after being confined to her PPE.

"Doctor Fell, her name is," Cole said. "Michaela Fell. One of the best, apparently. And she likes to let you know it, believe me."

"We've met," Ben said, and from the corner of his eye, he caught Freya's wry grin. "There's a knack to dealing with her."

"Care to share what that knack is?"

Ben smiled back at Cole, met his gaze, and offered him the best advice he could. "When I've worked it out, I'll let you know."

# CHAPTER NINE

"Ah, Detective Sergeant Savage," Michaela said when they approached. She finished her call and pocketed her phone, then nodded a silent yet cautious greeting to Freya before turning back to Ben. "I'm pleased to see you're fully dressed today."

"Morning, Michaela," Ben replied, and Freya smiled inwardly at the awkwardness of the situation.

Had it not been for her, the two may have been an item. After a series of unfortunate incidents, all of which involved Ben in various states of undress, the relationship had never come to fruition, and only by Freya's ability to manipulate the doctor's brilliant mind had the two remained on speaking terms. There was a funny side to be seen, and the only damage had been to Ben's pride. "Yep, fully dressed. What do we have?"

He had done well, Freya thought. She had half expected him to fluster and fluff his words to get over his embarrassment. But there were greater things on his mind, and the relationship with the doctor was well and truly off the cards.

"I can't give the cause of death. There are too many possibilities at this stage. We'll have to wait until the pathologist gets him on the slab." She held out her hand to her colleague, who Freya had seen before but hadn't yet been able to work out if they were a man or a woman. They handed Michaela a clear, plastic evidence bag containing a wallet. It was the type a young boy might carry nylon with Velcro fasteners. "There's your ID."

Freya reached out and took the bag while Ben pulled on a pair of disposable gloves. Then she handed it to him.

"He's local then," Freya said when Ben held up a cinema ticket for the Odeon. It was three months out of date, which was a good sign. Whoever the boy was, he was not simply passing through Lincoln with his parents.

"See it?" Ben asked.

"See what?"

"The number on the ticket. He's a member. They do those subscriptions."

"That's right, they do," Michaela added. "You pay monthly and get to go to the cinema as often as you want."

Freya called out to Nillson, who left Gillespie talking to a few uniforms and wandered over.

"Boss?" she said.

"Make a note of this number," Freya said, reading it out from the card Ben was holding up. "It's a membership number. Get onto the Odeon in Lincoln. Find out who it belongs to. Once you've done that, call it through to Chapman and have her call me with any details she can find. DS Savage and I will deliver the bad news."

"No problem," Nillson said with confidence, turning to head back to her car.

"And send Gillespie over here, will you?" Freya asked her, then returned her attention to Michaela. "Sergeant Cole suggested the boy drifted downstream. What are your thoughts?"

The doctor pondered the idea, glancing back at the body, then upstream to where the diving team's RIB was disappearing under the bridge.

"It's possible," she replied. "But that poses a challenge, doesn't it?"

"The search area," Ben concurred.

"From Lincoln to here? Must be eight or nine miles."

"At least," Ben agreed.

"Boss?" Gillespie said, coming to stand beside Ben.

The three turned to face the big Glaswegian, Ben being the only one who didn't have to look up.

"Have uniform take you to where the body was discovered. I'm not sure how much use it'll be, but I don't want to miss anything," Freya said.

"Aye, boss," the big man said, taking a sip of his coffee. "Alright, Doctor? I see we're keeping you busy, eh?"

"Hopefully it's not you keeping me busy, DS Gillespie," Michaela replied.

"Well, aye. Not directly, no. But, ah...forget it. I was just making a wee conversation," he replied, defeated by a single retort from Michaela. He nodded at Ben and then turned to walk away.

"You might as well take Cruz with you," Freya called out to him. "You never know. We might need him to knock on some doors. He's good at that."

Her voice must have carried because Cruz stopped his discussion with a uniform and looked up.

"You what, boss?"

Freya mimicked knocking on a door, then with her index finger painted a smile on her face, as if to say, *Door knocking, your speciality*.

"Ah, come on," he cried out, shaking his head. "Why do I always have to go knocking on doors?"

"Looks like you've got your work cut out," Michaela said.

"You and me both," Freya replied. "Call us if you find anything else, will you? I'll make arrangements to see the body with pathology."

The distraction had proved useful. Ben seemed to be more

communicative, and Freya gave their immediate future some consideration before she spoke.

"It's going to get busy. Are you up for this?"

He stared at her, as if reading between the lines. Now was his chance to bail or to call in some time off. The last thing she needed was for him to duck out of an investigation halfway through.

"I can always rely on Gillespie as a number two if you wanted to take some time."

"I don't need time. You're right. I need the distraction of an investigation."

"And your dad?"

"Like you said, Freya," he replied, although there was a hint of doubt in his eye. "I'm probably overreacting."

## CHAPTER TEN

IT HAD TAKEN LESS THAN THIRTY MINUTES FOR NILLSON TO contact the cinema, provide her details, and then receive the name of the membership number. She had passed the information on to Chapman immediately, who had found the boy's name and address, and the details of his next of kin, then relayed the information to Freya.

Freya had hoped for a little more time for her and Ben to develop more of a plan, but she couldn't argue with efficiency, and as a result, less than an hour after giving Nillson the instruction to look into the membership number on the cinema ticket, Freya and Ben stood outside what looked to be a council house on Park Lane, Washingborough.

"Who's doing this?" asked Ben, as Freya rang the doorbell and stepped back.

"And by that, I'm guessing you'd like me to," she replied.

"We could draw straws."

"It's okay. I've been the bearer of bad news for most of my career. Another instance won't make a difference," she replied, as the net curtain on the door twitched, and the door opened.

A man stood there peering out at them, but there was no

confusion evident in his expression. It was like he knew why they were there, and the grim nature of the conversation they were about to have.

"Mr Bird?" she said.

"Ah, good morning," he said, opening the door wider. "You'd better come in."

He stepped back, waving them inside, and then closed the door behind them, ushering them through the tiny little hallway into a small sitting room. The carpet was shabby but clean, and the two two-seaters were old, but the comfy type. The sort that seemed to get even more comfortable with age, if that was even possible.

The whole greeting part had flashed by before Freya had even shown him her warrant card.

"I'll get the kettle on," he said. "I imagine you'll want tea? Tea's always good for moments like this, I think."

Ben and Freya exchanged glances, then looked back at him.

"Tea would be good, yes. Thank you."

"I'll just be a moment."

"I'm sorry, but do you know why we're here?"

"Of course I do. I don't have the police knocking on my door every day, you know," he replied, appearing a little bemused, then slid off into the little galley kitchen. "It's a terrible thing. But you know, I'll come to terms with it."

The sitting room, it seemed to Freya, was the hub of the house. Not the kitchen, like in most family homes she visited. Every surface, from the wall shelves to the TV stand, featured photos and frames of all shapes and sizes. There were pictures of who Freya presumed to be elderly relatives back in the day, before colour photographs were common, and there were school photos showing their son in all his pre-pubescent glory. It was the first time Freya had seen the boy's face properly, and she found there to be a sadness about him. He was weak, or vulnerable somehow.

There was also a family photo on a tropical beach.

"That was last summer," the man explained from the doorway, carrying a tray of tea in a random assortment of mugs. "Beautiful, it was. I don't suppose we'll ever go back again, though."

He set the tray on top of a pile of newspapers and explained that Freya's was the mug with a picture of the A-Team on, and Ben's was the one with bright red lips printed on, as if somebody had kissed it with fresh lipstick. But the more Freya stared at it, the more she concluded it had to be somebody with lips like Angelina Jolie. Nobody had lips that full.

Their host sat on one couch and invited them to take the other, and it was only when he raised his own mug that Freya made the connection. Normally, she wouldn't give a hoot for what a mug said. She found the whole idea of printed mugs to be tacky and immature. But if the A-Team was on her mug, and there were lips on Ben's, she wondered what he had given himself.

*Lincoln River Tours*, the mug read, and there was a slogan beneath it that was too small to read. It appeared to be a cheap branding exercise, as much of the print had already worn off the ceramic.

"So then, I expect you'll want to go over it all again, eh?" he said, and slurped his tea loudly.

Eyeing Ben to see if he had also made the connection, Freya leaned forward and set her mug down on the table. There was no point looking for a spot, as there was none. So she just set it down on a piece of paper. In less than thirty seconds, ring marks on whatever bill it was she had used as a coaster would be the least of the man's troubles.

"Mr Bird, I'm afraid I have some bad news," she began. "Is your wife around?"

"Ah, she's out. Won't be back until later. But it's okay. I'll fill her in on all the gory details."

"Am I right in saying that you discovered a body in the River Witham earlier this morning?"

"Yeah," he said. "Well, it was one of my clients. But I took responsibility and called you lot. It's my tour and I don't shy away from such matters."

"Did you have a look at the body at all, Mr Bird?"

"I did. Well, from afar. Didn't get too close, if that's what you mean, and before you ask, no, I touched nothing. I've seen enough TV shows to know better. The girl saw it, and I turned Sally around to make sure."

"Sally?"

"That's my boat. I wanted to be sure. Then we just got out of there. I had these clients, see? A young couple. It upset the girl. I made the call to you lot and some fella in a uniform met us when we docked back at Brayford Pool to take a statement," he explained, taking another long sip of his tea. "I know it's morbid and all that, but this'll be good for business. Am I allowed to tell the papers, like? You know? I might get my tour mentioned. Drum up some business for the new season."

"Mr Bird, you have a son, is that correct?" Freya asked, and she nodded at several framed photos of the sad little boy.

"Aye, yeah. Simon. So?"

"Do you know where he is?"

Mr Bird shrugged and appeared a little confused. "At school, I expect. It's Monday. Where do you think he is?"

Freya said nothing. There was enough there for him to piece it together, but in case he couldn't, or some part of him blocked the truth from forming, she readied her next statement in her mind. She stared at him, grim-faced.

"Isn't he?" Mr Bird said eventually.

"You said the body was face-down in the water."

"Well, yeah, but..."

"I'm sorry, Mr Bird."

"What? Simon? No. You're wrong. It can't be him. I would have recognised him."

An explanation of how spending a night face-down in a river

can bloat and distort a body would have solved the man's confusion. However, no parent needs to hear that kind of description.

Fishing the clear, plastic bag from his jacket, Ben presented the wallet that was found in the boy's pocket.

"Is this Simon's wallet, Mr Bird?" he asked.

It was all the evidence the man needed. He set his tea down so hard that it sloshed over the papers and he took the bag from Ben's hand and held it to his chest. He sobbed once, then composed himself.

"We can arrange a Family Liaison Officer to come and be with you," Ben explained.

"Are you sure it's him?" Mr Bird said, his voice high with emotion as he clung to the hope that it might not be his son. "I mean... He could have dropped this. Anybody could have picked it up."

"I'm afraid we'll need you to make a formal identification," Freya said. "I'm so sorry to ask."

"See him, you mean?"

She nodded. "We need to be sure it's him before we begin our enquiries."

"Enquiries?" Mr Bird said, not following. He swallowed hard, and to his credit, he was holding his emotions back better than most. "He drowned, right? I saw him. I saw him there."

"There were marks on Simon's body that suggest it might not have been an accident," Freya said, and the man's eyes widened with horror. "I must tell you, we're treating the death as suspicious until we can be sure."

"Suspicious?"

"Mr Bird, I'm sorry to ask," Ben said. "But can you tell us where you were last night?"

# CHAPTER ELEVEN

"That was awkward," Ben said, as he pulled on his seat belt. "We probably should have checked the statement from uniform."

Freya smiled weakly. "In all my years, and all the victims' parents I've spoken to, never has that happened."

She stared through the windscreen at the empty street ahead, where Simon Bird had most likely learned to ride a bike and had kicked a ball about.

"Sometimes, I wish I could go back to the very first time I had to do it," she said. "And I would write the name down somewhere. For them all."

"Make a list, you mean?"

"Of sorts. But more than a list. Memories. If someone were to tell me the names of all the times I've had to do that, I expect I could recall them all. Hundreds of them. I would remember some detail or another. A photo on the mantlepiece, or a barking dog, or something."

"Someone has to do it," Ben said. "And it's better that we do it. Not just some bloke in a tie and an off-the-shelf suit ticking boxes, or, even worse, a letter from HQ."

"Yes. Yes, you're right," Freya said.

"What next?"

"Can we get to the river from here?"

"I think so," Ben said. "There's a bridge. Five Mile Bridge. What are you thinking?"

"I'm thinking that Simon Bird most likely walked to the river. In which case, he probably entered somewhere near here."

She fired up the engine while Ben opened the map on his phone.

The Birds were not a well-off family. But the father, Hugo, seemed to be a decent man. Freya wondered what was going through his head right now. If he was on the phone to his wife. Would he tell her over the phone, or would he ask her to come home?

The curtain twitched when she glanced at the house, and she saw his form slink from view.

"Go to the top of the road and turn right," Ben said, snatching Freya from her thoughts.

"Hmm?"

"You okay?"

"Yes. Yes, I'm fine."

He nodded, clearly not believing her. "Top of the road and turn right," he repeated, and she engaged drive, then eased the big car on.

"Makes you wonder, doesn't it?" she said, leaving space for him to speak.

"About?"

Then she considered Ben's situation. He was a bachelor. He hadn't the faintest idea of what it's like to be a parent, and although Freya had never been a maternal mother, she had raised her ex-husband's boy as her own.

"It makes me think of Billy," she explained. "I'm not sure what I'd do if..."

"I can't believe the bloke didn't even recognise his own son, if I'm honest," Ben said.

"You and me both. Maybe he didn't get close enough?"

"He said it upset his client. Maybe he just got her out of there before he got close enough to recognise him?"

"Maybe," Freya said. "He took the bad news well, didn't he?"

"What do you mean?" Ben asked. "He was crying his eyes out."

"How many times have you had to do that?"

"I don't know, Freya. I didn't know I was supposed to count."

"What I'm trying to say is that, yes, he was upset. But there was something off about his reaction. Don't you think?"

"You don't think he might have—"

"I'm not suggesting anything. But we can't rule anybody out at this stage, can we?"

"You're heartless sometimes, Freya. We've just told the bloke his son is dead, and you're wondering if it was him who did it."

"I'm not wondering anything, Ben. I'm just stating the obvious. Until we rule him out, he's a suspect, just like anybody else. He has the means. Maybe he has a motive?"

Ben shook his head in disbelief and Freya smiled at his reaction. He must know she was right.

"The first task in any murder investigation is to eliminate the family," Freya explained. "Ask Chapman to check him out. And the mother too. What secrets have the Birds got we need to know about? We need the victim's social media checked out, if he had any. Who did he interact with frequently? Did he have an argument lately? You know what kids are like these days. Their entire lives are documented in one form or another. If something happened, it might give us a start."

"I thought you said I was running the investigation," Ben said, not with malice or any negativity. But it was a valid question.

"You are," Freya replied. "But as far as Granger is concerned,

I'm SIO. Those are the things I want to see get done. What did you have in mind?"

"What did I have in mind?" he repeated. It was unlike Ben to buy time to consider his response. It was perhaps a sign his mind was distracted. "The social media thing is a good call. And the parents. I mean, we're going to need to know their movements. The father said he was at his boat. Let's confirm that."

"And finding where Simon Bird entered the water?"

"Yeah. That makes sense," he replied. "And that just leaves a few unanswered questions."

"Such as?"

"Time and cause of death."

"We'll need to pay Doctor Bell a visit," Freya said with another smile. "Your favourite pathologist."

"Turn left here," Ben said, pointing at a small side road on a tight bend. "If I'm honest, I'm not looking forward to that."

After passing a few houses and some industrial units, the landscape cleared into open fields. The Range Rover absorbed the blows from the deep potholes, so Freya kept her foot down to see how it would cope with the rough terrain.

"Ah, come on. It won't be that bad," Freya told him, remembering the doctor's face when she saw Ben in nothing but a pinny after losing the bet with Freya. "She sees naked men every day."

"She sees dead naked men, Freya. Dead ones," Ben said, holding onto the dashboard as they passed a particularly rough piece of road. "Not full-grown adult males with a pulse."

"Once you've seen one, you've seen them all," Freya said, unsure if she was smiling because of the banter, or because she was enjoying putting the car through its paces. "And besides, nobody saw anything except your backside when you opened the door to Michaela. And maybe a glimpse of something else when the wind caught your pinny. But it wasn't a lot. I swear."

"Well, when we do see her," Ben said, as they neared Five Mile Bridge, and he pointed to one side for her to stop the car, "let's keep it strictly business. I've got enough bloody distractions right now. The last thing I need is you two laughing like hyenas."

He climbed from the car before she could reply and was already walking over the first of two bridges, which spanned a drainage channel running parallel with the river. She waited a few moments, giving him some time to himself before following. She wouldn't run. It wasn't in her nature to chase after anybody. So Freya strolled, taking in the scene of the open fields and waterways. She found Ben staring down at the water.

It wasn't a wide river by any standard. Wide enough that it needed a footbridge to cross. Wide enough that two boats might pass side by side with care. And it was straight. Straight enough that the Romans might have overseen the course it carved through the landscape. The side where they were standing had a footpath, or a towpath, running beside it. The other side was open fields.

Ben gave a loud sigh.

"Do you want to go right, and I'll go left?" he asked.

"Not really," Freya replied, pointing at the bridge. "I want to go up there."

In place of a stairway, the bridge builders had installed a ramp that zigzagged up to the crossing, which Freya presumed to be for disabled access or bike riders. She strolled towards it, leaving Ben to follow, which he did.

It was nearing midday, and the spring sky was still tainted with stains of winter. Heavy clouds lined the horizon, and what had started as a blue sky that morning was now a featureless curtain of grey. It was as they reached the centre of the crossing, some ten metres above ground level, that the wind took effect. Freya leaned on the handrail, gazing upstream towards Lincoln.

"Do you really think he started this far upriver?" Ben asked, leaning on the rail beside her.

"Who knows? He could have. If we have to walk the length of this river, then that's what we'll do."

"The footpath," Ben said, as it had just caught his attention. "Maybe somebody saw him?"

"With all those reeds?"

"It's possible," Ben replied, and he made a note on his pad, which he was just putting back in his pocket when his phone rang. "It's Gillespie," he announced.

But Freya wasn't listening. Something had caught her eye. She was heading for the far side of the bridge.

"Gillespie," Ben called out, as he followed Freya, gesturing at her to ask where she was going in such a hurry. He put the call on loudspeaker, which was irritating, as the wind caught Gillespie's microphone now and then, and rasped loudly. "Where are you?"

"I'm at the site," Gillespie replied. "Watching the dive team. Bugger that, Ben. Looks bloody freezing."

"Is there much to see?" Ben asked. Freya was only just listening, vaguely following the conversation. Her mind focused on the exact spot she had seen from the bridge.

"Ah, looks like a river, Ben. I can see the spot where the wee lad was found. The reeds have been flattened. Other than that, mate, there are no footprints on the bank, nothing," Gillespie said.

"What have you got Cruz doing?"

"I've got him walking up and down the riverbank looking for places to get in and out of the water. How about you two? How did the parents take it?"

"Better than expected. We're just upstream in Washingborough," Ben replied, and he caught Freya's attention with a wave of his hand, then gave her a questioning look. "Hold on, Jim. The boss thinks she's seen something."

Freya had stopped three hundred yards from the bridge.

"I have seen something," Freya replied, then after climbing down to the water's edge and parting the reeds ahead of her, she looked back at him. "I'm no David Attenborough, Ben. But if there's one thing I know about nature, it's that there are no straight lines. Tell Gillespie I need a boat up here. There's something in the reeds."

"Something in the reeds?" Gillespie said. Unlike Ben, Gillespie had a habit of repeating what Freya had said, buying time to think of something useful to say. But nothing useful followed. "Like what?"

"Something long, straight, and very oar-shaped," Freya replied. "Now, get me that bloody boat."

# CHAPTER TWELVE

Gillespie and Cruz arrived shortly after the divers had retrieved what Freya had thought was an oar, but had since been advised was a paddle.

"More precisely," Sergeant Cole said, examining the paddle with a curious eye. "It's for a paddle board."

"What, you mean one of those things you stand up on?" Gillespie asked. "Like a surfboard?"

"Like a surfboard, but bigger, yes," said Cole.

"So where's the board?" Ben asked, and all of them, Freya, Ben, Gillespie, Cruz, and the boatmen, all peered downstream.

"I don't suppose you passed a paddle board on your travels, did you?" Freya asked, to which Cole shook his head grimly. "Which means we're going to need to search downstream as well."

"Bloody hell," Gillespie muttered. "It could be out in the North Sea by now."

"It could be, you're right," said Freya. "And if Simon Bird was actually on that paddle board, it could have vital evidence on it."

She looked up at Ben. It was his investigation, and therefore his decision to make.

He nodded, as if reading her thoughts. "Sergeant Cole, how

far downstream can you guys go? And more importantly, how quickly?"

Cole digested the question, glanced at his colleagues, then made his suggestions based on his experience dealing with water-based crimes.

"We can go down as far as Boston. From there, we'll need the local team involved. There's a short stretch of water after Boston before the river opens up into the sea. These little RIBs aren't cut out for it."

It was Ben's turn to digest the information, and if Freya was correct, he'd be wondering how quickly he could get Chapman on the case. Thankfully, Cole hadn't made sergeant just by passing an exam, and he had more to offer.

"We can get the Boston team on board. I'll have them check from the estuary back upstream, and we'll head downstream. We'll meet somewhere in the middle and hopefully one of us will have a paddle board in tow."

"You're a legend, Sergeant Cole. Thank you," Ben said. Then, while he had the floor, to Freya's delight, he took full advantage of it. He turned to Gillespie and Cruz. "Jim, get that paddle to the CSI team. We need prints and anything else they can find. Cruz, take a walk upstream."

"Eh?" Cruz said, his standard response before moaning about a particular task.

Ben jabbed his thumb over his shoulder. "Get up there. If Simon Bird was on a paddle board, he didn't enter here. There are too many reeds. Most likely, he will have found a clearing."

"On my own?"

"Yes, on your own. What, do you want me to hold your hand?"

"Well, no. But..."

"But what?"

"Well, I'll be stuck here, won't I?"

"Have you got a phone?" Ben asked.

"Yeah, course I have."

"Good. When you get to Lincoln, call a taxi."

"What are you going to be doing then?"

If the question had been directed at Freya, she would have closed the young DC down with a single glare. But Ben had far greater tolerance for Cruz's lack of respect for seniority.

"DI Bloom and I will be going to see the body. Unless of course, you want to do that?" Ben asked. "We'll watch her open up his chest, check his lifeless lungs for water, and cut into his stomach to see what he had ingested. Maybe you could cast a spell and bring him back from the dead?"

Cruz's expression changed to one of absolute abhorrence. He glanced at Gillespie, then back at Ben, wide-eyed. "No. No, you're alright." He pointed in the direction of Lincoln, and immediately started to back away. "I'll call you if I find anything."

"You do that," Ben replied, and they watched the young DC walk away, making a show of examining every inch of riverbank he passed.

"Boston just confirmed," Cole said, handing a radio back to one of his colleagues. "We'll head down there now. If it hasn't washed out to sea yet, we'll find it."

"Thanks, Cole," Freya said, and Ben too voiced his gratitude.

"Aye, lads. Good work, eh?" Gillespie added.

With that, the little outboard motor kicked in and the divers tore off down the river, pushing a bow wave as they built speed.

"What was all that about?" Gillespie asked, and he nodded at Cruz, who by now was a hundred metres away, crouching to examine the ground. "You know? All that about him casting a spell, or what not? Am I missing something?"

"No," Ben said, and Freya noticed the smile in his eyes. "No, Jim. You're not missing much at all, really."

"Boss?" a little voice called out from upstream. Cruz was a hundred yards away, waving his hands, then pointing at the ground. "I've got something."

He held his hand up as they approached, in case they trampled the scene. And it was a good job he did. The grass had been flattened, and it was the one spot that would have been easy to get into the water.

Gillespie snapped on a disposable glove, stooped to pick up a cigarette paper, and then again to collect the cardboard wrapper it had come in. Small, rectangle sections had been torn from the material, a tell-tale sign somebody had used it for the roach end of a joint.

"Smoking dope?" Ben said, sounding surprised. "At thirteen years old?"

"They get younger and younger, right?" Gillespie added.

"Bag them up," Freya said. "Let's get CSI down here. There are footprints everywhere, and if they can find the remains of a joint, we might be able to get some DNA from it."

"Aye. I'm on it, boss," Gillespie said.

Standing back, Freya surveyed the scene. The space at the water's edge had clearly been trampled, and the surrounding area too. Plus, a few metres away was a larger area of flattened grass. It was as if somebody had been lying down or rolling around on the ground.

"Do you see it?" Ben asked Freya, and both Gillespie and Cruz followed his gaze.

"If you ask me, it looks like somebody had a wee party."

"Or a fight," Cruz added.

"But why get on a paddle board?" Ben asked. "I doubt it's the fastest means of escape."

"We don't know if he got on a paddle board. Not yet anyway. At the moment, all we have is a body and a paddle," Freya said.

"Right. But let's assume he did. I mean, he got from here to Tattershall somehow, right?"

"Right."

"So, let's say he was here with his killer. Maybe he was being bullied right here? Maybe he got away?"

"Oh, right," Cruz said, allowing sarcasm to flavour his tone.

"He was just strolling down here with a paddle board, got bullied, then made his getaway?"

Ben stared at him. All six-foot-something of Ben looming over the young DC with the big mouth.

"Sorry," Cruz said.

"No," Ben replied. "No, you might have something there. That's what we need to do. We need to establish why the paddle board was here in the first place. Look at this place. This isn't one or two people messing around. This is several people. Several schoolkids, all having a smoke away from prying eyes. One of them rocks up with a paddle board. Where did he get it?"

Freya nodded. "Ben's right. We can guess at why Simon Bird was out on the water with the paddle board all we like. But that's not going to solve anything. We need to talk to the kids. For that, we need to know who brought the paddle board."

She stared at each of them in turn, finding Cruz with a confused expression on his face.

"What's wrong, Cruz?"

"Oh, nothing."

"Cruz, I don't have time for games."

"I was just wondering how we go about doing that. You know? Finding out who the paddle board belongs to. We don't have any suspects. It's like we have the egg, but no chicken."

Both Gillespie and Ben screwed their faces at the analogy. But Freya felt a smile spread across her face.

"What would you do, Cruz?" she asked. "Let's say you lived near the river. You wake up one morning and decide to go paddle boarding. What do you do?"

He shrugged.

"Ask my mates if anyone has one?"

"It's a possibility," she replied.

"Buy one?"

"You're a schoolkid. You don't have much money."

"Do I have enough to rent one?"

"I don't know. How much are they to rent?"

Cruz shook his head, pondering the question with a casual glance up and down the river. In the end, he shrugged. "I don't know, boss."

"So there's your next job," Ben added, stepping to regain control of what Freya had promised was his investigation.

"What?" Cruz said, pulling a face that said he wasn't looking forward to the task.

"Find out where we can rent one from," Ben said. "And see if they've lost any recently."

# CHAPTER THIRTEEN

IT WAS NEARLY AN HOUR LATER, WHEN AN ENTIRE CHAIN OF communications had taken place, that Ben and Freya stood outside a pair of double doors at Lincoln Hospital. The pathologist had called Chapman to advise them that a preliminary post-mortem had been carried out, and Chapman, knowing that Freya would be driving, had called Ben, who then relayed a message from Freya to advise the pathologist that the victim's father would need to identify the body later that afternoon.

Moments after the call, Ben's phone had rung again, and Chapman had advised Ben of two updates. The first was that the press had somehow managed to get wind of the boy's murder. That wasn't necessarily a problem. The public had a right to know. However, whenever the press was involved, Granger was closer to the investigation. Which meant pressure to find results fast.

The second event was even less positive, and Chapman delivered the news with trepidation. Doctor Bell, the pathologist, was, as far as Chapman could make out over the phone, less than impressed with the short notice, and had asked Chapman to make sure Ben and Freya knew that the little boy found in the river was not the only work she had to do today, and that she would be talking to them when they arrived. It hadn't seemed so bad on the journey to the hospital, but now they were there, Freya was not looking forward to finding out exactly what the good doctor had to say about it.

It was no use explaining that it was a murder enquiry, and they needed to act fast, and for that they needed information fast. This was Doctor Bell they were talking about.

Ben sucked in a breath and pushed the mortuary buzzer to let Doctor Bell know they had arrived. They heard the buzzer inside, but when Ben withdrew his finger, the noise continued. He hit the button again, but still the buzzer continued.

"Who is it?" a voice said through the intercom, barely audible over the persistent buzzing.

"Hi, Doctor Bell. It's Ben Savage and Freya Bloom. We've come to see—"

"I know who you've come to see," she replied. "I'll be a moment."

"Nice one, Ben," Freya said, and a few short seconds later, the door was opened by a calm and collected Doctor Bell. Although, beneath her unnaturally pleasant exterior, the tattoos, piercings, and white smock, Freya knew she was a seething wrath. Doctor Bell, with her heavy Welsh accent, had a tongue like a fork, and was prone to voice her opinion, whatever the subject. She gave the doorbell unit a whack with one of her plump fists and the buzzer stopped.

This was going to be a challenging meeting and one wrong word could unleash the Welsh dragon.

"Well," the doctor said, her voice quiet yet menacing, "if it isn't Cagney and Lacey."

"Doctor Bell," Freya said, summoning a smile from somewhere within. "How are you?"

"Busy is what I am. Well, I was busy this morning."

"But not now?" Ben asked hopefully.

"No. Not now, Ben," she replied, holding the door open with her bright red Croc. "Now I'm extremely busy and have very little time for chitchat."

"I fear we may have some part to play in that," Freya offered.

"I fear you do, too. What do you think I do here, sit and wait for the Dicks from the Sticks to send me a body? Eh?"

"I'm sure you can appreciate–"

"And if that wasn't enough, now I have to find a clean smock and watch a grown man identify his son."

"May we?" Freya asked, gesturing they would like to go inside instead of having the conversation in the corridor.

"You may," Doctor Bell said, after a prolonged stare into each of their eyes.

"Your hair is looking good," Ben said.

It was a running theme with the doctor that each time they saw her, her hair was a different colour. It was all part of a charity she had set up to help her mother through cancer. This week, it was a fiery orange, but Ben was famously poor at small talk with women, and his choice of timing was exceptionally bad.

"Don't even think about paying me a compliment in the hope you might win some favours, Benjamin Savage. Now then. You know where the PPE is. I'll see you inside. As it happens, I've carried out the prelim. It'll be short and sweet. That's good news for you, good news for me, but bad news for the little lad on my table."

"Understood," Ben said, doing his best to conceal a smirk, but failing miserably.

"I'll see you inside," the doctor said.

"What the bloody hell is the matter with you?" Freya hissed as soon as the door was closed and they were alone.

Ben fetched the gowns, masks, and hats from the cupboards and tossed her a set.

"What?" he said. "I was just paying her a compliment. You say it every bloody time."

"Yes, I say it every time, but I choose my moments. I don't do it when she's riding her bloody high horse, do I? I do it when the time is right. You really have no clue about women, do you?"

He shrugged. "I'm single, and the only naked woman I've seen this year is you."

"And that will do you no favours," Freya said, supporting her statement with a raised index finger. She pulled on her gown and hat. Then, before she donned her mask, she had a thought. "At least she said it'll be quick."

"It'll be quicker if you two stop your nattering and get out here," a voice called out from inside the theatre.

Ben and Freya exchanged nervous looks.

"Can she hear us?" Ben whispered, his eyes wide.

"Yes, I can hear you fine," came the reply. "The intercom is stuck on. Now then, do you want to see this boy, or shall I put him back in his drawer? The poor lad's had a rough weekend as it is."

"Ready?" Freya asked, as Ben was tying his gown behind his back.

He gave up, leaving a mess of a knot that would be near impossible to untie with his hands behind his back. But that would be an issue he would have to deal with later. They entered the theatre, and Freya was pleased to hear classical music playing through a little speaker.

"The Marriage of Figaro," Freya announced, as they drew near the stainless steel bench on which a blue sheet covered a boy-shaped mound. "One of my father's favourites."

Doctor Bell said nothing in reply. Her eyes were closed, and she seemed to be lost in the melody. It was only as the tune came to its glorious conclusion that she opened her eyes and slowly peeled back the blue sheet that covered the boy. It was the first time Freya had seen him in full, only glimpsing him at the dock-side in Tattershall and unwilling to disturb the CSI team as they worked.

In death, he looked peaceful, although the darkness around his eyes seemed a permanent feature. It was as if he hadn't slept for days or weeks. He was a thin boy, underweight, from what Freya could see, and his arms were delicate, which, when looked upon alongside his face, gave him a gaunt and starved appearance.

The standard Y-section had been made across his chest, from each shoulder to the centre of his breastbone, and then down to his navel. Perhaps because of her irritancy, the doctor had left him like that for Ben and Freya to see.

The doctor retrieved a pen from her breast pocket. It was the type that had four colours to choose from, each one selected by depressing the corresponding button near the top of the pen. It was the type of pen Freya would expect to find in a schoolgirl's pencil case, not in the hands of a forensic pathologist.

"See here," the doctor said, indicating the trachea in the boy's neck with the tip of her pen. "CT scans show signs of fluid. The same can be found here, here, and here." She pointed to the boy's sinuses, nasal cavity, and an area close to his ear.

"What does that mean?" Ben asked.

But the doctor ignored him, as was often the case when she was providing her professional opinion. She waved her hand over the open cavity, specifically around the one remaining lung. "Here, we have ground-glass opacity. I've popped one out already, but I'll spare you the gory details. You can see from the remaining lung how large it is. Not a good sign, if you ask me."

Freya suppressed the urge to comment on how she would have preferred to study a single lung on a bench than stare into the open cavity of a dead boy. "Does that indicate..." she began, but the doctor hadn't finished.

She moved her pen down the boy's intestines. "Swollen, eh? See that, do you?"

"I guess so," Ben said. "Isn't it supposed to look like that?"

Doctor Bell stared at him as if he was some kind of imbecile. She shook her head slowly.

"No, Ben. No, it is not supposed to look like that. The small intestine and stomach are swollen. Any idiot can see that."

She slid her pen back into her breast pocket, taking the time to ensure the little clip was fixed to the material of her smock, then set her hands on the bench, silently indicating that she was now ready for questions. There were only really two questions Freya needed answering for now. There would be more later. But until the father had identified the body, they could do very little with any news.

"Cause of death?" Ben asked, which Freya deemed a suitable question, but the doctor rolled her eyes and gave another of those patronising head shakes.

"He drowned, Ben," Freya said, enjoying a polite smile from the doctor in return. "I've seen this a few times."

"Right," Ben said. "Might have been nice if you could have mentioned that, instead of letting her think I'm an idiot."

"Her?" the doctor said.

"You," Ben replied, then caught himself and came back at her with his next question. "Time of death?"

A sharp intake of air suggested it wouldn't be a straightforward response.

"Less than twenty-four hours, judging by the rigor. The temperature of the water is a factor, obviously."

"Obviously," Ben added.

"And the condition of the gastronomic organs suggests loss of blood flow for at least eight to ten hours."

"So somewhere between ten and twenty-four hours?" Ben suggested.

"Then there's the rectal temperature."

"The what?"

"The rectal temperature. It's the temperature inside the boy's—"

"The body loses around one and a half degrees every hour

after death," Freya added, saving the doctor from explaining the ins and outs of her work to Ben. "Fahrenheit."

"But wouldn't the water affect the temperature?"

"It might," the doctor said. "But if you want my opinion, which I imagine you do, as you're here asking me the questions, then I would say this boy has been dead for twelve to fifteen hours."

"Twelve to fifteen. What does that give us?" he asked, checking the time on his phone. "Somewhere between nine p.m. last night and midnight."

"Midnight swimmer, was he?" Doctor Bell asked. "One of those wild swimmers?"

"Wild swimmers?" Ben said.

"Will you be repeating everything I say, Ben? If you are, I'll leave gaps for you to join in."

"Sorry," Ben mumbled, reddening as he did.

"Wild swimmers," the doctor continued. "Strange lot. Go swimming outdoors. In rivers and such."

"Brave," Ben said, hoping to regain some kind of credibility with the doctor.

"Brave? Lunacy, it is. That's what swimming pools are for. Shall I show you the bacteria I found in this boy's stomach?"

"No. No," Ben said, "I'll take your word for it."

"We have no reason to believe he was wild swimming. Not at this stage, anyway."

"No. No, I should think not," Doctor Bell said, giving Freya a brief nod.

"The medical examiner suggested there might be some bruising?" Freya added, to which the doctor's top lip twitched, as if Freya had just stolen her moment.

"Doctor Saint?" she asked.

"Yes. Yes, that's him," Freya said, remembering the man on the dockside.

"He's one of the better FMEs. And he's right. There is some bruising. But not where you'd expect to find it."

She retrieved her multi-coloured pen from her breast pocket again and waved a small circle in the air around the boy's neck. "Now then," she said, with a flick of her eyebrows like she was about to tell a campfire story. "You can just see them here. I can't turn him over because... Well, it's obvious why. But can you see here, this bruise, and the corresponding bruise on this side?"

Both Ben and Freya followed the pen like they were entranced, then nodded in unison as two small schoolchildren might nod to the teacher.

"If this boy had been strangled, you'd see bruising here, and here," the doctor continued, showing the area near the front of the boy's neck. "However, these bruises suggest something altogether different. Far more sinister, they are."

"Somebody held the back of his neck?" Ben suggested, and the doctor pointed her pen at him excitedly.

"Yes. Yes, Ben. He was held here, like this, see?" She grabbed the back of Freya's neck, not as softly as Freya might have hoped, considering this was just a demonstration. "And he was forced down."

Freya lurched forward as the doctor gave the last part of her re-enactment.

"I get it," Ben said. "I get it."

The doctor let Freya go, but grabbed onto her arm.

"Now then. See here?" She waved her pen over the areas her fingers and thumb had gripped her, and although Freya couldn't see them, she was pretty sure there would be two marks there. Two white patches of skin that were slowly regaining colour.

"Hence the bruising," Ben offered.

"Hence the bruising," the doctor concluded, although Freya was unsure if she was repeating what Ben had said for dramatic effect, such was her way, or because Ben had repeated what she was saying earlier. Either way, she was glad the demo was over.

"Is there anything else you can tell us?" Freya asked, keen to get out of there. Too much of Doctor Bell's company was rarely a treat.

"I've scraped the fingernail, but I doubt we'll find much there." She held up one of the boy's hands with practiced care. "Short. Bites them, he did. Terrible habit, that."

"I guess the water would have washed any evidence away," Ben muttered to himself, with a last glance at the dead boy's face.

"I'll forward the results, and the toxicology, of course. But you know how long they take. You'll have solved it, and I'll have somebody else on my slab before the results come back."

"I do hope not," Freya said. "We do try to keep the bodies to a minimum, Doctor Bell."

"I'm sure you do," the doctor replied. "I'll see you out."

She covered Simon Bird with the sheet, then ushered them towards the door. Ben began to untie his gown, and the doctor caught him fiddling with something behind his back.

"Oh, I was going to mention," the doctor began. "We're having a little get-together at my house. This weekend, it is. I thought I'd return the favour, seeing as you invited me to Ben's strip dancing party."

"Oh lovely," Freya said, and Ben just turned his head, holding his tongue. "What's the occasion? Birthday? Shall I bring a cake?"

"No, as it happens. It's a goodbye party for my mum. You know? The sickness and all that."

"A wake?"

"No, not a wake. She's not dead yet. She starts her new treatment soon. Stronger injections, you know?"

"Right," Freya said, not really following why they would celebrate that.

"Said she wants a party to see her off. Just in case she doesn't come out of it. She swears blind it'll be the one that sees her off."

"But a party?" Ben said, clearly not thinking before he spoke.

"Yeah. A party. You know, in her own words, if the good lord is going to take her, then she'll go with a smile on her face."

"Right," Ben said, mirroring Freya's response.

"Anyway. I'll text you the address and time."

"So, do people bring gifts to these types of parties?" Freya asked, wanting to show the woman some kind of support. "I'm afraid this will be a first for me. I'm quite looking forward to it."

"Looking forward to it?" the doctor said, a look of disgust on her face. "It's a death party. She might never come back."

"Well, not looking forward to it, as such," Freya said, back-tracking. "But, you know? I'm keen to send her off with a smile."

You could have cut the air with a spoon. The doctor stared at her, as if she was questioning Freya's intelligence with just that single, penetrating look. Her face was expressionless, save for her mouth, which hung open in incredulity.

"Just bring your wallet," Doctor Bell said. "I'll be taking dona-tions. Cash only, though. I'm not bloody Aldi."

And with that, she closed the door, leaving Ben and Freya alone in the reception. Ben sighed audibly through pursed lips, and Freya leaned on the back of the visitor couch.

"Thank god that's over," Ben said. "A bloody death party? Is she a complete lunatic?"

"I can still hear you," Doctor Bell called out, and Ben winced for the second time that day.

"Help me out, will you?" he said, and he turned so that Freya could untie him. But the knot was a mess. She gave it a tug but that only served to tighten it. "Cut it, or rip it or something. Just get the bloody thing off me."

Freya searched for something to cut the strings with, but found nothing. In the end, she rubbed her hands together, bent him over the couch, and prepared to rip the strings from the gown. After all, how strong could it be?

Ben gave a small groan at her first tug, and by the time Freya was getting into her stride, with the cords wrapped around her hands, he was groaning with every effort she made, until they groaned and moaned in unison, with Ben bent over, holding onto the couch for support, and Freya pulling with everything she had.

Then the theatre doors opened.

They both looked up to find Doctor Bell in the doorway, a bemused expression on her face.

"What is the matter with you two?" she asked, and then, to add insult to injury, she gave them her final head shake of the day.

## CHAPTER FOURTEEN

"I don't know how she does it," Freya said when they had both climbed into the car. She sat back, still reeling from the meeting with Doctor Bell. "I've never met anybody who can put me on edge like that."

"I feel like I've been violated," Ben added, and he too sank back into the plush, leather seats and rested his head on the headrest.

"It's definitely a murder, though."

"One hundred percent."

"What are your next steps?" Freya asked.

"I'm just going to sit here a while. At least until my pride, dignity, and self-confidence return."

"That could be a while," Freya said. Neither of them moved during this interaction. The car was silent and still, and outside, the world seemed to pass by oblivious to their trauma.

"Are you going to go?"

"To the death party?" Freya asked. "Yes. Yes, I think I will."

"It's at her house. You know that, right?"

"Yes, so?"

"It's going to be like walking into the arms of death."

"She asked for our support. What can we do?"

"Oh, I don't know. We could say we're working," Ben suggested, putting his hands behind his head as if he was settling in for a nap.

"Don't you feel that little pang of guilt? This is a woman's death party. She might not recover."

"For crying out loud, Freya. Listen to yourself. It's a death party. What the bloody hell is a death party? I've never heard of one. And do you know why I haven't heard of one?" Ben asked. "Because normal people don't have them. Normal people just go through the motions of sickness. Sure, there are risks. Society is aware of the risks. The doctors tell us if a procedure, or a treatment, has risks involved. But we don't celebrate it. We don't even talk about it. We just make whatever plans we need. We make sure our loved ones are taken care of the best we can, and we go for it."

"It's kind of nice, though, don't you think?" Freya mused, and Ben's silence spoke volumes. "No?"

"No, Freya. It's bloody sick is what it is."

"Oh, come on. Her mother is going in for treatment. She might never come out again. The least we can do is give her one last send-off. Some happy memories for her to carry into theatre, or whatever it is."

"And what if she survives?" Ben said. "Then what? What if we see her on the street? 'Oh, hey, Mrs Bell. Remember me? I was at your death party. Glad to see you're still alive.'"

At that moment, Ben's phone rang. He fished it from his pocket, hit the button to answer the call, then activated the loud-speaker before resting his head back on the seat.

"Chapman?" he said lazily. "How's it going back there?"

"Hi, Ben. All quiet here. Just the way I like it, thanks."

"So you don't fancy coming to a death party?" Ben asked.

"Eh?"

"Nothing. Don't worry," he said with a sigh. "What have you got for us?"

"I've been going through Simon Bird's social media accounts. He's not very active, but he has a Facebook account. I've checked Instagram, and he's not on there, which is weird, because Facebook is more of an older generation thing."

"Older generation?" Ben said. "Should I have an account?"

"Not that old, Ben," she quipped, which was unusual for Chapman, who was known for being reserved, polite, and professional. She was in a good mood. "It looks like he blocked several other users. In fact, he's blocked more people from seeing his profile than he has actual Facebook friends."

"What does that mean?" Ben said. "I'm a Neanderthal, remember?"

"Well, on Facebook, you connect with people. When you add somebody as a friend, you become Facebook friends. Simon Bird had a total of twenty-five Facebook friends."

"Right?" Ben said, trying to draw more information from her.

"He blocked fifty-something people."

"Maybe he was just cautious?"

"No. No, see, I've been looking into it. I searched TikTok too."

"TikTok?" Ben said. "Isn't that the video thing? You know? Attention-seeking girls showing off their bodies to the rest of the world?"

"Well, yes, and no. It's a lot more than that. Anyway, I found an account dedicated to Simon Bird."

"So he had a TikTok account?"

"No, it doesn't belong to him. It belongs to somebody else. And the videos are horrible. Every one of them has been put up there to ridicule the boy. There's even one of a lady sunbathing, and the words 'Simon Bird's mum' plastered over the top of it. Hundreds of people have liked it."

"Liked it?"

"Don't ask," Chapman said, who clearly didn't have the energy to explain how social media worked to Ben. "The point is, I think Simon Bird was being bullied."

"You mean like having his head flushed down the loo?"

"No, Ben. It's worse than that. Bullying has evolved since the dark ages when you were at school. It's about public humiliation. There are tons of videos on here, Ben. Somebody even leaned over the washroom stall and filmed him... You know?"

"No. No, I don't know. Filmed him doing what?" Ben said, winking slyly at Freya.

She could picture Chapman. Even sitting on her own with nobody to overhear, the polite, mild-mannered DC would be uncomfortable with toilet talk.

"Alright," Freya said. "We get the picture. Do we know who this account belongs to?"

"No. I've passed it over to the tech guys at Lincoln HQ. It's an anonymous account."

"That could take them days to trace," Freya said. Her knowledge of social media was limited, but compared to Ben's, she was a guru.

"I did have an idea," Chapman added, which made Freya sit up and listen.

"Go on."

"Well, although the person who set the account up is anonymous, there are tons of other people liking the video and making comments about Bird."

"How does that help us?" Ben asked. "It's not the other people we need. It's the person who set the account up."

"Exactly. If we assume the culprit posts these videos, and all his or her friends like the video, then we can assume that the only person who hasn't liked the video is the person who set the account up. It might be nothing, but it could lead us somewhere."

"Do it," Freya said. "It's a bloody brilliant idea. I've asked Gillespie to drop a paddle off to CSI. I'll get him to go to the school afterwards to talk to the head. If we can identify his peers, and understand if there are any groups we should be concerned with, we might pin the culprit down."

"No problem," Chapman agreed. "I'll go through each of these videos and see which people like them all. We can assume they will be the kids closest to whoever's done this."

"Call me when you've made some progress. Thanks, Chapman. Brilliant work."

Ben ended the call and was about to pocket the phone when it rang again. Gillespie's name showed on the display.

"Jim?" Ben said, again diverting the call to loudspeaker. "Were your ears burning?"

"Hey, Ben. No. Should they be?"

"We mentioned your name, that's all."

"Ah, I don't like the sound of that. One wee bit."

"It's nothing major. As soon as they have identified the body, we need you to go to the kid's school. Talk to Chapman. She'll point you in the right direction."

"Oh, aye. You need me to break the news?"

"Yeah, that, and talk to the head about any little cliques."

"Cliques? You mean like gangs?"

"I doubt very much if the headteacher will appreciate us referring to groups of their children as gangs, Gillespie," Freya added.

"Oh, aye. Yeah. Got you."

"We just need a list of kids in his year group, and who hangs around with whom."

"Whom?" Gillespie repeated.

"Yes, whom. It's a word, DS Gillespie. Look it up."

"Right," he replied, then cleared his throat to hide the sound of his amusement. "How's it going, anyway? Did you get to the morgue?"

"We're certain it's a murder. All we need now is for Doctor Bell to let us know when the father has been to identify the body. We're just lining up a few lines of enquiry."

"Drowning?" Gillespie asked. He had a way of using a single word to ask a question. It was a bad habit and poor use of the English language, in Freya's opinion. But more often than not, she let it slide. Not everyone was afforded the same degree of education as her, and she counted herself lucky in most instances.

"He drowned, yes. But was helped."

"Oh, aye. The bruises on the wee lad's neck? He was a little boy, for Christ's sake. Who does that?"

"Chapman has a theory he was being bullied. If she's right, then there may be a link there."

"Ah, hence my visit to the school?"

"Exactly."

"Did the father not say anything about it?"

Both Ben and Freya were silent for a few moments. It hadn't even crossed Freya's mind, and judging by Ben's expression, it hadn't crossed his either.

"No, funnily enough," Ben said. "But then, why would he? I mean, if you'd just been told your boy is dead, would you think of that?"

"Aye, but you told him he died under suspicious circumstances, right?"

"We did, yes."

"And surely you asked him if he could think of anyone who might have had reason to hurt the lad?"

"We asked all the right questions, Gillespie," Freya said, her tone a little sharper than she had hoped. "I can assure you, this isn't the first time I've had to deliver bad news."

"Aye, well," Gillespie muttered quietly. "I was just brainstorming, you know? Shooting from the hip and all that."

"Yes, well, next time, maybe I'll be sending you to deliver the news."

"How did he take it, then? Was it bad? I hate that. Had to do a few with DI Standing. Awful. Just bloody awful."

"He took the news better than expected," Freya said, and even as she spoke the words, she could recall Hugo Bird's admirable composure. "A little too well, in my opinion, but then it takes all sorts. Grief hits us all in different ways."

"Did you hear who he was?" Ben asked Gillespie, as if they were two blokes standing at a bar discussing last night's football match. "The dad?"

"No. Should I? What, is he famous or something?"

"Not famous, Jim," Ben said. "He was the bloke driving the bloody boat."

"No."

"Yep."

"But–"

"It was him."

"And he didn't–"

"Nope."

"Aye, well, I'm with you, boss," he said. "He's one to keep an eye on for sure."

——————

# CHAPTER FIFTEEN

——————

Back at the station, Freya gave them all a few minutes to check emails and grab a drink, and then she nodded at Ben. He gave her a quizzical look in reply, with an accompanying shrug, to which she replied with a nod at the blank whiteboard. This back and forth was in complete silence, and just when she expected Ben to voice a question, he pointed at himself with raised eyebrows.

Freya's response would be, she hoped, as clear as she could make it. She rolled her eyes and nodded, at which Ben tapped his watch and mimicked a phone call. Freya read that little mime to mean he was waiting for Anna Nillson to call, after which they would know for sure whether or not the body belonged to Simon Bird.

It was two-fifteen, and the viewing had been scheduled for two o'clock. The call was imminent. Such matters rarely took longer than fifteen minutes.

She nodded once, then set about their lines of enquiry. Her reasons for allowing Ben to run the investigation were twofold. The first was to give him a distraction from whatever was wrong with his father. The second was to bring him along further. He was more than capable of running the show. In fact, he'd led the investigations while Freya's predecessor, DI Foster, had been dying of cancer, and it was a well-known fact that Ben was due to be moved up into the DI position when Freya had come along. So he was ready.

But unless she was careful, his motivation and confidence may slip. And given that DC Gold was probably considering a shift in her career, and that Detective Superintendent Harper, more affectionately known as Arthur for his ability to only do half a job before handing it over to somebody else, had been off with a mystery illness for months now, changes were imminent. Freya had worked for enough factions, departments, and units to know that top brass enjoyed taking advantage of a move to make big changes all at once, as opposed to smaller, incremental changes throughout the year. If changes were to be made, then she wanted him to be ready. If Harper retired, or died even, which wasn't unlikely given his age, Granger would move into his position, leaving Freya the opportunity to step into the DCI position. That left a big hole that she didn't want top brass to fill with any old officer they could find. The position belonged to Ben. She may have delayed his career by arriving, but she sure as hell wasn't going to let somebody take what was rightfully his.

"Okay, okay," Gillespie said finally, and he tossed his pen onto his desk in defeat. "I can't work it out."

"Work what out?" Chapman asked, without breaking her flow in typing, yet turning to look at him.

"The magic thing. I heard it clear as day as I came out of the stairwell."

"I don't think you did," Chapman replied, feigning a confused expression.

"Aye, I heard it. It's not a word you hear every day, not in our line of work, anyway."

"You must have heard wrong," Cruz said, reddening. He glanced around the room for the others to back him up.

"Yeah. Must have heard it wrong," Ben agreed. "We told you. We were talking about Cruz's latest trouser accident."

Cruz rolled his eyes and inhaled loudly. He couldn't argue with it. Cruz had wet himself at least twice in the past six months, so it was a credible, albeit embarrassing, excuse.

"When?" Gillespie asked, and he eyed Cruz as he might a suspect, seeking the tiniest tell-tale sign the young DC was lying.

"Oh, at the weekend," Cruz said, and he looked to Ben for support.

"Oh, aye?" Gillespie said, moving to get into Cruz's line of vision. "You just wet yourself, did you? No reason. One minute you were walking down the road, and the next you just–"

"You said it was in bed, didn't you, Cruz?" Ben said, coaxing Cruz into embellishing the story.

"Yeah. Yeah, that was it," he said. Then he added, "Pfff. I need to sort it out. See a doctor or something."

Gillespie nodded, although it was clear he didn't believe a word of what was being said.

"On your own, were you?" Gillespie asked. "I thought you told me you stayed over at your wee lass's place?"

"I did, yeah," Cruz said, and behind Gillespie's back, Ben shook his head, running his finger across his neck, telling him to stop talking. "It was only a bit, though. You know?"

"No," Gillespie said. "So if I went downstairs and found her, she'd tell me, would she? She'd back you up?"

"No, don't," Cruz said. "She doesn't know."

"So, what you're saying is that you wet the bed with her lying beside you?"

"No, she wasn't there. She was out. With her mum."

Ben gave Freya a wide-eyed look of complete disbelief.

"Out with her mum?" Gillespie said.

"Yeah. I was on my own."

"In her house?"

"Yeah."

"And you wet the bed?"

Cruz lingered for a moment, but he'd come too far to get out of it.

"Just a bit."

"And you expect me to believe that?"

"Don't say anything to her, Jim. Please, mate."

"Alright," Gillespie agreed.

"Oh Christ, thanks, Jim. She'd go nuts if she found out–"

"But I want something in return."

"Eh?"

"I want something in return. All these secrets I keep having to carry for you. They're becoming a bit of a burden, if you know what I mean?"

"Like what?" Cruz asked, with more than a little trepidation.

"Oh, I don't know. Why don't you fetch me a coffee from the kitchen, and I'll have a wee think about it?"

"A coffee?"

"To start with, aye. I'll think of my recompense while you're out there. You know? I'm feeling a wee bit better already, just at the mention of coffee."

Cruz stood and pushed back his chair. "Alright. I'll get you a coffee. But you have to promise."

"Oh, it's coming on again," Gillespie said, rubbing his temples. "It's this weight I'm carrying. It's growing heavy on my mind. I think I'm going to have to tell someone one of these secrets–"

"Alright, alright. I'm going," Cruz said, just as Ben sat forward in his chair, studied his phone, then gave Freya a serious look.

It was the call they had been waiting for. The call that would either set them all in motion, or leave them hanging there until a positive ID could be sought. Ben collected his phone, then sat back in his chair, staring directly at Freya as he answered it. All eyes were on him, and Chapman, with her fingers poised above her keyboard, bit her lower lip in anticipation.

"Nillson," he said.

He avoided putting the call on speaker, which Freya took to mean that Hugo Bird could probably be heard in the background. Listening to a father grieve over the death of his child wasn't at the top of anybody's agenda. It was those things that Ben did that made him stand out. The little touches that demonstrated his experience and his understanding.

"Are you okay?" he asked. She would be. Nillson was a tough nut to crack. "Well, thanks for letting me know. I'll see you back here, then. Right. Cheers, Anna."

He set the phone down on his desk before looking up and meeting the stares from the team.

"It's him. It's Simon Bird."

# CHAPTER SIXTEEN

At the whiteboard, Ben glanced around the room. It had only taken Nillson twenty minutes to get back, which left one empty seat, a glaring hole in the team that Ben tried not to think about.

"So, here's where we are," he began. "At approximately seven-thirty this morning, Simon Bird was discovered floating face-down in the River Witham, near Tattershall. The man who discovered him was his father, Hugo Bird, who, as a tour boat operator, happened to be passing."

"I thought it was his passengers?" Gillespie called out, and he checked his notes. "A young couple. Harry Cousins and Debbie Glover."

"That's right. The girl saw the body, so Hugo Bird turned the boat around to take another pass. From there, he returned to Brayford Pool, calling the emergency services along the way," Ben explained. "As you all know, we attended the scene at Tattershall and have subsequently found a spot on the riverbank where we think Simon entered the water. A paddle was found nearby, believed to belong to a stand-up paddle board. The paddle is now being examined for prints."

Ben took a moment to take a sip of water, catching an approving nod from Freya as he did.

"Hugo Bird has now confirmed the body is that of his only child, Simon Bird. What we need now are lines of enquiry. DC Chapman has discovered evidence of bullying on social media. Gillespie, you're going to attend the school to understand if there are any groups of children we need to be aware of."

"Aye, Ben. I've got the name of the school. I'll head down there after this."

"Good. Nillson, I want you to go and talk to the young couple on the boat. See if their story matches with Hugo Bird's."

"Will do," she replied, and Chapman handed her a piece of paper, presumably with the details of where the couple were staying.

"Cruz, when we're done here, go upstairs to CID. We need some flyers printed up."

"Flyers?"

"We need a call for witnesses. If we're right, and Simon floated down the river on a board without a paddle, somebody may have seen him. It's a popular spot for dog walkers and joggers."

"Right," Cruz said, looking pleased with the task. "That's simple enough."

"Have a few hundred printed off," Ben continued.

"Eh?" Cruz's pleased expression soon faded as he waited for the rest of the instruction.

"Then I want you to stick them onto every lamp post, street post, sign post, or whatever you can, along that riverbank."

"From Washingborough to Tattershall?"

"Wherever you can find a place."

"That's miles."

"The lane that runs from the main road to Five Miles Bridge," Ben continued. "Do you remember it?"

"Yeah," Cruz said, appearing confused now and more than a little worried.

"There are some houses down there—"

"Oh, you have to got to be kidding me?"

"Knock on the doors. See if any of them have those doorbell cameras. The same applies to the industrial units down there. One of them must have a camera up."

"Why do I always have to go door knocking?" Cruz asked, sighing heavily.

"Because you always moan about having to go door knocking, DC Cruz," Freya said, stepping in to save Ben's flow. "When you learn to stop moaning about door knocking, then maybe I'll give you something with a little more responsibility."

"Aye, as long as it's not making coffee," Gillespie said, raising his mug. "This is bloody awful."

"I want footage," Ben said, raising his voice. "Anything we can get. I want to know who's been down that lane in the past twenty-four hours. I don't care if they walked, drove, rode, or if they went down there on a bloody space hopper. I want the footage. Is that understood?"

Cruz nodded, then sulked.

"Right. We've all had a little while to think about some angles here. Let's hear your ideas," Ben said.

Chapman raised her hand, as Freya thought she might.

"I've just had confirmation that the dive team has found a paddle board down in Boston."

"Excellent," Ben said, and he clapped his hands once to get the excitement going. "Have uniform collect it and take it to be examined. What else do we have?"

"I found a little place that rents out kayaks and stuff," Nillson said. "I was wondering if they might do boards, too."

"Good shout," Ben said, nodding his agreement. "Can you get down there this afternoon?"

"Sure, I'll go after I've spoken to the young couple."

"Excellent. Right then, DI Bloom and I will go to see the boy's family. Hopefully, this time we get to see the mother. I want to understand a bit more about Simon and the whole cyber-bullying thing. Chapman, can you help DCI Granger with the press? He'll need some notes on where we are."

"No problem."

"Let's meet back here in the morning and swap notes."

The flurry of activity that usually followed a briefing passed, and Ben was writing up the board. He'd written Simon's name in the centre and linked Hugo Bird and his wife Sally with a straight line. To one side, he created a bullet list. *Bullied. Paddle board. Father found him.*

"Not much to go on, is it?" Freya said.

"Ah, it's normal at this stage. We'll get there," he replied, sounding far more positive than he had done only that morning.

"You did well."

"Is that a compliment?" he asked.

"Sure."

"It's not my first briefing," he replied, turning to face her.

"Of course," she said, remembering the first time they had met formally. Ben had been giving a briefing on a girl's body that had been found on a nearby beach when Arthur had led Freya into the room. Shortly after, Arthur had taken the case from Ben and handed it to Freya. "It wasn't meant to sound patronising."

He smiled, but was clearly in the zone. "Lucky I didn't take it that way, then."

"I'll just use the washroom," Freya said. "Then we'll go and see the Birds, shall we?"

"Sounds like a plan to me."

The incident room squealed open and slammed shut as normal. Ben replaced the lid on the pen, stepped back to admire the board, checking he hadn't missed anything, and then grabbed his coat and made his way to the fire escape stairs to wait for Freya. He was just about to open the fire escape door when it swung open and he bumped into somebody.

"Whoops, sorry," he said. He took a step back and found a familiar face staring up at him. "Jackie?"

"Ben, hi," she said, and then peered along the corridor to make sure they were alone. Then she stepped back into the stairwell. "How's it going? I hear there's been a murder."

"News travels fast. The press even know."

"I saw Gillespie in the car park," she explained.

"Oh, right?" Ben muttered. "A young lad. Found in the river."

"He said you're all over it. Led the briefing too, I hear."

"Just Freya keeping me on my toes, I guess."

"Nice one, Ben. I'm pleased for you."

"What about you? How's the course going?"

"Oh, it's amazing, Ben," she began, then stopped herself. "It's different. You know? Like, really helping people through stuff and getting them to talk. I feel like it's a cross between being a spy and a social worker."

"Nice analogy," Ben said, with a little chuckle that finished with a long, empty, and awkward pause.

"Has she said anything? DI Bloom?"

"What about?"

"Me. On this course."

"Only that you won't be in this week."

"But she doesn't feel like I'm abandoning ship?"

"Why would she?" Ben lied, with all the best intentions.

"I'm just trying to better myself. I need to progress, you know? Trying to open a few doors. I just feel like I'm letting her down."

"So, are you looking to transfer?"

Just then, Freya's heeled boots announced her approaching. Ben glanced back to see her walking along the corridor from the washroom, drying her hands on a paper towel, which she cast into the kitchen bin.

"I'll just grab my things, Ben," she called out, then disappeared into the incident room, with the usual squeals and bangs of the doors.

"I'd better go," Jackie said, as she moved back toward the stairs. "I don't think I can face her."

"You don't have to go," Ben said, with a quick glance over his shoulder to make sure Freya wasn't coming.

But Jackie was already on the stairs.

"Let's meet up," he said, leaning over the handrail.

She stopped on the little landing and glanced back up at him.

"Sure," she said. "I'll call you."

"Make sure you do."

She disappeared down the rest of the stairs and out through the door into the car park.

"All set?" Freya said from behind him. She peered over the handrail. "Who were you talking to?"

"Nobody," he said, and thought about buying a few moments for Jackie to get away. He re-entered the corridor, calling back over his shoulder, "Hold on one sec."

"Where are you going?"

"Just grabbing my laptop," he replied, and heard Freya call out that he never takes his laptop anywhere, questioning why he would take it now.

He collected the laptop from his desk and was stepping through the open incident room door when he stopped and cast a sweeping glance across the room, his gaze settling on Jackie's empty chair. He hadn't noticed before, but there were no pens, no pads, and there was no trademark empty coffee cup with her lipstick on.

"Shall we go?" Freya said from the fire escape door. She eyed him curiously as Ben made his way back towards her clutching his useless laptop. "You okay?"

"Yep," he replied with a sigh. "Let's do this."

# CHAPTER SEVENTEEN

"I'M LOOKING FOR A MR BOORMAN," GILLESPIE SAID THROUGH the glass in the secondary school reception. He flashed his warrant card as discreetly as he could, then pocketed it.

The school was nice. It was clean too. Much cleaner than the various schools he'd been thrown out of when he was growing up. The open office space behind the receptionist reminded him of the incident room, and all the pretty, middle-aged brunette had to do was lean back and call out to a colleague, and she got the answer she was looking for.

"I'm afraid he's not around right now," she said. "Can I help at all?"

"Aye, yeah. Maybe. You could tell me when he'll be back?"

"Can I ask what it's regarding?" the lady said.

"It's regarding one of your pupils," Gillespie explained, leaning forward to keep his voice low. "And I think it's best to talk directly to him. It's a wee bit sensitive."

"Oh. Well, maybe I can book you an appointment?" she said, with a smile, and she too leaned closer. "Love your accent, by the way."

"Mine?" he replied, astonished. Nobody had ever told him that. Not as far as he could remember, anyway.

"There's something about a Glaswegian accent," she said with a little laugh, then studied a calendar on her screen. "Now then, let me see."

"Will he not be back today?"

"Possibly. Mondays are a bit hit and miss with him, I'm afraid. It's the academy meetings. I don't know why they happen on a Monday of all days."

"The academy?" Gillespie said. "What academy is that, then?"

"The academy the school belongs to," she replied, as if everyone knew where the headteacher would be.

"The school is an academy?"

"Yes, of course. We're part of a wider group of schools. We're part of an academy."

"Isn't it just a school? In my day, schools were just schools. You either went to the one near your house, or you went to the next closest one."

"Things have moved on since you and I were at school. You'll find most schools these days belong to an academy. It adds a layer of management across the top."

"Right, so it's a business now, is it?"

"Yeah, kind of."

"What are the benefits of that?" Gillespie asked. "I mean, are they run any better?"

"Well, most likely."

"So the kids' education is better, is it?"

"No, the curriculum is the curriculum. It's stipulated."

"But they learn more?"

"No, the teachers are the same and the lessons are just as long."

"So, how is it better? Is the food better?"

"The food hasn't changed because of the academy, but trust me, it's a lot better than you and I would remember it."

"Right," Gillespie said, with an accompanying smile. "Things were simpler back then, eh?"

"I suppose they were," she replied.

"So, where do I find this Boorman fellow?" he asked, and he gave her a wink.

"This Boorman fellow is standing right behind you, sir," a voice said.

The lady behind the desk smiled up at him, pleased with herself.

Gillespie turned to find a tall, lean man studying him from Gillespie's worn but comfy boots to his warm but tarnished jacket.

"And you are?" the man said.

"Gillespie. Detective Sergeant Gillespie. Might we have a wee word? Somewhere private. Your office, maybe?"

Boorman was a little taken aback by Gillespie's introduction. His eyes widened slightly and he glanced down at the receptionist.

"What's this about? I've a pretty busy day."

"Aye, well, it's probably best if we talk in private."

"I see. On your own, are you?"

"I am. It's very important," Gillespie explained. "Why don't you lead the way, eh? Then we can get this over and done with."

Gillespie offered the lady another wink as Boorman led them both towards a set of double doors, swiping his card to enter.

"Ah, excuse me," the woman called, and both Gillespie and the headteacher turned to find her waving. "You'll need to sign in, I'm afraid."

"Sign in?"

She slid a tablet through the gap under the window.

"Rules are rules," she said, in her best teacher-like voice.

"Am I going to be called out at register?" Gillespie asked, as he entered his details. "Or maybe I'll join assembly."

"I'm afraid you've missed today's assembly," she said, and there was something in her eye that suggested that when she was at school, she was one of the cool kids. Probably rolled her skirt over at the waist to shorten it, chewed gum, and smoked cigarettes at break, he thought. He slid the tablet back, and she studied his details, offering a polite, "Mmmm," sound. "Thank you, James."

"It's Jim," he corrected her, and the headteacher coughed politely.

Gillespie watched as the woman set the tablet down and prepared to carry on with her work. He didn't move a muscle, and her eyes rolled around to stare at him, before her eyebrows raised in question.

"And you are?" he said, adopting his best teacher-like tone. It was a gamble. In fact, it was more than that. It was damn right inappropriate, given the circumstances for his visit.

But opportunities are there in life for the taking. And he was damned if he was going to pass on this one.

"Busy," she said finally. "Very busy."

"Well, it was nice to talk to you, Very," Gillespie said. "Maybe I'll see you again."

He found it odd that a woman as pretty as she was appeared surprised at his attention. She even blushed. She had enormous eyes, a cute button nose, and an infectious smile.

"I'll look forward to it," she replied.

"I am rather busy," Boorman explained from the doors he was still holding open, signalling the end of the interaction.

He led Gillespie through a corridor and then produced a set of keys to unlock a door just four down from the reception. The office was enormous, too large really for one man, Gillespie thought, when he considered how small Granger's and Harper's offices were. A large potted plant, despite occupying one corner of the room beside the window, was the focal point. It was a palm, of that Gillespie was sure. Its broad leaves reached out across Boorman's plain but large L-shaped desk, upon which was a laptop, a notebook, and three pens, all lined in together like soldiers facing the firing squad.

A bookshelf filled one wall, and at a glance, the books all appeared to be the self-help type. *Theory of Motivation* was the title of one, and another was titled, *How to Win Friends and Influence People*.

Boorman waved a hand at one of the two guest seats, which, compared to the plush, leather chesterfield armchair he lowered himself into, might as well have been an iron maiden. Gillespie dragged it closer to the desk, turning it so he could sit on the hard, wooden chair side-on to Boorman, and lean on the desk.

"Well, then. We have five minutes. How can I help?" Boorman asked, interlacing his fingers.

"You have a pupil named Simon Bird," Gillespie stated.

"That's correct."

"I'm sorry to say we found his body this morning."

Boorman was still for a moment, as if he was digesting the news. He shook his head a little.

"I'm sorry. Did you say Simon Bird has died?"

"I did. I'm sorry to have to be the one to tell you. It's never easy."

"And his parents?" Boorman began. "Do they know?"

"That's all taken care of. I'm not sure how much you know about the process, but we can't begin our investigation until the body has been formally identified."

"Investigation?"

Gillespie inhaled long and hard.

"We're treating the death as suspicious, Mr Boorman. I can't really say too much at this stage. But the father—"

"Hugo," Boorman added.

"Aye. Hugo Bird has identified the body. It's Simon. So now we can go ahead and look into why he might have been killed."

"I'm shocked. Truly, I am," Boorman said. He lifted his desk phone, punched a few numbers, then waited a few seconds. "Can we get two coffees in here, please? Thank you."

He set the phone down again, his hand lingering on the handset, then looked up at Gillespie.

"I'm sorry, if I was abrupt."

"No need to apologise, Mr Boorman."

"Desmond. Call me Desmond, please."

"Well then, Desmond, there's really no need to apologise. I've thick skin. Besides, how were you to know why I was here?"

"Yes, quite right. I thought one of our pupils might have smashed something, or caused havoc somewhere again."

"Happen often, does it?"

"More often than you'd think," Boorman explained, then shifted direction. "The parents mostly. Bad influence."

"Well, I probably know some of the parents then," Gillespie said. "In a professional capacity, of course."

"Sadly, I think that might be an accurate statement. Now then. What can we do to help?"

"One of our DCs suggested there might have been some bullying going on. Some online bullying, more to the point."

"Ah, yes. I heard about that. It was a TikTok account, wasn't it?"

"Aye, it was," Gillespie said. "You knew about it?"

"Of course. I had it shut down the moment I heard about it."

"The account is still open, Mr Boor... Desmond. It was still happening."

The headteacher sat back in his chair, shaking his head in dismay. "Bloody typical. They've probably just started another one. That's what they do, you know? The kids know all the workarounds. They know how to set up an anonymous account."

"We're investigating now. Our tech guys will find out who they are, sure enough."

"Well, I hope so. Whoever it was should be banned. And they'll be dismissed from this place too. I can assure you of that."

"The problem we have is that an investigation like this can take days. Weeks, sometimes. We really need to make progress fast. The first few days are critical."

"Yes. I understand," Boorman said.

The door opened, and the very lovely receptionist entered carrying two cups of coffee on a tray, with a few sachets of sugar and a teaspoon. It was the first time Gillespie had seen her in full, and the sight pleased him. She was a good-looking woman.

"Thank you," Gillespie said, as she slid one coffee closer to him. "Just what the doctor ordered."

"You're welcome," she replied, but without the accompanying flirtatious expression she had used to reel him when they had been alone. "Can I get you anything else?" she asked them both.

"No," Boorman said. "Please tell the others I'm not to be disturbed."

She closed the door behind her. Gillespie wasn't sure if it was the school environment, or it had just been too long since he'd been close to anybody, but he found himself pushing away the schoolboy infatuations to focus on the task at hand.

"And you think the cyber-bullying might have something to do with his death, do you?" Boorman asked.

"Maybe not directly. But we have to look at every angle. We've compiled a list of names that look at the social media posts and like them. What we'd like to do is run this list of names against your list of names to identify who's missing."

"I see. And the missing name will be the culprit. I like it. It's a good idea."

"It's not infallible. But it'll give us a start. Ideally, what I'd like from you and your team," Gillespie said, with a sideways nod at the door, "is a list of every pupil in his year group, grouped into their informal peer groups. You know? Who hangs out with whom?"

It was the first time Gillespie had used the word whom, and Boorman didn't even bat an eyelid. Which meant he must have used it in the right context. Pleased with himself, Gillespie then sat back and waited for Boorman's response.

"You can have your list, Detective—"

"Sergeant Gillespie," he added, and he fished one of his contact cards from his top pocket. "Detective Sergeant Gillespie."

"Yes, well. You can have your list by the end of the day. I'll see to that," Boorman said, collecting the card from the desk and holding it up to the light. He peered over the card. "I might be wrong. But I have a good idea who's behind all the bullying."

# CHAPTER EIGHTEEN

F REYA AND B EN WERE ON THEIR WAY TO THE B IRD HOUSEHOLD, both of them lost in thought. Freya was enjoying the ride and the luxury of her new car, and she guessed Ben was mulling over one of three things; his father, Jackie, or the investigation. He must have sensed she was wondering what he was thinking, and he broke the silence.

"It's nice to be driven everywhere for a change," Ben remarked as he settled into the passenger seat. "I could get used to this."

"Well, don't get too used to it. I don't particularly want to rack up the mileage on this," Freya replied. "Besides, I rather enjoy being thrown around the inside of your car in these country lanes."

Ben glanced sideways at her, then stared ahead, wide-eyed.

"When you're driving fast," she added. "You know the roads, I mean. You have more confidence navigating the lanes. Not..." She sighed. "Not what you were thinking."

"Just checking," he said, his schoolboy grin curling the edges of his mouth.

"And anyway, if you crash your car, it'll do you a favour. If I crash this, I'd still be paying for it in two years' time."

"What's that supposed to mean?"

"I mean, your car isn't worth anything."

"Oh, well, I'm sorry it doesn't meet you expectations, your highness."

"That's not what I mean, and you know it. It's a perfectly splendid car. Especially for what we do. It doesn't matter if it gets a scrape or a knock. You'd barely notice it."

"Of course I'd bloody well notice it."

"It's an old junker, Ben."

"It's three years old."

"Yeah, and in that three years, you've put over a hundred thousand miles on the clock."

"Ah, it's barely run in. That's got another hundred in it, at least, before it packs up. Well, it *would* do," he said.

"Would do if what?"

"If it wasn't carting your ego around. I can see why you got one of these. You need it to get your massive expectations in."

It was banter, and Freya knew it. She enjoyed it, in fact. But he often made comments about her that made her wonder how much truth was in them.

They turned into the Birds' street, and she slowed to a crawl.

"I wonder if the news has spread yet," she mused aloud.

"Place like this," Ben replied, nodding. "Yeah. It doesn't take long."

"I just hope the press doesn't get wind of where they live. The last thing they need is the scavengers hanging around outside their house."

"Did they agree to an FLO?" Ben asked.

"Not that I know of," Freya replied, and she gave that question some consideration. "And even if they do, it won't be Jackie, Ben."

"I know," he said defensively. "I was just wondering if we could get someone on the inside. Might be helpful. Anna Nillson was an

FLO before she joined Major Investigations. You know that, right?"

"Yes. She told me once. She's moving up the ladder, and she'll do well. She's a smart girl. Switched on. Bloody fearless too."

Ben was about to say something, but paused, as if reconsidering.

"Do you think Jackie will be making a mistake if she transfers?" he said.

"I think Jackie Gold will do what's best for Jackie Gold, and we owe her our support, whatever her decision."

"But you've helped her a lot. You must feel a little responsible for her. I know I do."

"I feel nothing, Ben," Freya said, parking outside the Birds' house. "We're not here to feel, are we?"

"I guess not."

"Look. If you're asking if I'll be angry, or feel betrayed, then the answer is no," Freya explained, and she took a moment to peer at the house to make sure they had a moment to chat. "But if you're asking if I'll be disappointed, or sad to see her go, then yes. Of course I would. She's got a brilliant career ahead of her, whichever direction she takes. She's a single mother. She doesn't have the freedom that you and I enjoy. She needs to do what's right for her."

Ben nodded. She imagined he expected her to say something like that, and it wasn't until they were both out of the car and facing each other over the huge bonnet that Freya delivered the last word on the point.

"And you can tell her that," she said, giving him a knowing smile, "the next time she apprehends you in the stairwell."

# CHAPTER NINETEEN

"Mrs Bird?" Freya said, holding up her warrant card and offering a neutral expression. "I'm Detective Inspector Bloom. This is Detective Sergeant Savage. I wonder if we might have a word?"

Sally Bird was tall and could have once been beautiful, had it not been for her makeup, which Freya thought looked as though a twelve-year-old had applied it. Freya did, of course, factor in that the woman had likely been crying. But even so. She stepped to one side and gave a brief nod of her head to invite them into the house, then ushered them politely into the small lounge space.

"Is your husband around?" Freya asked, noticing the absence of life in the house. It was still, like the morgue they had been to earlier that day.

"He's gone out," Sally replied. There was a rasp to her voice, like that of a long-term smoker's. She stared at Freya through her greying fringe. "But we spoke. I know."

"We're doing all we can," Freya said. "We were wondering if you might be able to help with a few things."

"Why don't I make some tea?" Ben offered, and Freya took the seat she had taken earlier, encouraging Sally to sit opposite her. Ben slipped from the room, and Sally sat on the edge of the armchair, as if she didn't want to commit to it entirely. Like it was wrong for her to relax. But she would do one day. When the pain had eased.

"He said he even went to see him," Sally said.

"He didn't tell you he was going?"

"No. Well, I had some missed calls from him. But I always have missed calls from him," Sally explained, then shook her head. "I can't believe it. It's like I'm dreaming and Simon is going to walk through the door any minute."

"I've known people to lose loved ones, and they still get that feeling a decade later," Freya said. "I know this is a terrible, terrible time for you. But, Mrs Bird–"

"Sally. Please. Call me Sally."

"Sally, thank you. You see, when something like this happens, there are certain rules we have to follow. A process, if you will."

"I understand."

"I would have preferred to wait to speak to you both, but you see, we couldn't begin our investigation. I do hope you really understand. The first few hours are critical."

Sally nodded. She seemed a kind woman. A little lost, maybe. But kind.

"Usually, we wait until the next of kin has been advised before we can begin, but in this instance, we needed to be sure it was indeed Simon."

"And it was," Sally said. "Hugo said it was."

"So now we're moving forward. And I'm afraid that's where you come in."

Sally Bird looked up at Freya, wiped her eye, and rested her palms on her lap. She swallowed hard and steeled herself.

"We have several lines of enquiry, Mrs Bird. I'm going to take you through each one. I'll give you as much information as I can, and I'd like you, if you can, to tell me whatever you feel you can. Is that okay?"

The light rattle of tea cups coming together interrupted them, and Ben entered the room, settling two cups down on the messy coffee table. He left again, only to return with a small pot of sugar and a spoon.

"First of all, Mrs Bird, are you okay to answer our questions? We can come back if you'd like some time."

"No," she said abruptly, and her fringe seemed to jump into life with the effort. "I want to help you. I want whoever did this found."

Freya nodded, and Ben, as usual, prepared his notebook and pen.

"And before we start, I have to ask if they have offered you a Family Liaison Officer? I mentioned it to your husband, but…"

"They have, yes. Had a phone call a while back," Sally explained, taking the opportunity to blow her nose. "Somebody is coming. They said so. Said they'd send someone this afternoon. I don't really know what good they can do, though."

"They can be a great help. We call them FLOs," Freya explained. "You'll be surprised how much help they can be."

"We'll see. I only agreed as… Well, I'm on my own here, aren't I? Hugo isn't much use."

"Where is he?" Ben asked, and Sally shrugged.

"Who knows? Does what he always does when things get hard." She peered through her fringe again. "Runs away."

Freya offered her a sympathetic smile in return but chose not to dwell on any relationship issues for the time being. They would get to that when the time came.

"Did Simon own a paddle board?" Freya asked, and the use of past tense invoked a twitch in Sally's eye, like an annoying fly was buzzing around her. She dabbed her cheek with a tissue, then composed herself.

"You mean, like one of those surfboard things?"

"That's right. Did he happen to have one, or at least have access to one?"

Sally shook her head. "No. I mean, he knows how. Sorry. He knew how. He tried it on holiday. I have a photo somewhere," Sally said, and she began fishing in her handbag for her phone.

"It's okay," Freya said. "It's just that we found one nearby. We thought he might have taken it to the river with some friends."

"He didn't have any," Sally said, and she lowered her gaze to stare at the loose nail she was picking at. "Friends, that is. He kept himself to himself. He used to have one. Long time ago. But you know how kids are. I don't think he ever truly found anyone since. Never really let it get to him, mind. He was a strong lad. Had to be."

"Sally, I'm sorry to ask, but was Simon being bullied?"

The silence that followed said all that was needed to be said, but Mrs Bird added to it anyway.

"I don't know why," she began, her voice rising in pitch.

"It's okay. We don't have to talk about it–"

"Ever since he was young, I don't know... I mean, he wasn't the sharpest. Naïve, my old dad used to call him. He'd fall for anything."

"Children can be cruel, can't they?" Freya added, and Sally nodded, wiped the fresh tears away, then cleared her throat.

"He had learning difficulties," she explained. "Not just English and lessons, and that. But, well, everything. He'd button his shirt up wrong, or...or he'd put his jumper on inside out. Kids teased him. They pick up on those things, don't they? But they didn't know him. If only they'd known him. He was a kind boy. Sweet. He just wanted to be normal. You know? He just wanted to be left alone."

"Is there an individual that springs to mind?" Ben asked.

"An individual? No. It's a group of them. They live over the back here," she said, jabbing her hand to the rear of the house. "Next street. Gavin, his name is. He's the ringleader. Gavin Forbes. Rich family. Let him do what he likes."

Freya glanced across at Ben, who was making a note of the name, but Sally hadn't finished.

"They do stuff online too. I saw it. I had it taken down. Told the headmaster. What's his name? Boorman. Bloody disgusting what they put up there."

"We've seen it," Freya said, hoping it would stop the distraught mother from having to relive the horrors.

"You've seen what's up there now. But not before. The stuff I had taken down. Whole Facebook pages dedicated to my Simon. Pictures of him in the school showers after PE. I mean, who does that? How can anyone be so cruel?"

"I ask myself that question every single day of my life, Sally," Freya said.

"Twice I've had it taken down. I know it's him. I know it's that bloody Gavin. They've moved it now. It's on some other social media thing."

"TikTok," Ben said. "It's being taken down now, I believe."

"Yeah, well, they'll have to stop now, won't they?"

"Why would this Gavin Forbes do this to Simon, though? Was there an argument?"

"No. No argument at all. My Simon wouldn't say boo to a goose. It's that boy. Gavin. He's got something wrong with him. A screw loose. Do you know what I mean? They befriended Simon last summer. Or at least they pretended to. Came round, he did. Little pervert was watching me in the garden. Anyway, he came round and convinced Simon to empty his piggy bank for something. I don't know what."

"I'm sorry to hear that," Freya said. She'd heard it all before, but it got no easier. "So he took Simon's money?"

"Yes, for drugs, I bet. I reckon he told my Simon he could join their little gang if he coughed up. Heartbroken, Simon was. He said nothing, of course. Simon was very good at internalising everything. He dealt with things his own way. But I heard him. A mother knows. I know when he's upset. I know the sound of him crying into his pillow."

"Do you have any proof that Gavin Forbes was involved in the bullying, Mrs Bird?" Ben asked.

"Proof? No. Course I don't. If I had proof, I'd have reported him a long while ago. Maybe then we wouldn't be here now. Maybe then, Simon would be on his way back from school as we speak."

"We will investigate, Sally," Freya said. "I can assure you, if Gavin Forbes is guilty of anything, we'll find out."

"Yeah, well," Sally said. "It's all too little too late, isn't it?"

Ben glanced in Freya's direction, but she didn't look back. Her attention was on Simon's mother. She took a sip of the tea, then replaced her cup on the table, which she noted had been cleared a little since they were there earlier.

"Is there anybody else you can think of, Mrs Bird?" Ben asked. "Anybody at all that might have wanted to hurt Simon?"

Footsteps on the footpath outside approached the front door and a polite knock followed.

"That'll be the FLO," Ben said and, all too keen, he made his way towards to door. "I'll just get it."

Sally shook her head in dismay, then caved. She threw her hands in the air. "Oh, sod it," she said, and reached into her bag and produced a packet of cigarettes. Her trembling fingers fought with the packet, but she managed it eventually, then sparked one into life with a disposable lighter, and took a long drag. Only when that initial hit of nicotine had worked its magic did she say what she had to say. She stared at Freya through her fringe again, her sad eyes dark and pained. "Anybody who wanted to hurt my Simon has already done so."

## CHAPTER TWENTY

THE BIRDS' FRONT DOOR HAD SEVERAL PIECES OF FROSTED GLASS in a semi-circle. Ben peered through it at the figure on the doorstep, but couldn't make out any details. It looked like Jackie. It was her shape anyway. And the hair was right. But it had been so long since he had seen her in uniform that he couldn't be sure.

He turned the lock and gave the door a sharp tug, then stepped to one side, ready to invite Jackie in.

But it wasn't Jackie. It was another female officer, who looked Ben up and down, like he had somehow already offended her.

"PC Reed," she said. "Family Liaison. Are you Mr Bird?"

"No," Ben said. "Detective Sergeant Savage."

"Oh, I see. I was told to come—"

"And you were told right," Ben said. "You'd better come in."

She stepped inside and closed the door behind her.

Ben jabbed his thumb at the closed lounge door and whispered, "Mrs Bird is in there with DI Bloom. I'll show you the kitchen."

He led her through to the kitchen, and in a flash of pointing and gesturing, he told her all she needed to know. "Tea bags, coffee, and sugar are all kept in there. Sugar is in the lounge right now. Milk in the fridge. Use the green bottle. The blue one smells a bit funky. Kettle is over there."

"Right then," she said, and appeared as if she was itching to get started by talking to the victim's mother.

"Just give her a sec. DI Bloom is just finishing. I'll introduce you."

"Is it Ben?" she said, the question catching Ben off-guard.

He nodded. "Yes, why?"

"I thought I recognised the name. Savage," she said. "It's not a common name."

"No. No, it isn't," Ben agreed tentatively, making his suspicions clear.

"Oh, sorry. Gold. DC Gold. She was in with us yesterday. She's doing the course, right? The FLO course?"

"So I'm led to believe," Ben replied, doing his best at nonchalance.

"Oh, she's lovely, she is, and she speaks very highly of you. That's why I remembered your name. She'd make a bloody good FLO."

"She would," Ben agreed. "And, yes, she is lovely. A sweetheart."

"I still don't understand why she'd want to take a sidestep. She's a DC. We hardly ever get anyone come in from Major Investigations."

"She's a special case. As I understand it, she's just trying to improve herself," Ben said. "I mean, she's not actually going to transfer, is she?"

Reed shrugged. "I don't know. She didn't really say. All I know is, if she made the move, she'd have found her calling."

"Are we done?" a voice asked from the doorway. It was Freya, and she stood with her eyebrows raised expectantly, as she often did.

"Yes," Ben said. "I was just showing Reed where the tea and coffee is."

"Well, I imagine she would have been lost without you," Freya replied, then made a show of counting the cupboards. "Eight. And my guess is everything is in the cupboard above the kettle."

Ben looked at Reed, who stared at the floor like a naughty schoolgirl.

"Am I right?" Freya asked, clearly not willing to let it drop.

"Mostly," Ben said.

"Thought so. Well, good luck, Reed. Ben, make the introductions, and I'll see you in the car."

Without waiting for a response, Freya walked off, closing the door behind her. Ben led Reed into the lounge and found Mrs Bird taking the moment of peace to have a little cry.

He opened his mouth to speak, but Reed placed her hand on his arm and gave him a little shake of her head. Then, confidently, she knelt beside the grieving mother, and spoke.

"Mrs Bird? Mrs Bird, my name is PC Reed. I'm your Family Liaison Officer. I'm here to help you through this, okay?"

It was as if the entire ordeal had reached capacity. Sally Bird suddenly looked up at her, then at Ben, and then broke in a flood of wails and tears, and Reed, who had first introduced herself to Ben with a scathing assessment, now gave him a warm smile and flicked her head at the door, indicating that he should leave her to do what she did best.

Ben closed the lounge door, but instead of heading straight out to meet Freya, he lingered a while, listening in to what Reed was saying.

"Mrs Bird, this is a hard time for you. I understand that. I'm trained to deal with people in these situations. Now, I want you to listen to me."

A silence followed, and then Sally Bird blew her nose.

"Are you listening?" Reed asked, and Ben imagined Sally peering at her through her greying fringe.

"I want you to lean on me. Tell me anything. Tell me everything. Or just tell me nothing. I'm going to be right here beside you."

Ben smiled. Behind the door, it could have been Jackie in there. The tone was her all over. The kindness. The strength. All that was missing was Jackie's faint Scottish accent. But his mind filled that in.

"Now then. I'll make you a fresh cuppa, okay? Then maybe you can show me some photos, if you think you're up to it."

That was Ben's call to leave. He slipped through the front door, closing it quietly behind him, and then strode towards the car. Inside, Freya was deep in thought, and again, he felt the need for silence.

"Anybody who had wanted to hurt Simon had already done so," Freya said, before she'd even acknowledged his presence. "That's what Sally said when you went to answer the door. What does that mean?"

Ben gave it a second, then responded, "I guess it means exactly what she said. Anyone who had reason to hurt him, and others, as the case may be, had hurt him already."

"No. No, it's more than that. What does it mean to us?"

She hit the button to start the engine, but this time, she did not seem to relish that sweet rumble of power. She stared at the Birds' front door, lost in thought, and Ben had to follow her gaze to at least try to bring her back.

"Are you reading too much into it?" he asked.

"No. No, I'm not. Anybody who had reason to hurt Simon had done so already. So whoever hurt him, this final time, did so for a new reason."

"You mean, like a new argument or something?"

"Kind of. But not an argument. Not necessarily, anyway. Anybody who had reason to hurt him had done so already. He was killed at the weekend. When was the last social media post up about him?"

"Friday. It was the toilet thing," Ben explained.

"So the reason he was killed was for something that happened between Friday night and Sunday," Freya said.

"That's not really definitive. I mean, she couldn't know for sure there wasn't some outstanding reason for someone to hurt him."

"No, but she's right. If somebody wanted to get at Simon, they only needed to find him at school and hurt him, or post something on the social media page. This was something new."

She looked across at Ben, and her eyebrows rose again in anticipation.

"So? What we do about it?" she asked.

Ben digested her thoughts and processed the information before he spoke.

"What I'd like to do is go around to this Gavin Forbes' house and drag him down to the station," he said. "But why don't we see what Gillespie and Chapman come up with first?"

"Then what?"

"Well, if Forbes' name is not on the list, then he must be the one behind the social media."

"And if his name is on the list?"

Ben smiled back at her. "Then we drag him," he replied. "Sounds like he needs the wind knocked out of his sails."

_______

## CHAPTER TWENTY-ONE

_______

THE ADDRESS CHAPMAN HAD GIVEN ANNA NILLSON FOR THE couple on the tour boat stated an Airbnb in Canwick, a pleasant area on the south side of the village. Aside from the huge hill on which they had built Lincoln Cathedral, there was only really one other hill of significance within the city, and the house Anna was looking for was nestled into the side of it.

She guessed there to be at least five bedrooms, plus the converted stables. Tall trees cast long shadows across the property. The setting sun had painted the sky across the city a beautiful orange.

The front door opened before Anna had even climbed from the car, and who she presumed to be the owner of the house, a woman in her late forties wearing smart jeans and a loose-fitting, white blouse strolled over to her, her head cocked, as if she was waiting for Anna to introduce herself. Anna raised her warrant card as she approached.

"DC Nillson," she said. "I'm sorry to bother you."

"Not at all. Is there a problem?"

"I'm looking for a Debbie Glover and Harry Cousins. I understand they're staying here."

"Oh, right," the lady replied, glancing over to the stables. "I don't know if they're here. We don't really keep tabs on the guests."

"That's fine. Do you mind if I take a look?"

"Be my guest. Do you need me at all?"

"No. It's fine. I'll knock if I have any problems," Anna told her.

"It's the stable at the end," the lady advised, then remained standing in the driveway, watching as Anna approached the door.

Anna knocked three times, listening out for movement inside. She heard something. A shuffling maybe? Like someone was moving something around. Then the door opened to reveal a young Asian man pulling on a t-shirt.

"Harry Cousins?" Anna asked.

"Yes. That's me," he replied, glancing over his shoulder as a girl stepped into view.

"And you must be Debbie Glover?"

Anna raised her warrant card again.

"I'm Detective Constable Nillson. I was wondering if I could take a few moments of your time."

"Is this about the body?" Harry asked.

"I'm afraid it is, yes."

"We told the man everything we know," the girl said, opening the door further and edging in front of her man. "The copper at the dock. He made notes as well."

"Yes, I know, but we like to make sure nothing has been missed. You may have been upset. You could easily have forgotten something."

"I forgot nothing," the girl said. "I can picture him clearly."

"You saw him first. Is that right?"

The girl nodded, glanced at Harry, then back at Anna, like she was waiting for the next question.

"I'm afraid this is a major investigation. I just need to go over what happened with you. Is that okay?"

"It's fine," Harry said, giving a little eyeroll behind his girl-friend's back. "Do you want to come in?"

"If it's a good time, yes, please."

"We're just packing, actually," Debbie said. "There's stuff everywhere—"

"We'll find a space," Harry said, stepping back into the room. "We don't have to leave until tomorrow, anyway. It'll take her that long just to pack her case."

Debbie rushed in behind him, making a show of piling all her clothes on top of her suitcase. It took about three seconds for Anna to realise that the little suitcase beside the door, which was ready to go, belonged to Harry and the rest of the clothes, which looked like a Black Friday at Primark, belonged to Debbie.

She found a seat beside a little desk and appraised the room, trying to see past Debbie's clothes and makeup. The owner had retained the country feel, with a high, vaulted ceiling and exposed beams, while providing a contemporary feel with flat walls, modern furniture, and just enough soft furnishing to make some-body feel at home.

"Do you want to talk me through it?" Anna said. "Where and when did you meet Hugo Bird?"

With a quick glance at Debbie, who shrugged and sulked quietly, Harry sat on the edge of the bed, the only free space he could find, and began.

"It was about seven this morning. We'd arranged the early tour with Mr Bird, as we wanted to have the whole day to look around some more."

"You wanted to, more like," Debbie said, then looked across to Anna. "He's a nerd. He wanted to know all about the history."

It was as if she was expecting Anna to join her in ridiculing her boyfriend. But she didn't fall for it. She nodded approvingly at Harry.

"If you like history, then Lincolnshire is a great place to look around."

It was Debbie's turn to roll her eyes. She shook her head and began folding clothes, although Anna was quite sure the volume of clothes would not fit into the case.

"We had to wait a few minutes," Harry continued. "For the engine to warm up or something. But we must have got moving about ten past seven. We went east, under a couple of bridges and out of the city into the countryside. I don't know how long we'd been going for. Maybe an hour. Maybe less. But it was Debbie who saw it. The body, that is. Isn't that right, babe?"

Debbie nodded, gave them both a cursory look, then carried on folding clothes.

"I didn't even know what it was at first. It just looked like a bunch of clothes in the reeds," she said while she worked. "But we asked him to turn around to check."

"And I'm guessing he did? And that's when you realised what it was?"

"Sort of, yeah," Harry explained. "He didn't want to at first, though. He was talking about one of the old abbeys. But we convinced him. And he turned around. And, well, as soon as we realised what it was, he sped away."

"Why do you think he did that?"

Harry nodded at Debbie. "He didn't want Debs to see too much. He's actually a decent bloke. Weird, but alright. You know?"

"Ruined our day, though," Debbie said. "Don't forget that."

"How so?" Anna asked. "He was trying to stop Debbie from being upset?"

"We'd arranged to be collected at Tattershall," Harry explained. "We were going to the beach afterwards. But Mr Bird didn't want to turn back. Took us straight back to the city, so we missed our collection."

"It cost us a fortune," Debbie added.

"We got a fifty percent refund. Somebody died, Debs," Harry

said, then looked at Anna. "Sometimes she loses sight of the fact that a family out there just lost someone they loved."

"I am here, you know?" Debbie added, looking between them accusingly.

"He called the police on the way back," Harry explained, ignoring his partner. "When we'd gotten away a fair bit. He seemed to know the location and called the police. He told them where we'd be docking, and by the time we got back, a couple of policemen were there. That's when we gave our statements. I don't think there's very much to add, if I'm honest."

"You missed the part about him looking up my dress," Debbie said.

"He did not look up your dress, Debs."

"And the part about him giving us wine," she carried on. "I bet he doesn't have an alcohol license either."

"Debbie? What are you trying to do to the bloke?"

"I'm just saying, that's all. He's not as clean-cut as you make him out to be."

Harry turned to Anna, gave another eyeroll, to which she was becoming quite accustomed, and spoke frankly.

"He didn't look up her dress. I'm sure it was just a mistake as she was sitting down. But yes, he opened a bottle of wine. But if you ask me, it was more to cheer Debbie up than anything else. She was giving him a hard time about his boat and the tour. Honestly, I think he's an alright guy. He did the right thing."

"That's good to know," Anna said. "Where is it you're going next?"

"Home," Debbie stated, before Anna had even finished speaking.

"Where's home?"

"London. Back to normality."

"I'm going to have to ask you to stay a while longer," Anna explained. "You can't go home just yet."

Debbie stopped mid-fold, gave Anna a filthy look, then fixed her stare on her boyfriend, expecting him to sort the problem out.

"We've told you all we know," he said.

Anna spoke frankly, giving as much information as she dare.

"We're treating the investigation as suspicious," she said. "We might need to call on you to give further evidence. You'd be helping us out."

"Evidence?" Harry said, looking a little worried. "I don't understand?"

"This is a murder investigation," Anna said. "I'm afraid you two are the closest we have to witnesses."

# CHAPTER TWENTY-TWO

"You know this will be one of the harder investigations the team will have dealt with," Freya said to Ben as they drove down the little farm track towards Ben's house.

"What makes you say that?" he asked. "We've managed so far."

"Oh, I know that," she replied, as she brought the car to a stop outside his house. "But there's a severe lack of evidence. Even if Gavin Forbes turns out to be involved in the social media accounts, we'll have a hard time linking him to Simon Bird's death. It's just the way it is. I might be wrong. In fact, I hope I am wrong, but it doesn't happen often."

She gave him a tight-lipped smile.

"I hear you," he replied.

"It's not that we won't solve it. More that we have to be wary of certain things."

"Such as?"

"Motivation," she replied. "What normally happens when we first get stuck into an investigation? There's a flurry of activity, right?"

"Well, yeah. We assign tasks, split the workload, and we build momentum."

"That's it. Momentum. Unless we can define a few lines of enquiries, that momentum will falter. It's down to us to keep the team going. To keep feeding them new leads. Honestly, I've seen it before. The motivation drops in an individual and it spreads like cancer. Until half the team are moping about, kicking a can down the road. But one spark of a lead, and there's a surge of activity."

"And if that lead goes nowhere?"

"It's a rollercoaster, Ben. We can manage it. But let's just be aware that we may not sort this out so quickly. It could take months."

He nodded and sat back in his seat, staring ahead at his father's house. Following his gaze, Freya understood the danger of the distraction, but there was no point in avoiding it. The best way to deal with danger, she thought, was to face it head-on.

She killed the engine and pushed open the door. "Come on," she said.

"Eh? Where are you going?"

She didn't answer. Instead, she strode to old man Savage's front door, then glanced back at Ben, who was following but unsure why. Then she knocked three times, just as Ben would.

"What are you doing?" he hissed. "He's probably busy."

"That you, Ben?" a voice called out from inside.

Freya smiled back at Ben and called out, "It's me, Mr Savage. Freya. We just popped by to see how you are."

The door opened, and Ben's father stood there looking down at her. The old man was as lithe as she'd ever seen a man of his age. He didn't wear glasses, which helped him maintain the look of a man in his late sixties, rather than the early seventies he really was.

"I'm sorry about this, Dad," Ben started.

"Freya," his father said. "What a pleasant surprise. Come on in, won't you?"

She smiled back at Ben, who was shaking his head in disbelief.

"I thought it would be nice to have a little catch-up, if you have time, that is?" Freya said, entering the house where Ben had grown up for the first time.

"Time, yes. I've got time," he said, making his way through to the old kitchen. It was exactly how a farmhouse kitchen should be, in Freya's limited knowledge of interiors. "I always have time for you, my dear."

Ben closed the door behind them and followed them into the kitchen.

"I'll do that, Dad," he said, when his father went to fill the kettle.

"I can fill a kettle, boy," the old man said. "I'm not too far gone to make a cup of tea."

"I didn't say you were."

"No, but you thought it, didn't you?"

Ben was silent. It was interesting to see the dynamics between Ben and his father. Ben, an alpha male in every walk of life Freya had seen him in, tumbled down the pecking order in the presence of his aging father with just a handful of words.

"Now then," his father began, and he blinked a few times, as if he was trying to remember something.

"It's Freya, Dad," Ben said.

"I know her bloody name, don't I?" came the reply. "I was trying to remember if she had milk and sugar."

"You've never made her tea before, Dad. This is her first time in here."

"Is it?" he replied, and Freya nodded.

"It's okay. I'm always mistaken for somebody else."

"Well then, that'll be why I couldn't remember."

"Yes, and no, thank you," Freya said. Then, to clarify, "Milk, no sugar."

"Ah, just like Ben's mother used to have it."

"And probably half the population," Ben added quietly.

"Sorry?"

"Nothing, Dad. Did you get up to Bozeman today?"

"The young lady doesn't want to hear about the fields, Ben," he said. "She's come here to..."

He stopped mid-sentence and pulled a face as if he was trying to remember something, and it was on the tip of his tongue.

"Actually, I've got a little confession to make," Freya said, and felt Ben's burning stare. "I came to invite you to dinner."

"To dinner?"

"At the cottage," Freya added. "It's my way of saying thanks for letting me stay."

"You don't need to cook me dinner."

"I know. But I'd like to. And Ben. And Ben's brothers too. Jeff and James. All of you. I'd really like to."

"Well then. That's a hard invite to turn down. When are you thinking?"

"This weekend," Freya said. "Saturday. Shall we say six o'clock?"

"Six o'clock," he repeated, his voice re-energised. "You're on. Although, I doubt the Brothers Grim will come," he said, jabbing his thumb toward Ben's brothers' house. "It's hunting season."

"Hunting? Oh, I didn't know they hunted. Is it wild fowl?" Freya asked, remembering the shoot her father had taken her on as a child, with the deafening noise and what she deemed to be a total slaughter of birds.

"He means it's a Saturday night," Ben said, as the kettle came to a boil and clicked off. "Not the type of hunting you're probably used to."

"Oh," she said, feeling her cheeks blush. "Well, then it'll just be us three. I'll do something nice."

"I'll look forward to that. It's been years since one of Ben's lady friends invited me to dinner," the old man said. "Sugar?"

Ben's father held the teaspoon poised above the caddy, waiting for her to respond.

Out of the corner of her eye, she caught Ben's eyebrow raise in alarm. He stiffened.

"No sugar for me, thank you," she replied.

"We're just friends, Dad," Ben added, clearly feeling the need to fill the void that followed.

"Your mum and me were friends once too."

"Yeah, but... Dad, it's not like–"

"Then you came along," his father said, as he set a cup of black tea before Freya and offered her a wink. "That's when the trouble started."

"Dad–"

"Maybe I'll embarrass him and bring some photos. Got some nude ones, too," he said. "Mind you, you've probably seen it all already by now. People don't wait until they're married these days, do they?"

"You mean like you and Mum waited?" Ben said. "Besides, Dad, we're not together–"

"I have seen it, actually," Freya said with a smile, loving every minute of Ben's horror, which was apparent over his father's shoulder. "But bring them anyway. I'd love to see what he was like as a boy."

The old man laughed, which induced a coughing fit. He recovered moments later, still smiling. "You could always pin them up in the station. I'm sure the other girls would like a good laugh."

"Actually, most of them have seen him naked too."

"*Freya?*" Ben cried.

A wry smile crept over the old man's face, deepening the wrinkles around his eyes. "I thought he was the shy one."

"Oh, he's not shy, Mr Savage," she explained. "In fact, if he inherited his confidence from you, then I imagine you've got some stories of your own to tell."

The smile remained, as if the old man's face had set.

"I'm looking forward to dinner on Sunday," he said.

"Saturday, Dad."

But the old man ignored him.

"I think it's going to be a lot of fun," Freya said. "Thanks for the tea. It's perfect."

# CHAPTER TWENTY-THREE

J IM GILLESPIE HAD BEEN HOME FOR LESS THAN THIRTY MINUTES. He'd showered, dressed, and, out of habit more than anything else, searched his empty cupboards for something to cook, then resigned to getting a takeaway, again. The trouble was that getting a takeaway meant heading out and taking a stroll along the high street, which wasn't a problem. But he would have to pass the pub, and it was impossible to walk past the place without stopping in for a quick beer. He'd tried it before, even going to such lengths as crossing the street to avoid temptation. But that mean, old devil on his shoulder had always talked him into it, often with the argument that his food was never ready in the twenty minutes Mrs Chang always told him it would be.

He could always phone and ask for a delivery, but he'd tried that one before as well. He was far from a food critic. In fact, he'd eaten things that were barely discernible before. But cold Chinese food was not appealing in the slightest. Despite his proximity to the restaurant, he always seemed to be the last one on the delivery guy's list.

He was pondering this dilemma when his phone vibrated in his pocket, and when he pulled it out, he saw a number he didn't recognise had sent him a text message. It was probably work, he thought. So, sensing some new information, or a lengthy back and forth with Ben or Freya, he moved into the kitchen and flicked the kettle on. Dinner would have to wait for ten minutes. He opened the message and had to read it three times before he finally believed what he was reading.

*'Hi Jim. Sorry for messaging you like this. I was wondering if you would like to have a chat over a drink sometime??? J :)'*

"J?" he said aloud, but couldn't help a smile from forming. "Who the bloody hell is J?"

He considered his reply while he made a tea, then leaned on the worktop to read it again while he sipped at the hot drink.

It was the little smiley face she had added at the end of the message that got him. Who does that?

"Someone who has a kid," he said to himself. "Has to be. People our age don't do that, do they?"

He began his reply, setting to it as if he was a novelist who had woken with an idea for a best seller. A name beginning with J struck him.

"Jackie?" he said, with more than a little dismay in his voice. Then his mind questioned the doubt. Jackie was a pretty girl. She was more than pretty, in fact. She was a catch. But he thought it was well known that she only had eyes for Ben. And Ben, being famously clueless with women, had never taken her up on the offer. But why now?

Then he remembered seeing her earlier that day. She'd been in uniform and had called him over to ask about DI Bloom. Had that just been a rouse to get him on his own? *Women do that, don't they?* Little games, just to get five minutes with someone. She'd smelled good, too. She'd been wearing perfume. He hadn't even noticed at the time. But why now? Why make a move now?

"She's transferring," he said aloud again, recalling that she had mentioned an FLO course.

Well, if Ben wasn't going to show the girl a good time, he might as well try.

'Hi J,' he began. '*Drinks sound great. Where do you have in mind?*' His finger poised over the button to send the message.

But then he thought about Jessica in the coffee shop. The girl who served him. Not by choice, though, he admitted to himself. There were two girls who made the coffees in the little shop, and if the queue worked out that he would be served by the other girl, he always made an excuse for the person behind him to go ahead, as if he was responding to a message on his phone or searching his pockets for money.

He'd given her his number, too. A long while ago. He thought she'd just binned it. The wee lass must get a dozen numbers every day.

*Is it Jackie or Jessica?* he thought, then re-read his reply.

'Hi J. *Drinks sound great. How about tomorrow night at the Fox and Hounds near my place?*'

He re-read it, smiling to himself at his cunning ability to eliminate at least one of them. If J didn't know which pub he was referring to, then she must be Jessica. If they knew the pub, then she must be Jackie.

He hit send, then slurped his tea, grinning from ear to ear.

He strode through into the bedroom, with far more swagger in his stride than he had walked out with. He sprayed a little aftershave, checked his reflection in the en-suite mirror, and remarked on how good he looked. Good for his age, at least, the devil on his shoulder added. But the devil's work wasn't over yet.

Less than ten minutes later, he was standing at the bar of his local while Mrs Chang and her family cooked his egg-fried rice and aromatic duck. Twenty minutes, she had told him. Time enough for at least two beers.

The next message came through while Craig, the landlord, poured his first beer. He felt the little vibration in his pocket and did his best to conceal his schoolboy grin.

*'I was thinking of somewhere a bit more private. Somewhere nobody knows either of us, with a dark car park in case we need a wee bit of privacy.'*

"A wee bit of privacy?" he said aloud.

"You what, Jim?" Craig said, as he slid his beer towards him.

"Oh, nothing," Gillespie replied.

"You want some privacy?"

"Eh? Ah, no. I was just..." He held his phone up and justified his outburst with what he deemed a globally acceptable statement among men. "Women."

"Ah, I see," Craig replied, leaning on his side of the bar. "I had one of them once."

"Once?"

"Yeah. She left me for a younger man."

He ran his hair across his bald head and tapped his more than ample stomach.

"Right," Gillespie said. "I see."

"I'm glad, if I'm honest," Craig continued. "If I had stayed with her, I'd have been a nobody. Look around you. I'd have none of this."

Gillespie glanced around the near-empty pub. The walls still had drips of nicotine running down them in the corners from back when smoking was allowed in pubs and restaurants, and he'd seen bodies wrapped in newer carpets than what was laid out on the floor.

"Right," he said.

"Better off without them," Craig said. "That's what I say. What's the trouble? Maybe I can help?"

"I doubt it, Craig. No offense, eh?"

"Leave off. Come on. We're alone here. What's the problem?"

With nobody else at the bar to distract the landlord, Gillespie saw little option but to divulge his dilemma.

"This stays between us, aye?" he warned. "If you tell a soul, I'll have uniform down here in a heartbeat, and you'll be explaining where all that dodgy scotch comes from. Right?"

"Yep, sure," Craig replied, his hands held high as if surrendering. "My lips are sealed, Jim. I'm just trying to help, mate."

"Aye, well. It's like this, ya see. I've got two leads."

"Leads?"

"Aye, leads. Lines of enquiry," Gillespie said, raising his eyebrows to tell Craig to read between the lines.

Craig shook his head, not following.

"Ah, ya daft idiot. Two women."

"Two? What are you? Mad?"

"I'm not seeing either of them. They're just..." He searched for the right word.

"Just what?"

"Possibilities," Gillespie explained. "They're just on my radar, and I'm on theirs."

Craig shook his head.

"And you can't decide which one to go for? Blimey, Jim. You're a dark horse. Here's me thinking you were just some lonely, old copper who drinks too much, eats too much, and probably sits at home in his underpants watching Eastenders."

"You thought that about me?"

"Well, not exactly," Craig said, then moved the conversation on. "So, what's the problem? You've got two women who like you."

"Aye. One of them has texted me, but I don't know which, and I'm pretty sure she wants more than a wee drink in a wee little pub somewhere, if you know what I mean?"

"Like what?"

"Eh?"

"What else does she want?"

"Christ, man, do I have to spell it out for you?"

"Oh," Craig said, his eyes widening. "Well, what are you going to do?"

"I don't know. Meet her, I guess."

"What one do you want it to be?"

Jim gave it some thought. Either would be nice.

He shrugged. "I'm not bothered."

"Then what's your problem?"

"I didn't say I had a problem, Craig," Jim explained, downing the rest of his pint and sliding the glass towards the landlord. "It was my way of telling you I won't be in tomorrow night. Fill her up, eh?"

# CHAPTER TWENTY-FOUR

Freya knew what Ben was going to say even before she opened the door to him. She had left his father's house only an hour ago, and in that time had showered, dressed, and laid her notes out on the old dining room table.

"Did you have to?" he said, even before the icy wind that ran off the fields had caught her wet hair.

"I thought you'd enjoy that," she replied, turning to walk back into the living room.

He'd follow and close the door behind him. He always did. He could be like a dog with a bone sometimes. And earlier, she had teased him with a pretty big bone. Sadly, he hadn't the emotional intelligence to see through her plan. Just like many of the men Freya had met, he focused on the here and now, and less on the bigger picture.

"Enjoy it?" he said, entering the room behind her. "You invited my bloody dad to dinner."

"Well spotted," she said, musing over the scrawled notes that were spread over the table. She'd recreated the whiteboard in the incident room, with names on scraps of paper so she could easily move them around. "Does he like roast lamb, do you know? He strikes me as a lamb type of guy."

"Lamb?" Ben said. "You could give the old bastard a cheese and pickle sandwich and he'd think you were Gordon bloody Ramsay. Except for Christmas, he hasn't eaten a decent meal since Mum died, and that was decades ago. What the bloody hell were you thinking?"

"And ale? I bet he likes ale," Freya added. "I'll get some of that IPA in. Gillespie knows which ones are best. Remind me, will you?"

"Remind you to do what?"

"To talk to Gillespie. I want to know which is the best IPA to get for your dad. I want him to feel comfortable, don't I?"

"No. No, you don't. This is a mistake," he said. "All he's going to do is terrorise me. And what was the whole cup of tea thing about? Did we really have to go in there?"

"Well, as I recall, he did not actually invite you. I was just stopping by to see my landlord."

"You were poking your nose in."

"I was looking out for a friend."

"He's not your friend. He's my dad. And he can be a right awkward git sometimes. He can make my life harder than it already is with one vicious swipe of his tongue."

"I meant you, Ben," she said, turning to look at him for the first time. Judging by his groomed hair, clean but wrinkled shirt, and jeans, he'd also taken the hour to have a shower. He looked pretty good too, save for the shirt, which looked like he'd found it at the bottom of his wardrobe. "You scrub up well."

"Eh?"

"Apart from the shirt," she said, gesturing at the wrinkles.

"No. Before that. The bit about me being your friend."

"Well, you are, aren't you? If you're not, then why are you in my house?"

"Of course I'm your friend. I'm just saying. Why go to see him? My dad? What was the purpose?"

"To see for myself."

"What?" He looked confused. As if he couldn't comprehend that she might even be able to help.

"To see for myself. You know. The dementia thing. The Alzheimer's."

"Alzheimer's?"

"It's a form of dementia. One of the most common. I think you're right to worry about him."

"So you believe me?"

"I think you're right to have your concerns, Ben. I'll give you my full diagnosis following dinner on Saturday."

"What makes you so qualified, Doctor Bloom?"

"Ah," she said, smiling back at him. "Experience. Now, do help me out here. I'm pulling together some lines of enquiry for tomorrow."

"Hold on. Hold on. You can't just leave that there."

"Leave what where?"

"The experience thing."

"Ah," she said again. "You want to know who I saw go through it? By which you mean to gauge my relationship with the individual so you can yourself ascertain whether or not I'm fit to offer you any guidance?"

"Eh?"

"My dad."

"Your dad?"

"Alzheimer's," she said. "We don't speak of it much. But it was there."

"Oh. Sorry, Freya, I didn't know—"

"That's because I hadn't told you. But now I have. So there," she said. "Now, about these lines of enquiry."

"Was it bad?"

"Bad enough. How bad does it need to be? I mean, he could

function, if that's what you mean. He could talk, and he could cook himself dinner, although he rarely did. He was used to people cooking for him."

"Ah, I see," Ben said, mimicking her language. "That's the difference between your father and mine. My dad will still have to cook, clean, and fend for himself. Your father had people doing all that for him."

"He had people doing those things for him before they diagnosed him with Alzheimer's, Ben. And you're wrong. There's no difference at all. The hardest part of dealing with an illness like Alzheimer's is not the day-to-day stuff like leaving a room and forgetting your notebook, or walking into a room, for that matter, and forgetting why you went there. It's the memories. The long-term memories we might not draw upon every day. It's recalling the name of your dead wife, and the times you shared. It's seeing a face like yours, recognising it, but not being able to put a name to it, or make a connection. Getting your days mixed up, like your dad did tonight, is nothing, Ben. I told him dinner was on Saturday. Less than five minutes later, he said it was Sunday. That's nothing. If he is ill, and by god I hope he isn't, Ben, it's going to get a lot worse."

He was silent for a minute. The way he always was when he was thinking of the right thing to say, or shoving his emotions to one side.

"Why are you telling me this?"

"Because you need to be ready. Because if, and when, the time comes, you're going to need to take care of him. You're going to need to take care of his farm for him. He won't be able to drive machinery the way he does. He won't be safe in a field with livestock. He won't even be safe out in the fields on his own. Do you know what I'm saying, Ben?"

"I think so, yeah," he replied.

"Things will change, Ben. Your priorities will change."

"I'll talk to my brothers. See what they have to say about all of this."

"Say nothing just yet," she said, and she offered her kindest smile. "Let's get Saturday over with first."

"You mean Sunday?"

"No," she said, and she caught him smiling.

"I won't let it get to me. Not anymore. I'll deal with it," he said, and he flicked his head at the sprawl of notes on Freya's table. "There's people out there going through worse, right?"

"Right," she said, glad of his perspective.

"Now," he said, clearing his throat, "about these lines of enquiry."

## CHAPTER TWENTY-FIVE

SHE SMELLED GOOD, BEN THOUGHT, AS FREYA TURNED AWAY from him to get her head back into the investigation. And try as he might to join her in that headspace, there were too many distractions. What she had said about his father was rolling around his mind like an old bottle on the back seat of his car; a constant reminder that the problem wasn't going away. But at the front of his mind, he'd found a new distraction, or at least, reignited a distraction he thought he'd learned to live with.

She'd washed her hair and had removed her makeup. She had changed from her stylish work clothes into a pair of jeans. He liked her in jeans. They showed off her figure, but more than that, they showed a human side of her. It was that human side that had reignited this old flame. The flame he'd tried so hard to snuff out. She hadn't mentioned her father's illness before. But then, why would she? It wasn't something people shouted about, but in all their time together, during all those chats they had, and during which each of them had, at one point or another, been vulnerable, she had never said a word of it.

"Hugo Bird," she began, placing the palm of her right hand flat on the paper with his name on. "There's something not right with him," she said, turning to face Ben. "Are you listening?"

"Me? Oh, erm, yeah."

She gave him a quizzical look, then continued.

"As of yet, we have no apparent motive, but he had the means."

"The boat?"

"Yes, the boat. He may also have had the opportunity. He said he was at his boat until late, and his wife can't account for his whereabouts during the hours Doctor Bell suggested Simon was killed. I asked her while you were flirting with the FLO."

"Flirting?"

"We need to eliminate him from the investigation. Until then, he's on our watch list."

"He's the bloody kid's dad."

"I know," Freya agreed. "But it gets worse. If Sally Bird can't account for her husband's whereabouts, then he can't account for hers."

"No way."

"We have nothing to go on," Freya said. "I'm not crossing anyone off until we can be sure."

"What about the other kid? Gavin Forbes?"

"Yep, he's up there too. We're going to be calling in some favours for this one, Ben. Tech guys, the dive team, and CSI."

"Oh, joy," Ben said, referring to his episode with Michaela. "What's your plan?"

"My plan or your plan?" she said. "You're driving this one, remember?"

"My plan? Okay. First off, we get CSI onto Hugo Bird's boat."

"What for?" Freya said. "Simon didn't bleed, so there will be no blood. And it's his father's boat. His prints will be all over it."

"Then we focus on eliminating the parents. Excuse the pun, but they're muddying the waters."

"Okay," Freya said tentatively. "How do you suppose we do that?"

"I'd like to involve the FLO. She seemed experienced. She can offer us any insights into the parents' behaviour. The father said he was at the dock tending his boat for the next day's tour. He moors the boat at Brayford Pool."

"So?"

"There'll be cameras. We'll see him come and go."

"That's one for Gillespie," Freya said. "What about Sally Bird?"

"Mobile phone data. She said she was home all night. I don't see any other way of proving her wrong."

"Okay, it's a start," Freya agreed. "Ask Chapman to get on to the phone company. I seem to recall she was friendly with one of them."

"Oh, that's right," Ben said, remembering the first investigation Freya had worked on with them all. He clicked his fingers, trying to remember his name. "Sounded like a pop star."

"A one-hit wonder, you mean?" Freya said. "Chesney."

"Chesney, that's it. Yep, Chapman will be over him like a rash."

"In her knitwear?" Freya said, injecting an image of the very conservative DC Chapman wearing nothing but knitwear into Ben's mind.

"Did you have to take it down a notch?"

"Don't tell me you haven't wondered?"

"Wondered what?"

"About her love life," Freya said. "Chapman."

"No, Freya. I'm sorry to disappoint you, but I do not go around making assumptions about people's love lives based on what they wear. She's a friend, and she's a bloody excellent researcher too. I've never even considered her in bed."

"But if I asked?"

"If you asked me about Chapman?"

"Yeah, come on. It's just you and me here."

"What do I think she's into?"

"Yeah."

"Straight sex. At least five dates beforehand. Lights out," Ben said. "And he'd have to be clean. I mean, scrubbed clean."

"That puts you and Gillespie out of the picture, then, doesn't it?"

"Very droll," Ben said. "What about you? What's your assessment of Chapman's love life?"

She made a face as if she was considering the question, though Ben knew she would have an answer ready. It was just a game she was playing.

"I'm different. I'm female. We approach such matters differently to men."

"Oh, here we go."

"No, hear me out. I think she would be a considerate lover. I imagine her to be warm, and that she would aim to please."

"Aim to please?" Ben said, unable to hide the childish smile creeping across his face.

"What about me?" Freya said.

The question hit Ben like she had just slapped him around the face.

"You?"

"Yes, come on. You know me well enough by now. You've even seen me naked, which you keep reminding me about. What gets me going?"

She folded her arms, and by doing so, accentuated her cleavage. It was a distraction, and Ben knew it. When he tore his eyes away from her shirt, she was staring directly at him knowingly.

He smiled at the game she was leading him into and stepped closer to her, so close that he could reach out and pin her arms to her sides if he wanted. He leaned in until they were cheek to cheek, and he inhaled the smell of her hair, losing himself in the aroma of her perfume.

"Power," he whispered.

"Is that right?" she replied, and he noticed her back arching a little as she tilted her head back, perhaps waiting for a kiss. Perhaps not. He never knew with her.

"You thrive on it," Ben said, again, whispered. He inched forward, forcing her back to the table, and to his delight, she sat on the hardwood, parting her legs for him to close the gap between them.

But then something caught his eye, something in an image jumbled up with the papers. It was hard to be sure, and now wasn't the time. But damn his curious mind. "Are those photos from where the body was found?"

The moment died like a snuffed candle. There would be no bringing it back. Not now.

"What?" she said, her tone becoming more irritated.

Staring down at the papers behind her, his face and hers side by side, Ben inhaled once more. The scent would be his only take-away that evening. "The photo of the reeds. Who took them?"

"The dive team, I guess," she replied. And unlike any other woman he had known, she was no longer irritated, but curious. "I had Chapman print them for me."

"There's a knot in the reeds."

"A what?"

"A knot," he said, still positioned between Freya's thighs, but staring over her shoulder at the table. "It's hard to say for sure, but why would somebody tie a knot in the reeds?"

"You're...erm," she began, and patted his hips.

The moment had passed for good now. She offered him a look of solace, then slid off the table to see what he was talking about.

"Look," he said, dragging the photo across the surface. He pointed at the little tangle of reeds that could easily have gone unseen or been put down to the flattening that happened during the scuffle.

"You're right," she muttered, turning her back on him to study the image in detail, leaving him standing behind her, reminded of how close they had just come to altering their relationship.

*What was it she had said?* he thought to himself. *Things change?*

"We need to get these enlarged," she said finally, and snapped upright, turning to find him staring again. She offered another of those knowing looks and bit her lower lip. The pause in discussion was mere seconds, although it felt like days. Her. Standing there. No longer feverish. And him, with his needs and desires still clear.

Ben re-focused. "What if Simon Bird floated down the river on the board and was sent into the reeds before the river turned? Like the current sent him or something? That's what Cole thought. He was already miles from home."

"Scared and tired," Freya added.

"Yes. He would be scared. Maybe he tied himself to the reeds, so he didn't float away?"

"It would have been dark."

"He was waiting until morning. All he had to do was stay there until somebody found him."

"He would have been cold."

"Freezing," Ben added.

"But somebody came. In the night."

"Maybe he called out?"

"Or maybe they knew he was there?"

"He thought he was being saved," Ben said. "He thought he was being rescued."

"But instead, he was forced off the board and into the water."

"Whoever did this has a boat," Ben said. "Or at least has access to one. Nobody could wade through those reeds. It's too deep."

The back and forth reached a conclusion. The momentum faded, leaving a void. There was no need to voice the fact that Simon's father had a boat. But the fact was that along that stretch of river, many people had boats. From little rowing boats to small crafts, such as Hugo Bird's.

"Shall we eat?" Freya said, then met his stare. "I seem to have worked up an appetite."

# CHAPTER TWENTY-SIX

BEN HADN'T MENTIONED THE CLOSE CALL THAT HAD OCCURRED the previous night. Nor had he mentioned anything about his father. Freya had expected him to offer some kind of fumbled apology or explanation, and she was ready to quell his embarrassment. But he hadn't. They were nearing the station, and all he spoke of was the investigation. He was riled, ready to go. Focused.

Exactly how she'd hoped he would be.

She neither saw herself as a psychiatrist nor a therapist, although she'd seen plenty of them herself. But from the moment she had picked Ben up from his father's house a few days ago and witnessed the internal struggles he was dealing with, she knew he just needed a distraction. He needed to perform well. He needed to be part of something. The fabric of his own world, in which his father was the glue, was threatened. He needed a lifeline.

And Freya was so very glad to see him cling to that lifeline with everything he had.

She parked in the station car park and they entered via the fire escape as usual. At the top of the stairs, they were met with a hum of activity. Laughter. Loud voices.

But surprisingly, none of the voices were Gillespie's, who,

historically, could normally be heard at the centre of a debate. Freya was reminded of the time when the entire team was engaged in a heated debate about the best chocolate bars, and even the usually quiet Chapman had joined in, voicing her opinion.

In the first-floor corridor, they walked slowly, both of them with their heads cocked to hear what the discussion was about.

"Vinegar, salt, then mayonnaise," Cruz said, his voice lacking depth, like that of a teenage boy's. "That's how it was meant to be."

"No, no, no," Nillson said. "Salt first, then the vinegar, then the mayonnaise. What do you think, Chapman?"

"I think you're both wrong," she replied in that calm fashion of hers.

"You don't put the sauce on first?" Cruz asked, his tone conveying utter disgust. "That's just sick."

"Nope. I agree with putting the vinegar on first. Because then the salt sticks to the chips. But mayo? No. Not on chips. Ketchup is what you need."

"Oh, come on," Cruz said. "Ketchup is dead. There's been a mayo revolution since you last had fish and chips."

"My cousin mixes mayo and ketchup," Nillson said. "Makes a burger sauce thing. Bit weird."

"Also," Chapman continued, clearly not having finished making her point, "the ketchup goes in a dollop on the side, not all over the chips."

"No way," Cruz said. "Nope. That's not how it's done."

"I agree," Nillson said. "It has to be all over."

"Alright, listen," said Chapman. "Let's agree to disagree on the ketchup or mayo part. But Cruz and I are right about the vinegar first."

"Eh?" Nillson said.

"You're outvoted," Cruz added, and Freya imagined him shrugging in consolation.

"Still, what's more important is the *delivery* of sauce," Chapman continued. "If you spread it all over the chips, you have absolutely no control over how much you get on each one. Some of them have almost no sauce at all, yet others are soaked in the stuff. What you need is a little dollop on the side. Not too much, you can always add more. But when you chuck it over your chips, you have absolutely no control."

"You're a control freak," Cruz said flatly.

"It's a tried and tested arrangement. Try it sometime."

"Oh Christ, guys. Can we just keep the talk of chips and vinegar down?" Gillespie said, and through the windows in the incident room doors, they saw the Glaswegian raise his head wearily.

"What about kebabs?" Cruz said, grinning from ear to ear.

"Oh God, no," Gillespie moaned, letting his head drop back into his hands.

"Nice, long, tender strips of doner meat, dripping with fat."

Gillespie groaned.

"Garlic sauce," Nillson said.

"Burger sauce," Cruz replied. "What about that, Chapman? Are you a dollop girl with a kebab, or do you go in with lashings of sauce?"

"I'm not a dollop girl at all, Gabby," she said, clearly a little disturbed at the thought of how the phrase could be construed. "As it happens, kebabs require a slightly alternative strategy to chips."

"Ha, there. See?" Cruz said.

"But it's not burger sauce," she said, and then turned to Nillson. "And garlic sauce? No."

"Shall we break this up before Gillespie shows us all what he had for dinner last night?" Ben suggested, as Freya pushed open the door and grimaced at the squealing hinges.

The room fell quiet. Three heads turned to face them. Gillespie remained with his eyes closed and head lying on his outstretched arms.

"Are we ready?" Freya asked. "We're running a murder investigation here."

"I'm ready, boss," Cruz said, like an annoying yet underachieving teacher's pet.

Nillson nodded, settling back in her seat, while Chapman finished off whatever she was typing.

"Good," said Freya, and she gave Ben the nod.

She made her way to her desk, hung her coat on the back of her chair, and opened her file. Ben, meanwhile, had tossed his jacket onto his desk and was standing beside the whiteboard.

The room waited for him to speak.

"Before we start, there's something I just want to clear up," he said. "Gillespie, are you awake?"

"Aye, Ben. I'm just resting my eyes a little," he replied, and raised his hand as a sign of life.

"A little too much to drink last night?"

"Eh? No. I didn't touch a drop."

"Good," Ben said, and he smiled at the team. "In my opinion, as humble as it is, a tender, juicy doner kebab, dripping with fat, requires a healthy dollop of chili sauce all over it. So it runs down your fingers and gets into any cuts. Chili sauce, so hot that it burns your chest on the way down and lights a fire in the pit of your stomach."

"Oh, Christ," Gillespie muttered, and he stood, wobbled a little, then crashed through the incident room doors heading toward the washrooms.

———

# CHAPTER TWENTY-SEVEN

———

"Simon Bird," Ben started, tapping the whiteboard with the end of the marker. "We know he was killed around midnight on Sunday night. We've got minimal lines of enquiry, but we have come up with a theory that I'd like to progress."

"Does your theory involve Gillespie driving?" Nillson asked.

"The first casualty of war is the plan, Anna," Ben said. "I'm not putting him behind the wheel of a car today. Cruz, he's with you."

"Eh? me?"

"Yes. You can drive, can't you?"

"Well, yeah, but–"

"So, he's with you."

"Oh, don't tell me I'm going door knocking again, boss. Why do I always knock on doors?"

"Talk to Sergeant Priest downstairs and ask him to send a couple of uniforms to Washingborough. I want the Birds' neighbours spoken to. I want to know if anyone saw any of the Birds coming or going, and I want times."

"Yes, boss," Cruz said excitedly. It would be the first time, that Ben could recollect anyway, that he hadn't been assigned the dreaded door knocking duty, and he was clearly overjoyed. "So, what am I doing? I could always shadow you guys? You know? Learn a few things."

"You're sticking flyers on posts. Get the print-outs from CID and take Gillespie. I want a flyer on every post along that tow path."

"Sticking flyers up?"

"It's an important job, Cruz. Is there a problem?"

"No," he said, as a child might.

"And you'll take Gillespie, yes?"

Cruz stared across at Gillespie's empty seat in dismay.

"I guess so."

"Think of it as having another pair of hands. Albeit a half-drunk and useless pair of hands."

"Hey, I'm not half-drunk," Gillespie said, as he re-entered the incident room and let it close with a bang.

"Completely drunk?" Cruz suggested.

"I'm right as rain. Must have had a dodgy pint or something. I just needed a wee power nap. It'll take more than a few pints of ale to break Jim Gillespie," he said proudly. "What have you got for me, Ben?"

"You're not driving. You're with Cruz."

"Eh? Sticking up flyers? What am I? Twelve years old?"

"You're over the limit and I can't have you driving or talking to people."

"You can't let him actually work," Nillson said. "He's half-drunk."

"I think we all deserve the benefit of the doubt every now and again, Anna. It's not like this is a common occurrence. If it happens again, however, then I'm sure Jim will understand when he's taken off the investigation," Ben replied, and he took the photo of the reeds from Freya's open file. "Chapman, find the digital file for this image and have it enlarged."

Nillson craned her neck to see what the image was of.

"Reeds?" she said.

"Not just any reeds, Anna," Ben replied. "Reeds that have been knotted."

"Why would they be knotted?" Cruz asked.

Ben returned to the board, pondered the question for a moment, and after a quick glance at Freya, he spoke.

"Imagine this," he began. "You're Simon Bird. For one reason or another, you're on a paddle board."

"So we do think the board is connected to him, do we?" Cruz asked.

"Just hear me out," Ben replied, holding his hands up in defence. "For one reason or another, you're on the paddle board. You've lost the paddle, which we know because we found it miles upstream from where he was found. Which means you're at the whim of the current. Maybe you see people on the footpath and you call out to them? Cruz, that's where your flyers come in. The current takes you miles downstream, and as the river turns, you float close to some reeds. So you grab onto them. You call out, but nobody comes. From where you are, you can see the setting sun. The temperature drops, and you begin to wonder if you'll be there all night. All the while, the river is pulling you away. It's tugging at the board. You've been there hours now, and all you want to do is sleep. The anxiety, the adrenalin, and the panic have left you exhausted. So you tie a knot in the reeds and slip your arm through. Then you can lie down and rest. The current isn't so strong that it would pull you away. So you lie there, waiting for help to come. Waiting for the sun to rise. Hoping someone will come along."

"Aye, but someone did come along, didn't they?" Gillespie said. "They came along and throttled the poor wee bastard. Drowned him."

"The question is who, out of all the people that might have wanted Simon dead, had access to a boat? Who knew he was there? It's our job to find out," Ben said.

The delivery, in Freya's opinion, was exceptional. He had placed them all there. He'd empathised, and he'd put them all in the shoes of Simon Bird.

"Aye," Gillespie added, his sombre, gravelly tone rumbling its way into Freya's thoughts.

"Gillespie, Cruz, you're on flyers and CCTV from the houses and industrial units on the lane leading to Five Mile Bridge," Ben said. "What did you find out yesterday?"

Gillespie nodded at his laptop. "I saw the headmaster yesterday. A Mr Boorman. I've got a list of every kid in Simon's year, along with who they hang around with."

"Good, send it to Chapman to correlate with the social media accounts."

"Aye, will do. But there's more."

"Go on," Freya said.

"A name. Someone who Boorman feels is worth looking into."

"Well, don't just leave it there, Gillespie," Freya said. "Tell us."

"Forbes," he said. "It's a lad named Gavin Forbes."

# CHAPTER TWENTY-EIGHT

"Right, let's bring the boy in. Nillson, that's a job for you. Take a uniform with you and have someone collect the parents. Or one of them at least."

"No problem," Anna replied.

"How did you get on yesterday, anyway?"

"The rental place was closed. By the time I'd finished with the two witnesses, I was probably too late."

"Ah, the witnesses. What did they have to say for themselves?"

She took a deep breath, seeming a little unsure of how to describe her visit.

"They're an odd couple, that's for sure. He's a history nerd. She's a shopaholic, from what I can see. One of those girls who takes selfies at every opportunity, regardless of where they are."

"I know the type," Ben said. "And it was the girl who saw the body, wasn't it?"

"Yeah. Although, they said Hugo Bird was reluctant to turn the boat around at first."

"Why would he be reluctant?" Freya asked.

"I don't know. They said he was keen on showing them one of

the old abbeys, or something. Said he got excited about the history."

"And when they convinced him to turn around?"

"As soon as they saw it was a body, he put his foot down. Or whatever the equivalent boat terminology is. Harry said he thought Hugo was just protecting Debbie from getting too much of an eyeful. He said he did the right thing as far as he was concerned."

"Not much help, then?" Ben said.

"They corroborated Hugo Bird's story. I've asked them to stay around for a few days."

"That must have pleased them," Cruz said. "Thanks for spotting the creepy dead body on the creepy early morning tour boat, and by the way, can you hang around for a few days?"

"I'm sure they'd prefer to stay in Lincoln for a day or so, rather than be dragged all the way back up here," Chapman offered.

"Right," Ben said, clapping his hands together once. "Let's recap. Lots of talk, but not much in the way of progress. Chapman, what are you doing?"

"I've got the list of pupils from Simon's school. I'm going to see if I can identify the owner of the social media account that was set up to bully Simon Bird."

"Good. Can you also get hold of any CCTV footage from Brayford Pool? I want to see if Hugo Bird did indeed go to his boat on the Sunday night, and if he did, what did he do?"

Even from four or five metres away, Ben could see how neat her handwriting was, as she added another line to her to-do list.

"Cruz. Talk to me," Ben said.

"Eh?"

Ben gave a sigh. The young DC often showed great promise. He was an intelligent lad, with an uncanny ability to recite facts from documentaries he'd seen or discussions he'd heard. But his attention span was akin to that of a five-year-old child.

"What are you doing, Cruz?"

"What, right now?"

"Today, Gabby. Today. What are you doing today?"

"Oh, right. Jim and I are heading down to the river for a fun-filled day of sticking flyers up on posts."

"Then what?"

"Then, once Jim has sobered up–"

"Oy," Gillespie said. "I am not drunk."

"Okay, once Jim's hangover has worn off, we'll see if any of the houses or industrial units at the top of Five Mile Lane have CCTV."

"Good. Anna?"

"I'm bringing in Gavin Forbes. When I've done that, I'll head down to the rental place."

"Right. DI Bloom and I will focus on the parents. At this stage, we need to eliminate individuals from our enquiries. Starting with the parents. Hugo Bird said he was at his boat the night Simon was killed. Chapman, that one is on you to prove. Sally Bird said she was at bingo. We'll take care of that one. We'll head down to the community hall and talk to somebody. Nillson, you're on Gavin Forbes."

A childish smirk spread across Cruz's face. Had Freya not sat forward in her chair, delivering one of her trademark stares of incredulity, he might have even voiced the joke inside his head.

"Cruz, Gillespie, you're starting the search for witnesses and checking for CCTV. And remember, if you happen to see anybody while you're out, don't be shy. Talk to them. Especially dog walkers and joggers. They may have used that route on Sunday night."

"Aye, Ben," Gillespie said, sounding less than thrilled to be with Cruz all day. "Permission to grab a decent coffee from the wee shop up the road before we start?"

"If that's what it takes to get results, then do it," Freya intervened. "And next time you go for a pint after work, try not to have a dodgy one."

"I'll do my best, boss," he replied.

Ben looked at each of them, then nodded.

"Good. Let's meet back here at three p.m. and see where we are."

# CHAPTER TWENTY-NINE

W HEN DS J IM G ILLESPIE WALKED OUT OF THE STATION AND climbed into what he could only describe as the smallest car ever made, his face was sullen and his movements slow. But two minutes later, after he had convinced Cruz to stop at the wee coffee shop on the high street, he was a new man.

Sure, he'd had a few beers while he had waited for Mrs Chang and her family to prepare his dinner, and sure, the elation from the text messages had amplified the effects of those beers. But he was far from hungover, and whatever stain the alcohol had left on his abilities that day was all but wiped clean with the promise of seeing the lovely Jessica and watching her make him a coffee. Having to work with Cruz had been a bit of a setback, but once again, the thought of seeing Jessica took the edge off that.

It was mid-morning, and a queue had formed. In Gillespie's opinion, they served the best coffee for miles. Which wasn't hard, as the only alternatives open to him in that particular part of rural Lincolnshire were the station kitchen, a petrol station outside of Woodhall Spa, and a self-serving machine in a one of the Co-op supermarkets.

He joined the queue, towering above the rest of the people in it, and counted his position. He was sixth. Which meant that, all orders being equal, Jessica's colleague would serve him. And just as that thought ran through his mind, the person at the front thanked them both and idled out of the door, leaving just four people in front of him. It wasn't just a case of being an odd or even number, he had learned. He also had to factor in the orders the customers ahead of him were asking for. If Jessica's customer had asked for two or more coffees, then the balance could shift easily. What he needed was somebody behind him in the queue, so that, should he happen to be destined for Jessica's colleague, he could make an excuse and fall back a spot, guaranteeing him to land in front of the delightful Jessica.

Thinking fast, he leaned out of the cafe door and whistled to Cruz, waving to catch his attention.

The other customers all turned at the noise, and Jessica smiled shyly. Cruz, however, was listening to the stereo, and was happily bopping along inside the parked car.

"Cruz?" he called out, keeping his voice as low as he could. But Cruz was in full flow. He had even begun waving his hands around. *How the bloody hell does a man dance inside a car?* "Gabby?"

Still nothing.

The queue dropped to three people, with the last customer ordering just a black coffee and a flapjack. With no other alternative, Gillespie pulled his phone from his pocket, found Cruz's number, and hit the button to call him.

Inside the car, Cruz stopped his dancing and checked his phone. Then, with a look of utter bewilderment, he stared out of the window, shrugged, and shook his head, as if to say, "What?"

Gillespie pointed at his phone and gestured for Cruz to answer the call.

"Hello?" Cruz said, in a tone that suggested he didn't know was calling.

"It's me," Gillespie said, trying his hardest not to let his agitation get the better of him. "Can you come here, mate?"

"Eh?" The radio was still playing, and Gillespie could hardly hear him.

"Can you come here?"

Cruz was still staring at Gillespie as if he was an idiot.

"Turn the bloody music down," Gillespie said, far louder than he probably should have, and as a result, both Jessica and her friend, and the three remaining customers, all stared at him.

"Sorry," Gillespie said, raising his hand in an apology. "It's my friend. He's a bit dim-witted."

The music quietened on the other end of the call and Gillespie took a breath to calm himself, before lowering his voice and addressing Cruz.

"Can you come here, please?" he said, as nicely as he possibly could.

"Eh? What for?"

"I just need to speak to you."

"You are speaking to me."

"Aye, I know that. But I'd like to speak to you here," Gillespie said, turning away from the queue and covering the handset with his free hand.

"Oh, for god's sake," Cruz said, and he made a show of switching off the engine, climbing from the car, and stretching. *Stretching? He's only been in the car for two minutes.* Then he took the time to lock the car, even though it was twenty metres from the front of the cafe.

"What?" he said, as he approached Gillespie.

"I figured you could get your own coffee," Gillespie told him.

"Eh? I don't want a coffee."

"Yes, you do," Gillespie said, widening his eyes to encourage Cruz to play along with him.

"Eh?"

"DI Bloom wants a coffee. So why don't you get hers, and I'll get mine?"

"Eh? Why?"

"Because it'll be quicker," Gillespie said, through gritted teeth.

"You got me out of the car for that?"

"Just join the bloody queue, Gabby."

"Alright, alright," Cruz said. "Jesus. One hangover and you're like Jekyll and bloody Hyde."

The customer in front of Jessica thanked her, then balanced his three coffees and made his way out, giving Gillespie the opportunity to make a show of holding the door for him.

"Why are you acting weird?" Cruz said, as the person next in line moved across to Jessica's station. She smiled briefly at Gillespie and Cruz.

"I'm not acting weird," he growled, doing his best not to move his lips.

"Eh?"

"Oh, for crying out loud, man. Will you just shut up?" Gillespie said, and that stain caused by the three suspicious ales he'd had the previous night returned. It was like somebody was holding the coldest ice cube known to man in the centre of his forehead.

"Who's next?" Jessica's colleague asked, and Gillespie cursed inwardly. If Jessica's customer only wanted something quick, he'd be lumbered with the colleague. He took a step back to stand beside Cruz, equalising his chances.

"What are you doing?" Cruz asked, his voice loud and irritating. So bloody irritating.

Gillespie pretended not to have heard him, and focused on his peripheral, where he was studying Jessica's every move. There were two cups being prepared, whereas her colleague only had one to deal with. He could be in with a chance.

"It's great you're going to help me stick those flyers up," Cruz said. But to Gillespie, his voice was distant, like in a dream. A bad dream. "I walked for miles yesterday. I doubt anyone ever reads them anyway."

"And I'll take a bit of that carrot cake," Jessica's customer said.

That bought him another minute at least, as Jessica prepared the paper bag and the cake slice, and was asking which piece the customer would like.

She was lovely. Her hair was shining today. She must have washed it, Gillespie thought. Then he wondered how it might smell.

"I mean," Cruz continued, from that faraway place, "if anyone saw a lad floating down the river, they'd have called the police, surely?"

"Floating down the river?" Jessica's colleague said, as she took the payment from her customer. That was when things started to go very badly. Her customer turned around to stare at Gillespie. She was a middle-aged lady, good-looking, and she clearly looked after herself.

"I heard about that. It was in the papers."

"They're police," the colleague said, then looked back at Gillespie. "Are you working on it, then, are you?"

"I heard it was a lad from Washingborough," the customer said. "I heard some other boys put him up to it, then watched him float down the river."

It was all well and good to be polite to citizens, but the conversation was threatening Gillespie's plan.

"Aye, well," he said. "That's another team working on that."

"Eh?" Cruz said, and Gillespie casually stood on his foot, applying more and more weight until Cruz's confused expression morphed into something altogether different.

"Who's next?" Jessica said, as her customer left. Gillespie didn't bother holding the door. He stepped straight over to her, smiled, and then, after a few seconds, she spoke.

"You okay, Jim?" she asked.

"Aye, yeah. Never better," he replied. "You're looking happy this morning. Had a wee bit of good news, did you?"

"Good news?" she asked, cocking her head.

"Aye, you're all beaming and that. It's nothing. I was just saying, that's all. You look good. You look happy."

It was the annoying colleague who broke the silence, as Jessica's eyes darted from her to Gillespie and back again.

"Oh, go on," she said. "You might as well put him out of his misery."

*It was her,* Gillespie thought. It must have been her who sent the text. And with only Cruz, Gillespie, and the two girls left, they could probably talk quite openly about it.

"Aye," Gillespie said. "Go on. What's got you full of the joys of spring then?"

Jessica stammered. She looked away, her face reddening.

"Ah," her friend said. "I'll do it, shall I? It's her boyfriend."

"Her what?"

"Her boyfriend," she said. "He proposed last night, and she's been grinning like a little schoolgirl all morning."

# CHAPTER THIRTY

THE COMMUNITY CENTRE CAR PARK WAS NEAR EMPTY, SAVE FOR a small hatchback parked close to the main entrance. Freya parked beside it and killed the engine. Ben was out of the car searching for CCTV before Freya had even collected her thoughts. He was fired up still, and that pleased her.

She climbed out, retrieved her coat from the back seat, and pulled it around her. Spring had definitely arrived, but the mornings still had a chill to them.

"Why was he there?" Ben asked over the bonnet of Freya's car. He leaned on the Range Rover and stared at her, seemingly oblivious to her contemptuous look. "If we knew why Simon was there in the first place, then we might catch a break."

"Do you mean, by understanding why he was by the river, we might understand why somebody might have wanted to hurt him?"

"Well, yeah. Of course."

"Do you think maybe the reason somebody wanted to hurt him was because he leaned on their new car?"

Ben stood up straight, glanced at the little community hall, and gave the car a mock shine with his sleeve.

"I just don't get why he was there in the first place. His mum said he had no friends. The headteacher said Forbes was the one behind the bullying. It's easy to imagine Forbes and his little clique lying by the river smoking drugs, but why was Simon there? Unless Gavin Forbes told him to come down with the promise of hanging around with them."

"Sally Bird said Forbes lured Simon into the group before. Maybe he was up to his old tricks?" Freya said.

"Everything we've got is based on a bloody theory," Ben said. "We need to start talking to people."

"It's a fog," Freya told him.

"A fog?"

"Haven't you heard that expression before?"

"I know what a fog is, Freya."

"In crime. Police work. The fog. It means you can't see the end of the road, only a little way ahead, and even then you don't know if you're heading in the right direction. All you can do is take one step at a time and keep looking ahead."

"Sounds a little like the rest of my life."

"Oh, I doubt that," Freya said. "In fact, out of us all, I'd say your path is the clearest."

"Oh great. So you've analysed my life now, have you?"

"Not analysed," she said, rolling her eyes at his dramatic response. "But I do understand you. Thousands wouldn't, but I do."

"This fog," he replied, ignoring her insight into his life. "Do you ever get lost in it?"

"Frequently," she said. "Sometimes you have to go deeper and deeper into it, just to learn where it was you took a wrong turn."

"And where was your wrong turn?"

"I get the feeling we're not talking about Simon Bird here," she said, but nodded, going along with the conversation for the sake of conversation. "Probably when I was in London. When I met my ex-husband."

"Oh," Ben said, sounding surprised. "I thought you were happy at some point."

"At one point, I thought I was happy. I thought he was what I wanted. I thought he needed what I needed. You know? To round my life off. A husband. He already had a child, so that ticked a box that I was never willing to tick myself. But if I'm honest with myself, I should have walked away. I should have thought about the fog. Hindsight is twenty-twenty, right?"

"So they say."

She gave a little laugh at how easy it was to absorb Ben's questions and deflect her insecurities onto him. It was he who now felt as if he was probing too deep.

"But I had to venture through that fog. Eight years of walking blindly until I found clarity. A break in the clouds, as it were."

"Eight years. That's a long time to be lost."

"Oh, I wasn't lost. Not all the time. I was on a path. I was heading somewhere. But the little break in the clouds offered me a chance to look back. And I could see into the distance. I could see another path. That was my moment of clarity. That was when I realised I'd taken a wrong turn."

"You've really thought about that metaphor, haven't you?"

"The trouble is, Ben," she said, ignoring his flippancy, "we're all walking through the same fog. There are millions of us, all navigating the same fog. We may walk the wrong path for a while. We may meet people and alter their path. And in turn, they may meet somebody else, and alter theirs. Do you see what I'm saying?"

"Are you referring to your ex-husband's son?"

"I am. But not just him. My ex-husband. Who knows what he could have done had he not met me? That's one of the wonders, isn't it? We take a path and we tell ourselves to stick to it. We have no idea of the damage we're doing to other people's journeys."

"Or the help we're giving. It works both ways," he said, clearly reflecting on how each of them had helped the other during the past six or seven months since Freya had moved to Lincolnshire.

"Exactly," she said. "If an alternative path presents itself, and we feel the urge to venture down it, then we should. After all, if we're walking blind, what does it matter which path we walk down?"

They had spoken so long from inside the fog analogy that the real world around them seemed odd for the first few moments after they had stopped.

"No cameras," Ben said.

"Maybe there's a register," Freya replied, and she left him wondering about the fog while she approached the main doors.

A small ramp catered for wheelchairs, and one of the two doors was unlocked. The foyer, a five metre by five metre square room, smelled of disinfectant, and nearly every inch of wall space had been taken up with flyers, posters, and pin boards.

"We ought to get Cruz to pop by and leave a flyer," Ben suggested.

"That's if he can find room to pin it anywhere," Freya replied. Then, catching herself sighing heavily, she called out, "Hello?"

Ben pulled open a door, glanced inside, then closed it again. "Cleaning cupboard," he said. Then he called out louder, "Anyone home?"

A head poked out from a doorway, just as Freya was approaching it, and she startled the older man.

"Now then," he said, once he had recovered from his little fright. "Can I help at all?"

"Good morning, sir," Freya said, showing him her warrant card. "I'm Detective Inspector Bloom. This is Detective Sergeant Savage. We were wondering if we could talk to the person who runs this place?"

"Which one?" he replied, then caught Freya's slightly confused expression. "It's a community centre. The community run it."

"Okay. And who would have run the place on Sunday night?"

"Sunday? That's bingo night," he said. "That's me."

"Ah, good. Now we're getting somewhere. We're making enquiries into one of your customers," Freya said, unsure if customers was the correct term.

"Customers? Do you mean one of our members?"

"That sounds more like it. Her name is Sally Bird."

"Sally?" he said gravely. "Oh, aye. We all know Sally."

"Oh, is she popular?"

"You could say that, aye."

"Well," Freya said, noticing a hint of contempt in his tone, "you'll understand the importance of our questions, then."

"Thought it might have something to do with her. Terrible thing, that."

"You've heard then, have you?"

"It's all over the local rag. Hard not to hear about it. It's certainly set some tongues wagging, I can tell you."

"Sally mentioned she was here on Sunday night. Is that right?"

"Sunday, Sunday, Sunday..." he murmured, staring up at the ceiling while he thought. Then he thrust his index finger out. "Ah, yes. Sunday. Sally was here. She won the thirty-ball game. Twenty quid."

"The thirty-ball game?"

"It's a shorter, faster game," the man explained. "I think that's all she took, though. I don't recall seeing her after that. In fact... No. She left soon afterwards. She often leaves early."

"Did she say where she was going?"

"Not to me. I was on stage pulling my balls out."

"You were pulling your balls out?" Ben repeated, presumably for clarification. "On stage?"

Innuendoes such as that were often lost on folk of the older generation, Freya mused. Not for a lack of a sense of humour. In fact, some of the dirtiest minds she had ever come across had been in the older generation. But terminology differed from generation to generation.

"Yes. Calling the numbers. You know? It's bingo, man. Haven't you ever played?"

"I haven't, I'm afraid. But I'm aware of the rules," Ben said, not hiding his smile.

"Right. Will that be all?"

"May we please take your name?" Freya asked.

"It's Dennis," he replied, as if they should have known the infamous Dennis and his infamous Sunday night stage act. "Dennis Stone."

"Thank you, Dennis," Freya said, offering him a grateful and encouraging smile. She turned to leave, gesturing for Ben to lead the way. But then she stopped at the doorway and turned to find him staring after them. "Just one more thing. Do you happen to recall what time Sally might have won her game?"

"The thirty-ball?"

"Yes. That's it. Would you have any idea what time that was? You said she left soon after."

"We always do the thirty-ball in between two longer games. Not everyone likes the thirty-ball, see. Too fast for them. Plus, it gives the older folk an opportunity to spend a penny."

"Right," Freya said, surprised at how much thought went into arranging a bingo night.

"Must have been sometime between nine and nine-thirty," he said. "I know that because we played quite a few games that night, and I didn't lock up until gone midnight."

"Midnight?" Freya said, hearing the alarm in her own voice.

"Aye, yes. Midnight. By the time we've packed the chairs away and whatnot."

"And your balls," Ben added. "You must have packed your balls away."

"Yes, and those," the old gentleman agreed. "I always give them a wipe down when I'm done with them. All those people in the room. The moisture in the air makes them sticky, you see."

Behind her, Freya saw Ben turning away, presumably unable to hide his childish grin. Dennis looked after him, then up at Freya. "Is he alright?"

"Yes, he's fine. We're just keen to get to the bottom of this investigation," Freya said. "We're all a bit riled up over this one."

"Aye, well. Aren't we all? He was a good lad, that Simon. Didn't deserve to go like that."

"You knew him?"

"Aye, yeah. We all knew him."

"I imagine everyone knows everyone in a small community like this," Freya said.

"We used to. Not so much these days. Too many unfamiliar faces. New money. But we knew Simon. Simple Simon, they used to call him. You know? On account of his..." He tapped his head with his forefinger.

"He had learning difficulties, as I understand it," Freya said, steering the conversation onto more politically correct terms.

"Aye, well, if that's what you call it. In my day he were simple. Gullible. Naïve. It's sad. A tragedy, if you will. But I've seen it before. Boys like him. They don't get far without a helping hand or two."

"Sadly, there seemed to be more hands holding him down than helping him up," Freya mused aloud. "Thank you, Mr Stone. You've been a great help."

He nodded his goodbye, and once more, Freya had another thought.

"Sorry, one more thing. We're having some flyers printed. A call for witnesses," Freya explained. "May we use your board? You never know. One of your members might have seen something."

He glanced at the board and seemed to search for a space, then nodded solemnly.

"I'll find a space for it," he said. "I'm sure somebody must have seen something. You'd be surprised what people see and keep to themselves."

Freya raised her eyebrows at the statement. But Dennis Stone retreated to the office, turning on the threshold.

"Good day," he finished.

# CHAPTER THIRTY-ONE

"Thank god we didn't send Gillespie or Cruz to do that," Ben said as soon as they got back into the car.

"Bless him," Freya said, then turned to stare at Ben, who seemed to read her thoughts.

"We're still walking blindly through your fog, aren't we?"

"The point is we're still walking. As long as we keep moving, Ben. That's what matters," Freya said. "Have somebody stop by and put some flyers up. I think we might catch a lead here."

"Oh?" Ben said, and Freya realised he had already left the community centre when she had said her goodbyes to Dennis Stone.

"Something he just said. Something about how we'd be surprised at what people see and keep to themselves."

"That's ominous."

"Yes. Yes, it is," Freya said, but her phone ringing broke her chain of thought. She retrieved it from her pocket and stared down at the screen. "It's Nillson," she said, before clicking the green button to answer the call. The call was routed through the car's Bluetooth system. It was crisp and clear, as if Nillson was in the back seat.

"Ma'am?"

"Go ahead, Nillson. I'm here with DS Savage."

"I just thought you should both know," the young, feisty DC began. "We've got Forbes. He's on his way to the station now."

"And his parents?"

"Uniform have picked his mother up from work."

"Good. See to it they have a duty solicitor if they need one. If they have their own, which I very much doubt, then make the arrangements. I want to question him as soon as I'm back, and I don't want to wait."

"Will do, ma'am," came the reply.

"How is he, anyway?"

The line was quiet for a moment, while Nillson considered her response.

"Angry," she replied. "At least he was angry at the school. But you know how kids are. It's probably a front to save face. I wouldn't be surprised if he's crying his eyes out right now, wondering what's going to happen to him."

"Me either," Freya agreed. "Okay, good work, Nillson. We'll catch you later at the station. In the meantime, see if you can get some kind of report out of the tech guys on what they've found so far. We've got twenty-four hours with the lad. I don't intend on wasting a single second of it."

"Ma'am," Nillson said, by way of confirmation, then killed the call.

Freya sat back in her seat, hoping for a few seconds of head space. But Ben, who had said nothing during the call, was ready with a distraction.

"Another few steps forward, into the thick fog?"

She gave a little laugh. "That's right. Another few steps. Then a few more. That's all we can do sometimes."

"You're not sounding confident, Freya," Ben said. It was out of the blue. Almost an accusation. "The boy. Forbes. You're having doubts."

"Am I?" she replied. "Well, thanks for letting me know what's going on in my mind."

Ben said nothing. He just stared at her, one eyebrow cocked.

"Alright, alright. You're right. I do have my doubts. But it's just the fog, Ben."

"Do you want to air those thoughts?"

"Not right now. What about you? You're not sold on the idea of it being Forbes either, are you?"

"He sounds like a toe rag. And if it is him behind the social media, then he clearly had it in for Simon. But there's one thing that doesn't stack up for me."

"Go on."

"Well, how did Forbes get to him? I mean, if we go by our theory that Simon Bird floated down the river on a paddle board, tied himself to the reeds, and waited for help to come. Then whoever killed him must have had access to a boat."

"Yes, we ascertained that last night."

"So then Forbes must have access to a boat. Or at the least, another paddle board. And even then, was he supposed to have paddled back against the current?" Ben said. "It's bloody miles."

"Oh, Ben," Freya said, and sighed. "Sometimes I feel like your mind works completely differently to mine. It's like you're another species altogether."

"And the rest of the time?"

"It's like we share the same brain," she said. "All we can hope for from Forbes is for him to clear a bit of the fog. My concern right now is why Sally Bird left bingo early. Where did she go? What did she do?"

"And more importantly," Ben added, "why didn't she tell us?"

# CHAPTER THIRTY-TWO

"THIS IS RIDICULOUS," CRUZ SAID, VOICING HIS OPINION OF THE task for perhaps the sixth time in as many minutes. Gillespie rolled his eyes. He was glad for the mundane task. It gave him time to consider the blow he'd taken earlier.

He felt betrayed, although he knew it was unjustified. How could she? A boyfriend? But what about the flirting? He'd even given her his card and asked her to call him.

"What's the matter with you today?" Cruz asked.

"Eh?" Gillespie replied, slipping out of his own little world.

"Bloody hell, Jim. How much did you have last night?"

"I didn't. Well, I did. But just a few. Three, in fact. I'm just..."

He stopped. Cruz was alright. Sure, he was a little dim and was a walking definition of the word naïve. But he wasn't the type of mate Gillespie felt he could confide in. He lacked the ability to think before he spoke, rendering him terrible at keeping secrets.

"Just what?"

"Thinking, Gabby. Thinking. You know? It's what you do when you face a conundrum."

"A conundrum?" he replied. "Ah, come on. Let's hear it. I'm good at conundrums. I always get them."

"You always get them?" Gillespie said.

"Yeah, you know. Before the adverts on Countdown. Nine letters and a clue. I'm pretty good at it. My mum reckons I've an analytical mind."

Gillespie stared at the lad in disbelief.

"Not that type of conundrum, Gab."

"Alright," Cruz said, undeterred. "Well, you know what they say, a problem shared is a problem halved."

They moved along the towpath towards the next post.

"I'm not sure you're the right person to help with this one, little fella. It's of a..." Gillespie gestured the hourglass shape of his ideal woman with his hands. "It's of a sexual nature."

"Right," Cruz replied. "And you don't think I can help with that?"

"You're not exactly known for your talent with the opposite sex, mate. I'm okay, leave me to it. I'll get to the bottom of my little conundrum. I haven't been beaten yet."

"Excuse me?" a voice said from behind them. Gillespie turned to find a man wearing shorts and a t-shirt. He was jogging on the spot, and made a show of hitting a button on his smart watch before removing his headphones. "Are you putting these flyers up?"

Gillespie looked him up and down, then glanced down at the wad of flyers in Cruz's hand.

"Well, we're not taking them down, son," he said.

"Oh," the man said, and he stopped his annoying jogging on the spot. He was obviously out running but didn't appear to be breathless in the slightest. He was either super fit, Gillespie thought, or he'd only just set out. "It was just that I may have seen something. I'm not really sure."

"Okay," Gillespie said, and he nodded for Cruz to take notes. "Do you want to tell us what you saw? At this stage, any information could be helpful."

"Well, I was out for my daily run. I run here every day, you see?" he said, and Gillespie caught a whiff of an accent much like DI Bloom's. He was well-spoken and sounded more like a public schoolboy than a local. "I saw a group of kids. I'm sure I did. They were about a mile back that way."

He jabbed his thumb over his shoulder, pointing back the way they had come, which correlated with the team's theory and the spot Cruz had discovered where the paddle was found in the reeds.

"There were four or five of them."

"Four or five?"

"Yes. One couple was lying on the grass, kissing."

"So boys and girls?" Gillespie said.

"Well, yes. There were two girls if I recall. One was lying with one of the boys, and the other was sitting a few feet away."

"Which leaves two boys," Gillespie said.

"Yes. One of them was in the water with a type of surfboard thing. An SUP, I think. I've seen them on holidays."

"A stand-up paddle board?" Cruz said.

"Yes, that's it. He wasn't on it. But he was holding onto the leash thing."

"And the other lad?" Gillespie asked.

"He was on the bank. I thought he was helping him at first. You know, those things can be hard to stand up on."

"Right," Gillespie said. "But now you don't think he was helping?"

"I don't know. That's the thing. I wasn't really paying much attention. I was out–"

"For your run. Yes, I get it," Gillespie said. "And what time was this?"

"Well, I prefer not to run in the dark, and I definitely don't run after dinner."

"So, late afternoon?" Gillespie said. "Is that safe to say?"

"Yes, I think so," the man said, and he smoothed a lock of his black hair across his head. "Wait. I know."

He reached into his shorts, putting his hand down the side of his leg, and looked up at the sky, as if he was feeling for something.

From the corner of his eye, Gillespie saw Cruz pull a slightly concerned expression, and then take a step back. But the man's hand emerged with a mobile phone. He held it up for them both to see. "My phone," he said. "I use an activity app."

"An activity app?" Gillespie repeated.

"Yeah. I record all my workouts. Distance, time, heart rate. You name it, I record it."

"Right," Gillespie heard himself saying, thinking that the man really should get a hobby. "And how is that going to help?"

"The time," he replied. "I know I average around four and a half to five minutes per kilometre. And I know that from my house the bridge is about a kilometre."

"Right," Gillespie said again.

"Well, don't you see?" he said, holding his phone up to show Gillespie a screen full of figures and acronyms. "It says here that on Sunday afternoon, I started my run at three-fifty. Which means that I would have reached the bridge at three fifty-five."

"Give or take thirty seconds or so," Gillespie added, following along.

"Exactly. So that means I would have seen the group of kids sometime between three fifty-five and four o'clock."

"And your phone tells you all that, does it?"

"Well, yes. Look. It's all here."

"I'll take your word for that, Mr...?"

"Green," he replied. "Jeffrey Green."

"Jeffrey Green. Make a note of that, will you, Gabby?"

"Already on it, Jim."

"Is it helpful?" Jefferey asked.

"Well, aye. At this stage, anything is helpful. We need to build a timeline of the victim's movements. So, aye. I think it is helpful. Nifty little app, that."

"Oh, well, I'm glad. I was hoping not to waste your time."

"Ah, it's definitely not been a waste of time. So, are you just starting your run, or...?"

"Just finishing, actually. I don't usually like to stop. It messes with my data. But, given the circumstances..."

"Aye, well, it's definitely been worth it," Gillespie said. "Listen, you said you lived a kilometre from the bridge."

"That's right," he agreed, then pointed in the lane's direction. "At the top of Five Mile Lane. You can't miss it. It's an old cottage. Pretty little thing."

"You wouldn't happen to have one of those doorbells with a camera on it, would you?" Cruz asked. "I mean, you're into your gadgets and that."

"Ah, I've seen them. They look great, don't they? Sadly, the cottage is listed. Grade two. I couldn't drill the hole to run the cable."

"Shame," Cruz said. "Thanks anyway. It was just a long shot. We're going to be heading up there after this. We'd have probably knocked on your door."

"Oh, right," Jeffrey replied. "I don't have the doorbell camera, but I do have cameras on the side of the house. They're wireless."

"Oh really?" Cruz said, giving Gillespie a sideways glance. "Do you think we could swing by and take a peek?"

"Erm, yeah. Sure. Shall we say in an hour?" he replied. "That gives me ten minutes to get home, thirty minutes to shower, and twenty minutes to get lunch going."

"Do everything by the clock, do you, Mr Green?"

"I'm a trader. I have to."

"A trader, aye? The markets, you mean?"

"Yes. I have to be ready for when the markets come online."

"So, you work from home?"

"Yes. I have a little office overlooking the fields."

"You just sit at home all day? Trading?"

"Well, there's more to it than that. I have to read the papers, watch the news. You know? Stay up to date with politics and business."

"And go for a run?" Gillespie said.

"Yes, of course. It's quite a sedentary way of earning a living. So I try to get moving when I can."

"Sounds like I'm in the wrong job," Gillespie mused aloud.

"Well, it's not quite as simple as that—"

"You sit at home, read the papers, watch the news, and go for a run?"

"You make it sound so mundane."

"Mundane?" Gillespie said, with a little chortle. "Not mundane. That's a life goal right there. Of course, I wouldn't put so much weight on the running. But the rest of it... I envy you. I'd rather be sitting at home reading the papers than walking an endless path with him."

He nodded to his left, indicating Cruz, who voiced his objection with a sudden, "Oy!"

"Listen. It might sound like a simple life. But I can assure you it's not. At least you know how much you'll earn today. My earnings are at the whim of the American dollar right now. And with everything that's going on in the world, that means quite a few sleepless nights."

Gillespie tried his best to understand what the man was saying. How was the American dollar relevant? How did politics affect his earnings?

"Right, that makes me feel a wee bit better," Gillespie said, offering a very practiced smile that said, *Right then. We'll be in touch.* "Right then," he said. "We'll pop round in about an hour, when you've showered, lunched, and stuff."

"It's number five," Jeffrey stated. "In case you can't find it."

"That's perfect. Thank you, Mr Green," Cruz said.

"Perhaps I can make the footage ready. You know? Download it from the cloud in advance. It might save a bit of time."

"That would be great," Gillespie replied, then nodded his goodbye.

Less than thirty seconds later, as Cruz fixed yet another flyer to yet another post, Gillespie turned around, and just caught sight of Jeffrey Green as he rounded a bend.

"Bloody hell. Look at him go. I'd have a coronary if I ran that fast. You'd have to fetch the dive team to come and get me. There's no way an ambulance could get down here."

"Who's to say I wouldn't just roll you into the water," Cruz muttered, as he pulled one of the cable ties tight. "I might actually make it through the day without being insulted."

"Nah, I doubt that. There'll always be someone to insult you, Gabby," Gillespie said, and received a tired eyeroll in reply. "Listen, I was thinking—"

"You were thinking?" Cruz said, and a panicked look spread over his face. "I don't like it when you think, Jim. It always turns out badly for me."

"No. It'll be fine. Listen. How about I go and knock on the doors? You know? Get the CCTV. And you carry on here?"

"What? Do this on my own, you mean?"

"Aye, yeah. It'll be grand. We'll finish faster."

"But I'll be on my own," Cruz stated. "Again."

But Gillespie had already turned around and was heading in the opposite direction, back towards the lane.

"You'll be fine. Stop whining," he called out. "We'll be back at the station early. DI Bloom will think we're the bloody A-Team."

Gillespie had taken a few steps when he heard Cruz's little voice called out, "You just want all the glory. You know this is pointless."

"When have I ever stolen any glory, Gabby?" Gillespie called out, then stopped and turned to give one more reassuring look. "Oh, and Gabby?"

"What?" Cruz replied, sulking like a schoolboy, which he pretty much was.

"I'll see you in about two hours. Pick me up at the top of the lane," Gillespie said, doing very little to hide his glee. Then he nodded at the river. "And try not to fall in."

# CHAPTER THIRTY-THREE

"Try not to fall in," Cruz muttered to himself. He yanked another cable tie tight.

He stared at the flyer, wondering if anybody else would take notice of them. At the top, in large, bold letters, they read, WITNESS APPEAL. Then alongside a photo of Simon Bird was a description of events, watered down so as not to give too many details away. It read like a press release, and Gab guessed it was probably based on the press release Granger had issued.

With countless more posts ahead of him, he began his lonely stroll along the towpath. It could have been worse, he thought. It could have been raining.

Forty-five minutes had passed, and he was succumbing to the solitude. His outlook had shifted from being forced to tie flyers to posts on his own to enjoying a stroll along the river. And he was getting paid for it. On the whole, things could have been a lot worse.

The only two negatives were, he considered, that he had to stop every few hundred yards to stick a flyer on a post, thus breaking his trail of thinking. But the return journey would be better. He could really lose himself in his thoughts.

The second negative was, of course, the idea of having to collect Gillespie when he was done. It wouldn't be so bad if the massive Scotsman didn't take every opportunity to ridicule Gab or insult him. They got on just fine, but when the insults started flying, Gillespie was like a dog with a bone. And he shuddered to think what would happen if he found out about what he had told the others a couple of days ago.

Annoyed with himself for giving into them, he kicked a stone along the path. If Gillespie found out, the entire station would find out, and then Hermione would learn that he'd spoken about what they did and no doubt assume that he'd been bragging about their sex life. She would blow it all out of proportion, and probably dump him, and all for a few minutes of Gillespie's joy.

He stopped at the next post and set his wad of flyers down. Then he set about cable tying the flyer to the post. He'd found a technique that seemed to work with just two hands now that Gillespie wasn't helping him.

A squeal of brakes from behind startled him and he spun around to find a man on a bicycle coming to a stop.

"You police?" he said.

"No, I'm just doing this for fun," Gab replied, then backtracked, as he always did when he let his emotions run his mouth. "Yes, I'm with the police. Can I help?"

"These flyers. The kid. I think I saw something."

"Oh, really?" Gab said, pulling the cable tie tight.

He stepped closer to the man and appraised him. He was one of those Lycra men Hermione had been joking about when they had passed a line of cyclists on the way to the cinema a few weeks ago. What had she called them? Mamils, or something. She had said it stood for middle-aged men in Lycra. He twisted his feet to release his shoes from the pedals, and then climbed off his bike, slowly removing his gloves. Gab's eyes were instantly drawn to his obscenely tight shorts, and wondered if it was a crime to have something like that on show in a public place.

"What was that then?"

"I should probably talk to somebody in charge," he said, removing his helmet and running a hand across his shaved head. "Do you have a number I can call, or should I just dial the number on the flyer?"

"You can talk to me," Gab said, seeing an opportunity to bring something to the briefing other than reporting the successful sticking up of a few hundred flyers.

"Are you running the investigation?"

"Well, not exactly. But I'm on the team."

"Can I speak to your boss?" he said. "Was that the fellow back there? Big chap. Grumpy looking."

"Him? My boss?" Cruz said with a laugh. "No, I've sent him off to knock on some doors. So whatever it is you have to say, you can say it to me."

He seemed a little unsure and glanced furtively over his shoulder. "Well... I suppose."

"Look. Do you have anything to say or not? I'm quite busy here."

"It's just that..." he began. "Last Sunday. Late afternoon time. I saw someone."

"You saw somebody?" Gab repeated, coaxing him to say more.

"Look. I don't know if it was anything. It probably wasn't."

"Any information at this time could be helpful, sir," Gab said, stealing Gillespie's line and adding in the salutation for a more professional appearance.

"I saw a bloke. A man. Down there on the bridge," the man said, and he pointed back toward Five Mile Bridge. "I know it's wrong to say, but I ride here a lot, and all I normally see are joggers, dog walkers, and kids. That's it. So when I saw him—"

"The man?" Gab added for clarity.

"Yes. When I saw him, he just stood out like a sore thumb. He didn't have a dog. At least, I didn't see one. He wasn't running. In fact, he was wearing smartish trousers."

"Smartish?" Gab said.

"Yeah, you know. Trousers, like suit trousers. But not as smart. As if they were off the shelf and badly cut," he said, then pointed at Gab's trousers. "Kind of like those."

"These?"

"Yeah, you know. Just normal trousers."

"Right," Gab said, doing his best to hide his irritation. "So you saw a man wearing poorly fitting trousers, and you think he might have something to do with a murder investigation because he didn't have a dog and he wasn't jogging."

"Yes. No. It's more than that. There was something about him. Something about the way he walked. He kept looking around. It was like he was waiting for somebody, or hiding from someone. Up to no good. Does that make sense?"

"I know what you mean. Can you elaborate on his description a little for me?" Gab asked. "Do you remember what colour hair he had? Was he wearing a jacket? Was he big or small?"

The man shook his head. "He didn't strike me as big or small. So I guess he was about average."

"Okay," Gab said, making a note of the comments so far. "And his jacket?"

"I can't remember. Honestly. Maybe a tweed jacket, or a sports jacket. You know? Like a blazer."

"And can I take your name and some contact details? It's just in case we have to ask you a few more questions."

"I suppose so. It's Steve. Steve Wilks," he said, then offered his phone number. "I'm just up in Branston. It's about a mile or so from here."

"Thanks, Mr Wilks," Gab said, feeling like he'd done a pretty good job of getting the information. "If we asked you to identify the man, would you be prepared to do so?"

"You mean in a line-up?"

"Well, we'd prefer to do it digitally first. I'm not saying it would come to that. But just in case."

"Yes. Sure. Anything to help. It's a bloody shame. Such a waste of a life."

"Yes. Yes, it is," Gab agreed. "Well, thank you, Mr Wilks. We'll be in touch."

As Mr Wilks was climbing back onto his bike, Gab couldn't help but notice how he manhandled himself into position, adjusting his Lycra shorts. Gab grimaced and looked away, shaking his head. On any other occasion, he might have internalised a rant about the man's indecent appearance, but the promise of taking some good news to the briefing had elevated his mood considerably.

He bent to collect the pile of flyers he'd set down at the foot of the post, just as a breath of wind caught the first few and sent them fluttering down the path. Before the rest of them took off, he grabbed the thick wad, and then scrambled to collect the loose three.

He caught two just fine, but the third had fluttered into some reeds beside the water.

Annoyingly, he couldn't just leave it. It clearly belonged to the police, and he could only imagine Granger's face as he presented the local newspaper a few days later, showing a headline, 'Police Pollute River.'

It was just out of reach, so he got down on one knee and outstretched an arm. The flyer was nestled into the reeds, just inches from the tips of his fingers. He sighed and resigned himself to lowering a foot down. If he could find a sturdy clump of reeds to stand on, he might get away with it. He tried a few spots before settling on what he deemed to be the sturdiest of all the clumps of reeds available. Then, gradually, he transferred his weight.

It was holding. He stretched out, fingers tantalisingly close to the flyer as it fluttered in the breeze.

That was when he saw it. A bag. A sports bag of sorts in bright yellow. It was tucked into the foot of the bank, out of sight. The only reason he could see it was because he was virtually standing in the river now.

He snatched it up and slung it onto the bank, then with his confidence high, he turned and grabbed at the flyer.

And that single careless act was both his undoing and fuel for an unending barrage of Gillespie's taunts.

# CHAPTER THIRTY-FOUR

THE ADDRESS CHAPMAN HAD PROVIDED ANNA WAS A DOT ON the map application on Anna's phone. A tiny dot surrounded by green fields, with a thick, blue stripe indicating the river running left to right beneath it. Twice she had to pull over to the side of the lanes to check she hadn't passed the turning, but each time she discovered she was still heading in the right direction.

Then she saw it. A faded, wooden sign, homemade, by the look of it, informing passers-by that Witham River Rentals was the next left. She indicated, took the turn, and immediately had to pull to the side to avoid colliding with an oncoming Transit van. The driver, a man in his fifties with a weathered face, gave her an accusing look as he passed, then stopped at the top of the road, indicating to turn left.

Anna eased back onto the road, the sound of the long grass scraping the underside of her car. A few minutes later, the road opened up into a small car park with what looked like a converted barn at the water's edge, and beside that, tucked into the adjacent field, a pretty, little cottage.

The barn was signed, 'Witham River Rentals' and was just as tarnished as the sign at the roadside. To one side of the car park, a few old boats sat dormant on trailers like some kind of marine graveyard. Decay had set into the hulls, while the parts of the boats that had been above the waterline were all covered with old tarpaulins, like skeletal remains in a morgue.

The only vehicle parked on the property was an old Land Rover, which was equally dogged-looking, but even Anna knew the old beast would likely still be running, even if it was two decades old. She parked beside it and climbed out, only to find the main entrance locked. So she had a quick glance around to see if anybody was nearby, then slipped around the side of the barn.

The scene that greeted Anna was as she had imagined it to be. Boat parts and engines littered a little outdoor workshop area, which was no more than a wooden frame covered by corrugated plastic sheets. Machinery for lifting items was stored in various places; chains, hooks, slings, and hoists, plus a wide variety of steel shackles. And there was rope. Endless amounts of off-cuts. The larger lengths had been coiled and hung from various places wherever was convenient. But scattered in the corners and resting on workbenches were smaller lengths.

The property was set close to a bend in the river, where the waterway was wider and presumably deeper. A wooden dock provided access to the water, which Anna guessed was for the people who rented the water equipment to get in and out. A little rowing boat had been tied up and rocked gently on the calm river.

She found a pedestrian door at the rear set beside a pair of larger doors, and she gave the handle a try, not expecting it to be unlocked. But it was. She shoved it open.

"Hello?"

No response.

"Hello, is anyone there?"

Again, nobody replied. It was dark inside, with just a few slices of weak sunlight highlighting the dust in the air. The stench of damp wood and sweat tainted the space. She peered into the gloom, identifying a rack of canoes against one wall. Or were they called kayaks? She never did know the difference between them. It was clear that the owner had put some effort into the work-shop. The main reception bench had been built to replicate an upturned rowing boat. Perhaps it had originally been an upturned boat?

A line of old oil drums housed oars and paddles, and another rack was laden with what looked like more than twenty life jack-ets, or buoyancy aids, as she had heard them being called before.

And then, at the far end of the barn was a single stand-up paddle board standing on its end. It must have been nearly ten feet tall and leaned against the wall, nestled into a corner. Beside it, stacked in a neat pile at least five feet high, was a pile of bright yellow holdalls, each one marked with a number that had been stencilled on with indelible marker. Then she noticed the paddle board had an identical number stencilled at one end.

She made her way over to the stack of bags and unzipped the one closest to her. Inside was a roll of heavy, rubber-like material. It wasn't exactly rubber. It was some kind of PVC. She reached out and touched the board, and to her surprise, it wasn't solid like a surfboard. It was inflatable. The bags, she assumed, each contained a deflated paddle board.

She thought about Simon Bird, and how he might have taken the paddle board to the spot a few miles up the river. Until now, it had been assumed that somebody had dragged or carried it to the spot by the river where Freya found the paddle. But this changed things. If the board was deflated and in a holdall like these, then somebody could have easily stowed it somewhere to collect later.

"Now then," a voice boomed, startling her. She spun to find a man silhouetted in the doorway. "Back for more, are you?"

He let the door close behind him, and he took a slow step forward, moving behind the counter, closing off any exits Anna had.

"Are you Michael Doughty?" she asked.

"It doesn't matter what my name is," he said, edging closer to her. He passed through one of those slices of sunlight, revealing a hardened and weathered face, a few days' growth, and cold, dark eyes. It was the driver of the van that she had passed. He must have turned around once he'd seen her and driven back. "What matters is that you're in my workshop."

"I'm with the police," Anna said. "We're investigating a murder."

He cocked his head to one side. "Prove it."

But Anna couldn't. Her bag was on the passenger seat of her car, and she hissed a curse under her breath.

"It's in my car," she said, and made to step around him. But he sidestepped, blocking her path, and a grin grew across the uneven surface of his face. "Are you going to let me get it?"

"No. You'll run."

"Why would I run?"

"Because I've caught you red-handed, you thieving little bitch."

"What?" she said, suddenly very aware that the situation could go very wrong very fast. "I'm a police officer. Let me go to my car, and I'll prove it."

"You're one of them, aren't you?"

"One of who? You're making a mistake."

"You've been nicking my stuff. Who are you? His big sister?"

"Who's big sister? Mr Doughty, I am Detective Constable Anna Nillson. I'm with the Major Investigations Team investigating the death of a young boy on this river a few days ago." She jabbed her thumb at the stack of paddle boards. "We found a paddle board. A paddle too. I was wondering if you had rented one out to anybody recently."

He looked her up and down, suddenly unsure of himself.

"Rented, no," he said. "Had them stolen? Yes."

"You've had a board stolen?"

"Them. Plural," he said, a string of saliva joining his tongue to the roof his mouth when he spoke.

"I'm not here to steal your property, Mr Doughty," Anna explained calmly. "I'm here to help solve a young boy's murder."

He said nothing, seeming to take his time in deciding. He scrutinised every inch of her, from her boots, across her black leggings, her leather jacket, and then her hair, which she kept pulled back in a tight ponytail while working. She wasn't out of the woods yet. He had the look of a man who would take what he wanted, and from what she'd heard so far, he clearly bore a grudge.

"Will you let me get my warrant card?" she asked, keeping her voice as low and calm as she could.

"I'll come with you," he said. "You might outrun me. But you won't outrun Bo."

"Who's Bo?" she asked. "Or is it better that we're not introduced?"

# CHAPTER THIRTY-FIVE

Bo turned out to be forty kilograms of German Shepherd, who watched Anna from the van's passenger seat. He didn't bark or growl. He just watched her curiously. That way dogs do, when they're deciding if you're the alpha, or if they are.

Michael Doughty waited by the corner of the barn while Anna fetched her bag, and then she presented her warrant card, thankful she could refrain from letting her hands shake.

He nodded.

"Alright," he said. "You'll have to forgive me. I was just defending my property."

"From what?"

"I told you. Thieves," he said. "Vermin, they are. Come here when I'm not about. Take my property. Hard enough to scratch a living these days without having little bastards break my locks and take my kit."

"You said you had lost some paddle boards?"

"Aye. That's right," he said. Anna guessed he was from Northern Lincolnshire, on the border of Yorkshire perhaps, because of his slightly thicker accent. "Have they taken anything else?"

"Not that I've seen. I know it's kids. Anyone with half a brain would have taken the tools. I know what they do. They take them, fool around on the river, and then throw them away. It doesn't matter to them, does it? They didn't pay for them. Wouldn't surprise me if they're not lying punctured at the bottom of the river."

"And when did you last notice one missing?"

"It's not the boards I noticed. It was the lock. Prised off the door with a jimmy bar or something. If I get my hands on them before you, I can assure you..." he said, pointing his finger at Anna.

"You can assure me what, exactly, Mr Doughty?" Anna said. "You'll do well to remember this is a murder investigation."

"Aye, well. I'll not be putting up with this much longer. My patience is wearing thin enough."

"Well, your patience is going to have to hold up a little while longer. We've got a young lad lying dead in a mortuary."

He tore his eyes from hers and stared at his van, averting his gaze for as long as he could.

"If I'm honest, Mr Doughty, I'm surprised you get enough business to keep going. I could barely find you, and the river isn't exactly busy."

"I've got a kiosk up at Skeggy. Keep all my kit here," he said, nodding at the little cottage. "Where I can keep an eye on it."

"Oh, right," Anna replied. "That seems to work well."

"You what?"

"Have you reported the thefts to the police?"

He pulled a face at the mention of the word police, like he'd just eaten a rotten piece of fruit.

"What's the point in that? You're hardly likely to help me out, are you?"

"You said you had tools in the workshop."

"Aye, that's right."

"What are they for?"

"Mending stuff. Engines, and the like. I run a small trade for the local boats. You know? Services and the like. Keeps me busy during winter when the beach trade dies down. Nobody rents kayaks or paddle boards in winter, do they?"

"I guess not," Anna replied.

"Aye, well. The boats still run, don't they? If it weren't for me, they'd have to take them down Boston for a service. Long way that."

"So you thought you'd capitalise on the traffic?"

"No law against ingenuity, sweetheart."

"It's DC Nillson," she said. It seemed they had come to a stalemate. She'd tried the softly-softly approach, and had met his aggression tone for tone, yet still he was a brick wall. "When did you notice your lock was broken?"

"Saturday," he said, the answer ready and waiting on the tip of his tongue. "Before that, last week."

"Time?"

"Afternoon. Two-ish."

"Any cameras?"

"Did you see any?"

"No. But then I wasn't looking for them."

"Well then."

"Well then, perhaps you ought to get some," Anna replied. "Either that or call the police and let us deal with it."

"Ah," he said dismissively, and averted his gaze again. Clearly he had a deep mistrust of the police.

"Perhaps you could tell me where you were on Sunday night?"

"Me?"

"Can you see anybody else?" she said, matching his earlier rhetoric.

"Sunday night?"

"From, say, six o'clock onwards."

"Sunday at six?" he said, feigning giving the question considerable thought. Then he stopped the charade and stared at her, his top lip curled over as if the dog had just broken wind. "At home."

"Can anyone corroborate that?"

"Can they what?"

"Can you prove that?"

"I live alone."

Anna glanced at the van then back at him.

"Bo and me. It's just us."

"What did you do?"

"Watched a film," he said, as if he was daring her to contest the fact.

"Which one?"

"Can't remember," he said, and then Anna raised her eyebrows questioningly.

"You're not doing yourself any favours."

"Pearl Harbour," he said, after a while. "It was on Netflix."

"And after that?"

"Bed," he replied.

She searched his eyes for a hint of a lie but found none.

"Are you going anywhere anytime soon?"

"Well, I was supposed to be on my way to Skeggy."

"I don't mean your business in Skegness. I mean, are you going on holiday anytime soon?"

"Holiday? The season's starting. I don't have time for a holiday. I've got to pay for replacements boards, you know?"

Anna nodded and fished a card from her warrant card.

"If you think of anything that might help," she said.

He eyeballed the card, gave a little chortle, then pocketed it. Anna climbed back into her car under the scrutinising stare of Bo the German Shepherd. She started the engine and lowered the passenger window.

"One more thing," she called out, and he raised his eyebrows in anticipation. "If you lose another one, be sure to call me, won't you? We're on your side. It's worth remembering that."

# CHAPTER THIRTY-SIX

"What the bloody hell is that smell?" Freya asked, raising her voice to be heard above the squealing incident room door. The room fell silent and the door slammed closed. She stared at Ben, who draped his coat over his chair, grimacing at the stench.

"Don't look at me," he said. "I just walked in with you."

"It smells like a sewage farm. Chapman, are the washrooms backing up again?"

"I'm afraid not, ma'am," she replied, and she flicked her eyes over to Cruz and Gillespie.

Gillespie was covering his face with his hands, and his body jolted from the laughter he was trying so hard to hide.

Cruz, however, had turned beetroot-red and had a face like thunder.

"Cruz? Is that you?"

That was it. Gillespie broke. He burst into laughter, removing his hands to reveal a face equally red as Cruz's, but with tears running down both cheeks.

"Is somebody going to explain what that is? Or do we need to call some kind of doctor?"

Cruz inhaled and let the breath out through pursed lips.

"Cruz?" Freya said. "Have you had another accident?"

Gillespie stood and walked to the far end of the room in an attempt to get control of himself.

"I fell in, boss," he said.

"You fell in?"

"The river. I slipped," he said. "Should I go and change?"

"No," Freya replied. "No, you can stay like that. Chapman, open a window, will you? Gillespie, can you pull yourself together, please? I want a briefing. We are running a murder investigation here, you know."

"Aye, boss," he said, his voice high in pitch from trying to restrain his laughter. He coughed and cleared his throat, then tried again. "Aye, boss. I'm coming."

"Good. Ben, do you mind if I run this one? I want to be quick."

He shook his head. "You're the boss," he replied.

"Good. Where's Nillson?"

"She's on her way back," Chapman said. "She called in about twenty minutes ago."

"I'm here," came a distant voice, and the incident room burst open. "Oh my bloody god, what the hell is that smell?"

Gillespie turned away and took a few deep breaths to control himself.

Chapman averted her eyes and continued typing, doing her best not to get involved.

"It's me," Cruz said. "Of course it's me. It's always me."

"Have you had another accident?" Nillson asked, with her hand over her nose as she passed him.

"No. I have not had another accident."

"He fell in the river," Ben said.

"You fell in? What are you, ten years old?"

"I got too close," Cruz explained. "I was putting a flyer on a post. Alone, I might add."

"Alone?" Freya said, and she sought Gillespie's attention for a reason.

"Aye, well," he explained, "we thought it best if we split up."

"You thought it best," Cruz said.

"You know," Gillespie continued, "I went and knocked on the houses, seeing as Gab here seems to have an aversion to that particular task. Which left him to put the flyers up."

"Despite my specific instructions," Freya said.

"Well, aye, but—"

"Next time I ask you to do something, I want it carried out to the T," Freya said, keeping her tone short. She was all up for having a laugh, but when they were faced with a murder investigation with almost nothing to go on, now was not the time.

"Aye, boss," Gillespie muttered.

"Let's hope you can at least redeem yourself with some sort of contribution," Freya said.

"Eh?"

"What did you find?"

"Oh, aye. Well, I met this bloke. A Jeffrey Green. He's a trader. Works from home. Cushy number, if you ask me. Anyway, he said he was out running and saw a group of kids around four o'clock. They were down by the river at that spot where you found that paddle."

"At four o'clock?" Ben said. "That's eight hours before he died."

"I'm just telling you what the man told me," Gillespie said. "He's got a camera on the side of his house. It's to protect his garage. That's where he keeps his classic car. A nineteen sixty-six Jaguar E-Type. Mint condition, it is too. He showed it to me. Beautiful, it is."

"Oooh nice," Nillson said, and everyone turned to stare at her in surprise. "What?"

"I didn't have you down as a classic car enthusiast," Gillespie said.

"Are you kidding? That's one of the most beautiful cars ever built."

"Are we going to focus on Simon Bird, by any chance?" Freya asked.

"Aye, sorry, boss," Gillespie said. "Anyway, I checked the footage. And what do you know? Simon Bird walks past the house at three thirty-five that afternoon, heading in the direction of the river."

"That's interesting," Freya said. "It's much earlier than we had thought. What was he doing all that time?"

"I don't know what he was doing. But I can tell you that when I checked further back in the footage, four more kids had walked past twenty minutes earlier."

"Four?"

"Aye. Four."

"That must be Forbes and his mates," Freya said. "Did you bring the footage?"

Proudly, Gillespie produced a USB stick from his pocket and held it up for them to see.

"It was one of those cloud-based security systems. He had to download all the footage. Lucky he had one of these lying around. Said we could have it, too."

Seeing an opportunity to identify the four individuals, Freya seized the USB stick from Gillespie and handed it to Chapman. "See if you identify them from their social media accounts, please."

"Will do, ma'am," she replied.

"Anything else, Gillespie?"

"Nope. That's me," he said, clearly happy with his news. He stared up at Freya as if he was asking if he'd redeemed himself, as per her original statement. But she gave no sign either way.

"Right, who's next?"

"I'll go," Nillson said, then continued without waiting for any kind of response. "I paid a visit to Michael Doughty, the owner of a little water sports business down on the river towards Tattershall."

"Water sports?" Cruz said. "On the river?"

"That's what I thought too. But he has a little kiosk up in Skegness. Probably too small to store the gear there. Plus, he's had a few break-ins recently. He's lost a few paddle boards."

"Why are people stealing paddle boards?" Freya asked.

"He thinks it's kids, on account of them leaving the expensive tools and nicking the fun stuff. Plus, this is something I wasn't aware of. The paddle boards are inflatable."

"A blow-up surfboard?" Ben said, almost mocking the idea. "Isn't that just a Li-lo?"

"No. You'd be surprised. He had one there inflated. It was soft to the touch. I mean, it's inflatable, but it was rigid. You could stand on it easily. But the key part is this. When they're deflated, they fit into a holdall." She held her hands about two feet apart to show the size. "About so big."

"I hadn't considered that," Freya said, cursing herself for missing the obvious. "Gillespie, are any of the kids carrying bags in the footage?"

"No, boss. Nothing like that."

"Which means they collected it on the way."

"The bag was stolen on Saturday, as well," Nillson explained. "So whoever stole it must have stashed it somewhere."

"Somewhere between the houses at the top of Five Mile Lane and the river," Gillespie said.

"There's another thing," Nillson said. "Well, two things, really. He doesn't have an alibi. Claims he watched a movie then went to bed."

"Right?" Freya said, sensing something rather substantial coming her way.

Nillson smiled. She was good. A real asset to Freya's team. And she was enjoying her spot in the limelight.

"He has a little rowing boat moored out the back, and he's mad as hell that somebody keeps stealing his stuff."

# CHAPTER THIRTY-SEVEN

"Okay," Freya said, moving over to the whiteboard. She wrote Michael Doughty's name to one side and circled it for emphasis. "What do we know about this man?"

"I know one thing," Ben said and the team all turned to stare at the big man at the back of the room. "If Simon Bird got into the water near Five Mile Bridge and was found down near Tattershall Bridge, where the divers were, he would have floated right past Doughty's property."

"Doughty could have seen him and gone after him," Freya said.

"Or he could have killed him in his workshop and then dumped the body after dark," Ben said. Then he turned to Nillson. "It's the old cottage on the river, right? The one with the little jetty?"

"That's it."

"I know the place," Ben said. "It's in the middle of nowhere. Nobody would have seen a thing."

"This is good, guys," Freya said, enthused by the progress. "We've got four kids walking to the river and Simon Bird following twenty minutes later. We've got a stolen paddle board and a disgruntled owner. It's adding up. What else do we have?"

"I've got the names of those four kids," Chapman said, and with a last flourish, she hit the ENTER key on her keyboard, and the printer jumped into life. "Gavin Forbes, Julie Yates, Tess Mitchell, and David Stills. According to the headmaster's list, these four are close friends, and according to the social media account, they all liked, shared, and commented on the rogue social media account."

"All of them?" Freya asked.

"All except one," she replied, grinning.

"Don't tell me. Gavin Forbes?"

"Looks like he's heavily involved," Chapman said.

"Yes, and he's downstairs enjoying the comforts of Sergeant Priest's finest one-bedroom accommodation. I think it's time we interviewed him. Good work, Chapman. Ben, shall we?"

There was a scrape of chairs as the briefing came to an abrupt close, and Chapman resumed her loud typing. But rising above the sudden activity, a throat was cleared. It was almost theatrical. Freya, who was bent over her desk collecting files ready to hit Gavin Forbes with, peered up. Cruz was staring at her, his eyebrows raised and a wry smile on his face.

The others must have sensed the change in the mood too, as they suddenly stilled.

"I haven't told you what I found out yet," he said.

"You fell in the river, Cruz," Freya said.

"I haven't told you *why* I fell in the river."

"Because you're an imbecile?" Gillespie asked, but Cruz ignored the comment, choosing to keep his attention focused on Freya.

"Aright. Go on then, Cruz. If you have something to contribute, I'd be glad to hear it."

There was something about the way he stared at her. Something in his eye that told her this was important. And the fact that he'd waited until the very end to say so suggested he thought it to be the climax of the briefing.

"A man," he began.

"A man?"

"On the bridge. Wearing off-the-shelf trousers and a tweed jacket. He wasn't jogging or cycling. He wasn't walking a dog. He was just loitering by the bridge."

"And who told you this?"

"A witness. Said he saw him while out riding his bike. I've got his contact details, and he also said he could identify him, given the chance."

"That's pretty good, Cruz," Freya said, sensing that the man wasn't the showpiece. "So now we have a man hanging around close to where Simon, Gavin, and the rest of them were."

"And something else," he said as he reached down for a small rucksack by his feet. Freya had seen it there earlier, but had assumed it was his work bag or a gym bag. He let out a sigh of satisfaction as he dropped it onto his desk.

"A bag?" Freya said.

"Not just any old bag, boss," he said, and he stood, unzipped the bag, and tipped the contents out onto Gillespie's desk.

"Hey," Gillespie said, and he looked up at Freya for some kind of support. But she gave him none. She watched, intrigued as to what Cruz had found. "It's just a load of muddy, old clothes."

"Not just any muddy, old clothes," Cruz corrected him, then stared at Freya like he'd just solved the answer to the mystery of the universe. "These clothes belong to a teenage boy."

"They're yours then," Gillespie said with a smile. "Now you've got two sets of muddy, old clothes. The set you're wearing, and these."

At any other time, the rest of the team may have laughed at Gillespie's joke. But Freya wasn't laughing, and neither was anybody else.

"Not just any teenage boy, I'm guessing," Freya said to Cruz.

"No, boss," he replied. "These clothes all belong to Gavin Forbes."

"How can you be so sure?" Nillson asked. "Gavin Forbes doesn't strike me as somebody whose mother writes his name on the tag."

"They are his," Freya said, nodding at Cruz. "That's the yellow hoody he was wearing when he videoed Simon Bird in the washroom. Don't you remember? Whoever took the video brought their arm into the shot. When they grabbed onto the stall to pull themselves up."

"And they were wearing a yellow hoody," Nillson said.

"That's assuming it was Forbes that videoed him," Ben said.

"Cruz, turn that bag around a minute," Nillson said, peering across the bank of desks.

Cruz did as she asked, still delighting in his moment of glory.

"That's the bag the paddle board was in. I saw them in Doughty's place. An enormous pile of them. Forbes must have stolen the board and hid it near the bridge."

"Well," Freya replied, sliding off the desk she was perched on, "there's only one way to find out. Let's go and see what he has to say."

While Freya and Ben collected what they needed for the interview, Gillespie donned a disposable glove and held up the hoody against Cruz.

"Aye, see. It's a perfect match, look."

The moment of elation the find had evoked was waning, and the others were getting back into their work. But Gillespie wasn't finished, even despite one of Freya's coldest stares. He grabbed a rolled-up pair of jeans by one of the belt loops and let them unfurl beside Cruz's leg. It wasn't the seemingly good fit that caught the team's attention. Nor was it the look of utter despair on Freya's face. It was the sound of something landing on the floor as the jeans unrolled. Something hard. A sound they weren't expecting.

"What's that?" Ben said, looking under the desk. He reached down and picked it up, all the while his eyes set firmly on Freya.

She cocked her head to one side, waiting to hear what it was. And then he held it up.

"A mobile phone?" Cruz said. "I didn't see that before."

"Did you touch the clothing?" Freya asked.

"No, boss. I thought it best not to. I just recognised the hoody."

"Good," she replied.

Gillespie held out a clear, plastic evidence bag from his pocket, and Ben dropped it inside.

"Cruz, this one's for you. Take this to the lab. Don't come back until you know who it belonged to and what's on it," Freya said.

"What if it doesn't belong to Gavin Forbes? There's more than one yellow hooded sweatshirt out there," Nillson said.

Marching over to the whiteboard, Freya snatched up the marker and set to work. On one side of the board, beneath Gavin Forbes' name, she added the names of the other three kids.

"Right. What do we know about these four individuals?"

"Sally said Forbes was giving Simon a hard time," Ben said, still standing in the doorway.

"Right," Freya agreed.

"And the headmaster said he was trouble," Gillespie added.

"Okay, good. An independent character reference, but not enough to get CPS on board. What else do we have?"

"The clothes," Cruz said. "I mean, I know they don't necessarily link Forbes yet, but they were found tucked into the riverbank between where Simon got into the water and where he ended up. That's got to count for something."

"If they are his, then yes. They might. Same goes for the phone. But we don't have a motive for him. I mean, bullying is one thing. But murder is a big step."

"We have the opportunity, boss. I mean, we can be sure Forbes was with Bird on the riverbank. We've got them on CCTV and we've got witnesses."

"There was only one paddle board," Freya countered.

"Right, but what if Forbes went after him? He knows which direction the river flows. All he has to do is find a way to get down there."

"Doughty said that more than one board has been stolen," Nillson added.

"But how many were stolen on this occasion?"

"Just the one," Nillson said.

"Seems unlikely. It's weak. We need more," Freya said. "Something else."

"So let's search his house," Ben suggested. "Let's see what he has to say in the interview, then search his house. If he has one of the other missing paddle boards, then he has the means."

"Michael Doughty thinks the kids are stealing his boards just to have some fun with them, then burst them. You know what kids are like."

"There's no harm in looking," Freya said, then moved onto Michael Doughty's side of the board. "What do we have here?"

"A motive," Nillson said, almost immediately. "You should have seen him. He's an angry man, and I think he would take matters into his own hands."

"Agreed," Freya said, and she placed a small M beside his name.

"And he has a little rowing boat," Nillson added.

"Yep," Freya said, and added another M. "Opportunity?"

"He said he watched a film and went to bed."

"Alone?"

"Yes, boss."

Freya added an O beside his name.

"So why don't we just go and pick him up?" Cruz asked. "He's our man. Three strikes."

"If," Freya began, raising her voice a little for effect, "we didn't have all this," she said, and waved the pen over the left side of the board, where Gavin Forbes and his mates were listed, "then I might agree. But something isn't sitting right. We need more on Doughty. When we bring him in, we'll have twenty-four hours. I want concrete proof."

"Plus, we still haven't eliminated Sally Bird yet," Ben said.

"Yeah, but come on. The boy's mother?" Nillson argued.

"Ben's right," Freya said. "If Doughty has a decent lawyer, he or she will look for other avenues. They'll try to sway the jury's confidence. We need to focus on all other angles just as much as we're focusing on him. All other angles being Gavin Forbes, and if I'm honest, I'm still amazed it's been two days already and we still haven't eliminated Sally Bird. I don't know about you. But that rings alarm bells to me."

She waited for a response from the team, but received only agreeable nods.

"Okay, then let's see Forbes. See what part he had to play in all of this," she finished.

# CHAPTER THIRTY-EIGHT

"Right, then. Who's doing what?" Gillespie asked, as Ben and Freya were leaving the incident room.

It was an odd question and the wrong one to voice, which he knew the moment the words left his lips. By right, as a DS, he should have assumed some kind of leadership role in Freya's absence. But he'd seen the look she had given him while he was ridiculing Cruz, and was hoping to regain some of her confidence. He couldn't help himself. The lad was just an easy target.

She stared around the room, then back at him, and it was all he could do to help Cruz repack the little bag. He was gloved, and he hoped she could at least see he was following procedures.

"I would have thought that much was obvious," she said.

"Aye, well," he replied, folding the yellow sweater, ready to hand to Cruz. "I was just wondering. That's all."

She nodded, then addressed the room.

"Here's what I want done. Chapman, look into Doughty. See what you can find on him. Nillson, get onto Sally Bird. I want to know where she went after bingo. And talk to uniforms, see if the neighbours saw anything. Cruz, you're taking that lot to the lab, and when I say stay there until we know who it belongs to and what's on it, I mean it. I don't want to see you until then."

"Yes, boss," he said, sounding a little frightened.

And that was fair enough. She'd been patient. But clearly that patience was wearing thin. And worst of all, she'd saved Gillespie until last.

"And you, get down to the school before they all go home for the day and bring all three of the kids here, along with their parents. I want statements from all of them."

"Aye, boss," he said.

"Questions, anybody?" she asked, and stared at everyone in turn.

"Good, let's tighten this up. No more messing about. A young boy is dead, and it's down to us to find out why."

She pushed through the doors, and Ben followed, leaving them with an expression that said, 'You did that to yourselves.'

"You idiot," Nillson said, glaring at Gillespie.

"What did I do?"

"You've put her in a mood. That's what you've done."

"Me? How have I put her in a mood?"

"By messing about. You're always messing about, Jim," she said. But then her expression dropped as the incident room door swung open behind him. The squeal of the hinges seemed prolonged. Tortuous even.

"Afternoon," a voice said. And the voice was delightful. Angelic, almost. "I just caught Ben and DI Bloom on the stairs. There's a woman on a mission if ever I saw one."

Gillespie didn't turn. He stayed facing the window with his back to the doors, unsure of what to say, especially in front of Chapman, Anna, and Cruz.

"Yeah, you can blame Jim for that," Nillson said.

"Eh?" he said. "Ah, come on."

He gave in and turned to face Jackie, who was smiling in the doorway. She stared back at him, her mouth curled into a wonderful smile.

"Nothing changes then, eh?" she said, seeming to hold Gillespie's stare for longer than she normally would. Or was he imagining it?

It had to be her who had sent the text. If it wasn't Jessica, then it must have been Jackie.

"How's the course going?" Chapman asked, and Jackie broke the prolonged gaze to respond.

"Amazing," she replied. "There's a bunch of psychology stuff you have to learn. Like how to tell when someone's lying, or what to look for when you think someone could be suicidal. I mean, it's not the same being out there getting your hands dirty, but you can really make a difference."

"You planning on moving then, are you?" Cruz asked. It was the question on Gillespie's tongue, but he dare not ask it for fear of putting the wee lass on the spot.

"You're not backward in being forward, are you, Gabby?" Jackie replied. "I'm just opening doors. That's all. It's a string to my bow. And if the force is going to pay for me to learn all this stuff, then the way I see it, I might as well take it."

"Right," Cruz said. "But isn't it a bit of a step backward?"

"That depends if you're talking about climbing the ranks as a detective, or progressing my career," she replied, stepping into the room. She pulled a face, like she'd drank sour milk. "Oh, my god. What's that smell?"

"That's Gab," Gillespie replied, before anybody could defend him. "It's my fault, really. I left him unsupervised. Fell in the river. Lucky he didn't drown, if I'm honest."

Cruz rolled his eyes and shook his head. "He's just jealous that I found a key piece of evidence and he didn't."

"A key piece of evidence? You found a wee bag with some clothes in. I got the CCTV footage. That was me."

"Sounds like everything is still the same as when I left it,"

Jackie said. "Anyway, I just swung by to say hi. See how you're all doing."

"It's not the same," Chapman said. "Without you, I mean."

It was a lovely thing to have said, and Gillespie wished it was him who had voiced it.

"Yeah, it's weird, isn't it?" she replied. "This is the first course I've done for a while."

"I was thinking about doing the advanced driving course," Nillson said, which was typical of her. She was more of an action hero than any of them.

"It's worth doing while you've got the chance," Jackie said, then smiled at them all. "Right then. I'll be off. I'll see you all next week."

The team wished her well and the incident room doors closed behind Jackie. Almost immediately, Chapman and Nillson began discussing if Jackie would be back or not. But Gillespie had to seize the moment. He stood and darted for the door, then ran to the fire escape and leaned over the handrail.

"Hey, Jackie," he said, despite his mind telling him to go back to his seat and finish what he was doing.

"Hi, Jim. You okay?" she asked, staring up at him.

"Aye, yeah. Grand, actually," he replied, but then he was out of conversation. The seconds ticked by and the awkwardness grew with every one of them.

"Jim?"

"I was wondering," he began, although he did not know what it was he wondering. "Are you seeing anyone right now?"

"Excuse me?"

"Sorry. I was... I mean, I saw someone. Thought it was you. You know? With a fella and that."

"Oh, you know me, Jim," she replied, smiling. "I only have eyes for one man."

She winked and then continued down the stairs.

"See you later, Jim," she called, and then the door to the car park opened and slammed closed.

"See you later?" he said, wondering if she'd meant that she would indeed see him later, or if she was just using the phrase, *see you later*, like some people did. And she only had eyes for one man. Was that him? Or was that Ben? Or was it her son?

The entire station had known about her childhood crush on Ben. But years had passed and neither of them had done anything about it. They were close friends, and nothing more.

He wandered back to the incident room and stopped at his desk to collect his jacket and his files.

"You off, Jim?" Chapman asked, as he approached the door in silence. His mind was still reeling over Jackie's comment, and Chapman's question pulled him from his thoughts.

"Eh?"

"Are you off out?"

"Oh, aye," he said, as he pulled open the door. "I'm going to head to the school to round up those kids. Chapman, can you get a uniform to meet me there with some transport?"

"Yeah, I'm going to head off too," Cruz said, grabbing the little rucksack. "I'm going to take my little haul to the lab."

"Will you drive there, or go by broom?" Nillson asked.

Cruz glared at her, but a glare from Cruz would have little bearing on a woman like Nillson, who Gillespie had seen tackle bigger men than him to the ground. She shrugged him off.

"I'd better go and see a grieving mother and ask her some questions she doesn't want to answer. Wish me luck."

"You should see what the FLO has to say," Chapman suggested. "There's one at the house. She might have heard something."

"That's not a bad idea," Nillson replied, as Cruz shuffled toward the door with his prize piece of evidence. "I might just do that."

The door swung closed behind her and Cruz, leaving Gillespie alone with Chapman.

"Do you ever get the impression everyone knows something you don't?" he asked.

Chapman, in her knitted cardigan and pretty blouse, removed her glasses and let them hang from the little chain around her neck.

"No," she said. "I know you might think I'm just plain old Denise Chapman, but not a thing happens in this place that I don't know about. I'm always here, and I hear everything."

"What's this about Cruz and the magic stuff?"

"Ah," she replied. "That's none of my business."

"I thought you said you knew everything."

"I do." She laughed. "But it's not my place to say."

Not knowing what they were discussing was beginning to annoy him. The fact that secrets were being kept seemed unfair. But it was clear Chapman wasn't going to give in and tell him. But maybe she could enlighten him on another topic, he thought.

"How well do you know Jackie?" he asked.

# CHAPTER THIRTY-NINE

SERGEANT PRIEST, THE CUSTODY SERGEANT, HAD ALLOCATED them interview room two, the second of just two interview rooms in the small, rural station. When Freya entered, holding the door for Ben, she found Gavin Forbes, his mother, and duty solicitor, all waiting.

Gavin was sullen and stared at the floor between his feet. He was wearing his school uniform, which, for a boy who apparently caused as much trouble as he did, was surprisingly neat. The trousers were clean, the shirt was bright white, and the blazer was almost immaculate. The only thing tainting his appearance was his tie, which was skewed to one side to allow him room to undo his top button.

His mother was equally well turned out, Freya thought. She wasn't quite catwalk-ready, but she retained more than a measure of her former looks. She was one of those women who carried her age well, dressed in a smart blouse and a short-ish skirt, with tasteful heels, and a brown belt to finish the look.

The duty solicitor, however, looked very much like every other duty solicitor Freya had met. The suit was off the shelf and of very poor quality. In her opinion, half-inch of shirt cuff should show below the jacket cuff, but in his instance, the jacket came down to near the man's thumb. The shoulders were too wide too, making the man look as though he had borrowed his big brother's suit.

Freya took the seat nearest the door, opposite Gavin, leaving Ben the seat beside the wall so he could control the recording. While Ben prepared the machine, Freya quickly scanned her notes, making a show of rearranging her files. There was no need, of course, but it would all add to the effect. The frustration inside Gavin Forbes would be building. Increasing the chances of him saying something he might regret.

"Before we begin," Freya said, looking between Gavin and his mother, "we'll be asking some very serious questions. I expect you to be honest in your answers if you hope to be released anytime soon. Is that clear?"

"I'll be advising Mr Forbes of his responses," the duty solicitor said. The statement surprised Freya. She had expected him to be the type to remain quiet until the questions got awkward, and then advise his client to begin a mind-numbingly boring episode of 'no comment'.

Ben gave her the green light, and the recording device emitted a loud, robotic sound, preventing anybody from speaking too early.

Freya began by stating the date and the time, and then introduced herself, signalling to Ben that he should do the same. He knew the drill.

"Detective Sergeant Ben Savage," he said, and then waited for the man in his brother's suit to follow.

"James McCoy. Legal Counsel."

They waited for Gavin Forbes to speak. And when he did, he did so with far more gusto and a little less bravado than Freya had been expecting. He spoke loud and clear, but restrained any demonstration of content or anger, as was normally the case when interviewing young persons, particularly those who are guilty.

When the boy's mother had introduced herself, Freya prepared to begin.

"Gavin Forbes, before we begin, I need to remind you of your rights. Please listen carefully. You do not have to say anything, but it may harm your defence if you do not mention when questioned something you later rely on in court. Anything you say may be given in evidence. Do you understand?"

The boy nodded.

"Do you know why you're here, Gavin?" Freya said, opting for a soft approach, given the boy's mature responses so far.

"Not exactly. A policewoman came to the school. She said you want to question me."

"And are you aware of the crimes we're investigating?"

He nodded slowly. "It's Simon, isn't it?"

"Simon Bird, yes. Are you aware that he died two days ago?"

Again, Gavin nodded.

"Do you know how he died, Gavin?"

He looked up at his mother, who checked with the solicitor, then nodded for him to answer.

"Drowned, didn't he?"

"That's right," Freya replied. "I must tell you, however, that we believe his death was not an accident. We're treating the incident as suspicious."

"Suspicious?"

"This is a murder investigation, Gavin."

"A murder investigation?" he said, sitting up straight in his chair and looking to his mum for support. "I didn't murder him. The last I saw of him, he was floating down the river."

"When was this?" Freya asked.

"Sunday."

"Can you tell us what happened on Sunday?"

The boy's breathing had become heavy. The word murder would do that people, and was not necessarily a sign of guilt.

"He got on the board. He dropped the paddle, and then..."

Gavin stopped, his face a look of utter dismay.

"Go on, Gavin," his mother said.

"We chased him. We ran along the river beside him. For a bit, anyway."

"Sorry, Gavin, can we start from the beginning, please? Where were you, exactly?"

"Down at the river. Near the bridge."

"Why were you there?"

"We always go there."

"And who were you with?"

The question should have been a simple one. But for a seasoned troublemaker, naming names was hard to do.

"Do I need to remind you of the seriousness of this investigation?" Freya said. "You won't get anybody into trouble. We just need to know who was there."

He sighed, then glanced up at his mum. "David Stills."

"Who else?" Freya said, looking across at Ben, who was making a note of the name, even though they already had the names.

"Julie Yates and Tess Mitchell."

"Is that it?"

"Yeah."

"And what time did you arrive at the riverbank?"

He shrugged. "I don't know. Half three, I guess."

"And was Simon already there?"

"No. No, Simon came along a little while after."

"Do you smoke cannabis, Gavin?" Freya said.

His eyes widened, as did his mother's.

"No. No, of course not."

"It's just that we found some cigarette papers by the river. Did your friends smoke anything?"

"No, of course not."

"Okay, okay. I was just asking. We've sent them off to the lab, anyway. We'll soon find out who they belong to."

"It wasn't me, Mum. Honest," he said, in reply to his mother's glare.

"We also found a paddle. The type that one might use with a stand-up paddle board. Do you know what I mean?" Freya said, and she slid a photo of the item out from her file. "One of these."

"Okay," he replied.

"Have you seen this before?"

"I've seen one of them before."

"But this particular paddle, Gavin. Have you seen it?"

"I'm not sure. They all look the same."

"Ah, that's where you're wrong. And I thought the same. But if you look closely, you'll see this one has been marked with a number five on the handle."

He shrugged.

"Where did you get the paddle board?" Freya asked, slipping the photo back into the file and preparing to present the next one.

"I didn't. Simon brought it."

"Simon brought the paddle board with him, did he? He carried it down there?"

"It was in a bag. He pumped it up."

"As I understand it, though, Simon wasn't one of your close friends, was he?"

"He wanted to be. He was always hanging around us."

"So how did he know you would be there? I mean, I'm sure he wasn't carrying a paddle board around on the off-chance he might meet you and your friends."

Gavin sighed and stared at his feet.

"We arranged to meet there," he said. "Simon was boasting about how good he was at it."

"When was this?"

"The week before. At school."

"But you said you weren't friends. Why would he boast about that to you?"

"He saw me try it. He saw me fall in."

"So you did already have the board?"

"No. No, this was a different one."

"But you don't have a paddle board," his mother said. "Where did you get the board, Gavin?"

"It was Dave's. He got it," Gavin replied, averting his eyes. "He took it to the river last weekend."

"Well, the good news is that David Stills will be on his way here shortly. I'm sure he'll corroborate your story, Gavin," Freya said, and there was a flash of guilt in the boy's eyes. "Tell me what happened this Sunday. You've told me you arranged to meet Simon there. What happened, exactly?"

"He just got on the board and the current took him."

"Without a paddle?" Freya said. "The paddle that Simon needed? The paddle that just may have saved Simon's life was found in the reeds, right beside where you and your friends were lying in the grass. Didn't you offer to throw it to him?"

"Yeah, of course we did. He said he was okay. He said he could get it. But he couldn't reach it in time. Then I guess the river just swept him away before we could do anything."

"So how did the paddle end up in the reeds?"

"I threw it for him to catch."

"You threw it for him?"

"Yeah. But it fell short. I don't know. It was too late by then, anyway."

"Because Simon was already floating away?"

He nodded and reverted to staring at his feet.

"May I suggest we break?" the solicitor said. "My client is clearly suffering."

"From guilt," Freya added.

"Hey," the mother said, stepping in to defend her son. "He's not done anything wrong."

"He's just admitted to letting Simon Bird float away down the river to his death, Mrs Forbes. And he did very little to help the boy."

"What was he supposed to do? Jump in after him?"

"How about trying to call for help? You do have a mobile phone, Gavin, I presume?"

He nodded.

"And where is it?"

He shrugged. "I lost it."

"You lost it?"

Again, he nodded. "Last week sometime."

"I see. And did any of your friends have mobile phones?"

"I suppose so. You'll have to ask them."

"Did anyone call for help?"

"I don't know."

"Oh, come on, Gavin," said Freya. "You just watched Simon Bird float down the river. You must have been just a bit concerned."

"We didn't think he was going to drown, did we?" he snapped. "We're not complete morons."

"But you thought it would be a good laugh to watch him scared out of his wits being carried off towards the sea?"

"You don't understand," he said. "It wasn't like that."

"So how was it? Was this just another prank on Simon? Another video to post on your social media account?"

He stared up at her. That got his attention.

"That's right, Gavin. We know all about the social media accounts. The bullying. I wonder if you know, though, that cyberbullying is an offence. As far as I can make out, you were terrorising the lad."

"You're making it sound far worse than it is," the mother said.

"I'm telling it exactly how it is. Your son made Simon Bird's life a misery. You had one account shut down already. So you started another."

"I didn't," he said. "That wasn't me."

"So who was it?"

"I don't know."

"But you were aware of the account. I mean, you were aware of the videos of Simon while he was in the washroom, for example. Or the one of him in the shower after a PE lesson?"

He shrugged.

"You took those videos, didn't you?"

He glanced across his mother, ashamed, who in return stared at Gavin in disgust.

"You videoed another boy in the shower?" she said, shaking her head at her son. "What's the bloody matter with you?"

"It was just a laugh, alright."

"At Simon's expense," Freya added. "As was the video of him in a washroom stall."

"Gavin?"

"It wasn't like that, Mum–" Gavin complained.

"I can list several other videos," Freya said.

"It wasn't me–"

"Do you own a yellow hooded sweatshirt?" Freya asked.

"What?" Gavin replied.

"It's a simple question."

"Yes, he does," the mother said, and for the first time, Freya felt she had an ally in her.

"I saw the same yellow sweatshirt in the video of Simon Bird in the washroom stall. Whoever was taking the video was wearing it."

The duty solicitor spoke up, "If I can just add that more than one yellow sweatshirt exists, Inspector Bloom–"

"Oh, shut up," the mother told him. "Of course it's his. We will not lie our bloody way out of this, or get out of it on some technicality. If my boy has done wrong, then he'll bloody well own up to it."

"I'm glad you see it that way," Freya said, offering a curt nod. "Perhaps Gavin would like to explain why we found the sweatshirt hidden in a bag, along with several other items of clothing and a mobile phone? Perhaps Gavin can explain the bag as well? It's the same bag the paddle board came in."

"Eh?" Gavin said, panic setting in. "Where?"

"Why don't you tell me?"

"I don't know. I haven't seen that hoody for days."

"I suppose you lost it with your mobile phone, did you?"

"I don't know. I put it in the wash. I didn't really think about it."

Freya studied his face, searching for some tell-tale sign of a lie. She found nothing but genuine panic.

"Okay," she said. "We found the bag about a mile away from the spot where you claim to have last seen Simon Bird. It was tucked into the riverbank. Hidden from sight."

"I didn't put it there."

"The clothes were wet and muddy, and I'm sorry if this sounds presumptuous, but Simon's body was found a few miles further on. We have to explore the possibility of your son, Mrs Forbes, murdering Simon Bird, and then hiding the evidence."

Mrs Forbes' expression was grave. But to her credit, she came across as reasonable. She considered Freya's statement, mulled it over for a few moments, then swallowed and spoke directly to her son.

"Did you?" she said. "Did you hurt Simon? If you tell the truth now, it'll make a difference."

The boy looked hurt that his mother could even think such a thing. He shook his head in disbelief.

"No, Mum. I don't know why this is happening. I haven't done anything," he said, then sighed. "We nicked a paddle board from that place down the river."

"When?" Freya asked.

"Last week. I did it. Not Dave. It was me."

"Was this the board that Simon was on?"

"No, this was before. I don't know where the other one came

from. But everything else I told you is true. Simon wanted to show how good he was. We thought it would be a laugh to watch him fall in. That's it. He got on the board and just..."

"Just what, Gavin?" Freya asked.

"Floated off," he said. "That was the last time I saw him."

# CHAPTER FORTY

"I can't believe you let him go," Ben said, as they approached Freya's car.

The sky was darkening, but the days were getting longer. Only a month ago, at the same time, the whole car park would have been pitch black. It was at this time of year that his father would normally be making the most of the extra daylight.

"Where's he going to run?" Freya said. "Besides, being at home with his mum will be more of a punishment than making him sit in a cell for another twelve hours. In fact, I imagine he'd rather be in the cell."

They climbed inside and both sat quietly for a moment.

"I need a large glass of wine," she said.

"Need or want?" Ben asked.

"Need," she replied. "I hate it when kids are involved. It's bad enough the victim is a young boy, but when we interview young suspects, it's just wrong, isn't it?"

"Do you think he's guilty?" Ben asked. He admired Freya's profile, trying to read what she was thinking. Although, she had a way of keeping her deepest thoughts very close to her chest.

"Yes," she said, and she hit the button to start the car. "Of something. But not murder. Theft, yes. Plus, I suspect he's broken a few laws around violating Simon Bird's privacy and uploading indecent images of minors to various social media platforms. But murder? No. I don't think so."

"So, how do you explain the clothes and the bag?"

"I think if he is involved, then it's a stunt gone wrong. Another prank, maybe? Who knows? Maybe they set it up for Simon to float down the river and filmed the whole thing to post on social media?"

"Manslaughter, then?" Ben said, and Freya nodded.

"If he's unlucky, yes. If the jury takes into consideration his other offenses. Death by misadventure would be my guess, though. But he's going to need a better lawyer for that."

"That's not going to sit well with Simon's parents."

"No. No, it isn't."

A gentle vibration in Ben's pocket caught his attention.

"It's Nillson," he said. "She just texted me. All four of Gavin Forbes' friends are on their way here right now, complete with parents."

"I was hoping we could deal with them tomorrow. I need some time to think about Gavin Forbes. Something isn't quite right."

"You let Gavin go. If we wait until tomorrow, he'll have told them his story."

"You're right," she said, reaching for the door handle. "Sorry. It's going to be a late one."

But just as she reached to turn off the car's engine, her phone rang. The call came through the car's Bluetooth system.

"Freya Bloom," she said, and stared at Ben while they waited for the caller to identify themselves.

"Ah, DI Bloom," the voice said, in that highly distinguishable Welsh accent they had both come to love and fear. "I was hoping you'd answer."

"You called me, Doctor Bell. Why wouldn't I answer?"

"Well, I know how busy you are, see? Thought I'd just let you know about a recent development, I did."

"Recent development?" Freya said. "With the Simon Bird investigation?"

"Yes. Although, I'd brace yourself. It's not the most pleasant of news I have to deliver."

"Go on," Freya said. "I'm used to dealing with unpleasantness."

"I suppose you are. What with working with Ben all day every day."

"Oy," Ben said, making his presence clear.

"Oh. Afternoon, Ben," Doctor Bell said, without an ounce of regret in her tone. "I was just saying I have some news for you both."

"Go on," Freya said for the second time.

"Well, it's a bit delicate, you see. I've just finished my examination, and it's quite clear the boy was interfered with."

"Interfered with?" Ben said, and he met Freya's concerned stare with his own.

"Somebody raped him, Ben. Recently."

"Are you sure?" Freya said.

"I'm certain. Although, the damaged blood vessels had begun healing, which suggests it happened a while ago."

"How long?" Ben asked.

"A few days. A week at the most."

"That doesn't fit," Freya said, clearly thinking out loud. But Ben understood, and he agreed.

"Rape doesn't fit in with any of our suspects," he said, then addressed Doctor Bell. "I don't suppose–"

"No DNA, Ben. No. It's been too long, I'm afraid. The poor boy would have had several bowel movements by the time he was killed. Plus he was in the water."

"And it definitely didn't happen at the time of death?" Freya said.

"Oh, I'm sure of it. The body doesn't heal that fast, even in someone as young as Simon was."

"It does paint a whole new picture, though, doesn't it?" Freya said, again thinking out loud.

"It does," Doctor Bell said, as if she could see Freya's thought process, and agreed wholeheartedly.

"What?" Ben said.

"Shall I tell him, or do you want to?" Doctor Bell said.

"No, feel free. I'd be interested to see if your picture looks like mine."

"Righto," she said, then cleared her throat. "It's the bruises on the back of Simon's neck, Ben. We thought they were from somebody holding him under the water."

"But they might not be," Ben said, seeing where she was going with the idea. "The bruises could have been made–"

"While he was being raped," Doctor Bell finished for him. "Yes. See what I mean? Not pleasant. Not pleasant at all."

"Unpleasantness is our business," Freya said. "Doctor, thank you. That's exactly what I was thinking. We'll be in touch if we need anything else."

"You're welcome," she replied. "I'll leave you two to ponder that thought."

The call ended and the screen on the dashboard returned to the standard display.

"He might have drowned, then," Ben said.

"He might have," Freya agreed.

"If it's not a murder investigation, do we hand it over to CID?"

"Not yet, no. I want to explore all avenues first. I want to talk to Gavin Forbes' friends to make sure the stories match up. I want to see what Nillson finds on the boy's mother, and I want to know what Chapman finds out about our man in the rental shop. If they all hit dead ends, then fine. We'll hand it over. But until then, I'm treating this as a murder enquiry."

She stepped out of the car and leaned inside for her bag.

"I suppose that glass of wine will have to wait," she said, a little disheartened. "If you wanted to go home and talk to your dad or your brothers, Ben—"

"He'll still be there when I get home," Ben replied.

"I always thought that. Don't take time for granted. You'll be amazed how fast it goes."

He considered it for a moment. But the idea of facing his worst nightmare was not an attractive one.

"I think I'd rather keep the distraction going until I can actually help him in some way."

Freya gave him a look as if she was just about to offer another pearl of wisdom that bordered on being motherly. "Shall we go and interview four teenagers and see which one breaks down first?" she said instead.

"You're so going to hell," Ben joked, and she eyed him as if she was gauging his ability to focus on the task at hand.

"Ain't that the truth," she replied, her expression softening. "And when I get there, every sorry soul I've ever put in prison will be waiting for me."

# CHAPTER FORTY-ONE

T HE THREE YOUTHS WERE KEPT ISOLATED FROM EACH OTHER TO avoid the risk of them exchanging stories. David Stills and his mother were in interview room one, Julie Yates and her mother were in interview room two, and Tess Mitchell was waiting in a spare office with her mother a few metres from the custody desk.

"All ready and waiting for you, ma'am," Sergeant Priest said. Priest was a Yorkshire man through and through. He seemed to grumble the words as a single baritone syllable.

"Were they any trouble?"

"None at all. In fact, it's nice not to be spat at, insulted, or verbally abused for a change," he replied, with his usual Northern candour. "I'll take guests like that any day of the week, if you can find them, that is."

"Thank you, Sergeant," Freya replied, peering through the window in the spare office door. Tess Mitchell looked terrified. Her swollen eyes stared up at Freya, wide and somehow hopeful. "Although I have a feeling that things could get ugly at any moment. Kids are unpredictable, emotional, and they don't hold back when the tears begin."

"They say never work with animals or children, don't they?" Priest said.

"And for good reason," Freya replied, taking another glance through the window at the timid, little creature inside.

"Do you want to start with her?" Ben asked.

"No. No, let's talk to the others first. This one needs a little more ripening," she said, then turned to face him. "I'll bet by the time we get to her, she'll tell us everything we need to know. But it'll be good to see what the others have to say first."

"To gain an objective view, you mean?" Ben said, following along with her plan.

"Something like that," she said, and led them through to the corridor. She stopped outside interview room one. "We may as well get the other boy out of the way. He's more likely to have corroborated with Forbes."

They pushed through into the room, and immediately, Mrs Stills stood up. It was more out of courtesy than aggression, and it pleased Freya to see some of the old ways were still being practiced.

"Please," Freya said, gesturing for her to take a seat. "I'm terribly sorry to have kept you waiting, but I would like to begin by thanking you both for coming voluntarily."

"Voluntarily?" the young boy in the chair muttered, shaking his head. If any of them were going to give Freya a hard time, it would be him. "They dragged me out of class for this."

"Dragged might be an overstatement," Freya said. "But you got here. I'm grateful. It's a terrible crime we're investigating. Any help you can offer will be very much appreciated."

"Sit up, David," Mrs Stills said, slapping his thigh with the back of her hand. "Have some manners."

Begrudgingly, David sat up in his seat and rested his arms on the table. After Freya had given him the nod, Ben hit the record button, stated the date and time, and asked the attendees to introduce themselves. The process took all of two minutes, by which time, David was growing ever more concerned.

"Why is this being recorded?" he asked. "Don't I have to give you permission to record me?"

"David–" his mother began.

"It's okay, Mrs Stills," Freya said, holding her hand up to prevent the boy being reprimanded. "Actually, David, no. This is a criminal investigation. I'm more than happy that you, in some shape or form, are involved in our investigation, and therefore, we need to record what you say for when the matter is presented in court."

"In court?" he said, but Freya was on a roll. This was her chance to break the barrier he had built and get a glimpse of the truth.

"Of course, the alternative would be for me to arrest you. But, at this stage, I don't think that would be helpful to any of us."

"Arrest him?" Mrs Still said.

"Now, David, do you understand you are below eighteen years old, and therefore are entitled to an appropriate adult?"

"Yes," he said, and glanced across at his mother.

"I'm his appropriate adult," she advised. "Can you please tell me what's going on here?"

"All in good time," Freya said. "David, perhaps you'd like to tell us why you're here."

He stared at her blankly and shrugged.

"I was told it was because of what happened to that poor lad," his mother said. "You know? The Bird boy. Simple Simon."

"His name was Simon Bird," Ben said, his first words in the interview.

"And I directed the question at your son, Mrs Stills," Freya added, then waited for the boy to speak. He was a good-looking boy, with the type of skin tone that tans with ease. Freya remembered a girl at her own mundane public school that also had that European complexion. She also remembered how jealous she had been during the summer months, when she seemingly only had to step outside for a few minutes and would become radiant. As opposed to Freya, who, during her childhood years at least, was forced to find shade beneath the oak trees for fear of burning.

In a few years, she mused to herself, he would have no problems with the girls, and in a decade or two, he would have them falling at his feet.

"It's because of Simon, isn't it?" he said.

"Kind of," Freya agreed. "But before we get to Simon's death, I'd like to know a bit more about the stolen paddle boards."

"The what?" his mother said.

"Stolen paddle boards, Mrs Stills. Oh, sorry. Didn't you know?"

David glared at her, then turned away, knowing full well there would be no escaping the subject now.

"Have you been at it again?" she said to her son. "Look at me when I bloody well talk to you."

"What? No," he said. The two single-word sentences were aimed at his mother, conveying his frustration. He turned back to Freya. "I know nothing about a paddle board."

"But you know what a paddle board is?"

"Of course I know what a paddle board is. I'm not a dummy."

"Can you use one?" Ben asked.

"Eh?"

"A paddle board, David. Can you use a paddle board?"

"Yeah, I suppose so. Who can't?"

"I can't," Freya said. "Ben?"

"Nope," Ben replied with a theatrical shake of his head. "Could Simon Bird use one, David?"

He shrugged. "I guess."

"You see, one of the problems I have is that we've had reports of several paddle boards being stolen from a business close to where Simon was found."

"Right?"

"David, you can give up the games. Gavin told us Simon was on a paddle board."

"Gavin did?"

Freya nodded. "My question is, where did he get it from?"

"I don't know. How am I supposed to know?"

"Well, you might want to know that Gavin also told us you both stole a paddle board from the business I mentioned."

"Yeah, but not the one Simon was on," he cried out in defence, and Freya felt the corners of her mouth wanting to reach upwards. But despite his emotions getting the better of him, it wasn't really a time to offer a smile. He sighed, realising his mistake, and turned his face away from his disappointed mother.

"You told me you'd stopped all that," she told him. "You wait 'til your dad hears about it."

"Oh, I think your husband will have far more pressing matters on his mind, Mrs Stills," Ben said.

"Like what?" David muttered, and he peered up at Freya through his long fringe.

"Like the potential for his son to be arrested as an accomplice to manslaughter," Freya said, closing her file and sitting back in the chair. "Your son, Tess Mitchell, Julie Yates, and, of course, the main act. Gavin Forbes."

# CHAPTER FORTY-TWO

"You can't do that," Mrs Stills announced, and any sign of her previous hospitality had been replaced with hostility.

"Oh, I think we can, Mrs Stills. You see, we have CCTV footage showing your son and his three friends walking towards the river less than half an hour before Simon Bird."

"So? That's not evidence–"

"And we have a statement from Gavin Forbes confirming that the four of them agreed to meet Simon Bird, so he could show them all his paddle boarding skills."

"Simon Bird? He's not a friend of my David's–"

"No, he's not. But as I understand it, they thought it would be a good laugh to watch a poor, sad boy fall into the river. A boy who would have given anything to have a friend. To be liked. To be a part of something."

"It was just a laugh," said David. "That's all it was. Nothing more. Just a joke. We didn't know he would die. We didn't know he would get swept away."

"Hold on, hold on," Mrs Stills said, raising her finger at Freya and Ben. "Do you mean to tell me that you knew this all along?"

"I haven't concealed anything."

"It's entrapment. That's what this is."

"I can assure this is not entrapment, Mrs Stills. I merely wanted to see how freely your son would tell us about it."

"What for?"

"As an indicator that might tell me if he's hiding something else, or if he's been honest. As it happens," Freya explained, "I've had to drag every bit of information out of him. Which tells me he has more to say. So, we can either stay here for as long as it takes, or I can have him arrested."

"Arrested?"

"You might want to call hubby, if it comes to it. We'll be keeping him in overnight."

"Overnight?"

"As long as it takes," Freya said, this time surrendering to the smile. "Of course, the sooner he comes forward and tells us what happened, the sooner he and his friends can go home."

"My friends?"

"Yes, Tess and Julie. They're being held in the different rooms."

"But they didn't do anything," David said.

"Which implies that somebody did," Freya said, folding her arms on the table. "So I suggest you get talking, David Stills, or none of you will be going anywhere for the foreseeable future."

"Oh, come on–"

"David," his mother snapped. "Will you just listen to the woman?"

"They'll never speak to me again," he moaned. "You're asking me to..."

He stopped mid-sentence, hanging on the crucial word.

"To what?" Freya asked. "Betray Gavin? You know something."

"No. I was going to say you're asking me to tell you so you can let the girls go home."

"Then I suggest," Freya began, "that it's time to decide whose friendship you value the most."

For the first time, David covered his face with his hands. It was a sure sign he was about to talk. Right about now, Freya thought, he would be silently considering the implications of what he was about to say.

"Shall we start with the paddle board you stole from Witham Rentals?" Ben suggested, and Mrs Stills' expression turned very grave indeed.

"It was last week," David said finally. "I thought it would be a laugh. You know? I was just down there on my bike."

"On your own?" Freya asked, and he nodded.

"Nobody else was about. It was that nice weekend we had. The hot one. I just wanted to be outside. So I rode along the towpath. I don't think I'd ever been that far down it. I kept telling myself I should turn back. But then, I suppose, I was just curious. That's when I saw the rental place. It had a boat tied up outside it. You know? Tied to a wooden post thing."

"A rowing boat?" Freya asked. "A little, wooden rowing boat?"

"No. This was bigger. The type that has an engine and a roof. It had a name on the side of it. I remember. The letters were painted in white paint."

"Do you remember the name of the boat?"

"No. I wasn't really paying it any attention. I was just curious. I wondered what was inside. So I stashed my bike in some bushes and had a look around the building."

"Was anybody there?" Ben asked.

"No. But the door was open. I remember the door being unlocked."

"So you went inside?" Freya said, and again, he nodded, while his mother shook her head in disgust.

"That's when I found the boards. There were loads of them. They were in bags. I didn't think it would matter."

"You took one, did you?" Freya said.

"Yeah," he said, ashamed. "And a paddle too. I had to ride back with them. Took me bloody ages."

His language earned him a slap on his arm from his mother, but that was the least of his worries.

"What happened to that board?"

"It burst," he said, with a carefree shrug.

"So, it's at the bottom of the river, is it?"

"Probably. The current took it."

"It was definitely burst, though?" Ben asked.

"Gavin put his front door key through it," he replied, nodding.

"Talk to me about what happened on Sunday, David," Freya said. "Was Simon part of your group?"

"Simple Simon?" he burst out and received another of those slaps from his mother. He flinched, then shook his head. "No."

"So why was Simon Bird on a paddle board? Why was he even there at the river?"

Freya was quite sure what Gavin had said was mostly true, but to have it confirmed would be helpful.

"He saw me," David started. "He saw us, anyway. Last week. He was on the other side of the river. He laughed when Gavin fell in. We all did, but..."

"But what?"

"Having us laugh at him is one thing, but Gavin wouldn't let someone like Simon laugh at him."

"Why not? Was Simon not worthy of laughing?"

"He just wasn't a friend, that's all."

"So what happened between last week, when you were playing on the paddle board you stole, and this week?"

The boy's lips clamped closed.

"David?" his mother urged. "Answer the police officer."

"Gavin confronted him. At school."

"When?" Ben asked.

"I don't know. Tuesday or something. I didn't write it down."

The comment earned him a glare from his mother.

"Go on," Freya said.

"He hit Simon."

"He hit him?"

"He always hit him. Everyone did. Not on the face. On his arm. You know? Like a dead arm. But Simon said something. He never did himself any favours. He always answered back. He always provoked him. So Gavin pinned him to the ground until he cried. Simon said he could paddle board better than him. He said the only reason Gavin couldn't do it was because he's stupid."

"So Gavin arranged for a demonstration, did he?"

David nodded.

"Where did the board come from?"

"That wasn't me," David said. "I only took one. I don't know where it came from."

"Did Simon bring it with him?" Freya asked. "Because we have CCTV footage that shows Simon walking along Five Mile Lane. He wasn't carrying anything."

"It was stashed in the field behind the towpath. The paddle was there as well. I didn't even know it was there until Simon arrived."

"So, who got the board from the field?"

"Gavin did. Simon too. They both got it."

"So they both knew it was there?"

"Yeah."

"But you didn't?"

He nodded.

"And the girls?"

"They didn't even know we were meeting Simon. It was going to be a surprise. We thought they'd enjoy seeing Simon get wet."

"Or perhaps you thought they'd stop you bullying him if they found out about it?"

He stared up them, shrugged, but confirmed nothing.

"David, how did the paddle end up in the reeds?"

"The paddle?"

"We found it in the reeds. It's in the lab now being examined for fingerprints. So please, think about what you say next."

"Gavin," he said. "Gavin threw it there."

"Why didn't Simon have it with him?"

There was a pause while David considered what he should say.

"Simon said something. I didn't hear what it was. He said he'd say something. Tell us all something we didn't know."

"Right," Freya said, waiting for him to finish the story.

"Gavin got up and was going to hit him. Simon had nowhere to go. He got onto the board without the paddle, so Gavin tossed it into the reeds."

"And poor old Simon just floated off downstream, did he?"

"We chased after him, but we got the bridge and..."

"And what?"

"We stopped."

"Why?" Ben said. "Why stop? You could see Simon was in danger."

"We saw someone. On the bridge. A bloke. He even looked down at Simon. We thought he'd help him."

"And you thought that you'd get in trouble when he finally helped him?"

Another shrug, this time delivered with very little conviction.

"Did you know the man?"

"No."

"But you recognised him?"

"No. I didn't see his face. None of us did. He was walking away from us."

"Can you describe him for me?" Freya asked.

"Don't know. Not really."

"Was he in running clothes, maybe? Or jeans?"

"A jacket. You know, like an old man's jacket. But he wasn't old. Not really."

"A blazer?" Ben said.

"Yeah. It was flapping in the wind."

Freya nodded. That was the second time she had heard about a man on the bridge.

"Can I go home now?" David asked.

Freya considered the question and her alternatives.

"You can go on one condition," Freya said.

"What?"

"You hand over your mobile phone."

"Eh? You can't take that."

"I can take what I need to take. Especially when we have evidence that you contributed to the cyber-bullying account. So you can hand it over voluntarily and you'll have it back when we're done, or we can get a warrant, and you *might* get it back when the investigation is over."

"Getting a warrant may take some time, too," Ben added. He looked across at Freya. "What do you reckon? An hour?"

"Two or three, I would imagine. At this time of day, at least."

"The what? Cyber-bullying?" the mother said, but Freya didn't look at her. She held her hand out, waiting for the boy to give her the phone.

He slid the phone from his pocket. It was an old model with a cracked screen and looked as though it had been used in a game of football as the ball. He slid it across the desk to Ben.

"Are we going to find anything on there we shouldn't?" Freya asked, and he shook his head. "I saw the posts about Simon."

"You even liked and commented on them," Ben said.

"But that's all. I didn't take the videos," he argued.

"I'll be checking your story, David. And we'll have our team look into your phone," Freya said, then gave his mother a nod. "Take him home. He's had enough for one day."

The woman didn't need telling twice. Two chairs scraped backwards across the smooth, concrete floor, and she held the door for her son to leave. Then, leaving Freya with a nod of appreciation, she followed.

"So Gavin Forbes wasn't telling the exact truth," Ben said, when the recording had stopped.

"I didn't expect him to. But a lad like that," Freya said,

nodding at the door in reference to David Stills, "he's not a bad lad. Not really. He's just mixed up in the wrong crowd. I'm quite sure he's telling the truth."

"Who's the bloke on the bridge?" Ben asked. "Cruz said something about a man as well."

"He's either no concern of ours," Freya said, collecting her file in her hand, "or he's everything for us to be concerned with. My money is on him being the paddle board guy."

"Michael Doughty?"

"Yes, him. In which case, he's everything for us to be concerned with."

## CHAPTER FORTY-THREE

So far, it had taken Jim at least an hour and a half to clean his house. At first, he had set out just to clean the kitchen, the lounge, and the bedroom. But after a quick glance in the bathroom, he'd decided that needed a good going over too. The toilet was now freshly bleached, the shower had been scrubbed, and the floor was clean enough that he could have eaten his dinner off it. That's if he had even stopped for dinner, which he hadn't. There hadn't been time. The bedsheets needed changing, or, as he joked to himself, the old sheets needed burning.

After the usual fight with the duvet cover, during which he had put it on the wrong way round once, inside out once, and finally the right way, he'd worked up a sweat. The laundry that had been scattered across the floor was now sitting in a heap in the bottom of his wardrobe, and when he backed out of the room, he sprayed a single spray of aftershave.

"Right then," he said, moving into the kitchen.

Then, after a quick glance at the takeaway cartons that were building up, he decided the bin was too small, and they warranted a new bin bag, which, once filled, he tossed into the back garden where it landed beside the wheelie bin. Once he'd cleaned the kitchen worktops, he squirted washing-up liquid onto the floor, grabbed the old mop, remarking on how new it looked even four years after he'd bought it, and doused it in the sink beneath hot running water. Another ten minutes later, and the kitchen now smelled as fresh as a...

He checked the washing-up liquid.

"Lemon," he said, and sniffed the air. "Smells more like Chapman's handbag than a lemon."

But there was little time for him to dwell on the scent. The important thing was that the room was cleaned, and all he had to do now was the living room. He groaned at the sight of more takeaway cartons and considered taking them and the bag he'd thrown outside to Mrs Chang in search of a recycling discount. But he didn't. He bagged the cartons up, and the bag landed in the garden beside the first one. He plumped the cushions, blew the dust from the surfaces and gave them a wipe with his cuff, then blasted the vacuum around for a few minutes. Vacuuming always made the house smell clean, even if it wasn't.

He stood back, admiring his work, and considered having a beer to mark his achievements. That was when he realised; he'd forgotten to pick up the wine. He checked his watch. It was six-thirty. She'd be here in thirty minutes, whoever she was, and he still had to shower.

"Right," he said aloud, then decided to leg it down to the pub to grab a bottle.

He snatched his keys and his jacket and ran out of the door. Even at the slow speed he was running, he caught a whiff of himself. Cleaning was harder work than he'd given it credit for, and he'd have to sacrifice his sparkly, clean bathroom to have a shower. There was no way J, or anybody else for that matter, was going to let him get near her in this state.

He burst through the pub door and leaned on the bar. The pub was fuller than it normally was at that time of night, which was just his luck. A man and a woman were waiting for service, the man toying with a twenty-pound note, making small talk while they waited. Jim leaned over the counter, seeing if he could see into the back room.

"Service," he called, and the man smiled at him. It was a casual smile, but there were undertones that Jim recognised. It was a man-to-man smile that threatened some kind of action if Jim tried to jump the queue. The man had a woman with him, and he wasn't about to back down in front of her. He must have said something, and she gave a little laugh, resting her hand on his chest.

Jim ignored them, leaned over the bar again, and whistled. "Service," he called out.

"He's changing a barrel," the man said eventually, and the woman standing beside him glanced Jim's way, appraising him from his boots up to his sweaty head of hair.

"Right," Jim replied. And with that, he marched past them, raised the bar flap, and ventured around to the fridges.

"Are you supposed to go back there?" the man asked.

"I haven't got time to wait all day. I'm a local. He won't mind," Jim replied, as he pulled two bottles from the fridge and tried to see the difference between them. The first was a Sauvignon Blanc, and the second was a Chardonnay. He held them both up in the light. The colour was slightly different. One was darker than the other. So he turned to the woman. "What would you prefer?"

"Excuse me?" she said, glancing around her to make sure Jim was actually talking to her.

"This one, or this one?" he said, presenting the right hand and then the left. "Which one would you prefer?"

"Actually, white wine gives me heartburn. I prefer a red."

"Aye, I get that. But if it didn't give you heartburn?"

"Well, what are they?"

"Eh?"

"What are they? That one looks like a Sauvignon, and is the other a Chardonnay?"

He glanced down at the labels.

"Aye."

"Well, the Chardonnay will be drier. It's not everybody's cup of tea."

"Right, so it's the Savvy one, then," he said, and began replacing the darker of the two.

"Who's it for?" she asked.

"A lady friend," he replied, not wanting to give too much information away.

"Well, what does she like?"

"I have no idea, sweetheart," he replied. Then, as he closed the fridge, he looked up at her from where he was crouched. "I don't even know who she is."

Seeing a strip of paper hanging from the till, Jim ripped it off, grabbed a pen from the little pot under the bar, and then wrote an IOU.

"You don't know who she is?" the man asked, and the confused look on his face told Jim he had never had a one-night stand, or probably a night of wild passion, in his life.

Jim signed the till receipt, placed it on the bar beside the till, and then grabbed his bottle. He was about to raise the flap once more when the woman spoke out.

"Erm," she began, and Jim was expecting her to voice her opinion about any old riff-raff stealing wine from behind the bar. He stared at her, mentally preparing himself to tell her to mind her own business. But her face said something altogether different. Her expression told him that, regardless of her man's lack of adventures, she had seen some action, and knew how to have a good night. "Just the one bottle?" she said, then winked playfully.

Jim looked down at the bottle in his hand, then back up at her.

"Aye," he said, and he bent down to the fridge to collect another. "You're right, lass."

"Enjoy your evening," the woman remarked as Jim raced past them, and to Jim's delight, a wry smile had crept across her face.

The interaction was very much to the distaste of her man, who looked on aghast.

At the door, Jim stopped and turned back to face the contrasting couple.

"If you see Craig," he said, and the woman turned to face him, "you tell him Jim Gillespie took two bottles of this stuff. He'll know who you mean. I live just down there in the corner house. The one without any flowers in the garden."

"You just left him a note," the man said.

"Oh aye," Jim replied. "But he'll never read my handwriting."

He gave them both a nod, then as he slipped from the door, he caught the woman's watchful eye, and returned the wink.

# CHAPTER FORTY-FOUR

Tess Mitchell and her mother sat side by side, while Ben and Freya resumed their positions. A new recording had started, and once again, Freya introduced the time, date, and attendees.

"I'd like to thank you both for coming," she began, hoping to win some favour with the girl's mother. Tess had been crying, and her eyes were swollen and red. "I'd just like to say that, at this moment, Tess, you're not in any kind of trouble. You can thank David for that."

"Dave? What did he say?"

"Just that you weren't really involved in what happened. However, we do know you were present when Simon Bird climbed onto a paddle board at the river last Sunday. So we'll need a statement from you. Please answer our questions accurately and honestly. All being well, we'll have you both on your way in no time."

"You didn't tell me you were there," the mother said to her daughter.

"I wasn't anywhere," the girl said, and immediately, Freya got the sense she was hiding something. "At least, not when it happened."

"You were at the riverbank on Sunday," Freya said. "Around three-thirty in the afternoon."

"Well, yeah. But he was okay then. We saw him. He was fine."

"And by fine," Ben added, "do you mean he was sitting on the riverbank having a pleasant time with some friends? Or do you mean he was floating down the river on a paddle board without a paddle?"

"Tess," the mother hissed, in utter disappointment, "you were with that boy again, weren't you?"

"No. Well, yeah, but I didn't know he was going to be there."

"Are you referring to David Stills?" Freya asked.

"No, not David," said Tess' mother. "He's a lovely boy. The other one. Forbes."

"Gavin Forbes," Freya said, pleased that the woman had volunteered a character reference for David Stills which supported her own views.

"That's him. Trouble, he is. Always up to something. I told her not to get involved with him."

"I'm not involved with him. He's David's best mate."

"Well, then you tell David you don't want to be around him."

The argument was taking place on the far side of the table, and Freya sat back, folded her arms, and caught Ben playing verbal tennis beside her. His eyes flicked from one side to the other as they argued, as mother and daughter often do.

"If we could get back to the matter at hand," Freya said, interrupting the mother in mid-flow. "We're investigating Simon Bird's death. We have a good idea of what happened and just need your daughter to corroborate what we've heard so far."

"I can't tell you what happened, exactly," the mother said. "But whatever it was, Gavin Forbes is behind it."

"I'd prefer to keep an objective opinion of the matter," Freya said, then turned to the woman's daughter. "Now, Tess, I can tell you this. We have CCTV footage showing the four of you walking along Five Mile Lane between three-thirty and four p.m. I have a statement claiming that the paddle board Simon used had been stashed in the adjacent field, and that Simon said something that upset Gavin Forbes, which caused Simon to escape on the paddle board. I also have a statement that indicates the four of you all ran after Simon as far as the bridge, where you stopped. Is that correct?"

She glanced across at her mother, then back at Freya, offering a slight nod of her head.

"For the tape, please," Ben said.

"Yes. That's all true."

"Why did you stop there?"

"There was a man on the bridge. Gavin said we'd better get out of there in case he called the police."

"Why would the police be a problem?" Ben asked. "Surely saving Simon would have been your priority?"

Tess said nothing, although her expression told Freya she had something to say, and had her mother not been sitting beside her, she may have found it easier.

"Is it because drugs were smoked, Tess?" Freya said with a sigh.

"Drugs?" the mother said.

"I didn't," Tess exclaimed.

"We're not questioning whether or not you were the one smoking the drugs, Tess. We're asking if that was the reason you stopped running."

She nodded. "Gavin said we'd better get out of there. Go home and deny we were ever there. He had some on him."

"Some drugs?" Ben asked, and she nodded.

"Just some weed."

"Some weed?" her mother repeated, her face a picture of disappointment.

"I know this is hard, Tess. I know you don't want to get anybody in any trouble, but a boy has lost his life. We need to find out what happened. What did you do when you saw the man on the bridge?"

"We waited for him to cross, then followed. It's the only bridge for miles. We thought he'd go after Simon, but he didn't. His car was parked on the other side of the water. So we waited for him to drive off. Then we ran. Julie and I, we ran back to her house. I don't know what the boys did."

"Do you have a mobile phone, Tess?" Freya asked.

"Yes, she does," her mother added. The disappointment had given her tone a bitter edge.

"Did you text either of them? David, perhaps?"

"A little while later. Yes."

"And what did he say?"

"Nothing. We didn't think anything of it. We didn't know what had happened to Simon. We were just glad to be away from there in case the police showed up."

"And where was he when he texted you?"

"He was at home. He said something about a film he was watching on Netflix."

"And was Gavin Forbes with him?"

"No. No, he was alone."

"Are you sure?"

"Yes. He's always different when he's alone. He sent me a selfie. He wouldn't do that if Gavin was there."

"A selfie?" Freya said. "Is it on your phone? Can we see it?"

"Oh, I, erm, deleted it," she replied, turning her head away to look at the wall.

"Oh, that's okay. I've got David's phone. Ben, can you fetch it for me? Perhaps Tess can show us which photo it was he sent."

"He would have deleted it too," Tess said with panic in her voice.

"Why? Why would he have deleted a picture of himself?" Ben asked, his hand inside the clear evidence bag which held David Still's phone.

"It wasn't a selfie, was it, Tess?"

Her mother's eyes widened when she realised what David must have sent.

"Tess?" she said. "What did David send you?"

"Nothing, Mum. It was just him."

"David could get in a lot of trouble for that, Tess," Freya said.

"It was just a joke. He meant nothing by it."

"Did he send you pictures of his body, Tess?" Ben asked.

She sighed, then gave a humph in defeat.

"He wasn't naked or anything. He's not like that."

"So what did he send you?" her mother said. "And did you send him...?"

She paused, unable to complete the sentence.

"No. Of course I didn't. He was in his boxers. That's all."

"Are the pictures indecent?"

"I need to see the pictures," her mother stated, suddenly developing an authoritative tone. "Hand me the phone."

"I'm afraid the phone is being held as evidence, Mrs Mitchell," Freya said. "The matter will be pursued, I can assure you. But before that, I'm wondering if your daughter has anything further to add."

Tess looked up. Her face was bright red and her eyes shone with tears.

"If David was alone," Freya began, "where was Gavin when you were sending each other photos?"

"He changed. When he saw the man, I mean. He looked worried. He said he was going home."

# CHAPTER FORTY-FIVE

The wine was in the fridge. Steam poured from the bathroom, and Jim appraised himself in the mirror, toying with having one or two buttons open at his collar. It was his lucky shirt. Lucky because it was his only non-work shirt, which meant that every single time he'd managed to find some female company, he'd been wearing it, rendering it lucky.

He opted for two open buttons and then toyed with his cuffs. Cuff links would be a little too formal. So he rolled his sleeves up once. Too baggy. Twice, too eighties. Three times. Yes, that was it.

"You'll do," he told his reflection. Then, with a last glance around the bedroom to make sure all was in order, he made his way through to the kitchen, stopping in the lounge when he heard his phone ringing. His heart sank at the noise. She'd better bloody turn up now he'd put all this effort in.

A gentle wave of relief washed over him when he saw Ben's name on the phone's display.

"Ben, how you doing?" he said, just as the doorbell rang.

He checked the time. She was five minutes early.

"Yeah, good cheers, Jim. Listen, I'm just with Freya going over the files. We're trying to put a plan together."

"Oh aye," Jim said, as he peered through the little peephole, but saw only a dark shape outside. "No rest for the wicked, eh?"

He pulled open the door, not knowing who to expect to be standing there.

Then recognition struck a bell in his mind, sounding alarms and whistles, the way a pinball machine might when the player found that hard-to-reach hole at the top of the board. It was good news. In fact, the more he looked at her, the more he was sure it was good news. But it was also bad. It was also very bad.

"We need you to do something for us tomorrow," Ben said.

"Aye," he said, and silently gestured for her to step inside, pointing at the phone as if to say, 'I'm just on the phone.' Then he felt stupid for doing so.

"We've had the statements from the kids that were with Gavin Forbes. We think there was a car parked near the bridge. Do you remember Cruz mentioning a man on the bridge?"

He waved her through to the kitchen, still reeling from the revelation of the mysterious J.

"Aye," he told Ben. "I remember."

She wore a long overcoat, buttoned to her chest, and a triangle of enticing, bare, pink flesh glared at him.

"We need you to go back to where you got the CCTV from. See if you can see anything."

"Aye, Ben. Aye," he said, as he opened the fridge door, took out a bottle of wine, and was about to offer it to her when she took it from him, being the one with two free hands.

"We haven't got details of the car yet. But there can't be many cars that go down that lane."

Deftly, she uncorked the bottle using the corkscrew she found in his drawer, and while she had her back to him, Jim studied her a little. She wore long, black boots that stopped just shy of her coat, offering a glimpse of nylon stockings.

"We'll be holding a briefing in the morning. When that's over, we want you to take Cruz with you."

She turned, bottle in hand, and took a long swig, staring him directly in the eye.

"Aye, Ben. Aye."

"Are you okay, mate?" Ben asked. "You seem a little distracted."

Setting the bottle down beside her, she bit down on her lower lip, took a half-step towards him, and began unbuttoning her coat. Button by button, she worked her way down the coat, holding it closed until the very last hole.

"I'm grand, Ben," Jim said, unable to believe what he was seeing.

She let the coat fall to the floor, revealing nothing but soft, white skin, and black, lacy lingerie beneath.

"You said the guy works from home, right?" Ben said.

Then she closed the gap between them, pressing herself into him.

"Aye, Ben. He does, aye."

Without warning, she reached up to his chest, took hold of his shirt in both hands and tore it open. Three little buttons from his lucky shirt landed somewhere with three gentle tinkles on the tiled floor. But now was not the time to complain about his lucky shirt being ruined. She ran her hands across his chest.

"What was that?" Ben asked, as she sought amusement elsewhere, and opened the fridge.

"Oh, erm... Nothing."

She found the can of squirty cream Jim kept then turned and smiled up at him.

"Are you on your own, mate?"

"Aye, I'm alone," he lied. "I'm just having a bite, you know?"

Tracing circles around his nipples, she then followed up with two large squirts of the cream, then with a sultry glance up at him, she licked at the cream.

"What you having?" Ben asked.

"Oh, erm... It's more of a dessert really," Jim replied, doing his best to control his breathing and to hide his growing excitement.

But nothing was going to escape her keen eye, and slowly, she dropped to her knees.

"Tell me you had a proper dinner first, Jim," Ben said.

She tugged on his belt with her teeth.

"No. I...erm, went straight for dessert."

"You need to watch those calories, mate. We're not getting any younger."

Suddenly, she snatched at the buckle and pulled open his jeans.

"Aye, Ben. You're right. But we've got to live a little, eh?"

With his shirt tails hanging free, his chest covered in what remained of the cream, and jeans open at the front, she straightened her legs, sliding up him, pressing hard into him as every part of her seemed to thrive at the touch of his excitement.

"You sound like you're in pain, mate. You're breathing heavy."

Standing before him, she took his hand and together they explored her body.

"I, erm... I've just had a busy wee night, that's all. Cleaning, you know?"

"Cleaning?"

"Aye. Cleaning," he said, as she flicked a bra strap off one shoulder. "Still got lots to do."

"Well, I'll leave you to it, then," Ben said. "We're aiming for an early start in the morning."

"Early start. Aye," he said, as she flicked the other strap from the other shoulder, teasing him.

"I'll catch you in the morning, eh?" Ben said. But Jim didn't get the chance to reply. She took the phone from his hand, hit the red button to end the call, and slid it onto the kitchen counter.

"A colleague," he explained, although the explanation was far from necessary.

With one hand, she took hold of the wine bottle, swigging from it feverishly, allowing it to splash down her front carelessly. Then, with her free hand gripping the elastic of his boxer shorts, she turned and led him along the hallway, past the lounge he'd spent so long cleaning, past the bathroom, and into the bedroom, where she shoved him onto the bed, took a swig of the wine, and without uttering a single word, she devoured him.

# CHAPTER FORTY-SIX

"If I didn't know better, I'd say Jim was having trouble," Ben said, pocketing his phone. "Sounded like he was doing a workout or something."

"Maybe he was," Freya said, without looking up.

She was sitting at her dining room table with every single file they had collated fanned out before her. In the past, she'd been accused of being messy, disorganised, or just downright lazy. But that was how she worked. There was no order to the files on the table, but the sequence of events was ordered in her mind. She just needed the files to hand when required. Having them fanned out gave her that perspective. "Who knows what that man gets up to in his free time? I shudder to think about it."

"He said he was eating."

"Well, it is dinner time," she replied. "Speaking of which. Are you eating with me?"

"I'm not hungry, if I'm honest," Ben said, staring through the window at the darkening sky.

Freya saw him gazing across the fields towards his father's house. His mood was as grey as the clouds on the distant horizon.

"Why don't you go and see him?"

"What's the point?" he replied. "I'll only annoy him, and he'll only make me worry. I might as well stay here with you."

"Oh, charming."

"Don't be sensitive, Freya. It doesn't suit you. Besides, whatever he's going through is out of my control. All I can do is pick up the pieces."

"Whatever he's going through might be out of your control. Or it might not."

"Could you be any more cryptic?"

"All I'm saying is that we should keep an open mind. He hasn't been diagnosed with anything. He's just got a little forgetful."

"You don't get it, do you?" Ben said, and there was a hint of emotion in his tone. "We're talking about a man who could, if he needed to, do every single one of those jobs on the entire farm. He can drive the machinery, he knows the schedule inside out, and if you asked him, he could tell you exactly who will be working in what field in six months' time. He is seventy-something and he's still stronger than I am. Do you know what I mean? A man like that doesn't just get forgetful. This is the start. I know it is."

"Yes, I do, as it happens."

"Go on then. What?"

"He's your hero."

"Eh?"

"He's your hero and you can't bear the thought of losing him. It's understandable. Although, I have to admit, I am a little disappointed in you."

"Why?"

"Well, I thought I was your hero," she said with a smile. "Go on. Talk to him. Make him a cup of tea, or whatever he likes. When was the last time you actually sat down and had a chat with him?"

Ben shrugged, ignored the humour, then stared back out of the window. "He's not a sit down and chat type of guy."

"Oh, I don't know. He seemed quite amenable to the idea when I was there."

"He didn't even know which day of the week it was, Freya," Ben replied. "But I'll tell you who knows what day of the week it is."

"Go on," Freya said.

"My brother."

She looked up at him, craning his neck to see out of the window.

"Is he coming here?"

"Looks like it."

"Which one?"

Ben turned to face her, his face a blank canvas for any emotion he wanted to paint.

"Both of them, by the looks of things."

"Both of them? Coming here?"

Freya glanced down at what she was wearing. Her fluffy slippers with her suit trousers were bad enough, but she had removed her blouse when she got home, and was wearing her oldest, warmest, dressing gown.

"I just saw my dad's old farm truck go past. Jeff uses it mostly," Ben said, clearly not sensing Freya's sudden dilemma.

Bolting from her seat, Freya just made the stairs when there was a knock on the front door. Three raps, almost identical to Ben's knock.

A face peered at the frosted glass, and if Freya hadn't known better, she could have sworn it was Ben peering through.

A second face joined the first, each of them squinting. Then one of the men waved.

"Damn," she cursed under her breath.

"Are you going to let them in then?" Ben called out from the living room.

She caught herself childishly mimicking him and sulked across to the front door. Despite knowing Ben for the past six months, she hadn't yet met the brothers who lived in the house on the far side of his dad's house. Ben spoke very little of them. Only that they had both followed their father in the farming business, one of them enjoyed dating apps and probably had every sexually transmitted disease under the sun, and the other rarely ventured out, preferring instead to stay at home at watch TV or play games.

After a breath or two to control herself, she opened the door, wiping the smile from her face, and instead choosing a neutral, surprised expression.

"Now then," one of them said, a standard Lincolnshire greeting Freya had learned very early on. He was as tall as Ben, but not as broad. His hair was longer and actually styled, whereas Ben's was just how it fell when it dried.

"Can I help at all?"

"Ben about?" the other said. He was shorter than his brothers, but as broad as Ben. He reminded Freya of a little tank.

Both had Ben's straight Roman nose and sharp features. Both were dark, like Ben, and both had his deep, confident voice.

"Do you mean is Ben here?" she corrected him. Poor grammar was one thing, but lazy dialogue was unforgivable.

"Yeah," came the reply. "He's not at home."

"Figured he's here," said the other.

"Now let me guess," Freya said, taking time to enjoy the moment. She pointed at the one on the left, the short, stocky one. "You must be James. Which means that you must be Jeff."

"Nope," the tall one said. "I'm James. He's Jeff."

"Which means that you must be Freya," the short one added.

"Whatever gave you that idea?"

"The slippers and the dressing gown," he replied.

"Excuse me?" Freya said, clutching her gown together.

"Ben says you live in them. Always wearing them, he said." He looked down at Freya's feet and pointed. "Slippers." He looked up at the gown she was holding together. "Gown. Which means you must be Freya," the taller of the two said.

"Hey, guys," Ben said, suddenly appearing behind Freya. "Come in."

It was one thing to have unexpected guests at her house, but it was another entirely to have Ben invite them inside. They sidled past Freya and congregated in the living room, leaving Freya to close the door.

She followed them into the living room, where she found the short one, whose name she had already forgotten, pouring over her files. Quickly, she scooped them into a pile.

"Do you mind? That's confidential police paperwork."

"Boy in the river?" he said, looking up at Ben, who gave him a curt nod. "Heard about that. Didn't realise he was abused, though."

"It's not common knowledge, so I'd appreciate it if you could keep that information to yourself. And next time you're invited into somebody's house–"

She stopped at Ben raising his hand. The taller one was waiting to say something, and the look on Ben's face was grave.

"What's wrong?" Ben asked him.

"It's Dad, Ben. He's not good."

"Has he fallen?" Ben asked, looking around for his jacket.

"No, no. Nothing like that. Well, not yet anyway."

"We're worried about him," the other said, the short one. "He lost the keys to the seed store today. Said he dropped them out in the fields somewhere."

"Where are the spares?" Ben asked.

"They were the spares. He lost the others weeks ago."

Sensing that Freya may have been a little hasty in her judgements, she waved her hand at the chairs.

"Do you want to sit?" she asked.

"No," the tall one said. "No, we won't stay."

"A drink, maybe?" she asked, but nobody answered.

"We just came to tell you we're holding a meeting. Tomorrow. You need to be there."

"A meeting?" Ben replied. "What for?"

"To make a plan. To work out what's to be done. He's going downhill, Ben. If he has to stop working, the place will fall apart."

"You've seen this, have you?" Ben asked. "You've seen him decline?"

"Well, we've seen bits, yeah. Johnny Grouch has been telling us for weeks. Said the old man's been making mistakes for ages now. Forgetting to order stuff. Losing keys. According to Johnny, Dad even drove up to Bozeman and forgot why he was there. We didn't believe him to start with. But it's getting out of hand. It was only once or twice a month at first. But now it's like Johnny's coming to us every other day."

"And you believe him, do you?" Freya asked. "You trust this Johnny man, do you?"

"He's been helping Dad since before we were born," the taller one replied. "He's like an uncle or something."

"We need you back with us, Ben," the short one said, and received a glare from his brother in return.

"I thought it would come to this," Ben said, unable to meet Freya's stare.

"We'll lose the farm, Ben."

"Are you two not able to manage the farm?" Freya asked. "I'm sorry. It's none of my business. Only that I just don't have a complete picture. And well, seeing as you're in my living room, discussing Ben's future."

"We need three of us. The farm's too big to manage."

"Well, a third party then?"

"What about Johnny?" asked Ben. "He's always wanted a share."

"Dad won't give it up. Not while there's breath in his body. He won't part with an inch."

"He doesn't have to part with it," Freya began, but Ben raised his hand again, indicating that the matter wasn't worth pressing.

"So?" the short one said. "You coming?"

"What time?"

"Nine. We'll get the farm hands going early doors, then meet back at our house."

"Will Dad be there?"

"No. He'll be up at Bozeman for the day. We've got eyes on him, though. Just in case, you know?"

Ben nodded. "Good."

"He always wanted you back, Ben. You know that, don't you?"

"He never said that. Not in so many words, anyway."

"No, but he did. He said it to us. 'One day, he'll be back,' he said. 'Before my time's up.'"

"He's always supported my decision to work outside of the farm."

"That's because he knows you'll be back one day," the tall one said.

"Is that right?"

"So you'll be there?"

Ben nodded and glanced up at Freya, and she smiled at him softly. He needed to be there. She wasn't going to stop him being a part of his heritage, if that's what he needed to do.

"I'll be there," he said, his voice dry and gruff.

"Alright," the short one replied. "That's that then."

They turned to leave and edged past Freya.

"I'll see them out," Ben muttered as he followed them, and Freya leaned on the chair, listening, and waiting for Ben to return.

"I see what you mean about her," one of them said, and Freya guessed it was the shorter of the two.

Her ears pricked and she straightened. What had Ben said about her? Other than the slippers and dressing gown comment, which he would be hearing about when the moment was right.

"Yeah, I can see why you're never home anymore," the other added.

"Shut up, Jeff," Ben said. There was humour in his tone, but it was faked. She knew Ben well enough by now to know his tones. There was a sadness to his voice that he would never admit to. Not fully.

The door closed in the hall and he appeared in the doorway a few moments later.

"Sorry about that," he said, moving over to the window to watch them leave.

"You don't need to apologise for anything."

"Well, I did. I realise they're not your cup of tea."

"Do I have a cup of tea?" she asked.

"You have a cup of Earl Grey, Freya. In a fine, white, bone China cup on a saucer with two little sugar cubes," he replied, then nodded out of the window. "They, on the other hand, are more your mugs of cold, weak, unbranded tea, with three helpings of sugar and a skin of milk on the top."

"Nicely put," she said, but the humour did little to elevate the mood.

"If they came here, there's definitely something wrong with Dad."

"Well, I guess you'll find out tomorrow."

He looked back at her, and she knew what he was going to say even before the words left his lips.

"There's a chance I might have to leave."

"I know," she whispered.

The idea horrified her. Never in all her career had she had the pleasure of working beside somebody so understanding, so calm, and so go-damn bloody attractive. She thought of all those times they had come close to breaking the limits of their friendship. Of all the times she had lusted after him, thought about him, even in those moments alone. Had she missed her chance?

"What will you do?"

"Life goes on," she replied, unable to utter a single word about how she truly felt, and resisting the urge to stride over to him and to make that moment count.

"Will you stay?" he asked, seemingly oblivious to the wanton expression on her face. "I mean, if Jackie goes as well? Things could be very different."

"Of course I'll stay," she replied. "We have a strong team. People move on. That's the way it works. Besides, I'll just have to have Gillespie by my side. I'm sure we'll be fine."

# CHAPTER FORTY-SEVEN

"Ah," Jim cried out, rolling onto his back to regain his breath. He felt as if he'd just been put through the force's required fitness test. Only this time, he'd finished with a grin on his face instead the usual vomiting. "That was insane."

She, however, had barely broken a sweat. Cautiously, she strode into the kitchen wearing nothing but her stockings, and returned moments later with her coat in her hand.

"Are you leaving already?" he asked, and realised that throughout the entire interaction, she had yet to utter a single word.

Instead, she reached into her coat, produced a box of cigarettes, and then lit one, tossing the coat and the cigarettes to the floor.

"I'm not done with you yet," she said, eyeing his naked, glistening body on the bed. He did his best to hide how hard he was breathing, then gave up and closed his eyes while he recovered.

Ordinarily, he would have told her he preferred for her to smoke in the garden, but that would entail her getting dressed, and he wasn't quite ready for that. Studying him from the doorway, she was as comfortable naked as she was fully clothed. Not that she had been wearing much to begin with.

"You didn't know it was me, did you?" she asked.

"Eh?" he said.

"You didn't know. I saw the look of surprise on your face."

"Aye, well, it was a bit of a surprise. But I had an idea—"

"Don't lie. You were expecting somebody else. It's okay. You can be honest."

"I had no bloody idea," he said, and gave a little, nervous laugh, which he covered with a fake cough.

"Disappointed?"

"Me? Disappointed?" he said, and looked her up and down. Sure, she was a bit rough around the edges, but she had to be five years older than he was, and she looked better than he did. He glanced down at himself then back at her. "Do I look disappointed?"

The comment raised a smile, and she blew smoke into the air, watching it disperse.

"How did you get my number?" he said.

"You gave it to me. At the school. Remember?"

"Ah, that's right. You made me sign in."

"Of course. You can't be too careful when there are so many young children about."

"Aye, agreed," he said.

She took another long drag on her cigarette, and the tip blazed bright orange in the low light.

"Can I get you a drink or something?" he asked, feeling odd that he would offer his guest a drink at this stage of the visit.

Slipping from the room, she disappeared into the bathroom. Jim heard the hiss of the burning cigarette as it hit the water in the toilet. The tap ran, the cupboard door opened and closed, and then she swilled mouthwash before emerging into the hallway, licking her lips.

"Thought I'd freshen up," she said, creeping toward the bed. "Before the second course."

Had he been given the choice, Jim would have opted to rest a while longer. Twenty minutes would have been nice. But, he told himself, duty calls.

She straddled his legs, teasing him back into action with the backs of her fingers tracing circles on his stomach and along the tops of his thighs.

"You're a piece of work, you are," he said, feeling his body react to her touch.

"I try," she said timidly. Then, biting her lower lip, she gripped his two most precious assets in her hand, staring him in the eye, unrelenting.

"Oh," he said, shocked at the sudden movement and significant discomfort, wondering if she was so forward that she might be into some kinds of weird games. That kind of thing had never really been his cup of tea, but given the circumstances, he'd try most things once.

"You will look after him, won't you?" she said.

He glanced down at her tightening hand.

"I try to look after them," he replied.

"I mean Gavin," she said, her tone serious, as if they were talking across a table in a coffee shop.

His mind wandered to Jessica in the coffee shop, thinking it was very unlikely she would be so forward, and even if it had been her that knocked on her door, he doubted she would be into the whole pleasure-pain thing.

"Gavin?" he said, only just realising what she said. "Gavin who?"

"Gavin Forbes. You know? The boy you interviewed today. My son."

"Ah well, it wasn't me that interviewed..." he began. Then his mind caught up with the conversation and he jolted her off him, and bounced off the bed to the window, suddenly finding the need to cover himself. All he could find to hand was the curtain. "You're what?"

"What's wrong?" she asked.

"Gavin Forbes? He's your son?"

"Of course. Who do you think I'm talking about?"

"Well, you can't be here," he said, hearing his voice rise a few octaves but caring little for it. "He's the main bloody..." He stopped himself from speaking and cursed himself inwardly. "You're his bloody mother? What are you doing here?"

She appeared completely relaxed, not surprised at all by his reaction, which told him all he needed to know. He'd been played. Well and truly played.

"No," he said, and she nodded. "No, you can't do this. Not to me. I've been good to you, haven't I?"

"And as I recall, I've been good to you?" she replied, giving his lower regions a furtive glance. He pulled the curtain tighter around him.

"I can't help. You've got the wrong man."

"I've got exactly the man I've wanted since I first clapped eyes on you, Jim. I just thought perhaps we could speed things up a bit, and you could help me out."

"Help you out? How can I help you out? I could lose my job over this."

"Oh, I wouldn't worry about your job too much. It's perfectly safe. However, if Gavin is arrested again–"

"Again?"

"Again," she replied with a nod. "Mr Boorman will have him expelled. I'll probably lose my job, and even if I don't, how could I possibly work there?"

"I don't understand," Jim said, although he understood all too well but could think of nothing else to say. "You used me?"

"You sound like a teenager, Jim. It's quite simple. You help

Gavin out. Make sure he gets off with a slap on the wrist. Nothing more. And I'll help you out."

"By not saying anything," he confirmed.

"By not saying anything," she agreed. "Do we have a deal?"

## CHAPTER FORTY-EIGHT

"RIGHT, LISTEN UP," FREYA SAID, CLAPPING HER HANDS ONCE to gain the team's attention. She stared out at them all, keen and alert, except for Cruz, who took every opportunity to glance down at his phone when he thought Freya wasn't looking.

But there was a gaping hole in the team. Ben's empty desk seemed larger than life. Noticeable, as if the strings of red and blue balloons were tied to the chair leg. There were no balloons, of course, but still, Freya's eye was drawn to it.

"Today we're making a splash in this case. And by a splash, I'm not talking about skimming a stone, I'm talking about a tsunami. Do I make myself clear?"

"Yes, ma'am," Chapman said. But nobody else uttered a word.

It was usual for Nillson to say nothing. She was too cool for school and gave Freya a curt nod as a response. And Cruz was paying more attention to his phone than what Freya had to say, something she would deal with shortly. But Gillespie? He was normally the loudest, with his gruff, "Aye, boss."

But he was silent. He was paying attention, at least. But he said nothing.

"Gillespie?"

"Aye, boss?"

"Are you on board with this?" she asked. "A splash? A tsunami?"

"I'm game if you are," he replied, with far less conviction than Freya was looking for. "You want me and Cruz to head down to Washingborough? Ben said something about CCTV."

"No. Change of plan," she replied. "You're with me. Ben is off today, in case you hadn't noticed."

He paled at the news but did his best to appear somewhat pleased.

"Unless, of course, you'd rather spend the day with Cruz?"

Surprisingly, he glanced across at Cruz, who looked up from his phone on hearing his name, pretending to be following what was going on.

"You'd rather spend the day with Cruz, would you?" Freya asked him.

"Well, the bloke knows me. We kind of bonded."

"You bonded with a witness?"

"I thought there was some kind of regulation against bonding with witnesses, boss," Nillson said, which raised a few smiles, and ordinarily would have invoked a retaliation from Gillespie. But again, he said nothing. Instead, he glared at her, his face a picture of guilt.

"Alright," Freya said. "You take Cruz. Nillson and I will talk to the parents. I'm pretty sure they have more to say than they've let on so far."

"Aye, boss," he replied, and his face seemed to regain some of the colour it had lost.

"Let's recap," Freya said, reengaging the team with another clap. "Simon Bird was found in the reeds on the riverbank between Washingborough and Tattershall. We know he drowned. We know he'd been sexually abused. And we know of at least two social media accounts set up with the sole purpose of bullying him. Simon Bird was not a happy soul. He had no friends. But in an attempt to make friends with Gavin Forbes and his little posse, Simon tried to demonstrate his abilities on a paddle board. However, from what I understand from the statements from Gavin's friends, Simon said something to rile Gavin. He threatened to tell the others something then he climbed onto the board to escape. Without a paddle, I might add."

"Why would anyone want to be friends with that lowlife?" Chapman voiced. "Gavin Forbes, I mean. Why would anyone want to be anywhere near him?"

"Yeah, I agree," Nillson said. "He needs a spell at Her Majesty's pleasure. That'd show him the life he's heading for. Should scare some sense into him."

"Oh, I don't know," Gillespie said. "He's not that bad."

The entire team turned to stare at him. Even Cruz looked up from his phone, a bewildered expression on his face.

"Not that bad?" he said.

"Aye, well. He's on the wrong path, granted. But maybe he just needs steering. You know? A slap on the wrist and loss of privileges."

"Simon Bird lost his life," Nillson said.

"Aye, I know that. But surely we don't think Gavin Forbes could have done that? He's just a kid."

"Let's try to stay objective, shall we, Gillespie? We work with the facts," Freya said.

She turned to Cruz, eyebrows raised, then cleared her throat. He glanced up at her, then pocketed his phone.

"How did you get on yesterday, Cruz?"

"The phone one hundred percent belongs to Gavin Forbes, boss. His email address is on it. Photos of him. Plus, the rogue social media account is on there, and it's signed in."

"So, he was behind the online bullying?" Freya asked, just for clarification.

"Looks that way, boss."

She cast a glance Gillespie's way then back to Cruz.

"Anything else?"

"Videos. The same videos that were posted on the accounts. Simon in the school showers, Simon taking a–"

"Alright, alright," Freya said. "Spare us the graphics. The facts are bad enough."

"So Gavin, it seems, is as guilty as they come, murder or no murder," Nillson said. "Still think he deserves a slap on the wrist, Gillespie?"

"Aye, well. The lad needs a wake-up call, alright. But that's all. Locking him up isn't going to solve anything. And it certainly isn't going to bring Simon Bird back. My money's on Michael Doughty. He's the only one with the means, motive, and opportunity."

"All the evidence points to him being involved. Even if it wasn't Gavin that held Simon Bird's head under the water, he had something to do with it. He was the reason Simon climbed onto that board. And in my book, that makes him guilty."

She watched Gillespie for a reaction to her statement, but he revealed very little.

"Still. Given the facts," she continued, "you're right."

"I am?"

"Michael Doughty is the only one with the MMO. However, until we can find a shred of evidence, we'll never get a warrant."

"So we need something on him?" Chapman asked.

"In the eye of the CPS, he's the victim of a crime, not a suspect. We need something to shine a different light on him."

"Well, I can tell you he's divorced."

"So am I," Freya said. "That's not a crime, as far as I know."

"But you weren't reported for interfering with a minor."

"Excuse me?"

From her seat in the corner, Chapman enjoyed a proud grin, the type that even professionalism and that great British stoicism couldn't hide.

"It's an old statement," Chapman said, reading off the screen. "Before everything was digitalised. But it's here. He was arrested under suspicion of abusing a minor. A young boy. Twenty-odd years ago."

"Tell me he was convicted," Freya said, but Chapman shook her head.

"Looks like the mother retracted the statement."

"Damn it," Freya said. "Is there nothing else?"

"Nope. Clean as a whistle since. I had to do some digging just to find this on him. Looks like our friend Michael Doughty used to go by the name of Michael Stone. I found a deed poll record created just after the sexual abuse case was dropped."

"Stone? That's the name of the old man at the community centre," Freya said. "He said something. He said something about being surprised what people see and keep to themselves."

"Do you think he was referring to his son?"

"I'm wondering if Michael Doughty is up to his old tricks," Freya said. "Good work, Chapman. Anything else?"

"Actually, yes. I was doing a bit of digging on Sally Bird, the boy's mother. Seeing as she has no way of proving where she was, I was looking through her bank records in case she had bought something, fuel or whatever."

"And you found something?" Freya asked.

"I think so. Although, it makes little sense. She rented a car. It's on her credit card statement."

"She rented a car? She already has a car. Why would she need to rent one?"

"That's not all. The same rental car was reported as being abandoned yesterday."

"Abandoned? Where?"

"Tattershall. At the little dock where Simon Bird's body was loaded onto the ambulance."

Freya digested the news with a few paces to the whiteboard and back.

"Alright," she said, raising her index finger. "Alright, we can work with this. We've got questions that need answering. That's all. Questions. Who abused Simon Bird? Who was the man on the bridge? Where was Sally Bird the night her son was killed? And why did she rent a car and leave it in Tattershall? All of those should lead us to a conclusion."

She stared around at the team. They were engaged, even Cruz. Just waiting for her instructions.

"Gillespie. Cruz. CCTV. Find the car the kids saw leaving the bridge."

"Aye, boss," Gillespie said.

"Good. Chapman, see what else you can find on Michael Doughty, or whatever his name is. Nillson and I are going to have a brief word with Sally Bird. I have a feeling she's hiding something. Grieving mother or not, she's going to talk."

## CHAPTER FORTY-NINE

THE LETTERBOX RATTLED FOR THE THIRD TIME, AND FREYA stepped back, peering up at the Bird house. The windows were closed and there was no sign of movement, not even a twitching curtain.

Nillson emerged from the side of the house a few moments later. "Anything?" she asked.

"No. She's not in. Hardly the grieving mother, is she?"

"She could have gone to a friend's house."

"She could have. You're right. But you'd think she'd answer the phone to the police officer investigating her son's murder, wouldn't you?" Freya replied. "Come on. We've got more than one fish to fry today. And I have a feeling this next fish is going to be a whopper."

They returned to Freya's car and the engine grumbled into life when Freya hit the ignition button.

"I'm going to need directions," she said, a little sheepishly. "Ben usually tells me where to turn."

"Gotcha," Nillson said. She relaxed into her seat and stared through the windscreen, waiting for Freya to move off. But she must've felt Freya's stare and returned the gaze quizzically.

"You're an excellent officer," Freya said. "Did anybody ever tell you that?"

"DI Standing rarely gave compliments," she replied. "I prefer to stay below the radar."

"Do your job and go home, you mean?"

"No. Not at all. I'm in this for the long haul," she replied with a smile. "And I'm not saying that because I'm with the boss. It's that way, by the way," she said, pointing in the direction they were facing.

"So you're looking to move up the ladder, are you?" Freya said, moving the car off.

"Eventually. When the time's right."

"Oh, trust me. The time is never right. You want my advice?"

"Go on."

"Take every opportunity you get. Get the promotion and fill in the blanks as you go. If you wait, you'll miss it."

"Is there an opportunity coming up?" Nillson said. "Is that why I'm with you today?"

"No. Well, not that I know of."

"What about Ben? Where is he? It's not like him to take a day off. I've never even known him to take leave."

"Ben's got a few family things to sort out," said Freya. "Nothing serious."

"Left here," Nillson said, guiding Freya toward the river. "Have you been invited to Pip's death party?"

"You heard about that?"

"Yeah, of course. Ever since that little soiree at your house, she's been all over me. Although, I can't say I've ever been invited to a death party. She is crazy, right? It's not just me."

"It's not just you, Anna," Freya reassured her. "I think crazy might be a little strong, but she's very different."

"Right at the top of this road," Nillson said. "Different is one way of putting it. She scares the bloody hell out of me."

"Scares you? I thought nothing scared you."

"Physically? You're right. I've got four older brothers. Psychologically? I've seen too many nutjobs go through the station. There are some absolute nutcases out there."

"You know, that kind of language could be construed as derogatory."

"Yeah, sorry, boss. It's an insult to all those who are medically insane."

Freya gave a laugh. She hadn't spent much time with Nillson, but in place of Ben, she felt her to be a good choice of partner, even if it was just for the day. The truth was that if Ben decided to abandon his career and help his family, she'd need a second pair of hands, and although Gillespie was next in line and the obvious choice, Nillson was a little more together. A strong contender.

"Do me a favour. Next chance you get, take the Sergeant exam."

She left Nillson to mull over her comment, and they rode in silence for a while, save for a few pointers from Nillson steering them in the right direction.

"It's this one," she said finally, straightening in her seat and pointing to a small turning off the lane. "All the way to the end."

Even as they approached the property, Nillson was preparing herself. She zipped her pockets, tied back her hair, and checked her boot laces.

"Expecting him to run?" Freya asked.

"I'm not expecting anything, boss. Except to be surprised."

"That's the best way," Freya replied as they emerged into a wide-open space with old boats on trailers to one side and what looked like a barn ahead of them with a pretty, little cottage beside it. A white van took pride of place closest to the adjacent cottage, so Freya parked beside it.

"What do you reckon? The barn or the cottage?"

A quick check of her watch, and Nillson stared at the cottage.

"The house," she said.

"Right then. You take the house, I'll take the barn," Freya said, as she pushed open the car door and dropped to the ground. She was pocketing her phone as Nillson stepped down. "Oh, and Anna?"

"Boss?" she replied.

"If you see him, call out, eh? I know you can handle yourself, but let's be on the safe side, given his history."

She took the instruction and deliberated for a few moments.

"Do you have the same conversation with Ben?"

It was a fair question, and there was no malice or resent in her tone.

"No. No, I don't. But then Ben isn't prone to rugby tackling fully-grown men to the ground."

"Touché."

"Besides, most suspects just drop to the ground at the sight of him. We don't have that advantage, and we're out here alone. So, we'll play it by the book, okay?"

"If you don't mind me saying," Nillson began.

"Go on."

"It's just that you don't strike me as somebody who worries about being out here alone."

"I wasn't," Freya agreed. "Until I found myself alone one day."

She winked, and leaving Nillson to ponder that cryptic clue, she made her way over to the barn. The sign on the frontage was weather-worn, as was pretty much everything in sight. There was very little of interest to Freya. Ben would have found the place fascinating, with all the ropes and engines and bits and bobs lying about. But Freya just thought the place dirty. Filthy, in fact.

But what was of interest was the little rowing boat moored to a small jetty in the river. It would take someone who knew what they were doing seconds to untie, cast off, if that's what they called it, and then get into the current. Simon Bird's body was found just a mile or so downriver, and he would have floated right past the property the paddle board was stolen from.

The barn door was unlocked, and on closer examination, Freya found the hasp and staple hanging by a single screw and mangled from being prized off. She pulled at the door then peered into the gloom. She had never been in a workshop that serviced and stored water sports equipment, but if she had been asked, she would have described the place to a tee.

Such businesses, in her opinion, were never destined to create millionaires. In her experience, the owners were extreme hobbyists looking to earn money from their passions. It was very admirable, and if they could pull it off and make a liveable income, good luck to them.

In the far corner, she found what she was looking for, a stand-up paddle board, beside a pile of bags that matched the one Cruz had found.

Each of the bags were identified with a number written with a stencil and a marker pen, and they were stacked with the number facing out. She crouched then worked her way through the bags, drawing the conclusion that numbers five and nine were missing. The bag Cruz had found in the river had been number five.

"Two missing," a voice said from behind. Startled, Freya flinched, turned, then stood to find Nillson standing there. "There's nobody about. I say we give the house a knock."

"I'm inclined to agree," Freya said with a sigh. "Come on. Let's see if he's home."

They returned to the front of the property with purpose. As far as Freya was concerned, when Doughty's record was factored in, they had plenty enough to arrest him.

"Call Sergeant Priest," she said to Nillson. "Give him our location and ask him to send a unit." She stopped at the cottage front door and rapped three times on the old, brass knocker. "We're bringing him in. Kicking and screaming if need be."

Nillson stepped away a few metres to make the call, and through the frosted glass, Freya saw a dark shape pass by.

"Mr Doughty. It's the police. Can we have a word, please?"

There was no response, and she caught Nillson watching as she spoke to Priest.

"Michael Doughty, I know you're in there. We just want to ask you a few questions," Freya called out. "I can always have a warrant brought down here. It's no skin off my nose."

At that, a bolt slid back on the far side of the door. Nillson ended her call and came to stand beside Freya. She was less than six foot, and in no way did she benefit from Ben's menacing size, but somehow, her presence was welcome. It gave Freya an odd sense of security.

The door opened a few inches and a man's face appeared in the crack.

"Mr Doughty," Freya said, opting for a cheerful yet patronizing tone. She flashed her warrant card. "Thought we'd stop by for a quick chat. Do you want to open up?"

"Now?" he said.

"It's as good a time as any. We haven't woken you, have we?"

"No."

"So, how about we get the kettle on?" Freya said. "Unless, of course, you have something to hide."

He glanced behind him then sighed audibly, and the door opened fully to reveal Michael Doughty dressed in nothing but his boxer shorts. He was a fair-haired man, with a hint of redhead in his beard and his chest hair. He stood tall, unperturbed by his attire, or lack of, in front of two strange women.

But it wasn't Michael Doughty's stare or state of undress that caught Freya's attention. It was the woman standing behind him over by the stairs.

Dressed in a man's dressing gown, her bare feet crossed for warmth, was Sally Bird.

"Ah," Freya said. "Two birds, one stone. Or should I say, one Bird, one Stone?"

## CHAPTER FIFTY

"Well," Freya said with a smile, "there's your surprise, Nillson. You said there would be one."

"It's not what it looks like," Sally said.

"No. Of course not. It never is."

"It's not. Michael's helping me."

"Is that what you call it?" Freya said. "Listen, I'm not here to police people's extra-marital affairs. I'm here to investigate the death of a young boy. So we can either come in and talk about it, or we can arrest you both and chat down at the station."

The two exchanged glances, then looked back at Freya and Nillson.

"Mine's a tea. White, no sugar," Freya said, as she stepped inside, gesturing for Nillson to follow.

"I'll, erm... I'll just get some clothes on," said Doughty.

"I'd be grateful," Freya told him, taking the opportunity to have a look around. The front door opened into an open-plan lounge and diner. The kitchen was through a small archway, built in a time when the average person was smaller than they are today. The cottage was probably listed. The furnishings were modest but tasteful.

"Where's the dog?" Nillson asked, and Freya froze. It would have been good to know about a dog before she had nosed around the property. Ben wouldn't have let a detail like that go amiss.

"It's my dad's dog," Doughty replied. "He's not here. I just walk him when my dad can't."

They waited a few seconds, just to make sure.

"It's perfectly safe to come in," Doughty said.

"I'll get the kettle on," Sally said.

"I'd be grateful for that," Freya told her, but before she followed her through to the kitchen, she gestured for Nillson to monitor Doughty. When she stepped through into the kitchen, she found it to be small. Just enough room for a couple to get by, although passing each other could be intimate.

Sally moved with familiarity, navigating the right cupboards to fetch mugs, tea bags, and sugar with ease. Then suddenly, as the kettle began to boil, she stepped over to Freya.

Freya held her ground.

"You're blocking the fridge," Sally explained, and cast her eyes down to the left.

"You seem to be quite familiar with the kitchen," Freya said, as she stepped back and Sally fetched the milk.

"If that's your roundabout way of asking how long Michael and I have been seeing each other–"

"It is," Freya said.

"Two years. Give or take."

"Two years. Wow. That would have made Simon..."

She hung on the last word, driving home her point.

"Eleven," Sally finished for her. "He was eleven years old when I started having an affair. There. I said it. Can we move on? Or do you want all the gory details?"

"Like I said, your affair is none of my business," Freya said calmly. "Unless, of course, your affair was, in some part, the reason your son was killed."

"It wasn't."

The response was calm yet defensive, but bordered on nonchalance.

"Your son is dead, Sally," Freya said, with as much empathy and compassion as she could muster. "He's gone. I've seen him. Your husband has seen him. He's gone."

"I know," she spat, and tugged at a roll of kitchen roll to wipe her eyes. "I'm his mother. Don't you think I'm hurting? It's all I think about. He's all I can see. I can't function. All I can think about is him."

"And your lover," Freya added.

"That's low."

"I say it as I see it."

"He's helping me. He loves me."

Before Freya said something she would regret, she took a breath, leaving Sally to finish making the teas. The older woman eventually slid a mug of tea towards her, then collected her own and settled into the corner of the worktop, cradling the mug with both hands. She looked tired. Clearly, and despite the dressing gown, she had made an effort with her appearance for her lover's sake. But the truth was evident in the lines around her eyes, and the slight tremble in her hands.

"Can I assume that when you left bingo on Sunday night, this is where you came?"

She nodded, then sipped at her tea.

"And you stayed here all night?" Freya asked.

"No. Michael had an early start. I left around eleven, or eleven-fifteen. Something like that."

"Why didn't you tell me, Sally? You could have saved us a lot of time."

"Oh, how could I? How would that have looked? Besides, it's not about me. It's about Simon."

She sipped at her tea again to hide her trembling lower lip, then blinked away a rogue tear that was forming.

"Seventy percent of murders in the UK are carried out by

someone close to the victim. Family members, friends, aunts, uncles, you name it, I've seen it," Freya said, leaning back to peer into the lounge, where Michael Doughty was descending the stairs. Nillson was blocking his way to the kitchen, and he peered past her anxiously as Freya returned her attention to the grieving mother. "That's why we try to eliminate the family straight away. So we can leave the family to grieve and channel our efforts somewhere useful. You should have told us. But we are where we are."

"You won't tell Hugo, will you?" Sally said.

"Your husband doesn't know? After two years?"

"It would kill him. He's not a strong man. Emotionally, I mean," she said, with a slight shake of her head. "He thinks he is. He thinks he's some kind of businessman. But really, he's not. He's..."

She stopped there.

"He's what, Sally?" Freya urged. "You can say it."

"A loser," Sally said. Her tone had lost any sign of loss and helplessness. The words seemed to come from her gut. "Michael, now he's a businessman. He has strength. Real strength."

But Sally's opinion of her husband bore little significance to Freya.

"Can you tell me why you rented a car, Sally? Especially when you have one of your own, which I presume is parked in a nearby pub car park. Am I right? In case Hugo comes sniffing?"

"Rent a car? Why would I rent a car?"

"I asked myself the same question. Especially given we found it down in Tattershall. Just a small boat ride away from here with a handy little dock to moor up."

"What are you saying?"

"I'm not. I'm asking questions, Sally. We checked your credit card statement. You rented a car from Lincs Motors."

"I don't know what you're talking about. I haven't rented a car. I've got a bloody car, and yes, it's parked up the road in the village."

"Well, your credit card suggests different. Does anyone else have access to your card, Sally?"

"Only Hugo. But he's got his own. He doesn't need my card."

"And does Hugo have his own car? I didn't see one at the house."

"No. No, we can't afford two. He rides into town. He's got a push-bike. He takes the towpath."

"I see. Well, I'm sure it will come out in the wash. I'm going to need to talk to Michael," she said. "But if I can ask just one more thing, Sally."

The woman nodded, and as if she knew what Freya would ask, she bit her lower lip in anticipation.

"Did Simon know about you and Michael?"

The lull seemed like it would never end. But it did. It was silent, and came in the form of a single nod of Sally's head, as she turned her head away to hide the inevitable tears.

# CHAPTER FIFTY-ONE

They sat in Michael Doughty's lounge. Nillson remained standing while Freya sat opposite Sally and Michael, who were holding hands. It was as if by doing so they had dragged Freya into their sordid secret.

"Michael, it might be best if we speak alone," Freya began, but the rest of her opening statement was cut short.

"Whatever you have to say to me, Sally can hear. We've no secrets."

"Well, if you're sure," Freya said, catching Nillson raise her eyebrows behind them. "You understand why we're here, don't you?"

"Not entirely, no," he replied, and the look he gave Freya dared her to accuse him.

"As you know, we found the body of a young boy not far from here. Just a little way up the river."

"Down the river," he said, correcting her.

"You're quite right," Freya said. "The thing is, Mr Doughty, he entered the water upstream, and he floated past your property sometime between four p.m. and midnight on Sunday night."

"So?"

"So, he floated by here, on one of your paddle boards."

"He stole it. I told you I lost some. I told you someone's been here," he ranted at Nillson.

"And we have no doubt the board was stolen. But that gives you a motive. Which is why we're here."

"A motive? You think I'd kill a young boy because he stole a bloody paddle board? Come on."

"You have a little boat out the back. I saw it," Freya said. "That's the means. The only thing left is an opportunity. According to Sally, she left here at around eleven p.m. on Sunday night. Leaving you alone. There's your opportunity."

"This is ridiculous. I know how the legal system works. Just because he stole a paddle board doesn't give me a reason to kill him. You're clutching at straws. That'll never stand up."

"You're right. You're totally right, Mr Doughty. We were clutching at straws. Until two keys pieces of information came my way. The first being your relationship," Freya said, and the two exchanged worried stares. "Of which I'm told Simon was aware. Is that right?"

Doughty nodded and spoke to Sally, "Do you want to explain, or should I?"

She shook her head. "You do it. I can't bear to say his name right now."

Doughty took a deep breath, made a show of holding Sally's hand even tighter, then stared Freya in the eye.

"He caught us," he began. "It was a week or so ago now. We were out by the river. I've got a little table. It's nice. When the wind isn't up, that is. Anyway. It was mid-morning. He must have seen us from the towpath. That's the only way I can imagine he could have found out."

"He was out this far? It's a long way from home for a thirteen-year-old."

"He does that," Sally said, then corrected herself. "Did that. Often. Go for walks and such. He'd walk all over."

"Did he call out when he saw you?" Freya asked.

"No. No, he didn't. We came inside hoping he hadn't seen us. He must have followed us."

"He came in the house?"

"No, I caught him looking through the window. We'd been inside for about twenty minutes. I went after him, but..."

"But?"

"Well, he got away," he said sheepishly, and Sally's face reddened.

"I see," Freya said. "I'm afraid all you've done is give yourself another motive."

"Eh?"

"He knew about your affair. What would happen if he had told his father? Sally's husband?"

"Hugo? Nothing. He's just–"

"He's just what? A loser?" Freya said, eyeing Sally to see if her expression gave anything away.

"Hugo brings his boat here. I service his engine for him and do a few bits. It's winter work, that's all. Not much call for rented paddle boards and kayaks in the winter months. That's how we met. Sally and I. Simon used to come with his dad. He used to be fascinated by the place. I guess it gave him quite a shock to see his mum here."

"Sally, did you talk to Simon about this?"

"I tried. Several times. But he wouldn't hear of it. Just shut himself away or went out. Disappeared for hours."

"Michael, I'm afraid it's not looking good for you. I understand you were here on Sunday night, but the fact remains that you had the means, motive, and opportunity to hurt Simon."

"He stole a paddle board," Doughty said, standing up and flinging his arms about. Nillson stepped forward, ready to grab him, but he calmed himself down. "I wouldn't bloody kill someone for stealing a paddle board. Or for keeping our relationship a secret. In fact, I've been asking Sally to come and live with me. Haven't I?" he said, and Sally nodded. "See. I want to tell Hugo. All this hiding around does none of us any good. My blood pressure is sky high."

"Sit down, please," Freya said, and to her surprise, he did as he was told, reaching for Sally's hand.

"Mr Doughty, what can you tell us about the allegations of sexual abuse?" Freya said. "Or should I call you Mr Stone?"

He stared at her as if she had just convinced him the earth was flat. Sally removed her hand from his and leaned away, her face a picture of horror.

"A small boy. About Simon's age," Freya said. "What can you tell us about that?"

"That was all lies. It was years ago," he began, and if Freya was honest, it wasn't the best opener. "It was false. Wrong. Damning." His breathing grew ragged and hoarse. "They got the guy. They locked him up."

"You were falsely accused, were you?"

"Exactly that. It was in the bloody local rag and everything. Destroyed me. Destroyed my business. Destroyed everything. But that was twenty years ago."

"Are you saying there was absolutely no evidence?"

"None at all. Of course there wasn't. Because I didn't bloody do anything. The charges were dropped. Course, by that point, it was too late. That's the hold they have, though. That's what you can do to a man. There doesn't need to be a shred of evidence. Doesn't even need to be a conviction. Bam. My whole life, gone. Friends, gone. Family? Disowned me. Never want to speak to me again. The only one that ever stood by me is my dad, and even that's at arm's length."

"Mr Doughty, you realise Simon Bird was sexually assaulted?" Freya said, then turned to the boy's mother. "And judging by your lack of emotion at that news, Mrs Bird, I can only assume you already knew about it."

She stared at the floor with tears rolling along the length of her nose. Car tyres crunched in the gravel outside, and Freya sucked in a long breath and looked up at Nillson, who gave her the nod, confirming the car outside was the uniforms Priest had sent.

"But I doubt he came to you, did he? I doubt he cried. He would have bottled it all up. Because that's what he did, isn't it? That's what you told me, Sally. He kept it all inside with the rest of the pain and suffering," Freya said. "I imagine you discovered it while during his laundry. That's how most parents like you find out–"

"Stop," Sally cried out. "Just stop."

But Freya was only just getting started.

"Here's what I think happened. I think Simon caught you both. I think him knowing about the pair of you somehow threatened you, Michael. So you punished him–"

"I beg your pardon," Doughty cried.

"I think you punished him the only way you know how," Freya said, raising her voice to be heard above him. "Then, last Sunday, you went to find him. But you were too late, weren't you? You were crossing Five Mile Bridge when he began floating away. So you raced back here, probably in time to see him floating past. You wanted to silence him. You couldn't have all that drama begin again, could you? No. No, you already started a new life once. A new name. A new location. There was only one thing you could do. So you killed him. You held Simon under the water."

"I did no such thing," Doughty screamed, and he jumped from his seat again, knocking the coffee table so hard an old newspaper that was resting on the little shelf beneath the table slid off, spilling its supplementaries across the floor by Freya's feet.

But it wasn't the fashion guide or the spring travel planner that caught Freya's eye. It was the little rectangle of plastic that was on the lower shelf.

She reached down and picked it up by its edges, and she studied the name on the front.

"Mrs S A Bird," Freya said. "Can you tell me how your credit card came to be here, Sally?"

Doughty was wide-eyed. He stared hopefully at Sally, who was equally dumbstruck.

"No. No, I didn't put that there," he said. "I've never seen it before."

"So how did it get there?" Freya asked.

He stared at her, panic forming in his eyes. He swallowed, then looked up at the door as a means of escape.

"What you do next could have a major impact on the rest of your life, Michael," Freya warned him. But she remained seated and calm, waiting for him to seal his own fate.

But he lingered too long.

Nillson was ready at the door, opening it just in time for the two uniforms to step inside and stop Doughty before he did something he would regret.

"Michael Doughty, I'm arresting you on suspicion of murder," Freya began. "You do not have to say anything. But it may harm your defence if you do not mention when questioned something which you later rely on in court. Anything you do say may be given in evidence."

"You can't arrest him," Sally protested. "He's done nothing wrong. It wasn't him. I know it wasn't."

"DC Nillson," Freya said. "Arrest her."

"What? You can't arrest me. I'm the boy's mother."

"And until you can prove me wrong, Mrs Bird," Freya said, "I believe you were an accessory. Nillson, nick her, and get Sergeant Priest on the phone. I want this house turned upside down."

# CHAPTER FIFTY-TWO

OUTSIDE MICHAEL DOUGHTY'S COTTAGE, FREYA AND NILLSON watched the uniforms load Sally and her lover into the waiting car. More units were on the way, along with a warrant to search the premises.

"It's a shame Ben isn't here to see this," Nillson said.

"It is. But he has bigger things on his mind," Freya replied, then moved the conversation on before Nillson asked a question she would have to refuse to answer. "Do you agree with my theory?"

"On Doughty? Yeah. It makes sense. If Simon Bird caught Michael Doughty and Sally in a compromising position, then he could have destroyed quite a few lives. I think Doughty ran after him. I think what you said was right. He caught Simon, and his urges took over. He couldn't help himself."

"And the man on the bridge?"

"It has to be Doughty. It takes about ten minutes to drive here from Five Mile Bridge. How long would it take to float down the river?"

"Except one thing makes little sense. Simon died at around midnight. He would have floated by here around four-thirty.

Whether or not Doughty saw him floating by, what happened in that seven and a half hours? If Doughty rushed back here, even if he had missed Simon floating by, it wouldn't take seven hours to row downstream with the current to where Simon was murdered. That's a hole in the timeline that any decent lawyer will pick up on."

"What about the car? Why did Doughty rent the car?"

"He must have planned it. When was the car rented?"

"On the Saturday," Nillson said, then she caught up with Freya's idea. "What if he knew it was Simon who had stolen the paddle board? He would have known Simon was a loner. He could have set it up somehow."

"That's good," Freya said. "Keep it going."

"He also would have known that Five Mile Bridge was the nearest part of the river to where Simon lived. What if he followed him there? But then stopped when he saw all the other kids?"

"It's plausible. And then what?"

"Well, the statements we have suggested the man on the bridge ran back to his car when Simon floated off. All Doughty had to do was catch Simon up. He headed him off here. Maybe he actually got Simon out of the water and held him until it was dark."

"When Simon's mother went home," Freya added, and they both stared at the workshop.

"How would Doughty have known it was Simon who stole the paddle board?" Nillson mused aloud.

They strolled around to the back of the workshop and pushed the door open. The idea that Simon Bird could have been held captive there during the seven hours cast the place in a new light. With the ropes, the shadows, and all the equipment, it was ideal.

"We're need CSI here," Freya said.

"I'll get onto it," Nillson replied, but then she cocked her head, staring up into the beams near the counter that was shaped like the hull of a boat. "What's that?"

Freya followed her gaze. A tiny, blue light flashed in the surrounding gloom, way above head height.

"That's a camera," Freya said. "It looks like one of those internet cameras. You know? Like the one Gillespie said the runner has on the side of his house."

"He told me he didn't have any cameras," Nillson said.

"Why would he lie?" Freya asked, needing no reply. "That's how he knew it was Simon who stole the paddle board."

"He must have installed it after David Stills stole the first one," Freya said. "Right? But he didn't fix the lock. He wanted them to come in. He wanted to see who it was."

She marched outside, more convinced than ever that Michael Doughty was their man. All they needed was CSI to find the forensic evidence to support the claim. They strode around to the front of the building where Freya's car sat beside Doughty's van.

"He wouldn't use his own van. That would be a dangerous move. So he used Sally's credit card to hire a car. Probably thinking that we wouldn't check her bank details. She's the mother, after all."

Nillson nodded in agreement.

"Everything points to Doughty," Nillson said. "But the only bit that makes little sense to me is the bag Cruz found. How would Doughty have got his hands on Gavin Forbes' clothes and his phone? What's the link between Doughty and Forbes?"

Freya eyed the Detective Constable. She was right. It was a fairly minor detail, but it carried enough weight to throw Freya's confidence off-balance.

Nillson left Freya to ponder the thought and browsed the skeletal remains of the boats on trailers parked on the far side of the little car park. There were several tarpaulin-covered trailers, all lined up as if they were waiting in line to be scrapped. Then her head cocked to one side, and she pointed.

"That's not a boat."

Freya followed her gaze.

"You're right," she said, and they both immediately made their way over to the line of retired water craft. Sitting between two small boats, perhaps disguised to blend in with the neighbouring trailers, was a vehicle. A heavy, blue tarpaulin had been pulled across it, with a few old, broken bricks weighing down each corner. Nillson kicked the bricks away from one corner, grabbed hold of the tarpaulin, and looked up at Freya.

"Are you ready for this, boss?" she asked, and Freya nodded.

She whipped the tarpaulin back to reveal a white Toyota hatchback. A layer of mud and grime covered the doors and the wings, but the tyres were inflated, and it appeared to be roadworthy.

A vibration in Freya's pocket distracted her, and while peering through the driver's window, she pulled the phone from her pocket.

"Gillespie, give me some good news."

"I've got the CCTV, boss," he said, sounding pleased with himself. "A car drove past at three fifty-five, heading toward the bridge."

"That has to be our man," Freya said. "And what time did it leave?"

"About five past four. And he was in a hurry."

"Can you see the number plate? Tell me you can get the number plate?"

"Sorry, boss. No can do. It's too blurred. I can send it to the tech guys, but the camera has a low frame rate. It's not really designed to capture high-speed images."

"Okay, okay. Send it. But at least tell me the make and the color. Actually, you know what? Don't tell me," Freya said, smiling inwardly. "Tell me it's a white Toyota hatchback."

"Eh? A what?"

"The car, Gillespie. Is it a white Toyota hatchback?"

"No. This is a Volvo boss. A grey Volvo estate," he said. Then, after a long pause, he cleared his throat. "What do you want us to do?"

"I want Gavin Forbes in for questioning again," Freya said. "We're missing something, and he knows what it is."

## CHAPTER FIFTY-THREE

THE INCIDENT ROOM DOORS SQUEALED OPEN WHEN FREYA burst into the room in a flurry of coat tails.

"Chapman, good work on Sally Bird. Do me a favour, stay in touch with Michaela from CSI. She's at Michael Doughty's property with her team right now. Nillson and I found a camera. I want to know what she finds."

"No problem," Chapman replied, dragging her desk phone closer as she prepared to make the call.

Nillson took her seat, opened her laptop, but waited for Freya's instruction. It was times like this that Freya needed Ben. He wouldn't have waited. He would have been pushing Freya to interview Doughty. But something wasn't right. The bag Cruz had found just didn't fit with Michael Doughty being the killer.

"Let's go over the facts," Freya said, very aware that two of her team were missing. She hadn't really noticed Gold's absence until now. But she was reminded of the part Jackie Gold played on the team. She was the heart and the kindness. She could get through to a youngster like Gavin Forbes with ease. "We know Simon Bird floated down the river at around four p.m. on Sunday. We know

Gavin Forbes was with him, maybe even scared him onto the paddle board. That makes him involved."

"Do you want me to get uniform to bring him in?" Chapman asked.

"Thanks, but no. I've sent Gillespie and Cruz," Freya replied. "We also know that Michael Doughty is in a relationship with Mrs Bird. According to Doughty, Simon caught them in the act and Doughty went after him."

"Oh God, imagine that?" Chapman said. "Poor kid."

"And given Doughty's history, there's a strong chance when he caught up with the boy, his urges took over."

"Hence the injuries Doctor Bell found," Nillson added.

"Right," Freya agreed. "That gives him a motive. I've seen the property. There's a good chance that if Doughty was the man on the bridge, he headed Simon off and held him in his workshop until after dark. Then he used his rowing boat to get rid of the body."

"But what about the bag with all Gavin Forbes' stuff in?" Chapman asked.

"Yeah, we thought the same," Nillson said. "Also, Gillespie found CCTV footage of the car our man on the bridge left in."

"Oh, really?" Chapman said, stopping her typing for the first time, and leaning forward to get the details.

"Grey Volvo," Nillson said. "Going too fast to see the plates, though."

"Grey Volvo?" Chapman repeated.

"The rental," Freya said. "What was the rental? If it's a grey Volvo, we're in luck."

"No. It was black," Chapman said, as she clicked a few times on her mouse. "Yep. Black Nissan."

"Bloody hell," Freya said. "Where has a grey Volvo come from? Hugo Bird doesn't drive. His wife drives an old hatchback. Doughty drives a van and has a white Toyota. And the rental is a black Nissan. Who owns a grey Volvo estate?"

"I can run some checks," Chapman said. "I might be able to narrow it down a little."

"Do it," Freya said, then returned to voicing their progress. "We also found Sally Bird's credit card in Doughty's house."

Chapman looked up from her keyboard. "So it was him that rented the car?"

"Seems to be," Freya said. "I think Doughty was going to use the car to get rid of Simon's body. But something happened. Something caused him to change his plans and dump Simon in the reeds."

"Unless, of course, Hugo Bird knew about his wife's affair," Nillson suggested.

Freya looked up at her, waiting for Nillson to back her statement up, as Ben would have.

"Just an idea, boss," she said.

It was a good idea, but her lack of supporting statement showed how far behind she was. What she needed was for Nillson to capture her attention with the statement, and then convince her of its plausibility.

Instead, Freya had to supply her own theory.

"Okay. Okay," she said. "We can work with that. Hugo knows the Doughty place well. He gets his boat engine serviced there."

"And he has a boat. If he knew when Sally was off with her lover, he could have easily taken a ride downriver and set Doughty up."

"Set him up?" Nillson said. "Do you think he could be that calculating?"

"He could have planted the credit card," Freya said. "Doughty looked surprised when I found it."

"Yeah, but come on. Sally was right there. He was hardly likely to fall to his knees and apologise."

"True, but it appeared genuine. No matter how well he fits our criteria."

Freya paced up to the whiteboard. They appeared to have

made no progress. Nobody had been eliminated, yet they had unearthed more evidence. It was chaos. In fact, it was so chaotic it was almost perfect.

"And we still have the issue of the bag Cruz found," said Nillson. "How does the bag fit into either Doughty or Hugo Bird being the killer?"

"It doesn't. That's the problem," Freya said. "And Hugo was seen on his boat in Brayford Pool the night Simon was killed. CCTV showed that."

"No, CCTV showed Hugo Bird leaving his boat at around eleven p.m. All we know is that his boat didn't leave Brayford Pool. Hugo left on his push-bike."

"He uses the footpath beside the river to get home. Sally said so," Freya said. "He would have known Michael Doughty has a rowing boat."

"That gives him the means and the opportunity," Nillson said. "But what's his motive for killing his own son?"

"We've got Michael Doughty. But before I interview him under caution, let's focus on Hugo Bird. First of all, he discovered the body. That doesn't make him guilty, but think about it. He's the boy's father. He'd want him to be discovered, rather than just floating there for days. He would have known he had a tour the next day, which would have given him the perfect opportunity to make sure his customers discovered the body. He could easily have rented the car. All he had to do was take his wife's credit card, ride down Doughty's place on his way home, and get inside. You saw the place. It's hardly Fort Knox, is it?"

"Yeah, but how would he know Simon was on the river on a paddle board at that time?" Nillson said. "That doesn't add up. And we still have the issue of Gavin Forbes' belongings in the bag. Michael Doughty had the means, the motive, and the opportunity. Hugo Bird had the means and the opportunity. But not the motive."

"Not that we know of," Freya said, meeting her stare. "But it feels right. It feels like we're on the right track."

"We've got Michael Doughty and Sally Bird in custody, boss."

"Well then, they're not going anywhere, are they?" Freya snapped, as she headed towards the door. "I'll be back in a minute."

"Ma'am," Chapman called out. "Before you go, that was Michaela from CSI on the phone."

"Okay?"

"The camera you found in Doughty's workshop. It's one of those that connects to your Wi-Fi, so you can see it even when you're out. From where it was positioned, the camera could see across the driveway, and the workshop."

"So that's how Michael Doughty knew it was Simon who stole the paddle board," Freya said.

"Not quite, ma'am," Chapman continued. "The camera is linked to an account owned by Gavin Forbes. It's the same email address the social media account used. They've looked at the phone Cruz found in the bag and the app is installed on there. It looks like Gavin Forbes set the camera up."

# CHAPTER FIFTY-FOUR

"Ah, Freya. Just the person," DCI Granger called out as she passed his office. She took a step back and peered through his open door, waiting for him to continue without committing to stepping inside his office. "I see you've brought in a Michael Doughty and the boy's mother."

"That's right, guv."

"Any reason the boy's mother is here?"

"Accessory, guv."

"Can we prove it?"

"I'm doing my damndest. I've got them for another twenty-two hours, unless, of course, CPS grant us an extension."

"What grounds do you have?" he asked, as Freya prepared to continue on to the washroom.

"What grounds? Her credit card was used to rent a car, she's in a relationship with the lead suspect, and she's lied about her whereabouts. Will there be anything else, guv? Only I'm in a bit of a rush."

"I need to give another press release tomorrow morning. I'd like to announce some kind of progress. You know what they're like."

"I'll give you an update as soon as I can," Freya replied, getting more desperate the longer she stayed there.

"Are you okay, Freya?" he asked.

"Just on my to the washrooms, guv. Women's stuff."

"Ah, well. You'd better go and..." he said without finishing, and gave her a wave of his hand to dismiss her. Then he called out to her, "Just get me that update, Freya. I need something to tell them."

"Leave it with me, guv," she called back, then burst into the washroom, just as her phone rumbled into life.

Ben's name displayed on the screen, and she both cursed and smiled inwardly, as she leaned on the basin, staring into the mirror as she answered the call.

"Ben," she said, trying her best not to sound breathless.

"Are you running?" he said, and she grimaced at her failure.

"Nope, I'm just... It doesn't matter. What's the news?"

"You first?" he said, sounding relaxed, as though he was sitting back in his armchair with all the time in the world.

"We've got Doughty and Sally Bird in custody," she said. "Chances are Doughty is our man on the bridge. But a few things don't stack up, so I'm just ironing out any creases before I interview him."

"What doesn't stack up?"

"The bag that Cruz found. Everything else points to him. He has access to the river. He had the opportunity. And given that Simon caught him and his mother in a compromising position a couple of weeks ago, I'd say he had the motive."

"Simon's mother?" Ben said. "What? The two of them were—"

"Yes, Ben. At it."

"So how does that give him a motive?"

"Doughty has previous charges dropped."

"What charges?"

"Sexual abuse. A little boy about the same age as Simon."

"No way."

"This was twenty years ago. Since then, he's changed his name and started a new life. As I understand it, he wasn't made to feel too welcome after the event, despite his apparent innocence. From what I gather, Simon caught his mother at Doughty's house and Doughty ran after him."

"And you think it was him who abused Simon?" Ben asked.

"There's a chance. Something isn't right. I know we're on the right track here."

"But no proof? You can't use a twenty-year-old report against him, especially if the charges were dropped."

"I know that, and you know that, but I can use it to apply some pressure on him," Freya said. "Hang on. You just said *I* can't. What happened to *we* can't?"

"Did I?"

"Ben? What's happened?"

"Oh, you know," he replied, the excitement gone from his voice.

The conversation had gone on for longer than Freya had thought, and she couldn't hang up now. She closed the cubicle door as quietly as she could and filled the toilet with paper towels.

"No, Ben. I don't know."

"Looks like Dad is going to have to wind it down. Johnny Grouch delivered some bad news today. Dad is going to take more of a management role."

"They need you to go and help?" Freya said, as she slid her trousers down and took her seat. "Tell me what happened. Every detail."

She muted her end of the call and listen to him as the pressure in her bladder eased. It had to be one of the greatest sensations the human body offered, she thought, mid-way through.

"Well, apparently what I've seen isn't the half of it," Ben said. "Do you remember what they said about him losing the keys to the grain store?"

Freya clenched, unmuted the call, and said, "Yep."

"Well," Ben continued, giving Freya time to mute the call and relax once more, "apparently, there are loads of stories. Lost keys. He even forgot to book the lorries last harvest. They had a hundred tons of wheat ready to go and nobody to collect it. It's a bloody miracle it didn't rain. Do you know how much that's worth?"

Freya grimaced, unmuted the call, and gave him a negative response, before resuming what she was doing as quickly as she could.

"The long and short of it is, Freya, I can't see a way around it. I have to help them out. It's the family business."

By the time he'd explained all this, Freya had completed her transaction and was pulling up her trousers.

"So you're calling to say you won't be back?" Freya said. She clamped the phone to her face with her shoulder and washed her hands, dreading the next part of the conversation.

"I thought you should know," Ben mumbled. "I can't see a way out of it."

"We're in the middle of an investigation, Ben."

"You've got Gillespie," Ben said.

"Oh, come on. He's inconsistent."

"What about Nillson? She's good. She's ready to move up."

"I have no doubt she's ready to move up. But..."

"But what, Freya?" he said.

"She's not you, Ben," she said. "I need you by my side. The only reason I've got through these past six months is because of you."

"Freya, come on. Don't say that. This is hard enough."

"I know. I know. It's unprofessional. But I have to say it. I feel like I'm on my own here."

"Freya—"

"What have you told them?" Freya asked. "Your brothers? What did you commit to?"

"I just said I'd talk it through with you."

"Do you want to meet up and talk about it?" Freya said.

"At the station? I'd prefer to come to yours or something."

"Meet me in the city. I'm on my way there now."

"Alright," he said, after a pause. "I can be there in about twenty-five minutes."

"Good. Meet me at Brayford Pool. I need to go and see Hugo Bird."

"Is that where he is?" Ben said. "Hang on. I'm not getting roped into the investigation, Freya. If I'm out then I'm out."

"You haven't quit yet," Freya reminded him. "And besides, he wasn't at home when I knocked."

"I know. I had a call from that FLO, PC Reed. She said neither Sally nor Hugo Bird have been seen all day. Seems pretty odd for a couple who just lost their son."

"Well, we've got Sally here," Freya said, smiling to herself at how easy it was to drag him back into the investigation.

"And Hugo?"

"Help me out this one last time, Ben. Meet me there."

He sighed audibly.

"Only if you promise me one thing."

"What's that?" she replied.

"The next time you use the loo when you're on the phone to me, you mute your microphone."

"I did," she said, hearing the indigence in her own voice. "Didn't I?"

"No, Freya. I don't know what button you pushed, but you certainly did not mute the call," Ben said. "I'll see you in twenty-five minutes."

# CHAPTER FIFTY-FIVE

"I SHOULD PROBABLY WAIT IN THE CAR," GILLESPIE SAID TO Cruz as they cruised Lincolnshire's country lanes on their way to Gavin Forbes' house. "You know? Just in case Ben or the boss call."

"Wait in the car?" Cruz said, panicking. "You expect me to go in on my own?"

"For Christ's sake, Gabby. It's not Al Capone we're bringing in for questioning. It's a wee thirteen-year-old kid. Surely you can handle a kid?"

"Well, yeah. But it's not protocol, is it?" Cruz said. "We're supposed to do it together. We're supposed to have a witness."

"Protocol?" Gillespie said. "Since when have you ever been worried about protocol? I seem to remember when it was you who wanted to wait in the car whenever we had to do something a wee bit risky. I didn't cite the bloody protocol at you, did I? Besides, we've got two uniforms meeting us there. They can be your witnesses, Gabby. Why are you making such a big deal out of it?"

"Me? You're making a big deal out of it. You're the one insisting on sending me alone."

"With uniforms," Gillespie added. "Anyway. I don't do it often, but I'm pulling rank. It's an order. Do you have a problem with that?"

"Well, no. But–" Cruz began.

"Ah, well, that's that then," Gillespie said. "You go and nick the kid. Hand him over to uniform. And I'll keep the engine running. We'll be back in time for lunch. Job done."

Gillespie turned into the road and made a show of searching for the right house, making it clear to Cruz that the debate was over.

"There it is," Cruz said, his tone sullen and sulky. "On the left."

Gillespie indicated, although the street was quiet, and let the car roll past the house, coming to a stop outside the house next door but one.

Cruz leaned forward to peer into the wing mirror, then looked across at Gillespie, confused.

"You overshot."

"Ah, we'll be fine just here."

"Aren't you going to reverse up a bit?"

"Eh? No. No need. You can walk the extra few steps. Won't do you any harm. Besides, uniform will park outside. It'll be easier to get the lad in the back."

"Easier?" Cruz said. "You said it yourself. It's a thirteen-year-old kid."

"Aye, but you know what they can be like. Spritely wee bastards, some of them. No. We'll stay here. I can keep an eye on things from here."

"You're up to something," Cruz said.

"Eh? Me?"

"Yeah. You're up to something. I can hear it in your voice."

"Ah, don't be daft, Gabby."

"You are. There's something you're not telling me."

"Ah, behave. You're the one with the secrets. All that talk

about magic and stuff. Don't think I'd forgotten about that. I know there's something you're not telling me, laddy. And I'll get to the bottom of it."

"You're trying to deflect the attention to me," Cruz said, and his unrelenting persistence told Gillespie he wasn't going to get away without giving the lad something to chew on. "You're avoiding the house. First, you don't want to go into the house. Now you're parked halfway down the road."

"I'm two houses away, Gabby."

"You're acting weird. You know something," Cruz said, just as the liveried car rolled past slowly. Gillespie jabbed his thumb over his shoulder, gesturing to the driver for them to park behind. But Cruz was unrelenting. "No. You're hiding something."

The police car had barely stopped when the front door of the Forbes front door opened and a familiar figure stepped into view wearing a towel dressing gown. She folded her arms and leaned on the door frame, her expression confident.

Cruz caught Gillespie looking in the rear-view mirror, and after a quick check of the wing mirror, saw what he was looking at.

"The boy's mother?" Cruz said. "Is that who you're hiding from?"

"Leave off, Gabby," Gillespie said.

"I'm right, aren't I?" he said, sounding as if he'd surpassed his own ingenuity. "You're hiding from her. It's written all over your face."

"You've got no idea what you're talking about," Gillespie said, watching Cruz study the woman in the wing mirror.

"Well, you'd better duck down, mate. She's coming this way."

Foregoing the rear-view mirror, Gillespie turned in his seat. Joanne Forbes was strolling towards the car, peering through the back window. He turned to face the front.

"If you want me to help, you're going to have to talk to me," Cruz said.

"Alright," he said. "Alright. She came to my house last night."

"You what?"

"I didn't know who she was," Gillespie explained.

"So you let a stranger in?"

"No. It's not like that. I thought it was..."

"Go on," Cruz said. "You thought it was who?"

"Somebody else," Gillespie said, watching her from the safety of the mirror now. He sank in his seat to hide behind the head-rest. "It's a long story."

"I've got a while. Why don't we start from the beginning?" Cruz said, enjoying every moment of Gillespie's torture.

"She told me who she is. But by then it was too late."

"You slept with her?" he shouted.

"For Christ's sake, Gabby," Gillespie said, hushing him.

"You slept with a suspect's mother?"

"Aye, yeah, I did. And I'm not proud of it. It was a mistake. A wee mistake, that's all."

"The boss is going to hang you out to dry, Jim."

"Aye, don't you think I know that?"

"What are you going to do?"

"I don't bloody well know, do I? I had planned on sending you in so I don't have to see her."

"Are you seeing her again?" Cruz said, clearly making a joke at Gillespie's expense.

"Ah, listen. She wants me to get her wee lad off. You know? See if I can sway things."

"You didn't agree to that?"

"No, of course I didn't. It's just that if Gavin Forbes is charged, then she'll make sure DI Bloom finds out about us."

"Oh, Jesus, Jim."

"I know, right?"

"I thought my secret was bad. You're screwed. Her son is as guilty as they come."

"Thanks for the vote of confidence," Gillespie said, eyeballing

Joanne. She was beside the liveried car being questioned by one of the uniforms. "Please, mate. Help us out here, eh? Talk to her. Get the lad in the car, and let's never speak of this again."

Cruz puffed his chest out and smiled.

"Alright. On one condition."

"Condition? You little—"

"Alright, if you don't want me to keep your dirty secret."

"Okay, okay," Gillespie said. "What's the condition?"

"You stop taking the piss out of me."

"Eh?"

"I mean it. No more sly digs at my size, at the way I am, or anything. In fact, not just no more sly digs. I want you to big me up to people. I want to be taken seriously and I can't do that with you making fun of me all the bloody time. Anything you know about me stays a secret. Or I'll tell."

"Jesus, what are we back at school now, are we?"

"I mean it."

"Okay, okay. No more taking the piss out of you."

"And?"

"And I'll big you up whenever I need to."

"And?"

"All your secrets are my secrets," Gillespie said with a sigh. Ridiculing Cruz was one of the highlights of his day. He'd just cut his daily laughter down by at least fifty percent.

"Good," Cruz said, his hand on the door handle.

"Wait," Gillespie said, with one eye on Joanne in the mirror.

"What?"

"What's the thing with the magic?" Gillespie asked. "It's been driving me crazy trying to figure it out."

## CHAPTER FIFTY-SIX

Freya felt as if she hadn't seen Ben for months, yet it had been less than a day. He sauntered over to where she was waiting, his long legs giving him a casual, albeit clumsy, gait.

"Alright," he said, refusing to meet her stare. He looked around at the boats and the line of restaurants and the cinema on the far side of the water, and he took a breath. "Seems like you're in a bit of a pickle."

"*We*, Ben. *We're* in a pickle."

He gave an unconvincing laugh. "Of course."

"Are you really going to do it?" she asked. There, she had said it. She had told herself she wouldn't press him, but the thought of him leaving was unbearable.

"Freya, don't," he said, then sighed. "Jeff said Dad's been on at them to get me to go back on the farm for months. He reckons Dad knew he was getting worse before any of us did. It's got to the point where he's making mistakes. Big mistakes. Dangerous mistakes. What am I supposed to do? He refuses to bring anyone else into the business. Even Johnny Grouch."

"Sounds like it's you who's in the pickle," Freya said. Then she found his wandering gaze and held it. "Finish this investigation with me. Go out on a bang, eh?"

He pondered it for a moment. Too long, she thought. But he nodded. "Alright. What are we doing?"

"Hugo Bird," Freya said, nodding at the line of boats. "He's got some explaining to do before we interview Doughty and Sally Bird."

"So let's do it," Ben said, and he led the way. His long strides forced Freya to walk fast. It was as if he didn't want to get too close. Or worse. That he was pulling away.

Brayford Pool offered ample mooring for the various boats that occupied the spaces. At one end of the dock, more than a dozen houseboats floated side by side. The rest of the mooring facilities were home to smaller pleasure crafts that bobbed gently on the calm water. There were small fishing boats, cruisers, and then there was Hugo Bird's tourist boat. It was old. Even from a distance, Freya could see it had weathered many a winter Lincolnshire storm.

A heavy diesel engine fired up from the jetty beside Hugo Bird's, and a man on a houseboat looked across at them. He finished coiling a length of rope, eyeing them with caution.

"Nice day for it," Ben said, and the man nodded a sour-faced greeting, then zipped his coat up and disappeared inside.

"I thought living in a campervan was bad," Freya said, eyeing the houseboat with disdain. "But at least it stayed still."

Ben laughed once. "It's all about perspective, I guess. There's always somebody with different problems to your own, right?"

"Right," she agreed.

They stepped onto the wooden jetty and made their way along, seeing Hugo at work on the boat, busying himself with maintenance.

"So, let me get this straight," Ben said. "Michael Doughty used to be called Michael Stone?"

"He changed his name following the sexual abuse allegations,"

Freya explained. "I'm not sure if that's public knowledge. So keep it to yourself. The last thing we need is for the press to find out."

"So he started over? A new life, as it were."

"Yes. From what Chapman told me, he took everything he had, bought the old house on the river, and started his business again. Witham Water Sports."

"You know, the thing is, I bet nobody even looked for him."

"Only his dad still speaks to him. Imagine that? Losing everyone you loved over a false allegation."

They came to a stop beside the boat, and beginning at Freya's feet, Hugo Bird's gaze worked its way up to meet her stare.

"We found the rental car, Hugo," she called out above the noise of the houseboat. It was a purposeful statement, designed to invoke an involuntary response, offering some kind of clue as to his knowledge of the rental. It even took Ben by surprise.

And for Hugo, it worked.

Hugo gave a sigh and dropped to sit on the side of the boat, then rested his head in his hands and sobbed.

Lifting her leg over the side of the boat, Freya stepped on and took a moment to get her balance. Then, with Ben holding the boat steady, she sat down beside Hugo.

"Do you want to tell me about it?" she said. "Start from the beginning. You'll feel better to get it off your chest."

She gave him a minute to collect his thoughts and control his sobbing. He wiped away the tears, but they continued to flow regardless, and he gave a loud sniff before exhaling through pursed lips.

"He was desperate and unhappy," Hugo started. "Simon, that is. I couldn't bear to see it. I was powerless to do anything about it."

"Why? Why was he unhappy? Because of the bullying?"

"Partly. He was like me. That's not exactly a joyous ambition, is it? Destined to become a worthless piece of dirt like me. Like my father too. We all are."

"You've got your own business, Hugo."

"My own business. It barely breaks even. I had dreams, you know? I had dreams I could start over. Take Simon and go somewhere new. Somewhere we wouldn't be losers." He raised his head from his hands and peered at Freya through bloodshot eyes. "I suppose you know about Sally?"

"I'm afraid you'll have to give me more than that," Freya said.

"The affair," he said. "Her and that bastard, Doughty."

"Yes. Yes, we found out this morning," she said, and he studied her expression, perhaps guessing that she had found his wife at Michael Doughty's house.

"Simon knew as well. Kept it from me. We were supposed to be buddies. He bloody well hid it from me. Let me carry on like everything was rosy. Like the bloody fool I am."

"I don't think he had much choice," Freya told him.

"Oh, he had a choice, alright. But he waited. He waited until I was on my knees. Until Sally had ignored dozens of my calls and I was broken. Then he told me. He pitied me. My own son pitied me. He never used to be like that. He never used to be so strong. But recently, he changed."

"In the past week or so?" Freya asked, and he nodded.

"Something happened. He got into trouble at school. He was late home. Detention or something. With the headmaster too. You know when your kid's in trouble when the headmaster oversees their detention."

"What did he get into trouble for?"

"Something to do with that Gavin Forbes lad. I don't know. But ever since then, he was different."

"Not last weekend?" Freya asked. "He didn't change last weekend?"

"No. It was during the week. I told you. The detention," Hugo said. "Whatever happened with Gavin Forbes changed him. He seemed to be in control suddenly."

"In control?"

"Yeah, like he'd had enough, or like he had found the strength to let the bullying and the name-calling just slide off him. Even Sally barking at him from the bottom of the stairs just made him smile, like it pleased him to see her angry. He was a different kid."

"And you?" Freya asked. "Were you upset with him for not telling you about your wife and Michael Doughty?"

The houseboat with the noisy diesel engine floated away from its mooring, and the chugging they'd had to shout to be heard above went with it.

"Of course," Hugo said, speaking quietly now. "Who wouldn't be? But it wasn't his fault. He wasn't trying to protect her, he was protecting me. He didn't want to see me upset."

"But you grew upset anyway," Freya said.

"Eventually, yes. When she disappeared and I broke down. It took a lot for him to tell me. A lot of strength, you know?"

He dropped his head into his hands again, clearly internalising his pain. Bottling it up.

"I can imagine," Freya said, then steeled herself. "Hugo, did you have anything to do with Simon's death?"

He stopped his sobbing long enough for him to look up at her. He didn't even wipe his eyes. Instead, he just looked appalled at the question.

"Me? Why would I do something like that to my own flesh and blood?"

"Did you try to frame Michael Doughty, Hugo? We found Sally's credit card in his house. We know he used to service your boat, so you're familiar with his property."

"Frame him?" he said, but his voice lacked conviction. He stared past Ben, perhaps gauging his chances of escape. But then he sighed again, and his demeanour altered. He was surrendering.

"The more you tell us, the easier this will be," Ben said.

"Simon came to me last week," he began. "I told you, he was like a different person. It was when I broke down. When he told me about Sally and...and that man."

Hugo stared between them, making sure they were both listening, and he told his tale with sincerity.

"What did he say, Hugo?" Ben asked.

"He told me everything was going to be okay. He said we should leave. You know? Like I said. Start a new life somewhere. Anywhere. It didn't matter where. Just the two of us. I asked him what had brought all this on and then he told me what he had been doing when he heard me crying."

"And what was that?" Freya asked, although she had an inclination of what he might say.

"He took me to his bedroom. He'd lined up all the pills in the house. My scotch from the cupboard downstairs was there. He was going to do it. But hearing me and seeing me like that, it showed him he wasn't alone. We were both miserable. We were both fed up. Don't you see?"

"I'm getting there," Freya admitted. "But go on."

"He said we could leave. He knew a way to make everything better. To make everyone pay."

"Make everyone pay?" Freya said. "Revenge?"

Hugo nodded. "He had a plan."

"What was his plan?"

"I don't know. He wouldn't tell me. He said if I knew then I'd be as guilty as him."

"So you knew he was going to do something serious?" Freya said.

"Well, yes, but I had no idea what it was. He said I was to meet him. In Tattershall. You know? The little dock there."

"I know it," Freya said, remembering the sight of the body bag on the wooden slats.

"Monday morning. That was when we were supposed to meet. He told me to bring everything I needed. We wouldn't be coming back. He told me that whatever happened, everything would be okay."

"Are you saying that Simon arranged everything?"

Hugo nodded and smiled fondly. "I always knew he was a smart kid. Deep down, like. I knew he'd break the mould. He could have been somebody, you know?"

"So Simon used his mother's credit card to rent the car?" Ben asked. "And no doubt had it delivered to Tattershall?"

"Suppose so," Hugo said, smiling proudly.

"And I suppose Simon planted the card in Doughty's house?" Ben said. "Is that possible?"

"It's poorly secured," Freya said. "He could have got in any of the windows."

"What about the bag?" Ben asked.

"What bag?" Hugo said.

"We found a bag with Gavin Forbes' clothing in. And his phone, too."

That's when it hit Freya. "The phone. The camera in Doughty's place was connected to the phone, because Simon had it. Gavin Forbes lost his phone. He said so. Simon was watching Michael Doughty's movements. He knew when his mother was there and he knew when Doughty was home."

"He was a smart kid, wasn't he?" Hugo said.

But Freya wasn't there to remember Simon Bird's devious mind.

"Simon set up the social media accounts, too."

"What?" Ben said.

"He created his own profile to implicate Gavin Forbes."

"But not the original accounts? He only had the phone one week."

"No. They were Gavin. That's why everyone thought the new accounts were Gavin too. Simon used the videos he found on Gavin's phone, plus all the photos, and remained anonymous. David Stills and all the others probably just presumed it was Gavin Forbes behind it. But Gavin wouldn't have known, because he didn't have a phone."

"Why would he do that?" Ben asked. "Why would he ridicule himself?"

"To implicate Gavin Forbes. It was an act of revenge. He knew we'd find the bag with Gavin's clothes in."

"Which Simon probably took from Gavin Forbes' washing line," Ben said. "Forbes said he put it in the wash and never saw it again."

"Exactly," Freya said. "Hugo, tell me about when your customers saw the body."

"Clients," he said, correcting her. "They were clients of mine."

"Just tell me, Hugo," Freya said, but he didn't speak. He stared at her, his mouth ajar as if he was just about to say something. "It was Debbie Glover who saw him, wasn't it? But you didn't know it was Simon, did you?"

He shook his head and inhaled, long and deep.

"I thought it was Michael Doughty," he whispered. "I thought Simon had done something dreadful."

"And that's why you turned around. That's why you brought the two of them back here, instead of stopping at Tattershall, wasn't it?"

"I couldn't meet him. I didn't know what to do," Hugo said, his voice rising in pitch. "He told me to meet him. I thought he was waiting for me there. But how could I, knowing what he'd done?"

"You thought the body in the water was Michael Doughty?" Freya asked him, and he nodded. "And even though he was your son, you couldn't go through with his plan to run away together."

"I thought he'd killed him. I'm not a wicked man. I know he was my boy, but..." He stopped mid-sentence and broke. "I couldn't be a part in that."

"I'm sorry to ask you this, Hugo," Freya said. "But you said Simon was suicidal. Do you think he could have drowned himself?"

"Why? Why would you say that? He was coming to meet me."

"Where his body was discovered, we found reeds tied together. I think he used the reeds to stop himself floating downriver."

"But he was meeting me."

"I'm very sorry, Hugo, but I don't think Simon had any intention of meeting you. I think he set up your escape as a parting gift. He had no argument with you. It was you and him against the world, right?"

"Right," Hugo whispered.

"I think Simon meticulously framed Michael Doughty and Gavin Forbes. But I don't think he ever intended to get in that car with you."

"He was thirteen years old," Hugo protested. "You're talking about him like he was a criminal mastermind."

"Not a criminal mastermind, Hugo," Freya said, with as much compassion as she could find. "But I think it's safe to say that the boy they called Simple Simon, your son, was a bloody genius all along. Sadly, I believe somebody scuppered his plans at the last minute."

# CHAPTER FIFTY-SEVEN

"Harry bloody Potter?" Gillespie said to himself, as Cruz closed the car door and called out to Joanne Forbes and the uniforms. He shook his head in disbelief, trying his hardest to focus on PC Larson and not Cruz in the image his mind had conjured.

The ordeal Cruz had put Gillespie through had caused a layer of sweat to form on his back, and he lowered the window to get some fresh air. It was times like this he wish he still smoked.

The events of the previous night played over in his mind. He could have stopped her at the door. He could have said no. But he was a red-blooded male. What was he supposed to have done?

He imagined the conversations with his superiors. DCI Granger would be mad as hell, but at least there might be a chance he'd understand a wee bit. But DI Bloom? No chance. There was no way she would listen to him explain he has needs and did not know who Joanne was when she rocked up at his door.

But then he'd have to explain the text messages. He'd have to explain that he had no idea who had texted him, who was coming round, and DI Bloom would see that as just plain old stupidity.

In the rear-view mirror, he saw the uniforms walking empty-handed to the car. Cruz strolled back to Gillespie's car, full of himself. He opened the door and climbed in, leaving the door open.

"All done?" Gillespie asked.

"He's not there," Cruz explained.

"Who's not where?"

"The kid. Gavin Forbes. He's done a runner."

"Oh, for Christ's sake, Cruz. I gave you one job."

"He was already gone. Your bloody girlfriend went up to his room to find him, and he wasn't there."

"She's not my..." Gillespie started, but then stopped and calmed himself. "Where could he have gone? Did she say?"

"No, funnily enough. She was too busy chewing my bloody head off for putting him through hell."

"Alright, alright, Gabby," Gillespie said. "Ah, Christ, the boss is going to lose the plot over this."

"I don't want to hear it, Jim. We've made our deal. We both know where we stand. I want to enjoy the peace and quiet for a while. I want to enjoy walking into the incident room without worrying you're going to make me look an idiot."

"Point taken. But don't you push your luck. With what you told me, I could destroy your relationship. If Hermione finds out I know about your sordid little sex games, she'll dump you before you've even had time to wave your magic wand."

"And I can destroy your career," Cruz said bluntly. "One quiet word in DI Bloom's ear. That's all it would take. It's not my fault the boy isn't there. And it's not up to me to talk to the boss. Over to you, Jim."

"Right," Gillespie said. "Stalemate."

"Right," Cruz replied. "She's been given a shoplifting case. It's big for her. I can't let you mess it up for her. CID could be her big chance."

Unused to being the one in control, Cruz adopted the expression of a smug winner. He reached into his pocket to answer his phone. Irritated, Gillespie had to look away, fighting the urge to shout Cruz's secret in the street, despite the consequences.

"DC Cruz," he said, and Gillespie hated this newfound confidence. "Yes. Oh yes. No, that's fine. Now? Yes, sure."

"Who is it?" Gillespie asked, but Cruz held up his hand, silencing him.

"That's great news," Cruz continued. "You're a star. I owe you one."

He ended the call, and Gillespie waited for him to explain who it had been.

"Well?" he said.

"Well, what?"

"Who was it?"

"Oh, the call, you mean?" Cruz said, enjoying his newfound status.

"Yes, the call," Gillespie droned, boring of the charade already.

"Oh, that was just my mates down at the lab, you know? Tech guys. Wanted to talk to me about something they've found on Gavin Forbes' phone."

"Something they found?"

"Yeah. Just some recordings. You know? Messages and stuff. They're sending it through now."

"Messages? What kind of messages?"

"Recordings," Cruz said with a casual shrug. "I'll have a listen when we get back to the station."

"He's sending them now?"

Cruz's phone pinged right at that moment.

"Is that it?" Gillespie asked. "Is that the message?"

"Yeah, I imagine so," Cruz said. "I told him to use my email address. He knows he can rely on me."

"Gabby?" Gillespie said.

"Jim?"

"Play the bloody message."

"Eh?" Cruz said, his usual childlike tone returning in the moment his concentration lapsed.

"It could be important. Play the bloody message."

"Alright, alright," Cruz said. He fumbled with his phone, his tongue worming its way between his lips with the concentration. "Here it is."

The recording was faint and raspy. Like the phone had been in somebody's pocket. The sound of heavy breathing was clear, despite the poor quality.

"Is that...?" Gillespie said, hanging on the last word. Not willing to verbalise what he was hearing.

"I think so," Cruz said, and they stared at each other in disgust. "It's Gavin bloody Forbes. He must have recorded him and his girlfriend."

"Jesus. What a sicko," Gillespie added. "Who does that?"

Cruz shrugged, clearly not seeing how perverse the act of recording the sounds of sex without consent actually was.

"Ah, Christ, he's really going for it, eh?" Gillespie said. "Turn it off, man. I don't need to hear that."

"Bring back memories from last night, does it, Jim?" Cruz asked, and he smiled that smug smile once more.

But then the recording altered. A male climax was audible over the recording.

"Ah, stop it, Gabby, will you?"

"I'm trying," he replied. "My phone's frozen. It won't stop."

The sounds got worse before they got better. The sounds of pleasured pain and relief all combined into a series of raspy groans.

"Oh, for God's sake. I can never un-hear that. It'll be with me for the rest of my sorry bloody life," Gillespie said, while Cruz still fought with the phone.

But then there was a voice. A voice so deep that it was impossible to believe it belonged to a thirteen-year-old boy or his girlfriend.

*"If you tell anyone about this, I'll see to it you suffer. Do I make myself clear, Gavin?"*

"Whoa," Cruz said, and he threw the phone onto the floor of the car in disgust.

"Was that...?" Gillespie started, but words failed him.

"I think it was, yeah," Cruz replied. He bent to collect the phone again and hit replay, the phone ironically responding to his commands now.

"Skip forward," Gillespie said. "I can't listen to that lot again."

He skipped to the last thirty seconds, glanced up at Gillespie, who nodded, then hit play.

*"If you tell anyone about this, I'll see to it you suffer. Do I make myself clear, Gavin?"*

They stared ahead at the empty road, but when Gillespie turned back to look at Cruz, there was a figure standing beside the car.

"Joanne?" he said, and wondered how long she had been standing there.

"What was that?" she said.

"Oh, nothing," Cruz said. "Police stuff."

"Are you sure?" she asked. "I don't believe you."

"Yep, just regular police stuff. Nothing for you to worry about, Mrs Forbes," Cruz said, adopting that confident tone once more.

"It's just..." she said, and she leaned on the car for support. "I know that voice."

# CHAPTER FIFTY-EIGHT

"ARE YOU TRYING TO TELL ME SIMON BIRD KILLED HIMSELF?" Ben asked, as they walked away, leaving Hugo Bird wallowing in his boat. Freya waited until they were a good fifty feet away before she replied.

"What are you suggesting?" she said, bringing them both to a stop beside a row of small boats. "What's the alternative? What does the evidence tell us?"

"The evidence tells us that Michael Doughty had the means, motive, and opportunity. We can't just back out because of what Hugo just said."

"But we can't press forward without evidence," she countered. "And when you strip away all other possibilities–"

"What's left has to be the answer. No matter how ridiculous?" Ben added. "Is that your take on Sherlock Holmes?"

"Not really. It's just logic."

"So who was the man on the bridge?" Ben asked and checked himself, reducing his volume. "We can't just let that slide. CPS will flag that as a risk to the prosecution."

"I'm not saying we should let it slide, Ben. I'm saying there must be an alternative."

"Like what?"

"Not what, who?" Freya said, scanning the car park where they had both parked.

"Well, we've got Michael Doughty in custody, along with Sally Bird. Gillespie is picking Gavin Forbes up. Hugo Bird is the only one left."

"Not necessarily," Freya said. "We've missed somebody. Somebody else links Gavin Forbes and Simon Bird."

"Like who?"

"Think about it, Ben. Michael Doughty is the perfect suspect, apart from the bag with Gavin Forbes' belongings inside. However, we now know that Simon fabricated the whole affair, and if it wasn't for one very important thing, I'd walk away right now."

"One important thing?"

"Well, two really. First of all, Simon fabricating the whole thing doesn't account for the man on the bridge, and it doesn't account for his abuse."

"Unless Doughty was actually responsible."

"I'm starting to doubt it," Freya said. "I believed it at first. But the more I think about it, the more it doesn't make sense. I had to bend the evidence to make it work. I had to look for a motive, based on a twenty-year-old arrest warrant, of which the charges were dropped."

"Freya, you're flitting from one suspect to another. We can't lock the whole of Lincolnshire up while we figure it out."

"I'm close," she said, holding her hand up to silence him. "I nearly bloody well had it."

"So are you saying Simon didn't fabricate the evidence? Or are we still carrying on with that theory?"

"Oh, he fabricated it alright. And he nearly made his escape, too. If it wasn't for the man on the bridge," she said, answering her phone on the first ring without looking at the screen, but holding onto Ben's attention long enough to deliver her final thought on the matter. "The man who abused him."

Then Freya brought the phone to her ear.

"DI Bloom," she said.

"Boss, it's Gillespie. Listen, I've got some news–"

"Gillespie, what colour did you say that Volvo was? The one on CCTV?"

"Eh?"

"The Volvo, Gillespie. It's not a hard question."

"Erm, grey, boss."

"Dark grey, light grey?"

"Ah, medium. I'd call it rain-cloud grey myself," Gillespie said, while Ben waited patiently for her to finish her call. "Listen, we've found something–"

"Shh," she hissed, finding herself studying Ben's quizzical stare and enjoying the connection. She hadn't realized how much she had actually missed him, despite him only being away for a morning. His presence relaxed her somehow.

"I've got a problem, boss," he said.

"Gavin Forbes is missing, and the mother is accusing us of scaring him away," Freya said.

A few moments of silence followed, during which Freya ran through the pieces in her mind to make sure. She put the phone on loudspeaker and waved Ben over to hear what was going on.

"How the bloody hell do you do that?" Gillespie said.

"There's a connection between Simon Bird and Gavin Forbes. Something nobody knows. A secret. Something terrible. That's why Gavin chased Simon onto the paddle board. Simon stole Gavin's phone, correct?"

"Aye, boss. That's what we think."

"He did," Freya said. "He stole the phone to frame Gavin Forbes. But he found something on it. Some kind of secret. Something Gavin wouldn't have told anybody."

"That's what I've been trying to–" Gillespie began, but she cut him off.

"He was being abused as well," Ben said.

"By the same person who abused Simon," Freya finished. "And while he was busy framing Michael Doughty and Gavin Forbes, he took the time to punish the abuser, too. Except it didn't quite pan out the way he wanted it to."

"Aye, yes," Gillespie said. "The abuser. The man on the bridge. I think I–"

"Yes. The man with the medium-grey Volvo estate that I'm looking at right now."

Ben turned immediately and followed her gaze to the car park.

She checked her watch, and then waited for Ben to return to the call, his eyes blazing red, ready to act.

"Gillespie, I imagine by now you're either on your way to the station or you're still at the house being grilled by the mother."

"Aye, boss. The latter of the two."

"You're with Mrs Forbes, then?"

"Erm, aye."

"She works at the school, doesn't she?" Freya asked. "On reception?"

"Erm, aye, boss."

"Ask her what car the headteacher drives."

They heard him cover the phone with his hand and then heard the muffled question. He returned a moment later.

"A grey estate car, she thinks."

"I see," Freya said. "Now ask her where he lives."

A similar lull to the first took place, but Gillespie's excitement was heightened when he returned to the call a second time.

"He's got a bloody houseboat," Gillespie said

"And he moors it at Brayford Pool," Freya finished, feeling all the pieces click into place.

"Aye, boss."

"Gillespie. Get down to Five Mile Bridge as fast as you can. Our headteacher knows we're onto him."

"How?" Ben asked. "We've only just worked it out."

"Because he left here fifteen minutes ago while we were talking to Hugo," Freya said. "And he's got Gavin Forbes on board."

# CHAPTER FIFTY-NINE

"Hold on, Where are you going?" Joanne said, when Gillespie started the engine. She clung to Cruz's door, preventing him from closing it. "Have you found him? Have you found Gavin?"

"We've got a lead. Get back inside, and I'll call you when we've got him."

Cruz tried to close the door, but she held on tight.

"No way. I'm coming with you."

"No, Joanne," said Gillespie. "You can't. This is police business."

But she remained steadfast, eyebrows raised, as if threatening to reveal Gillespie's faux pas.

"Oh, for God's sake. Get in the back," he said, ignoring Cruz's wide-eyed glare.

"Is everything alright?" a voice said through Gillespie's open window. It was one of the uniforms, eyeing Joanne suspiciously, his hand resting on his radio, ready to call for assistance.

"Five Mile Bridge," Gillespie said. "We're going to need an ambulance and backup."

"An ambulance?" Joanne said from the back seat, her voice

suddenly filled with panic. "Why? What's happened? What's happened to my baby?"

Gillespie pulled away from the side of the road and put his foot down.

"Nothing," he growled. "Not yet anyway. We think Boorman has him."

"Trevor Boorman? Why? What? I don't understand."

Gillespie gave Cruz a sideways glance, then bit the bullet.

"I'm sorry, Joanne. We believe Simon Bird was abused before he died. We think the man that did it—"

"No," she said, cutting him off.

"Was abusing your son, too. In fact, we know he is."

"The recording? Is that what that was?"

"You said it yourself. It was you who told us who the voice belonged to."

"Yes, but—"

"You didn't hear the full recording, Joanne. Trust me."

"Oh, my god. Oh my god," she said. "It's my fault. I should have been a better mum. It's hard, you know. Raising him. It's not easy."

"Nobody's blaming you. But we need you to stay calm. We're going to get him. We know where he is."

The entrance to Five Mile Lane was on a tight right-hand bend. Gillespie sped into the lane, grateful for there being almost no traffic. Beyond the few houses and businesses at the top of the lane, potholes dotted the road. He did his best to avoid them at high speed, but he inevitably hit a few.

In the back of the car, Joanne was growing hysterical. The questions came thick and fast, too fast for anybody to answer before she hurled the next one at them. Behind them, the liveried car followed at a distance.

"Joanne," Gillespie yelled, as he brought the car to a skidding stop in the small parking bay by the bridge.

She silenced.

"Just. Calm. Down."

She stared at him in the rear-view mirror, mouth ajar. Perhaps she was shocked into submission. Or perhaps she was about to break down. Either way, there was no time to find out. Gillespie was out of the car, and with Cruz at his heels, he sprinted to the bridge, searching upriver for the houseboat.

"There," Cruz said, pointing downriver. They'd missed him. The boat was five hundred yards away. Close enough for its rumbling diesel engine to still be heard.

Gillespie gave chase, passing the flyers Cruz had put up as they flapped in the breeze, and slowly but surely, he closed the gap.

"Boorman," he shouted, when he was close enough to be heard, and close enough to see two people on the rear deck. Both figures turned when they heard him shout. But only one stood, and that was when Gillespie saw what was happening. He sped on, his chest heaving with every pound of his heavy boots.

The figure that was standing leaned down, grabbed the second individual, and heaved him to his feet. It was Gavin Forbes, and as Gillespie drew closer, he saw the rucksack strapped to the boy's shoulders. The boy's knees seemed to buckle under the weight, so much so that the man, easily identifiable as Trevor Boorman, held him upright. He glanced back at Gillespie, who was catching fast. Then, in a last desperate move, he shoved Gavin Forbes backwards.

"No," Gillespie screamed, only fifty metres away.

The boy splashed into the water. But there was no struggle at the surface. The weight of the rucksack dragged him down almost instantly.

Torn between going after Boorman and the drowning boy, Gillespie's mind was made up in a flash. He pulled his jacket off as he ran and tossed it away, then without breaking stride, he dived into the freezing water, marking the faint ripples on the surface where he'd seen Forbes enter.

The river was only six-foot deep, ten at the most. But the icy-cold water sucked the breath from his lungs, and his boots were like rocks on the end of his legs. He took the biggest lungful of air he could, prepared to submerge, then dived, groping blindly for the boy's arms or legs, or anything he could find.

The current beneath the surface was strong. His lungs burned, and the visibility was limited to a foot or two at the most. He hung there, upside down in the water, his fingers gripping nothing but mud and weeds. His body screamed for air. He knew he had to resurface and try once more. But he held on a few moments longer. Long enough that his hand, just briefly, grazed cold human skin.

It was all he could manage. His lungs were at their limit. He kicked against the current, groping for another touch.

And there it was. A limp hand for him to clutch. He pulled himself closer, reached for the rucksack straps, and freed the boy's arms. Then, with everything Gillespie had left, he kicked up. As hard as he could.

Bursting through the surface, Gillespie gasped for breath. Gavin Forbes was limp in his arms. His face was paler than pale, and his lips were tinged with blue. With his hand beneath the boy's chin, Gillespie swam sideways to the bank, where Cruz was ready to help pull him out.

Two paramedics in green overalls were running along the towpath carrying boxes of emergency medical equipment, and in just a few moments, the four of them heaved Gavin's lifeless body from the river.

Exhausted, Gillespie rested his head on the riverbank. He regained his breath, while around him the paramedics fought to keep the boy alive. But it all seemed like a blur. Like a memory, or a dream.

He turned to look downriver, catching sight of the boat's tail end as it disappeared around a bend. And by the time he turned back to look at the fight to save the young boy's life, Joanne was standing there, blurred in his tears. But it was her.

# CHAPTER SIXTY

"Forbes was in the water. Gillespie got him out," Cruz said, his voice surprisingly calm for such an event.

"Is he breathing?" Ben said, talking loudly to be heard over the roar of Freya's engine. She was putting her new car through its paces, focused on the road ahead.

"We've got paramedics here. They're still working on him."

"What about Gillespie?" Ben asked.

"He's okay. He's a bloody hero. He dived right down. I thought we'd lost them both."

"What about Boorman?" Freya asked, her eyes never once leaving the road.

"We lost him, boss."

"You lost him? He's in a houseboat. It only goes about ten miles per hour, surely."

"He threw Forbes off. Strapped him to a rucksack full of bricks or rocks or something. Jim had to make the call. He chose the boy."

"And rightly so," Ben said. "We're going to head Boorman off at Woodhall Spa."

"You'll miss him. He's too far ahead, Ben."

"You sound sure."

"I walked the length of this bloody river, remember? He's got too much of a lead."

Ben looked up at Freya, doubtful if they could trust Cruz's judgement. But she nodded. "Where's the next river crossing?" she asked.

"Tattershall," Ben replied, then returned his attention to the call. "Cruz, keep us posted on Forbes. We're going to Tattershall to head Boorman off. Get in touch with Chapman. Tell her everything and make sure she informs DCI Granger. If this goes belly up, we'll need his support. Then find Nillson and get her on the road. Have you got all that?"

"I've written it down," Cruz said.

"Good," Ben replied. "Before you do all that, get hold of Sergeant Cole."

"Who?"

"The dive team that pulled Simon Bird out of the water. We're going to need some way of stopping that boat."

"Right. Got it."

"And Cruz?"

"Yeah?"

"Good work, mate. You're doing great. Look after Gillespie. Keep him warm and dry."

"Will do, Ben."

Ben hung up. "Well, this escalated quickly," he said. "I was at home with a cup of tea not two hours ago. Now we're chasing a murderer in a bloody houseboat."

Without looking at him, Freya smiled, still focusing on the road.

"What?" he said.

"You're a natural leader, Ben Savage."

"Shut up."

"You are. It's a bloody waste. That's all I'm saying."

"All I did was give his ego a bit of a rub," Ben said. "God

knows Gillespie will need him. That water must be bloody freezing. Can you believe he dived in to get Gavin Forbes out?"

"As it happens, yes. I can," Freya said. "He may have the sense of humour of a twelve-year-old, but he's got the heart of a lion, that man. It doesn't surprise me in the slightest that he risked his own life to save that kid."

"Yeah, well, let's hope it was worth it," Ben replied, glancing down at his phone, anticipating Cruz's next call. "You've got a good team behind you. You know that, right?"

"I know. But still. It won't be the same without you."

"You mentioned bringing Nillson on. Do you see her as your number two?"

The conversation wasn't the topic Ben would have chosen. But he was keen to hear how things would look after he had left.

"I told her she needs to take her Sergeant exam," Freya said. "I think she's ready for a promotion, personally. She just lacks something."

"Like what?"

"She's not Ben. I told you that before."

"We can't all be tall, dark, and handsome with exceptional detective skills," he said. But the joke fell flat on its face. "Well, that leaves you with Gillespie. Either that or they bring somebody new in."

"I don't want anyone new," Freya snapped, then took a breath, rolling her eyes. He'd noticed that before, the way she rolled her eyes, cursing herself for showing emotion. "I just want it to stay the same. I don't want it to change. I know that sounds immature. And yes, I know I should understand that people move on. I know that. But things are good right now. The team is good. More than good. Trust me. I've been in some pretty crappy teams before. I know when things are good. First, it was Jackie Gold leaving the team. Now it's you. I just..."

"You just what?" Ben asked.

"I feel cheated," she said after a pause. "That's all. I'll get over it."

"If I could stop my dad being sick, I would. You know that, right?"

"I know. I know."

"And I don't enjoy letting people down."

"I know that too," she said. "And you're not. You're not letting anyone down. Quite the opposite. In fact, I admire you even more for what you're doing. It takes a lot to give up what you're good at."

"I'm not doing it to be admired," Ben said, and he gazed out of the window to hide his watering eyes.

"I know that as well. But I can't help it," Freya said as they entered Tattershall. The roar of the engine died down to a quiet rumble. He hadn't realised how noisy the journey had been. She rolled into the car park where they had begun the investigation and came to a stop as close to the dock as she could.

In an instant, Ben had unclipped his seat belt and was about to open the door, when Freya stopped him with a hand on his arm, her manicured nails reminding him of the style, fashion, and grace she had brought to the team.

"I think the world of you, Ben," she said. "I don't know where I'd be without you."

"You'd be right here. Only you'd have that mad Scotsman Gillespie sitting beside you."

He looked out of the window again and blinked away a tear. He never had been any good with matters of the heart, considering himself more of a hands-on type of guy.

"No. No, I don't think I would. I don't think I would have lasted here in Lincolnshire without you."

"Now you're talking nonsense," he said, still holding onto the door. He turned back and was met with Freya's lips planted on his. She reached up and ran her hand across his face, prolonging the kiss.

It lasted forever, yet it was over far too fast. Her perfume seemed to fill his senses, and her touch was as soft and gentle as he had always imagined.

"I've wanted to do that since the moment I first lay eyes on you," she said, leaving him stunned, frozen to the spot and reeling from the moment. She opened her door, slipped out, and smiled down at him with sadness in her eyes.

He was about to say something, although he had absolutely no idea what would have come out of his mouth. Thankfully, his phone rang, and he answered it without looking at the screen.

"DS Savage."

"Ben, it's me. Cruz."

"What's the news, mate?"

There was a pause, a lull during which Ben could hear Cruz controlling his breathing. He put the call on loudspeaker and glanced at Freya through the windscreen.

"Cruz?" he said. "Talk to me, mate. Come on."

"He's alive, Ben. Forbes pulled through."

Ben got out of the car and put the phone on loudspeaker. "Oh, Jesus. Thank god for that. How's Gillespie doing?"

"He's okay. He's wrapped in a blanket with a flask of tea."

"No change then," Freya added, and Cruz gave a nervous laugh, unsure how to interact with the boss.

"Do you have uniform with you?" Ben asked.

"A couple. They followed us from the Forbes house."

"Call Chapman. Tell her to send more and have them lock the place down before the media arrive."

"Will do."

"Told you you could do it, didn't I?" Ben said.

Another pause followed, and Ben could have sworn he could hear Cruz beaming.

"Thanks, Ben," he said, and ended the call on a high.

"Come on," Freya said. "Let's wrap this up."

"I'm going to miss him, you know?"

She nodded but didn't reply directly. Instead, she seemed to study him as she leaned on the car. It was like they had been friends since childhood. That look. That familiar look.

"I'll let you have this one," she said, shoving off the car. "Let's send you off with a bang, shall we?"

# CHAPTER SIXTY-ONE

"This could be the world's slowest police chase in history," Ben said, catching Freya up on the bridge.

She was gazing upriver, where, not too far away, a single houseboat loomed towards them. The rest of the world seemed oblivious, which was how Freya wanted to keep things. The slightest hint of drama and the press would be there in a shot.

"Let's get Chapman on the line," Freya said. "I need her to drive this from the station."

Freya waited a moment then looked up at Ben. He was staring at her, seemingly confused.

"It was just a kiss, Ben," she said, then nodded toward the slow-moving boat and gave him a little smile. "Come on. He's getting away."

Ben pulled out his phone, dialled Chapman's desk phone, then directed the call to loudspeaker.

"Ben?" she said. "I thought you were off?"

"I am," he said. "I mean, I will be. I was, even. But I'm here now. I'm with DI Bloom. What's the latest on Sergeant Cole? Do we have an ETA?"

"I spoke to his team ten minutes ago. They scrambled immediately. They can't be far away."

As if on cue, a tiny outboard motor whirred in the distance. He turned downstream to face the direction of the sound and saw the tiny RIB in the distance.

"I think I see them coming. Have you spoken to Cruz?"

"Yeah. A while back. He seems to have things in hand."

"He does. He's done well."

"And Gillespie? Did you hear what he did?"

"I think DCI Granger will need to buy the entire team a round after this one, Chapman," Ben said. "Do me a favour. I need some uniforms down here in Tattershall, and an ambulance, just in case."

"Yep, no problem. Already on their way."

"Chapman?" Freya called.

"Ma'am?"

She glanced at Ben, holding his gaze.

"Have Michael Doughty released. And Sally Bird, too. Have somebody drive them home. I'll deal with the consequences."

A moment's silence followed before Chapman gave a curt, "Ma'am."

"You're a star, Chapman," Ben said. "Thanks for everything."

She paused again then spoke as if she hadn't heard him correctly.

"I'm just doing my job, Ben. This is what I always do."

"I know," he said, feeling Freya's stare bore a hole into the side of his face. "I just appreciate it. That's all."

"Right."

"Right then," he said. "I'll catch you later."

"Yeah," she replied, sounding unsure of what he had said, and she ended the call.

"Smooth, Ben," Freya said, and he pocketed the phone as Cole and his men sped beneath the bridge. But when he glanced up the river to follow the boat's course, he felt a sudden panic. "Oh god, Freya. Look."

A thick plume of black smoke spewed from the houseboat, now only two hundred meters away.

"He's set it on fire," Freya said. "He's bloody killing himself."

Ben ran from the bridge down to the riverside and sprinted up the path beside the water. He turned, running backwards for a few steps to call up to Freya on the bridge. Her phone was pressed to her ear.

"Get Chapman," he said. "Fire service."

Then he turned and ran the last one hundred metres. One of Cole's men was manoeuvring the RIB close to the houseboat with gentle nudges of the outboard, while Cole and another were boarding the rear deck, holding their jackets over their mouths to fight through the smoke. Inside, orange hues danced against the tiny windows. The curtains were ablaze, but from where Ben was, he could make nothing out.

He walked slowly, keeping pace with the boat, while Cole and his partner kicked through the door. They pulled at the shards of splintered wood, tossing them to one side. Then, with his jacket covering most of his face, Cole disappeared into the boat. His partner watched him, talking into the radio on his shoulder.

Waiting with bated breath, Ben looked on helplessly from dry land less than twenty feet away.

A few moments later, Cole reappeared, coughing and spluttering onto the rear deck. His partner pulled him away from the worst of the smoke, and he looked up at Ben, shaking his head.

"It's empty, Ben," he called, the effort inducing a chesty cough. He spat into the water and turned to look back inside. But by now, the entire inside of the boat was engulfed in flames.

"Empty?" Ben called back. "Are you sure?"

Cole was trying to take control of the boat, perhaps to steer it to the bank. But he was struggling with something.

Ben relayed the news to Freya with a single shrug of his shoulders, implying he didn't know where Boorman was. Freya was seventy-something feet away, and he could still read the confused expression on her face as she relayed the news to Chapman over the phone.

"He's tied the wheel to the handrail," Cole called out, holding up the slack end of a length of rope, and for the first time, Ben heard a slight panic in his voice as he looked ahead to where the boat was heading.

Ben followed his gaze. They were heading directly for the bridge.

He looked behind them, back up the river. It was arrow-straight for quite some distance. He looked back at the boat, following the line of its path. The fire was raging now. Only the front and rear decks were not ablaze. Cole and his partner were on the rear deck, but on the front deck, standing beside a coil of rope and a life jacket, were two bright orange Calor gas bottles.

"Get off the boat," Ben said.

"What?"

"*Get off the boat,*" he yelled.

"Hold on. I'm going to cut the rope," Cole said.

"There's no time," Ben called, seeing the flames reach up through the front deck, swallowing the bottles. "Get off. Gas bottles."

Even from twenty feet away, Ben saw the whites of Cole's eyes as they widened in horror and realisation set in. He had barely reacted, only his arms had reached for his partner, gripping him to pull him off the boat, when the scene in front of Ben seemed to implode, casting his entire world into orange flame, then grey smoke, then finally, the white nothingness that accompanies a dream.

And then there was only a darkness. An empty, black space with the acrid stench of burning hair in his nostrils, and a high-pitched whine ringing in his ears.

# CHAPTER SIXTY-TWO

THE SCENE HAD PLAYED OUT IN SLOW MOTION. FROM ATOP THE bridge, Freya had seen it all. Ben's confused look telling her Boorman was nowhere to be seen, Cole's struggle with the wheel, and the inferno raging through the boat. A fierce ball of flame had stretched the width of the river, as if it had been suppressed for a millennium and finally broken free of its constraints. The heat had been so fierce, Freya had felt it from over seventy feet away. So much so that she'd had to shield her face and her eyes. And when she looked back, Ben was lying a good fifteen feet from where he had been standing, and Cole and his partner were nowhere to be seen.

The little police RIB Cole had arrived on had overturned in the blast, and the officer driving it was now swimming to the bank.

And now the entire sequence of events replayed in her mind, slow and torturous, magnifying the details she couldn't bear to remember.

For the few moments after the blast, the world seemed to come to a standstill. A car stopped behind her on the bridge and a man ran to her side, taking in the scene of devastation below with a look of utter bewilderment.

She didn't even look. Paralysed to the spot, Freya could only stare into space. Horrified at what she saw. Somewhere inside her, the part that adored Ben, screamed to be by his side. Yet there was a fear at what she might find. A fear of losing everything all over again.

"Ma'am?" Chapman said over the phone, rousing Freya to a semi-functional state. "Ma'am, what's going on? What was that noise?"

Freya spoke slowly, keeping her voice as calm and controlled as she could. All the time watching Ben for the slightest sign of movement. Cole's officer had dragged himself up beside Ben and was checking his vitals.

"There's been an explosion," Freya said, numbed, but forcing herself to focus.

"Oh god," Chapman said, and the sound of her fingers on keys stopped momentarily.

"We need the fire service and more ambulances," Freya said. "As fast as you can. And call Lincoln HQ. Get the helicopter in the air. Boorman is on the run."

She watched Ben like a hawk, willing him to move. Even just a little. Cole's officer had pulled him into the recovery position and was radioing for help.

"On the run?" Chapman said, the sound of her fingers now tapping away at her keyboard coming clear across the call. "I thought he was on a houseboat?"

"He was. He set it on fire to distract us. Cole and one of his men might be injured."

"Is anyone else injured?" Chapman asked.

"No," Freya said, after a pause. She needed the team to focus. She spoke almost automatically, her entire attention focused on Ben. A twitch of his leg would suffice. A cough maybe. Or anything. But he was motionless. "No, everyone else is okay."

Somebody called out from the river below, and for the slightest of moments, through some trick of the mind, Freya heard Ben's voice. But it wasn't Ben. It was Cole. He had dragged his partner to the far bank and was calling out to the officer who had helped Ben.

Having dealt with Ben, Cole's officer was back on the riverbank, scanning the scene for Cole and his partner.

"It's a mess, Chapman. I don't know how we didn't spot him sooner."

"He wasn't on our radar, ma'am. He was Simon's headteacher. It's one of those positions you just trust, isn't it?"

"I guess," Freya said. "We thought he was killing himself. You know? Burning to death on a boat where nobody can save him."

"It wouldn't be the first time he's tried it," Chapman said.

"What do you mean?"

"I've checked his medical records. He's been in and out of therapy since he was a kid."

Freya digested the statement. She tore her eyes from Ben and she stared upriver.

"Ma'am?" Chapman said. "Ma'am, are you there?"

"I'm here," Freya said softly.

"Ma'am, I've just found something," Chapman said. "I know who Michael Stone was accused of abusing."

# CHAPTER SIXTY-THREE

"It's over," Sally said. She closed the front door behind her and leaned against it, closing her eyes to try to forget the ordeal. But there would be no forgetting. Not for months, years even.

Michael dropped his keys on the kitchen worktop then leaned on it, his head hanging between his arms like a dead weight.

She watched him, anxious for his mood. He hadn't said a single word to her. Not even in the back of the police vehicle when she had reached for his hand. He'd simply pulled it away, turning to stare out of the window instead. And now his brooding silence was a weight over the house. Not a dark cloud merely threatening rain. But the eye of the storm itself.

"I can't go back," she said, nudging him for some kind of interaction. "Hugo knows now for sure. And what with Simon... I don't think I can face it."

Michael said nothing. He didn't even move.

"Michael, talk to me. What do I do?"

"Do what you want, Sally," he said. His voice was low and moody. "That's what you always do, isn't it?"

"That's not fair—"

"Fair?" he said, shoving himself off the kitchen counter. He snatched a steak knife from the wooden block on the counter and turned to face her. "Fair? Is it not enough that my life has been torn apart once already? Is it fair that I should be put through it all again?"

"Michael, I didn't know—"

"No, of course you didn't. You were too busy thinking about yourself. When have you ever asked about my life? My childhood?"

"Never. But I—"

"And when have you have ever come here and asked me how I am? How was my day?"

"Michael, I'm sorry—"

"I saw the way you looked at me when that bitch found your credit card."

"What was I supposed to think?"

"I don't know. But you were quick enough to believe her. Is that who you think I am?"

"Michael, what's got into you? You're scaring me."

"Scaring you? Believe me, you've seen nothing yet. You don't know the half of it," he said, and he took a step toward her, seeming to fill the archway that connected the kitchen to the lounge. "You talk about leaving your husband like it's some kind of game. You talk about starting a new life with me, yet you don't even know me."

"Michael, I—"

"Do you?" he screamed.

"I... I thought I did."

"Tell me what you heard her say. Eh? Tell me what she said."

"When? I don't... I don't understand."

"Yes, you do. We sat there. On the couch. With the copper. She told you all about my history. She told you why I'm here. Why I had to leave my home, my business, and my family. Tell me what you thought."

"Thought? Well, I didn't believe her."

"Do you want to hear it? Eh? Do you want to hear what happened? Why I had to start again? Something you think is as easy as closing one door and opening another?"

"No, Michael, don't do this..."

He was standing in the centre of the room, the knife hanging limp by his side, and dark rings encircled his bloodshot eyes.

"Maybe you want to hear what I had to endure while I was on remand. Eh? Is that what you want? They tell you men convicted for...for these crimes are put in a special wing. Somewhere the other prisoners can't get at you. Somewhere you can't hear their taunts. It's true. We are. But they don't tell you how you have to walk past the violent offenders to eat or to shower. They don't tell you how easy it is for them to get at you. You think it's easy for them to find you on the outside? No. Out here is easy. On the inside, there's nowhere to run. Nowhere to hide."

"Michael, what are you saying?"

"When I was released, when the charges were dropped, I went home. What else was I supposed to do? Where else was I supposed to go? Do you know what I found?" he asked, closing the distance between them, and leaning in close so they were nose to nose.

She backed up against the front door with no means of escape.

"Scrawled across my front door in red paint. *Paedo scum*. In capital letters. They smashed my windows. Burnt my car. My life was over. My own family wouldn't talk to me. My sister. Even my own father took years to come around. Do you know how that feels?"

"I don't understand," Sally said. "You said it was all lies."

He stared down at her. The palms of her hands lay flat against the front door, and slowly, she slid her right hand along the wood toward the door handle.

But he gripped her wrist, twisted her arm, and snatched her off the door so she couldn't escape.

"You? You hurt Simon?" she whispered, her eyes wide.

"Is that what you think?" he whispered.

"I don't know. I didn't. But now–"

"But what? But now you've heard about my past. Do you think it was me? Do you think I could?"

There was a madness in his eyes that belied what she wanted to believe. Some hidden part of him she was yet to discover was rearing its ugly head.

"Do you think I hurt that boy, Sally?" he growled. "Eh? Do you think I did those things all those years ago?"

"I... I don't know," Sally muttered, terrified of who this man was.

He slammed his hand onto the door beside her head, and she squeezed her eyes closed, hoping, just hoping, that somebody would stop him. That this whole mess would go away, and Simon could come back.

"Eh, Sally? Talk to me–"

"Yes," she said. "Yes, I do. I didn't, but I do now."

"Ah," he said, his voice more of a breath. "Now you're getting me. Do you still want to start a new life with me? Eh? Do you still think it's easy to leave everything you've worked hard for?"

"No. No, it's not easy," she said through the tears. "But I would have."

She couldn't bear to look at him now. It was all she could do to stop the images of him and her own boy from crowding her imagination.

"And Simon?" he said at last. "Do you think I hurt him too?"

"I don't know."

He grabbed her wrist, forced the knife into her hand and turned it into himself, the point resting over his heart. His powerful hand gripped hers tight and pulled. His face contorted with the pain.

"Do you think I hurt Simon, Sally?" he said, letting fly small drops of spittle. "Because if you think I did, then so will everyone out there. And I can't go through that again. Not this time."

He increased the pressure on her hand, and his white shirt soaked up the first remnants of crimson. Slowly, his hardened expression softened. It was like a veil being pulled from his soul, revealing the true agony beneath him.

"If you believe I did it, if you believe it was me that did those things to Simon, then finish me. Now's your chance."

With his hand enclosed around hers, and hers around the knife, the force somehow exchanged, so that she was the driving force, and his hand merely the guide. He didn't scream or call out. In fact, he made no sound at all, save for the long exhale through flared nostrils as she drove the blade forward slowly. His body jolted once, twice, then stiffened, and he helped her, pulling her hand, coaxing her on.

"That's all I needed to know," he whispered as he clung to her, his strength already waning.

She gasped and froze, wondering if she should pull the blade from his chest.

But the job was done. His knees gave under his weight, and he fell at her feet, twitching. Then he stilled.

It was as if someone had lifted a weight from her shoulders, taking with it any remaining strength she had. His blood was the glue that held the blade to her open hand, and she dropped to her knees before him.

"Oh god, what have I done?" she whispered. "Oh god. Oh god."

The moment of clarity that struck her was grim beyond anything she had endured in all her miserable years. Whatever life she might have dreamed of was gone. Her only son was gone. Everything she had ever worked for, gone.

Her lungs felt as if they were half their size, and her head was light, like she'd finished a bottle of wine, maybe two.

The blood on the knife was already tacky, and she had to peel it from her hand to turn it. She hadn't the inner strength to force the same slow suffering on her own body, so she raised the knife, readying herself for the plunge. Preparing herself to fall onto it. Hard and fast, how death should be. Not slow like Michael's. Not slow like Simon's.

With a final intake of breath, she tightened her grip with both hands. She let her head fall back, unable to bear witness to it.

To the end.

She thought of Simon, and all she should have done for him yet didn't. But all she saw was his face, smiling back at her. Not smiling with love as a son should look upon his mother. But with joy at her suffering. At her end. At what she'd become.

If it wasn't Michael who stole the credit card, then it had to have been Simon who planted it.

"This is what he planned," she said aloud. "Simon. My own son. He set me up."

"Yes, he did," a voice said from the far side of the room. "He set us all up."

# CHAPTER SIXTY-FOUR

"What are you doing here?" Sally said.

"I'm not sure you'd believe me if I told you," he replied. His eyes were wide and black, and his chest heaved with what Sally could only imagine was adrenaline. He saw the knife in her hands, and the direction it was pointing.

"You can't stop me," Sally said, repositioning the blade. "I'll do it. I'll bloody do it."

He shook his head. "It's over, Sally. It's all over."

She glanced behind him into the hallway, her heart racing now. "How did you get in here?"

"The back door was open," he replied, and took a step into the room. "Michael must have left it unlocked."

At the mention of Michael's name, Sally froze.

"You know him?"

But he didn't reply. He took a step forward.

"Don't come any closer," she said, following his gaze to where Michael lay. At the sight of the body, his shoulders sagged along with the corners of his mouth. Then his dark eyes found her. "He was an animal," Sally said, holding the knife to defend herself. "A monster. He deserved it."

"He did," he said, and she saw the tears in his eyes now.

He took another step forward, and she shuffled backwards away from Michael, putting as much distance between them as she could.

"He told me," she said. "He told me what he did. He told me what he did to Simon. My boy. My son."

He gave a little laugh at the statement, and her anger. "I've known dozens of boys like Simon."

"Not like Simon. He was special. He was different. He was kind."

"He was a loser, just like his father."

"How dare you? He was my boy."

"He was the same as all the others," he said, sounding bored. "Weak."

"What?" she said, and something stirred inside her.

"Weak," he said again. "Weak, sad, lonely, and unloved."

"How dare you?"

"He never stood a chance," he said. "His dad's a loser, and you're nothing but a slut. Do you think I don't see it? Do you think I don't see kids like him all the time?"

"Stop it–"

"Attention seeking."

"No–"

"Do you think I don't know the signs?" he shouted, then nodded at Michael's body. "*He* didn't hurt Simon."

Suddenly, the front door rattled behind her. Somebody rapped on the wood three times, loud and hard.

"Open up. It's the police," a voice called out. It was the woman detective. Her posh accent was unmistakable. "Boorman. I know you're in there."

Sally glanced back at the door, and when she looked back at Boorman, he had closed the distance. He was standing beside Michael's body, staring down with a pitiful expression on his face.

"They're calling your name," she said. "Why are they calling your name?"

"I've done some bad things," he replied after a brief pause. "I've done some terrible things."

"Simon?" she whispered, feeling the pang of guilt squeeze her insides.

He just stared at her, sorrowful, saying nothing. But his expression spoke a thousand words.

"You?" she said, taking a step towards him, adjusting her grip on the knife.

"Boorman. Open the door," the detective called, rapping on the door again. Tyres crunched on the gravel outside, and a wash of blue light burst through the window, flashing across Boorman's face every other second.

But the police would not stop her.

"You let me kill him," she said, holding the knife out in front of her. He put his hands up in protest, but she slashed at him, catching his arm, and he stumbled backwards. "You watched me kill him. He was innocent, and you let me kill him."

"You know nothing," he shouted, as she placed the tip of the blade against his chest. She'd done it once. She could do it again. There was only one way out of this now, and if she was going to end it, she would end it on her terms. She pressed hard, forcing him back into the wall. "He's not who you think he was."

"How do you know him?" she whispered in disbelief. "Who are you really?"

"He's Trevor Boorman," that voice said, clear and articulate. Public school. And the female detective stepped into view in the rear hallway. Bloom. That was her name. She remembered now. Bloom held a hand up behind her, no doubt to stop the rest of the police from barging in. She stared down at Michael's body, then at the bloodied knife and Sally's bloodied hand. "Put it down, Sally."

"I don't understand," she said, fighting back the tears. It was over. One way or another, it was over. But she had to understand. She had to know.

"It wasn't Michael who abused Simon," Bloom said, and Boorman's eyes widened then focused on the blade pressing into his chest. "But he did abuse that boy twenty years ago. Didn't he, Trevor?"

Boorman steeled himself, biting down on his lower lip. His nostrils flared and his eyes were like saucers.

"You're the boy?" Sally said, staggering backward. "It was true?"

"He made me who I am," Boorman said, his voice thick with emotion. "He took everything from me. He did something to me. Changed me. I don't know what. I heard them talking."

"Heard who?" Sally said.

"Her," he replied, pointing at Bloom but not turning his attention from the blade. "I heard her on the dockside with your husband."

"So, it's true," Sally said, the knife a dead weight in her hand and every muscle in her body fatigued with the emotion. She stared him in the eye. With one move, she could end him. She could somehow make it up to Simon. Maybe he was looking down at them?

"It's over, Sally. Put the knife down," Bloom said, then stared directly at Boorman. "If you really want him to suffer as Simon did, then let him go to prison. Don't make it easy on him."

# CHAPTER SIXTY-FIVE

Two liveried cars transported Sally Bird and Trevor Boorman to the station, as Michaela led her team of crime scene investigators into the house clothed in white forensics suits. Michaela nodded once in recognition of a good job done as she passed.

"How did you know he would be here?" Nillson asked as she came to Freya's side.

"It was something Chapman said," she replied. "Something about how we implicitly trust certain members of society, because of who they are and what they do."

"I'm not following," Nillson said.

"She learned that Michael Doughty, or Michael Stone as he was formerly known, was accused of abusing a young boy."

"So?" Nillson said.

"Boorman was that boy."

"So it was true. The report from two decades ago?"

"It was, yes."

"So why were the charges dropped?" Nillson asked. "He should have gone to prison."

"Somebody else paid the price. There must be hundreds of

offenders out there who got away with it. Only this time, it'll come out in the wash."

"And thousands of victims whose pain and suffering are yet to be acknowledged," Nillson said, her top lip curled in disgust.

"They don't all end up like Boorman, Anna," Freya said. "They don't all tread the same path. Many victims manage to put it behind them, and although the memories never go away, they do find a way to move forward. Now and then, one falls through the cracks. The system fails them, and for one reason or another, they continue the cycle. If we understood it, perhaps something could be done to prevent it. Trevor Boorman will go to prison for what he did to Simon Bird and Gavin Forbes. But don't forget he was once the victim, and the system failed him too."

"I'm sorry. I find it hard to feel compassionate," Nillson said.

"So do I," Freya said. "And I imagine a jury will find it equally difficult."

The car park at the front of Michael Doughty's property was now a hive of activity. Uniformed officers blocked the narrow lane and guarded the exits, while Michaela and her team shuffled in and out of the building with boxes and bags of forensic equipment. A private ambulance was waiting to remove the body when the team had finished.

"Did you hear about Gillespie?" Nillson asked.

"I did," Freya said. "Cruz even called him a hero. You don't hear him giving praise like that very often. Not to Gillespie, anyway."

"As much as it pains me to say it, boss, I tend to agree. He might be an insufferable fool most of the time, but you have to give it to him," Nillson said, making her point abundantly clear. "Where's Ben anyway? I thought he would be with you."

Freya knew she would ask but was yet to come up with an answer. She hadn't wanted to tell the team what had happened to Ben. At least until Boorman was safely in custody.

She tried to smile at Nillson, whose intuition was clear in her concerned expression.

"Speaking of heroes," Freya said.

# CHAPTER SIXTY-SIX

Several miles upriver, Gillespie sat on the ambulance's rear bumper with a blanket draped over his shoulders and a fresh tea in his hand. His was one of two ambulances, and on the rear bumper of the second, Gavin Forbes sat in a similar position with his mother holding onto him like it was the first time she had ever truly held him.

"You're good to go," the paramedic told him. "How are you feeling?"

"Ah, I'm alright," Gillespie replied. "Thanks for the tea, eh? Warmed me right up, that did."

"Not a problem. You did a good thing today. You should be proud."

"I should," Gillespie replied. "Funny, eh? I don't feel it. I suppose you want me to move?"

"No. No, you stay there as long as you need to," the paramedic replied. "I'll be out here when you're ready."

"How's the lad?"

"He'll live to tell the tale," the paramedic said, staring over at the Forbes family sharing a moment. "It was close, though. Another few seconds, and who knows?"

Gillespie smiled up at him and nodded, having nothing of any value to add.

"I'll give you a few minutes to yourself," the paramedic said. "No doubt you'll have a hundred questions to answer."

But Gillespie's peace was short-lived. Seeing him on his own, Joanne gave her boy a squeeze and strolled over from one ambulance to the next. She plunged her hands into her coat pockets and wore a sheepish expression as she approached.

"I can't thank you enough," she said.

"Ah, it's nothing."

"Not really. You saved my son's life," she said. "I'd say that's far from nothing."

"I just did what anybody else would have done."

"No. No, you did far more than that," she said. "What I'm trying to say, Jim, is that I'd like to repay the debt. I don't know how, or what I could do, but–"

"Debt? There's no debt."

"Well then, maybe it's guilt that I'm feeling?"

"You were protecting your son. I don't agree with your methods, but your heart was in the right place."

"I used you."

"You did."

"But you had a good time, right?"

He stared up at her, amazed that she could even bring the event up.

"I'm sorry," she said. "I'm new to this type of thing."

"You didn't look new to it."

"I mean, I'm new to..." she began, then glanced back at Gavin, who was being tended by a paramedic. "Oh, forget it. Listen, I know he's not the best behaved kid out there. I know he can sometimes be a bit bullish, and I know more than anyone that he picked on Simon. But if he gets into any more trouble, I'm afraid I'd lose him. They'd take him away. He's not that bad. He just..."

"He just gets caught?" Gillespie said.

Her shoulders sagged. "I'm so sorry."

"Forget it. What's done is done. It doesn't look like he was guilty of anything other than being a bully. And as much as I can't stand bullies, he's got his second chance."

"I won't tell anyone," she said. "I know I said I would, but I won't. I owe you that much, at least."

"You're too kind," he said, with more than a hint of sarcasm in his voice. Then he relented. "Look, you did what you felt you had to do. Go and take care of him. And keep him out of trouble."

"I will," she said softly. "Take care of yourself, Jim."

"Aye. You too, Joanne," he said, as Nillson's car pulled into the little car parking area. "You too."

Cruz approached him as Joanne made her way back to her boy, and on seeing them both, Nillson joined them.

"How you holding up?" Nillson asked.

"Not too bad, Anna," Cruz said, completely missing the fact that her question had been aimed at Gillespie. "I'll be glad to get back to the station, though. My feet are bloody killing me. I swear I've walked up and down this river more times than..." He stopped when he saw Nillson's incredulous expression. "Oh, right."

Nillson turned her attention to Gillespie and waited with raised eyebrows for him to reply.

"Aye, I'm okay. I'll be coughing up river water for a wee while, but I'm alright."

"Glad to hear it," Nillson said as she scanned the scene. Uniforms and CID were out in force, cordoning off the area, and the paramedics were preparing to leave with Gavin and his mother. "Is that your girlfriend over there, Cruz?"

She pointed over to a few plain-clothed officers taking statements from passers-by.

"Aye, that's her. Waving her magic wand," Gillespie joked.

Nillson was wide-eyed. She turned to Cruz.

"You told him?" she said. "I thought you were worried he'd land you in trouble if he found out."

Cruz laughed. "I don't think Jim is going to be getting me in any trouble for a long while," he said, puffing his chest out. "In fact, I think I'm rather looking forward to the peace and quiet."

"Is that right?" Gillespie said.

"That's what we agreed," Cruz said, his confidence waning by the second.

"Agreed? I don't remember agreeing anything with you."

"You said that if I kept your secret, you'd keep mine."

"Secret?" Gillespie said, putting on his best confused expression. "I don't have a secret."

"You know?" Cruz said, nodding his head sideways towards the second ambulance. "Your secret."

"I don't know what you're talking about," Gillespie said. He stood, placed the plastic mug of tea on the rear step of the ambulance, and looked over to the second ambulance. "Hey, Joanne?"

The paramedic was about to close the rear doors, but her head popped out.

"DS Gillespie?" she said.

"Do you know anything about a secret?"

"A secret?"

"Aye. My colleague here seems to think there's some kind of secret or something."

She shook her head. "I'm afraid I don't know what you're talking about."

She smiled at Cruz sympathetically, then disappeared back into the ambulance.

"You know," Gillespie said, "I haven't spoken to PC Larson for a while now. Or should I call her DC Larson now?"

"No," Cruz said, his eyes wide. "No, Jim, don't."

"Excuse me, Anna," he said. "I'll just be a moment."

"No. You can't," Cruz said, running to keep up with Gillespie.

"Hey, DC Larson," Gillespie called out.

She stopped the conversation she was having, giving the passers-by the nod to leave, and she pocketed her notebook.

"Don't listen to him, babe," Cruz called out, doing his best to stay ahead of Gillespie. "I haven't told him anything. He's just causing trouble."

"I just thought I'd share some news with you," Gillespie told her, as he came to a stop a few metres from the three CID officers, and Cruz fought to both stay professional and protect the only relationship he'd ever been in.

"I'm sorry, babe," Cruz said. "I couldn't help it. Please don't hate me."

"Couldn't help what?" she said, clearly irritated about the attention she was receiving so early in her career in plain clothes. "What's going on?"

"I don't know what he's talking about, Hermione," Gillespie said, nodding at Cruz as if he was some kind of madman. "I just heard you were looking into the shoplifting thing. Primark, wasn't it?"

"That's right," she said.

"Any luck yet?"

"Nothing. CCTV images match none of the usual suspects. Why's that?"

"Nillson, do you still have the address of the Airbnb? You know? The one our witnesses were staying in?"

"Yeah," Nillson said, fishing her notebook from her pocket. "You think it's them?"

"Worth a shot. You said she had a mountain of clothes and only one case."

"Nice one, Jim," Larson said, as Nillson presented the page with the address on.

"That should get you a leg up, eh, lads?" Gillespie said, addressing her two new colleagues. They nodded, but were still a little distracted by Cruz. And Larson's attention soon turned to her boyfriend too.

"What were you going on about?"

"Me? Oh, nothing," Cruz said, waving his hand dismissively.

"Don't give me that. You apologised. What for?"

"Let's just leave it, eh?"

But it was clear who wore the trousers in the relationship when she cocked her head and narrowed her eyes, leaving Cruz little choice but to confess. All eyes were on him, and Gillespie was delighting in the young DC's obvious discomfort.

"I wet the bed a bit," he sighed.

"What?" she said.

"Just a bit," he explained. "While you were out with your mum."

Perhaps it was the shock? Or maybe it was the embarrassment. But Hermione Larson turned on her heels and walked directly back towards the car park, followed closely by two sniggering CID officers.

"She's going to dump me, isn't she?"

"What did you tell her that for?" Gillespie said.

"What else was I supposed to tell her? That I told everyone about our little role play in the bedroom?"

"Oh, I don't know. You could have thought of something else."

"Like what?"

"Anything, Gab. Anything. Tell her you forgot to buy flowers, or something."

"I couldn't think. I was on the spot. It's your bloody fault–"

"Stop," Nillson called out, and Gillespie stopped and turned to face her. Ordinarily, he imagined she would have enjoyed watching his and Cruz's little back and forth. But her face told a different story.

"What's up, Anna?" Gillespie said.

"Now that everything is back to normal, there's something you both need to know. DI Bloom asked me to tell you," she said. "There's been an accident. It's Ben."

# CHAPTER SIXTY-SEVEN

BEN DIDN'T LOOK LIKE BEN, FREYA THOUGHT. SHE'D SEEN HIM sleeping on many occasions. Usually in an armchair, which he filled, and usually even in sleep there was a strength to his appearance. Like a guard dog. He could open an eye at any moment.

But lying in a hospital bed with his head bandaged, he looked small. Dark rings had begun to form around his eyes, but from what the doctor had told her, he was going to be okay.

She closed the door to his room and pulled the visitor's seat close to his bed. Then, taking his hand in hers, she stared at him, wondering what was going on in his mind at the moment. Was he dreaming? If so, what about?

"If you can hear me," she began, "you saved Cole's life today. And his colleague. If it wasn't for you, they would have been hit by the blast. If you hadn't warned them, things could be very different."

She found herself stroking his finger with hers, and she marvelled at the difference in size.

"Gillespie saved Gavin Forbes' life too. You should both be proud. I know I am," she said. "In other news, we found Boorman at Michael Doughty's place. I realised Boorman was the boy

Doughty abused all those years ago. He must have overheard us when we were talking to Hugo on his boat. Sadly, we didn't bring in Doughty. Sally Bird got to him first. She's in custody now."

There were voices in the corridor outside, which Freya recognised. She had just a few moments alone with him.

"You'll never know the impact you've had on me, Ben. Half of me wants you to see sense and to stay with the team. But the other half, the selfish half, wants you to go. But only so we can have a chance. You and I. It's a choice, you see? We can't have both. There are rules against it. Just like with Cruz and his girl. I find myself torn, Ben. I'm afraid it's up to you to decide. You can leave the team and save your family business, or you can stay with the team and save lives. Both are important. Far more so than my own selfish needs and desires."

A knock at the door stopped her from saying any more. Still clutching Ben's hand, she waved the newcomer into the room, leaving Ben with a last word of advice.

"I'm sure you'll do the right thing. You always do," she said, then stood to greet his father.

"Ah, Freya. I thought I'd find you here," he said, and she stood, offering him the chair.

He waved it away. "No. You sit. Please."

"The doctor said he'll be awake soon," Freya told him. "It's a mild concussion. He'll be home tonight. They just want to keep an eye on him for a while. He's sedated."

"Concussion? How?"

"There was a small explosion," Freya explained. "Ben was knocked over and he hit his head."

"An explosion? Was anybody else hurt?"

"No," she said. "No, thanks to Ben, nobody else was hurt."

He gave her a quizzical look, urging her to explain.

"He saw what was going to happen and warned the other men who were nearby. They managed to avoid the blast."

"A hero, eh?" he said, his voice dry and aged.

"In more ways than one, Mr Savage."

He smiled at that, then his face hardened.

"I suppose he told you the news, did he? The boys are forcing me into retirement."

"He did, yes. We'll miss him."

"I shan't imagine he'll be saving many lives on the farm, Freya. Saving memories, maybe. Heritage. But not lives. I suppose you think I'm being selfish?"

"It's a choice only he can make," Freya said. "What I think isn't really important, is it?"

"But you would lose him. He's important to you. I can see that."

"And he's important to you. I think the important question is, what is it you're afraid of losing, Mr Savage?"

"Excuse me? I'm not sure I'm following," he said, a little taken aback.

"Are you afraid of losing the farm, or are you afraid of losing Ben?"

"I'm not afraid of losing anything–"

"Where are Jeff and James?"

"They're coming. They had to hand over to the labourers."

"And Johnny Grouch?"

"He's doing what I should be doing. I can't just drop everything, you know?"

"I imagine not," Freya said, offering a sympathetic smile. "You know, my father had dementia."

"I didn't, no. Why would I?"

"He was so far gone when he was diagnosed, he never knew anything was wrong. It was us that suffered. Those of us around him."

"Well, I hope it doesn't come to that. The boys, they think I'm sick. I tell them I'm fine, but they insist."

"You know, there are tests you can do to find out," Freya said, and she turned to face him. "Simple tests."

"I'm sure, I don't need any of that."

"Hold out your hands."

"Excuse me?"

"Hold them out. Your hands."

He did as he was told, albeit with trepidation.

Freya held them in her own, caressing the space between his thumbs and forefingers with her thumbs.

"Hmm," she said, then reached up to touch his cheek, again caressing his old, leather-like skin with her thumb.

Nothing happened.

"What are you doing?" he asked, backing away.

"It's just a thing a doctor might do. At least, they did back when my dad was sick," Freya explained. "Dementia often returns the patient to an infantile state. When you rub a baby's hand in that particular spot, their hand opens. It's a reaction. Nurses use it to check motor skills. The same with your cheek. If you did that to a baby, they would suckle. It imitates the mother's breast against their face. It's a natural reaction. You did neither."

"That doesn't mean anything—"

"No, it doesn't. You're right. And I'm not a doctor," Freya said. "But I'm a bloody good detective, and I can spot a lie when it's standing right before me."

"What are you saying?" he asked, as indignant and authoritative as he would have been three decades before.

"Your two sons let you drive here, despite several claims of accidents with farm machinery."

"They don't even know I came. Not yet. I wanted to see him with my own two eyes."

"That's what I thought."

"What's what you thought?"

"The legendary Johnny Grouch. The only man you can rely on. Your right-hand man. Your best friend, and who your sons claim to be like an uncle to them. He let you drive here, did he?"

"Who else was going to drive me?"

"And you found the hospital and the correct ward, somewhere that even I had to ask two people directions to find. Yet according to Johnny Grouch, you can't find a field you've owned your entire life."

"What are you saying, Freya?"

"You remember my name now, do you?"

"Talk fast or get out."

"You're not getting sick, are you?"

"Excuse me?"

"You managed to convince your sons you're sick. You convinced them you're going the same way as your own father. But you're not, are you? Your mind is still as strong as it ever was. You're just afraid of losing Ben. You haven't lost any keys, Mr Savage, or any fields. But you made your sons believe you had. You didn't leave the brakes off the tractor either, did you? You had your old friend tell James and Jeff you had. All you had to do was show Ben how forgetful you were. Little things, like forgetting your notebook. Getting days mixed up. All they did was add weight to the stories you had Johnny Grouch tell James and Jeff."

He stared at her, his eyes narrowed, as if he was trying to see the workings of Freya's mind.

"Mr Grouch has worked on your farm for how long now?"

"Decades," he replied.

"I imagine everybody trusts him?"

"Implicitly."

"Sometimes we trust people based on what they do, their role in society, or their history. Sometimes we trust them so much, we never stop to question them," Freya said. "I learned that today. I learned it the hard way."

"Is that right?" he replied, shifting his weight from one foot to another.

"So, tell me, Mr Savage. What are you afraid of? Losing the farm, or losing Ben? Because I can assure you," she said, "if you force Ben to give up everything he's worked for, and he finds out this is all one big lie, you'll lose him *and* the farm."

She stared at Ben, studying the lines around his eyes. He had his father's features but must have inherited his mother's heart.

"You have it all worked out," his father said. "It's you who is afraid of losing him."

"Yes. Yes, I am afraid of losing him," Freya said. "But I would never stop him from following his heart. I'd never stand in his way. But he saved lives today. Being a police officer is what he was born to do. Are you really going to take that away from him? Are you ready to risk losing him forever?"

He turned away, reddening, and leaned on the bed frame, staring at his son.

"I don't blame you," Freya said, collecting her bag from the chair and slinging it over her shoulder. She stopped beside the door and turned back to the old man, who refused to look her way. "But just do the right thing. For Ben."

# CHAPTER SIXTY-EIGHT

"Are you sure you're up for this?" Freya asked, her finger poised over the doorbell of a terraced house on the outskirts of Lincoln.

"I've been in bed for two days," Ben replied, pointing at his two black eyes. "Even an afternoon with mad Doctor Bell is better than staring at four walls."

"Even at a *death party*?" Freya joked as she pressed the doorbell.

He shook his head. "She's crazy. You just have to remember that. Brilliant pathologist. But crazy as a wagonload of monkeys. I imagine her mother is just as bad. I plan on keeping my mouth well and truly shut."

"Not when she's fed you a beer or two. You'll be insulting her in under an hour, Ben."

"Ah, that's where you're wrong. We've got dinner with Dad later. You don't really think I'm going to that half-drunk, do you?"

"I was going to get drunk just to get through the ordeal," she replied.

"Which ordeal is that? Dinner with my dad, or an afternoon

death party with a lunatic?" Ben asked. "Speaking of my dad. What did you say to him?"

"Nothing. Why?"

"He's been acting odd since I came out of hospital. He comes by to check on me. He's never done that. It's almost like he feels guilty about something."

Freya hit the doorbell again and the door opened before she had a chance to respond.

"Oh, I thought it was you," Doctor Bell said, pulling open the door and staring at Ben's bruising. "Still insulting people, I see."

"He was caught in an explosion," Freya explained. "Mild concussion."

"I wasn't talking about the black eyes," she said, tapping the doorbell and holding her mobile phone up. "I heard every word you said. As did everyone else."

"Everybody else?" Freya said.

"*Everybody*," she said.

"You've got a camera doorbell," Ben said, his eyes widening in embarrassment.

"Crazy as a wagonload of monkeys I might be, but I'm not quite mad enough to leave my dying mother at home with no security."

"It was a term of endearment," Ben said.

"Well, all I can say is that it's lucky you don't know what people say about you two behind your backs."

"Sorry, Pip. We didn't mean any offense."

"He didn't mean anything by it," Freya explained with the emphasis on Ben.

"It's okay. I expect nothing less from you two," the doctor replied, switching her gaze from one to the other. "Now then. Let's get inside, shall we? Oh, and try not to insult anyone else. Especially my mother. It's her party, after all, and she's not like me. She can be quite sensitive."

"We'll do our very best," Freya assured her, with a quick glance at Ben, who hid his amusement with a smile.

"That's what I was worried about," Doctor Bell said, holding the door open.

They followed her through to the living room, where, to Freya's surprise, she found a group of teenagers, each with their hair flopping over their eyes and some kind of metal band or slogan on their black t-shirts. Sat in the corner armchair was an elderly lady wearing a blue, knitted cardigan over a floral dress. Her cheeks were drawn in, and upon seeing Freya, she stopped talking to one of the teenagers and craned her neck in anticipation of her greeting.

"It's lovely to meet you," Freya said, holding out the little posy of flowers she had bought. "I thought you could take these in with you. You know what those rooms are like. I thought they might bring you a bit of cheer."

The old lady looked at the teenager she had been talking to, then politely back at Freya.

"Which room is that, dear?" she said, her Welsh accent even thicker than Pip's.

"The hospital room. I understand you're going in for some treatment."

"Some treatment?" she said. "Am I?"

"Yes," Freya said, and she had a sense of dread that wasn't unusual when dealing with the pathologist. And it looked like that sentiment was true across her family too. "You're Mrs Bell, aren't you?"

"Of course I am. Who did you think I was?"

It was then that the teenager sitting closest to the old lady leaned forward and caught Freya's attention.

"She's my grandma," she said.

"Right," Freya said politely.

"Pip is my sister," she added.

"Your sister," Freya said. "So this isn't Pip's mum?"

She shook her head.

Freya rolled the facts over in her head, deducing that the entire room was staring at her.

"Lovely flowers. How delightful," Pip's grandma said. "I'll get Pip to put them in some water."

Freya looked down at the teenager, feeling her face flush.

"I'm sorry. I thought—"

The teenager nodded. "It's okay. Mum doesn't much like flowers anyway. At least grandma will look after them."

"Can I get anybody a drink?" Pip said from the kitchen door. "The party girl will be in soon. Just swallowing her pills, she is."

Seeing an opportunity to move past her little faux pas, Freya called out to Pip, "I'll take a white wine, if there's any going."

"Did you bring any with you?" Pip said.

"No. I bought some flowers," she replied, and feebly gestured at the grandma beside her.

"I did say it was a BYOB death party."

"BYOB?"

Ben leaned in and whispered in her ear, "Bring your own booze."

"Drink flowers, can you, Freya?" Pip said.

"No," she said, feeling herself falling into another awkward conversation.

"How about you, Ben? Did you bring anything to drink?"

"No, I've been in hospital, remember? I'm off the booze."

"I can offer you both coffee or Ribena. Although, I wouldn't have the Ribena if I were you. Been in the cupboard for years, it has. With any luck, it'll be more like red wine by now."

"Ah, a coffee will be fine, thanks, Pip," Freya said.

"Make that two," Ben said.

"Decaf only, I'm afraid."

"Decaf coffee?" Freya said, feeling her stomach turn at the very mention of it. But then she felt the room staring at her. "Will be lovely. Thank you."

"Ben?"

"Decaf sounds good," he said, and Pip slipped back out to the kitchen.

Freya leaned in to Ben, keeping her voice low. "Christ, this is harder than I thought it would be."

"Just observe," he said. "Keep quiet and observe. It'll all be over in a while."

The doorbell provided a welcome distraction for the Bell family to turn their attention away from Freya and Ben. It was Pip's sister who opened the front door, and a loud, brash, Glaswegian voice boomed through the house.

"Thank god," Freya said, as Gillespie stepped into the room, followed closely by Cruz and his girlfriend, Larson, and then Jackie Gold, Denise Chapman, and Anna Nillson.

"Ah, well, look who it is," Pip said from the kitchen doorway. She turned back to the kitchen, presumably to address her mother. "You'd better hide the weed, Mum. The fuzz have arrived in force."

The team gave a polite laugh, and clearly thought nothing of it. But Freya, who knew the pathologist better than any of them except Ben, wondered how much truth there really was to that statement.

"Right then," Gillespie called out. "Where's the special girl?"

"She's coming through now," Pip called out from the kitchen, just as a woman who Freya guessed to be in her late fifties stepped into view, and smiled at the room.

"Here she is," Pip's sister said, getting up from her seat to give her mother a hug. She introduced her to the teenagers on the couch, who, to Freya's surprise, were well-spoken, polite, and even offered her a seat, which she declined.

Pip's mother wore a pretty, floral dress, which looked as if it had been bought when she was at least ten pounds heavier. And her makeup had clearly been applied by Pip's steady hand. The eyeliner was too heavy, the lipstick too thick, and if she wasn't mistaken, Freya could have sworn some kind of talc had been applied to pale the woman's skin.

"You look lovely," Freya said, when Pip's sister then turned her mother around to meet Freya's team.

"Well, I'll take that as a compliment, shall I?" she replied. "How did you expect me to look? How would you have had me? In a hospital gown with my backside hanging out, no doubt?"

"Well, no..." Freya began.

"You must be the detective. Bloom, isn't it?" she said, her keen eyes narrowing. "Told me all about you, Pip has. I'll be watching you."

Freya was sure it had been the chemo and drugs that had drawn the woman's face like a vacuum-sealed sachet of soup. But it was clear where Pip had inherited her eyes from. Just like Pip, her mother's eyes were wild and searching, scrutinising.

"I've heard a lot about you," Freya said, forcing a pleasant expression, but inwardly wishing she had declined the invite.

"Which makes you Ben," the woman said, turning to face him. She sized him up from his feet to his face, and if it wasn't for Ben's two black eyes, Freya was sure the woman would have reached out and grabbed him between the legs, to make extra certain. "Heard about you as well. You and her. Thick as thieves, you are."

"We work together," Ben said. "We're good friends."

"Right," she said, with an obvious volume of disbelief. "Just friends, are you?"

"I bought you this," Gillespie said, rescuing Ben from the woman's scrutinous glare. He held out a bottle of white wine. A Sauvignon Blanc, which Freya appraised as mid-range. A good choice for a man like Gillespie.

"You know the way to a woman's heart, you do," she said, and cocked her head, waiting for Gillespie to introduce himself.

"You can call me Jim, ma'am," he said, and he took her by the hand and kissed it, as if he was in a period drama, and the whole charade was fictitious.

"Well now," she said, and fanned her face with her free hand. "This one's a charmer. Single, are you?"

"Single as they come," he replied, proudly. Then he leaned in conspiratorially. "The way I see it, I'd be doing all the other girls a misjustice if I settled down. Know what I mean?" he finished with a wink, and Ben turned away, catching Freya's eyeroll.

By the time the rest of the team had been introduced, Pip had delivered the coffees in two huge Sports Direct mugs. Then, without attempting another conversation with Ben and Freya, she disappeared to tend to her guests.

Freya held the mug up.

"This is a pint of coffee?" she said.

"I know, right? Lucky it's decaf or I'll be climbing the walls."

"I can't drink it. I was just being polite."

Ben looked around and gestured behind them, where a large cheese plant was standing in the corner.

"Tip it in there," he said.

"I can't do that," she laughed, just as the mother came wobbling back through the living room and glared at Freya, dissolving her smirk like antacid in water.

"Something tickled you, has it?"

"Life tickles me, Mrs Bell," Freya replied. "If we can't laugh from time to time, what's the point?"

Mrs Bell agreed slowly and thoughtfully.

"Your daughter speaks highly of you," Freya added, looking for a way to break the uncomfortable stare. "You're lucky to have someone like her supporting you."

"You know where I'm going next week, do you?"

"To the hospital?" Ben said, clearly trying to come to her aid.

"That's right. You know I might not get out, don't you?" she said, then whispered with those wild eyes wide open. "I might take my last breath in there."

"I'm sure you'll be—"

"I'll be watching you," she said, cutting Freya off and pointing to the ceiling. "From up there."

She stayed that way for some time, beyond the point of awkwardness. Her head was cocked, and she was leaned in so close that Freya could smell the cheap wine on her breath.

"Look after my Pip, will you?" the old woman said finally, and Freya appraised her in her moment of weakness.

"Enjoy the rest of your party," she said after a thoughtful stare. "Don't worry about Pip. She's one of us."

"What was all that about?" Ben asked when Pip's mother had hobbled off.

"Ah, you know. Just girl's stuff. A heart to heart, as it were," Freya said, then caught Jackie's attention. "Gold. How did it go?"

Gold smiled back at her, unable to conceal her delight.

"I passed, ma'am," she said. "You're looking at the team's new dedicated FLO."

"Eh?" Cruz said. "I thought you were leaving?"

"Leaving?" Gold said. "Who told you I was leaving?"

"Well, the boss said..." Cruz began, then faltered.

"I said nothing of the sort," Freya explained.

"Hold on," Ben said. "But you didn't exactly put me right when I expressed my concerns."

"Of course I didn't," Freya said, feeling the warmth of a well-concocted plan coming together. "But it gave me a good opportunity to see which of you are hungry to progress your careers."

"Eh?" Cruz said, and he cocked his head, clearly trying to remember his actions over the past week.

"That's cruel," Ben said.

"Yes. Yes, it is. I have a mean streak. But I promise you, my intentions are always good."

A phone beeped and broke the silence between them, and Gillespie began tapping his pockets.

"Ah, that's me," he said, pulling his phone from his inside pocket, then he pulled a confused expression. "Eh?"

"Who is it?" Cruz said, craning his neck to peer at Gillespie's phone.

"Get out of it," Gillespie said, shoving him away.

But it was too late. Cruz had already seen the message.

"Hope you don't mind. I got your number from the barman. See you at seven. From the red wine girl," Cruz said. "Who's the red wine girl?"

"Ah, you know. Some girl I met a few days ago."

"Where did you meet her? You've spent all week with us."

"Ah, you know how it is," Gillespie explained, and he puffed out his chest as he pocketed his phone. "You've either got it, or you haven't."

"Got what?" Cruz said.

"Exactly," Nillson said with a laugh, then gave Larson an apologetic look.

"Right then, you horrible lot," Pip said, as she emerged from the kitchen carrying a cake that looked as though it had been decorated by a seven-year-old. She set it down on the table. "We're all here to celebrate the life of my ma, Ada Bell."

A few of the teenagers cheered, and the noise in the room grew as they each toasted Pip's mother, telling her how lovely she was, and how they would all remember her when she was gone.

"Christ, this is morbid," Freya whispered in Ben's ear.

But there was no time for Ben to respond. Suddenly there was a loud sob and Pip's mother fell into Pip's arms in what Freya deemed to be a real hug. A motherly hug. The hug of a dying woman. Of gratitude and guilt.

"Oh, Pip," she said. "Thank you. Thank you for all of this. For everything you've done for me."

"And that's my cue to leave," Freya said, slipping behind Ben and the team.

All eyes were on the dying mother clinging to her daughter, except those of the team, who all stared at Freya.

"Where are you going?" Ben hissed.

Over Pip's shoulder, Pip's mother eyed Freya knowingly, blinking away the tears.

Freya watched her for a moment, then gave her team the warmest smile she could muster.

"I don't do well with the whole mother daughter relationship stuff. I find it brings back bad memories. So, I'll see you all on Monday," she said, finishing her sweeping gaze on Ben. "And I'll see you at dinner. In fact, I'm rather looking forward to it."

"I'm not sure I am," Ben replied, and he glanced at Pip and her mother, and then at the team. "I don't think I'm ready to lose him. Everything changes, Freya. You realise that, don't you?"

"Oh, do try to be more positive," she said with deliberate flippancy, then, after a short spell of studying Pip's mother in her throes of gratitude, she left him with something to make him think. She stepped closer to him, leaned up so they were cheek to cheek, and whispered into his ear. "You might even enjoy it."

The End

The place was perfect. Exactly how she had imagined. There was silence, save for the wind rushing through the wild, tall grass. Her life was about to change forever, and the thought of what might be pulsed through her body.

The summer sun bore down on the ruins of Tupholme Abbey, lighting the old stone in hues of red and orange, and warming her naked skin. Her body tensed in the heat, and she arched her back against the old, tartan blanket, savouring the gentle breath of air and the touch of the cool grass between her toes, imagining his surprise when he found her. The thought of seeing him, of being alone with him with nobody to tell them it was wrong, or to stop them somehow, sent a wave of heat that coursed through her like electricity.

His footsteps swishing through the long grass around the old ruins were the delicate percussion to the thudding beat of her heart, and his silhouette against the sun as he stood before her was the shape of her dreams, her hopes, and of things to come.

"I see you started without me," he said. His voice was song-like, soft and silky, yet effortlessly masculine.

With the sun behind him, his details were obscured, shaded.

But she knew them, and if she closed her eyes, she could see them in her mind's eye. He bent to place the hamper down.

"I was keeping the blanket warm," she said. "What kept you?"

"I was chilling the wine."

"Wine? Really?"

"It's a picnic. We can't have a picnic without wine."

She shoved herself up onto her elbow, but stilled when he raised his hand.

"Stay. Don't move. Not a muscle, you hear?"

She nodded and lay back, leaning on one elbow.

"What else is in there?"

"A surprise," he said, and she heard the smile in his voice.

He dropped to his knees at her feet, allowing the sunlight to blind her once more.

"Close your eyes," he whispered, so she did, without even thinking.

Then she felt him close to her. His scent was the wildflowers and the air, and his breath the breeze. And his gift, the surprise he had promised, was the cool, soft touch of a tender strawberry on her lips. She bit down, carefree, and childlike, letting the juice cling to her dry lips.

He straddled her now, and she lay back as he poured the wine. The chink of glass on glass teasing her with what was to come. These delays. That was what he did. That was her opiate, and she found her hands clammy as she lay in wait.

But things were to be done properly. There was a way to do things, and those traditions should be followed. That was his way. When the time came, he would deliver, and she knew it. But by God she wished somebody would tell her body that. The ache beneath her stomach, the way one foot caressed the other involuntarily, and the way her mind wandered to how things might play out were all signs her early exploration had yet to wane.

She was ready for him. She'd been ready for hours. Since he'd first messaged her, in fact.

"To freedom," he said, holding a glass out for her to take.

"In a moment," she told him, and he set the glass down beside the hamper.

She rolled onto her elbow again to watch him a glee that was growing harder to conceal.

"I thought about you today," he said, resting his glass in the grass beside the blanket.

"I thought about you too," she replied, and found herself biting down on her lower lip again.

"I'm serious. I thought about us. You know? If it could work."

"You've got doubts?" she said, and the heat that twitched her toes and wet her palms dissipated, leaving only winter where summer had shone. "You have, haven't you? You're not going to go through with it."

"No. No, I am. I am," he said, and his touch ignited a candle flame, where only moments before, a fire had raged. "Forget I said anything."

"Forget? What's wrong?" she said, reaching for her clothes, but he stopped her, his hard grip clamping down on her wrist.

"I said forget it," he said, that silky tone replaced with a baritone rumble.

"You're going to do it? You're going to leave her?"

"Of course," he replied, and with a nudge, she was on her back once more, this time with him over her, smothering her. Possessive. "I made you a promise, didn't I?"

"You did."

"I won't let you down."

"Promise."

"I already did—"

"Say it again. Tell me. I'm not sure if I can go back now. Promise me. Promise me we can be together."

He lingered there above her, searching her eyes for some kind of truth. But there were no lies. She had herself bare in every sense of the word, and now she needed him to do the same.

In every sense of the word.

"Promise me," she said, growing impatient. She just needed to hear him say it. It had been a week since they had spoken, long enough for his mind to be changed.

"Shh," he whispered, leaning in to nuzzle her earlobe the way she had imagined him to. "Relax."

"Tell me," she breathed, and she felt herself succumbing to his spell. Her legs, with minds of their own, wrapped around him, pulling him into her. And she clung to him, feeling the tight muscles beneath his shirt.

It was all so familiar. It was as her dreams had been. His silhouette, his strength, his voice, and his smell were exactly how they would have been had she, by some divine will, created him herself.

He kissed her, and she was lost to his powers, with all thoughts of promises and the future cast away in an instant. And boy, could he kiss. Soft at first, and slow, as if he was simply preparing her.

But nothing could prepare her for the irony taste that followed, or the way his strength seemed to wane, and his weight pinned her to the blanket.

And the way his heavy breaths faltered and stuttered, which only moments before had been in harmony with her own. A duet. A chorus of passion that climaxed before the crescendo.

"John?" she whispered, her fingers groping his back for the source of the wet, sticky blood she felt. "John, talk to me. You're scaring me."

But he didn't move.

A breath came. An exhale, long and protracted. Final.

"John?" she said, panic taking over her senses. "John, get off. Please..."

But the only reply she heard was the ruins of the abbey, echoing her screams.

Then there was silence, save for the wind rushing through the long grass. And she was blinded by the sun, save for a few scant clouds hanging far above them. With his weight pinning her to the ground, she reached around him in a tentative embrace. But the sentiment was short-lived. Her fingers found something warm, wet, and yet tacky.

And she screamed once more, knowing that, just as she had thought, her life would never be the same.

# ALSO BY JACK CARTWRIGHT

**The DCI Cook Murder Mysteries**

A Winter of Blood

A Secret to Die For

**The Wild Fens Murder Mysteries**

Secrets In Blood

One For Sorrow

In Cold Blood

Suffer In Silence

Dying To Tell

Never To Return

Lie Beside Me

Dance With Death

In Dead Water

One Deadly Night

Her Dying Mind

Into Death's Arms

Join my VIP reader group to be among the first to hear about new release dates, discounts, and get a free Wild Fens novella.

Visit www.jackcartwrightbooks.com for details.

# COPYRIGHT

Copyright © 2022 by Jack Cartwright

All rights reserved.

The moral right of Jack Cartwright to be identified as the author of this work has been asserted by him in accordance with the Copyright, Designs and Patents act 1988.

All the characters in this book are fictitious, and any resemblance to actual persons living or dead is purely coincidental.

All rights reserved. No part of this publication may be reproduced, stored in a retrieval system or transmitted in any form or by any means, without the prior permission in writing of the publisher, nor to be otherwise circulated in any form of binding or cover other than that in which it is published without a similar condition, including this condition, being imposed on the subsequent purchaser.